Millie Adams is the very dramatic pseudonym of *New York Times* bestselling author Maisey Yates. Happiest surrounded by yarn, her family and the small woodland creatures she calls pets, she lives in a small house on the edge of the woods, which allows her to escape in the way she loves best—in the pages of a book. She loves intense alpha heroes and the women who dare to go toe-to-toe with them.

Jackie Ashenden writes dark, emotional stories with alpha heroes who've just got the world to their liking, only to have it blown apart by their kick-ass heroines. She lives in Auckland, New Zealand, with her husband, the inimitable Dr Jax, two kids and two rats. When she's not torturing alpha males and their gutsy heroines she can be found drinking chocolate martinis, reading anything she can lay her hands on, wasting time on social media or being forced to go mountain biking with her husband. To keep up to date with Jackie's new releases and other news, sign up for her newsletter at jackieashenden.com.

Also by Millie Adams

Dragos's Broken Vows
Promoted to Boss's Wife
Heir of Scandal
From Convent to Queen

Also by Jackie Ashenden

Newlywed Enemies
King, Enemy, Husband

Captured and Claimed miniseries

Christmas Eve Ultimatum
His Heir of Revenge

Discover more at millsandboon.co.uk.

CAPTURED AND CRAVED

MILLIE ADAMS

JACKIE ASHENDEN

MILLS & BOON

All rights reserved including the right of reproduction in whole or in part in any form. This edition is published by arrangement with Harlequin Enterprises ULC.

This is a work of fiction. Names, characters, places, locations and incidents are purely fictional and bear no relationship to any real life individuals, living or dead, or to any actual places, business establishments, locations, events or incidents. Any resemblance is entirely coincidental.

Without limiting the exclusive rights of any author, contributor or the publisher of this publication, any unauthorised use of this publication to train generative artificial intelligence (AI) technologies is expressly prohibited. HarperCollins also exercise their rights under Article 4(3) of the Digital Single Market Directive 2019/790 and expressly reserve this publication from the text and data mining exception.

® and TM are trademarks owned and used by the trademark owner and/or its licensee. Trademarks marked with ® are registered with the United Kingdom Patent Office and/or the Office for Harmonisation in the Internal Market and in other countries.

First published in Great Britain 2026
by Mills & Boon, an imprint of HarperCollins*Publishers* Ltd,
1 London Bridge Street, London, SE1 9GF

www.harpercollins.co.uk

HarperCollins*Publishers*, Macken House, 39/40 Mayor Street Upper, Dublin 1, D01 C9W8, Ireland

Captured and Craved © 2026 Harlequin Enterprises ULC

Princess, Pregnant, Prisoner © 2026 Millie Adams

His Forced Sicilian Bride © 2026 Jackie Ashenden

ISBN: 978-0-263-41825-5

04/26

Printed and Bound in the UK using 100% Renewable Electricity
at CPI Group (UK) Ltd, Croydon, CR0 4YY

PRINCESS, PREGNANT, PRISONER

MILLIE ADAMS

MILLS & BOON

CHAPTER ONE

"So, it's to be a loveless marriage, to a stranger in a strange land."

Princess Emerald of Basilia stared up at her older brother, King Onyx, his gaze dark and uncompromising as it ever was. And then to his left, at her brother's right-hand man, and her bodyguard, Andrei Ardelean.

He might as well have been carved from stone. He was a man who exhibited little emotion, unless you knew him. And Emerald and Onyx were two of the very few people who knew him. Sometimes, Emerald could even get a smile out of him. But not today.

"If you wish to look at it that way, Onyx," she said, staring her brother down, her rebuttal to his attempt at making her decision sound unhinged obviously irritating him.

"It is not how I *wish* to look at it," he said. "It is how it is."

"And what other *solution* do you see? King Lucian asked for me."

King Lucian, ruler of Alabria, The Sea Serpent of the Mediterranean. The most feared, loathed and reviled ruler in the string of islands that made up the Jewel Belt.

"You are my sister, you are not a political bargaining tool."

"Sadly, Onyx, I am. That's what it means when you're born into royalty, and you know that. We have to do what is best for the country. There is no other choice."

"There are many other choices."

"King Lucian is liable to bring his fleet of ships to our island and raid the place to take me."

Andrei shifted where he stood, his black gaze menacing. "He is welcome to try." Even after all these years of living in Basilia, he retained hints of a Romanian accent.

His parents had been fleeing a crime family, so the story went, and they had stowed away on a boat bound for Basilia, but it had sunk and they'd drowned.

Andrei was the only survivor.

He'd washed up on shore, and it had been her mother's and father's natures to take him in like he was their own. That poor, lonely orphan had become a symbol of the welcoming nature of their country. But she knew it had never really been about that. It was about love.

It was only after that that her father and mother had been killed in a car accident, and her brother Onyx had ascended the throne at the age of sixteen. Andrei had been part of the family by that point. Onyx had appointed him as her personal bodyguard, and so he had become her shadow, wherever she'd gone. The three of them were bonded together by loss. By trauma, and she could understand the pushback from them now. But both of them were far too pragmatic to behave this way.

They weren't *children*. Not anymore. They had to put away their fantasies of this place, being separate from the world and being their own personal haven.

They knew better than that. Onyx knew better than that, whatever he said. He himself was in a loveless marriage with a woman who didn't care for him at all. Emerald and Andrei both hated to see it, and Onyx wouldn't hear a negative word against his queen. Because he had chosen her for reasons of diplomacy. Nothing else, and that mattered to him more than anything. She understood that it was hard to watch your sibling take less than what they deserved, but she also understood why he'd done it. Ultimately, she respected him for it, because he was serving a greater need, a greater good.

That he didn't see her as worthy of doing the same spoke to the fact that however much he tried to pretend that he saw her as an equal, he didn't. It infuriated her. They were royal, they had a duty to their country above all else. Above all notions of love, passion or even personal happiness.

Her mother had given up everything she'd ever known to marry her father, and that marriage had united a kingdom.

How could Emerald do less? In honor of a mother who was no longer here, but who had shaped her in every way that mattered?

She decided to tell him as much.

"What's good for you is good for me. What's good for the future of the country is what I must do, just as you did when you married Circe."

"Don't speak ill of my wife. Do not compare her to a maniacal authoritarian."

"The rumors about King Lucian are simply that. Rumors. We don't know that he killed any of his wives."

"Even if he killed one of them, it's a wife too many. And anyway, they seem to always meet an end, don't they."

"There were only two. He's hardly Bluebeard."

"And this also isn't *A Thousand and One Nights*. You're not going to be able to tell him stories and keep him from doing what it is homicidal maniacs do."

She decided to ignore her brother's hysterics. She'd already reasoned out all of this. She'd been going over the logistics of an alliance between their countries for the past year. She'd first made contact with King Lucian six months ago, via email, and while he was difficult and mercurial she didn't think he seemed like a psychopath.

Though, maybe good psychopaths hid it well. She couldn't know for sure, and she felt it didn't benefit her to be complacent, but if she really felt that she was signing herself up for murder she wouldn't be doing it.

She believed him, ultimately, that what he wanted was an alliance.

Alabria was isolated, had very few alliances with anyone, and would make an excellent trade partner and military ally.

It was just that Lucian wanted marriage in exchange for those things.

She was a good negotiator. She always had been. She could think of no reasonable excuse to deny him what he was asking. There would have to be a better political prospect on the table, and currently, there wasn't.

So she'd agreed to the marriage.

It was signed. Notarized. Official.

Onyx's objections to it meant nothing.

Legally.

They meant something to her personally. But what she wanted personally wasn't the feature here.

She was a princess. With that came an obligation to duty and legacy. That was what mattered to her.

"The agreement that he sent over is very reasonable, and does not have a hint of homicidal ideation. The fact of the matter is, this is a great proposition, a boon for our country, and you know it."

"I don't like it. In fact, I would like to forbid you from doing it."

"Don't. We agreed that I wasn't going to be treated like I was inconsequential because I was younger, and a woman. I am one of your key political strategists and have been for years. I am not your spare, Onyx."

"Of course not. You never have been."

"Then let me do this. Alabria is the gateway to the Jewel Belt of the Mediterranean. Being able to move through that route freely would change the economy of our country. Alabria is bigger than we are. *He* is more powerful. I know you don't like to admit that there is any man on earth more powerful than you, but there is a point where ego becomes foolishness."

His lip curled, his offense apparent. "This is not about my ego, it is about your safety."

It was only then she let herself look at Andrei. His eyes burned bright with a sort of black flame that made her feel a world of things she didn't want to feel. That made her feel…

There was regret in taking this marriage offer, of course. There were so many things she hadn't done. So many things that she wanted that… They were impossible, and they always would be.

There was, in addition to regret, relief.

Relief that she would get the distance she'd never been

able to manage before. Relief that she would be safe from *this*. The tyranny of desiring what she couldn't have.

Even though her brother loved her very much, she would always have had to make a union that mattered politically. Always. She could understand why he was opposed to this, but even if it wasn't King Lucian, it would be another king here or there, a noble, a prince. Someone who could provide a beneficial alliance to Basilia.

"What are your thoughts on the matter, Andrei?" Onyx asked.

Of course he would ask Andrei. His adviser. The chief of his guard. His best friend.

Andrei shifted. "I don't like it. She could be putting herself in danger. I will not allow that."

"You are not in charge of me," she said. "Your job is only to protect me in the situations that I put myself into."

"Andrei will go with you," Onyx said.

"Excuse me?"

She couldn't imagine anything worse. She could not be followed into her new marriage, into the country by… She couldn't. The way that Andrei made her feel, the things that he aroused inside her…

Those were secrets that she kept locked down deep. For so many reasons they were impossible. They always had been. If her brother'd had any idea that she was lusting after the man sent to protect her, then he would no longer be her protector. He was like a brother to them, or rather he was supposed to be. The problem was, he had never quite felt that way to Emerald. At least not after she began to understand why men and women were different, and what made a man beautiful.

Andrei was beautiful.

He had black hair, deep olive skin and a perfectly sculpted face. The cheekbones and jawline of a model, but the ruthless intensity of a warrior. He was a puzzle. For no matter how long she knew him, she would never be able to get entirely down to the depths of him. He was a code that was impossible to crack. If somebody could have, it likely would've been her or Onyx. Given as long as they'd known him. But there were certain things he never spoke of, and emotions that he never showed.

He'd been sixteen, like Onyx, when the king and queen had died. Emerald had been twelve. She had been certain she'd seen tears glistening in his dark eyes that day, but he'd never spoken of it.

He'd never shown his emotion openly.

Even when he'd been a boy, lying in bed, just waking up to discover his parents were dead, his manner had been stoic. Grave.

It was his way.

But he hadn't left her alone in her grief. He'd held her while she wept, maintaining his own solid strength while she dissolved. Onyx had been the king, and while he'd been there for her as much as he could be, he'd been consumed with managing a whole nation rocked by the death of its monarchs.

Only Andrei had been able to concern himself singularly with her.

Theirs was a bond that defied words. And beneath that bond were feelings in her that defied what was possible.

"Of course I will," he said. "I will be a nonnegotiable addition to this envoy."

"But you live *here*," she said, panic rising inside her. "You can't uproot your entire life to follow me to another country."

"My service to the Crown is my life, Princess. Whether that service takes place here or in Alabria is of no consequence. You are my mission."

He was always doing things like that. Always undermining the emotional connection they felt they had with him. Always making it about duty and honor and his place. He wasn't royal, that much was true, but he was their friend. To her, he was a great deal more, whether he would ever know that or not.

Whether he would ever admit it or not.

You are my mission.

If he were any other man, it would be easy to take that as a declaration of some kind. But Andrei just meant that literally. She was a mission. A task for him to see to.

And he was ruining this. She needed to be away from him. She needed an ocean between them, a potentially psychotic husband between them. She didn't fear Lucian, because she'd gotten to the point where being near Andrei was the real source of her fear.

How long could she bend before she broke?

She was hoping to never test it.

"This is ridiculous. He's not going to make a political alliance with us and then *kill me*."

"I will assess the situation," Andrei said. "With your permission, Your Highness, I will send a missive to the Crown and let them know exactly what the princess will require as she evaluates whether or not she truly wishes to enter into this union."

"I've already agreed," Emerald said.

"And we shall add stipulations," Onyx said.

She threw her hands into the air, rage, desperation and her own throbbing heart making her lose control. "God spare me the interference of relentless alpha males."

She meant that in the most derogatory fashion possible.

Storming from the room didn't really help her case. She was trying not to be childish. But she had brokered the deal herself. It was a triumph of international relations. She was throwing herself on this altar, a sacrifice for the greater good of the country.

Well. That was exactly what Onyx was objecting to. But he didn't have the right. She wasn't weak. She knew that her duty was to the country. She knew where they were having difficulty, and she knew where she could make things better. Easier. King Lucian was the most difficult ruler spread across all the islands in this little belt of countries and principalities. She could tame him, then she could help everyone.

She remembered her mother, so beautiful and serene. She truly believed that her parents had loved each other, but she also knew that her mother had left a small village on the farthest end of the island that previously hadn't been joined together with the nation of Basilia. She had united the tribes there and the rest of the country. Had brought services to them. Had changed the lives of everyone for the better.

She wanted to be like her mother. She wanted to do something that mattered. Wanted to unite the nations. She had the opportunity to do that on an even grander scale.

It was her purpose.

What she knew about life was that it could be short and cruel. Even if she did meet her fate at the hands of King Lucian, she would've tried. Would've tried for a legacy that was bigger than herself.

The need to be her mother's daughter in this way was an almost desperate drive inside her. She'd lost her so long ago. This felt like finding a connection to her.

I'm the woman you would have raised me to be. If you had lived.

She heard heavy footsteps behind her, and she didn't even have to turn to know who it was. Her brother walked on top of the floor. He was silent. Years of royal training had turned him into an elegant panther. Dangerous, certainly, to some, but smooth. Andrei did not bother to conceal his presence, ever. He was a blunt instrument. A weapon. And he wore that proudly.

"You are making a mistake," he said.

She turned around, trying to steel herself for the impact of him. Even though she had just been looking at him, she knew that he would make her heart beat faster now that they were alone. Now that he was closer. She turned, and she was right. Her heart leapt into her throat like it was trying to escape. "That's not for you to decide."

"Perhaps not, but I'm telling you all the same."

"I am a princess," she said. "And you are nothing. You would do well to remember that." She immediately regretted those words the moment they came out of her mouth. She didn't mean them. But she was angry. Angry at these men for undermining her. Angry at Andrei for making her feel things that were so at odds with what she knew she needed to do.

It was the worst of both worlds. Not only was her plan being hijacked by the most controlling men she knew, but she wasn't getting the reprieve from Andrei she desperately needed.

She didn't look at him again. She refused.

She was going to prepare herself for the sea voyage to Alabria. King Lucian did not allow flights in or out of the country, unless they were his own. Everyone, including the citizens of the country, had to travel elsewhere by boat if they wished to fly somewhere. It had always been rumored that it was a show of strength. A way that Lucian let everyone know that in his country he even owned the sky.

She didn't care what it was. She wondered if the ship's journey would deter Andrei.

That made her feel guilty too. But she didn't ask, and she didn't look back.

She had made her decision. Whether her brother and Andrei supported her or not didn't matter. She was selling herself into marriage.

It was a choice that only she could make. And she had made it.

"You could forbid her to go." Andrei was leaning against the doorframe, rage churning in his stomach.

Emerald was being a fool. Very unlike her. She was the most devoted, levelheaded person he knew apart from Onyx. This was a rare miscalculation on her part, but it was one.

King Lucian was a monster. The very idea of that man laying claim to her…

He could not bear it.

"Certainly, I could. And then what? Lock her in the dungeon? You have met my sister. She is the smartest person I know. Smarter than the two of us combined when it comes to matters of negotiation and the economy. The trouble is, it is a very good deal that she's brokered."

"Fuck the deal," Andrei said. "What does it matter? If her safety is compromised…"

"She is also right about the fact that it has never been confirmed he is responsible for the deaths of his previous wives."

"They're also all dead," Andrei growled. "So they can hardly testify."

Emerald was the most precious thing in his world. He would kill for her. Die for her. Whatever was required of him. His devotion to her was complete.

He had cared for her, looked after her from the time she was young. This family meant everything to him. When he'd been taken into the palace he'd seen love for the first time. Real love that wasn't filled with trip wires and toxicity. Unconditional, beautiful love like they wrote about in stories and songs.

He'd loved his parents, because he knew nothing else. He'd loved his parents because he didn't know children shouldn't see violence—passionate or otherwise. He didn't know a father shouldn't strike his son, or expose him to the dark, twisted dealings of a criminal empire. His father had often showered him with praise, and that had made up for the times when being in his father's sphere was hard.

His own concept of love, of family, was so perverted that he'd been completely undone by the purity of the royal family.

It had changed something inside him, and he'd sworn an oath in his own soul to protect this family with everything he was.

He and Onyx were blood brothers. After Onyx's parents had died, Andrei had cut his palm, and Onyx had cut his, and they had shaken hands, solidifying their connection to one another. Emerald was something else.

His.

And yet he knew that she wasn't. She never could be.

His desire for her was anathema to him. He did his best to shut it off, to push it down, to push her away. He'd been put in charge of her after the king and queen had died. He'd been made her personal guard—though he'd been young. After all, Onyx was king at that same young age, in charge of an entire country. Andrei had ruled over Emerald's safety. He had protected her physically, and had been there for her through her grief. She had become the person who mattered most to him in all the world. A connection that was not familial, but felt soul deep in a way he would never have been able to put to words.

Then it had changed. The intensity of the feelings had always been there, but then that intensity had become deadly. Like a knife resting flat on flesh for years, suddenly twisted so the sharp edge sunk in, deep and terrible.

The great and terrible hunger that had taken over him during a dance at her eighteenth birthday party. An innocent touch of her hand against his and he'd been undone. The fierce need to claim her, to make her his, to take her until they were both breathless…

It had dogged him now for six years, this deep caring that had turned into something so much more obsessing.

He exhausted his sexual energies elsewhere, faceless, nameless hookups that he found shameful in the broad light of day, especially when he looked at her.

But there was nothing that could be done. He was not angry now because she was marrying someone else. That had always been what was destined to be. He was angry because this man, this mad king, could put her in danger.

"This is why you need to stay with her. Obviously if you think there is any real danger to her safety, I expect you to put a stop to things. Start a war on your way out if you have to."

Andrei crossed his arms. "I'm listening."

"You will gather intel for me. You will tell me everything, about the king, about the country, about the palace. If we have to have an international incident, then we must. If you think that he will be unkind to her, abusive in some way, if you believe that it is a place she will not survive, then at any point during the marriage, you will remove her, bring her back."

"I promise."

"I know that I can count on you. I have trusted you with my sister, and her safety since she was fourteen years old. I continue to trust you now."

He smiled, but it was not a genuine smile. Because if he had any idea that Andrei's feelings for Emerald had begun to change years ago, when she had begun to look like a woman, and her sweetness, her care had gotten beneath his skin in a way that no one and nothing else ever had, he would likely have Andrei thrown in a dungeon for the rest of his life. Beheading would be too good for him.

"I'm sorry about the boat trip," Onyx said.

Andrei shrugged. Yes, he felt cold terror in his veins when he thought about going out on the water. When he thought about what it had been like when the ship had begun to take on the ocean, until it was more water than boat. The way that the pressure of the sinking vessel had pulled him down, and the way his lungs had burned as he had swum endlessly in the wrong direction. How he had washed up on the shore, he couldn't say. It was a miracle, he had decided. Because there was no other explanation. But every other man, woman and child on that boat had died. And so, he had always found it to be a sharp-edged miracle. Because if the divine had saved him, then surely the divine could've prevented the boat from capsizing in the first place.

He had a long-standing rift with God over that.

"It is nothing," he said.

Because when it came to the choice between his own comfort and protecting Emerald, he would choose her every time.

And so he would choose her now. Above all else.

If he had to lead her into this marriage that she had chosen, he would.

And if he had to cut her husband's throat to save her, he would do that too.

The one thing he would never do, was put his hands on her.

CHAPTER TWO

SHE DIDN'T EXPECT to get so emotional packing up to leave the palace. She didn't know what she had expected. But her resolve was so firm, she'd sort of thought that it would carry her out of the palace, onto the boat, across the sea.

Now, standing on the dock about ready to board the ship, she felt...frozen. Like her shoes were made of cement.

"Princess," Andrei said, "the boat awaits."

The boat in question was a yacht, beautiful and streamlined and with every modern amenity that a person could ever want or need. It was Onyx's, and Emerald had never spent a lot of time on it. She'd taken short trips before but never anything this long. Well, and never to her potential doom, or to a marriage with a stranger.

"I know," she said, looking up at Andrei. "Are you okay?"

He smiled, but it looked more like a sneer. "I'm doing just fine. Why do you ask?"

She immediately felt terrible, because she shouldn't have even referenced the very real, and horrendous trauma he'd experienced as a child.

"No reason."

"Somehow, I thought as much." On wobbly legs, she began to walk up the gangway onto the boat. There was a staff member standing there with a tray of champagne waiting for them. "Oh, thank you," she said, taking the champagne and turning to look at Andrei. "Take one," she said.

"I do not follow orders," he responded. "Do I need to remind you?"

"That is strange, because you are here on my *brother's* order."

"I would be here no matter what Onyx advised. On that you can trust me."

He didn't take a glass of champagne, and she was certain that it was actually to antagonize her. At least it would be a comfortable crossing. All of her things had already been delivered to the plush cabin at the front of the yacht, where the views of the sea were glorious. The last time she had sailed on the ship Onyx had given her that room, and she had enjoyed it. But, she wouldn't go down there just yet. Instead, she opted to take her champagne to a lounge chair on the top deck and watch as they sailed away from Basilia.

She hadn't expected the grief. The tightening of her throat.

She was leaving all of this behind. This country where she had grown up, this jewel-bright treasure in the middle of the Mediterranean Sea. The only place that she had ever called home. The only place she had memories of her parents.

But she was doing it for her family. For her legacy. For her people. Onyx could come visit her, and surely she would be able to return home sometime. Surely.

She didn't have a chance to miss Andrei yet. Since it seemed that he was going to be her shadow this entire time.

Into her new life.

A ghost of everything she could never have.

She took an overly large swallow of champagne as the boat began to drift away from shore.

Conviction burned in her breast. She knew why she was doing this. She just had to hold on to that reasoning. To that conviction.

"Relaxing before your execution?"

She looked up at Andrei, dressed all in black, of course. "You are fun at parties," she said. "I know because I've seen you. Haunting the back walls like a wraith."

"Is this a party?" he asked.

"It could be. A beautiful yacht, gorgeous views, champagne. The only thing that's missing is other people."

"I never miss other people."

She laughed. "Of course not. Anyway, the more elaborate an event is, the more work goes into the security, I suppose."

"It is true."

She frowned. "What is my brother going to do without you?"

"I'm good at my job, Emerald. That means that anyone who has worked under me these past years is well trained in their position, and I leave behind competent people to coordinate the security of the palace. Only narcissists rule with such an iron fist that they cannot accept the assistance from those qualified around them."

"And you're not a narcissist," she said.

He wasn't. She was simply poking at him.

She did that with him, used humor, gentle and spiky depending on how exposed she felt, to make her footing feel sure with him. In return, he was dry. If you didn't know him, you'd miss that he was bantering back, because he did everything in the same, serious tone.

She knew him, though.

"No. I'm not. I am aware of my abilities, certainly. I am a realist. Not a narcissist."

He walked to the edge of the railing and grabbed hold of it, his knuckles white as he gripped it hard, looking out at the sea.

"I *am* sorry," she said. "About the sea voyage. I know that this isn't how you choose to travel, and it must be difficult."

There. She could be nice. She didn't need to bleed her desperation all over this situation. It would only make it worse. Complex feelings aside, and her irritation over all of the way this had played out ignored, Andrei was one of the people that she cared about most.

Bringing him with her should be a relief.

If she were normal about him, it could be.

"Nothing is difficult, Princess. I am more than able to accomplish my tasks. What happened is in the past." And yet still, he clung to that railing. His eyes on the water, not on her.

"Where are you sleeping?"

"I have a cabin," he said. "Your brother was overly generous in appointing lodging."

"Let me guess. You wanted to sleep on the floor in the coldest part of the ship so as to adequately suffer for not being royalty, and my brother insisted on giving you a bed."

He lifted a brow. "How did you guess?"

He released his hold on the railing, turned to face her, a smile curving his lips. So rare were those smiles. His long black hair fell into his face, and the wind pushed it off his forehead again. His cheekbones were hollow, his jaw sharp, his lips a source of great fascination. Full and mobile, and having the appearance of a man who should know how to smile and laugh often. They kept him from looking as severe as he was.

They had riveted her from the time she was fifteen or so. When she had truly accepted that Andrei was something different to her than a protector or a brother or a friend.

That he was, in fact, the most beautiful man she had ever seen.

She felt so ashamed of it, at least then. Her palms would get sweaty, her heart beating faster, and there was simply no way for her to understand those feelings. Why for him? Why so strong? There were different points where she had come to accept what those feelings were because he was an unrelated male in proximity. The truth was, she had very little access to men unencumbered. None, in fact. Even when she had gone to university in the city, Andrei had been with her. It was always him. Always. Part of her had always loved that. Part of her had loathed it.

How was she ever supposed to be normal, have a date, have a kiss, have sex, if the man who consumed her fantasies, who was out of reach even though he was only an arm's length away, was always there.

How?

The truth was, she hadn't figured it out. And now the answer seemed to be: She had to arrange a marriage for herself.

So now her first time, her first kiss, her first experience of sex, was going to be with... King Lucian.

He was reclusive. There were no images of him taken in years. The rumors were that he was scarred. That half of his face was hideously scarred from battles during brutal wartimes in his country. The other half was beautiful. A fallen angel's visage. He was older. Forty to her twenty-four.

But that really wasn't her biggest concern. His age was simply a number when compared to his potential brutality.

Though all of these things were consistent across time. Men were brutal, and they wanted young women to help bear their heirs. She wasn't unique or special in the grand fabric of the world, and certainly not in the history of royal unions.

She wasn't marrying him for his temperament, nor was she marrying him for the joy of sex.

The joy of sex might have to be something confined to her fantasies.

She really didn't need to be thinking about the joy of sex while Andrei stood there looking at her with those dark, molten eyes, and that mouth that had bewitched her for so long.

"Is there any way I can dissuade you from doing this?"

She shook her head. "No. Why do you need to?"

He walked toward her, and much to her surprise, took

a seat beside her in one of the loungers. "It has been my life's work to protect you. To keep you safe. I have followed you throughout your life. Every vacation you've ever been on, to university. And I will follow you here. I will guard you with my life, Princess, as I have done these past eight years. But it would be remiss of me not to ask you, to beg you, to reconsider."

"Andrei Ardelean? *Begging?* This is truly a momentous moment," she said, but her voice sounded breathless, and it was difficult for her to breathe.

He looked at her, his eyes black and hollow. "You are everything to me."

She was almost certain he hadn't spoken, that she had hallucinated his words, a trick on the wind.

At first she didn't react, because she didn't know how to. Didn't know if she should. But then she looked at him, her heart tripping over itself. He was staring at her with deep, focused intensity. He *had* said it.

But what did those words mean?

Was it *everything* as he was to her?

That seemed impossible.

"I trust you," she said. "I know you won't let anything happen to me."

"You didn't even want me to go with you."

She couldn't tell him. She couldn't tell him why she had wanted to leave him behind in Basilia. Why she was almost desperate to put distance between them. Did he have any idea how painful it was for her to go on and marry another man while he was right there. While she still had to see him. While she was still close enough to touch him, but never, ever could. Just like always.

Just like always.

"I *need* you to go with me," she said, finally, the closest thing to admitting she needed *him* that she would allow. "I see that now. Though, I do think you're going to have to look a little bit less suspicious of everyone and everything."

"I am there as your personal bodyguard. I don't think I need to look less suspicious at all."

"I do. Don't you think it would be better if they underestimated you. I mean, if there is going to be a problem."

"Perhaps. But if you're suggesting that I should play incompetent, I should warn you that I do not know how to do that."

"Incompetent at being incompetent? That sounds about right."

He made a short sound in the back of his throat and reclined in the chair. He crossed his arms over his broad chest, and she thought not to linger and notice every detail.

The strength in his shoulders, how his suit jacket pulled on his muscles. Andrei and her brother were addicted to the gym in the palace. They spent hours lifting weights and doing hideous amounts of push-ups and burpees.

They enjoyed pushing themselves to their limits.

Emerald did not.

Occasionally, she would watch a movie while walking on the treadmill. That was her version of fitness, and she was comfortable with it.

She often felt like Andrei and Onyx were attempting to sweat their demons out. Her demons took a different form. They didn't dog her physically. They were in her head, swirling around continually, day and night. Asking what her value was. Asking what she had done to make her life worthwhile.

At twenty-four, her mother had been a mother. She had been a queen. By thirty-one, she was dead. She wondered if all of that had felt like enough for her mother. All the things she'd done. By comparison, Emerald hadn't done very much.

"What do you see your legacy as, Andrei?"

He looked at her out of the corner of his eye, but otherwise didn't move. "My legacy?"

"Yes. Surely you feel like there's something you need to accomplish. Something you want to leave behind. We both experienced death at a very young age. I feel like it makes you think about it. And you experienced two times what I did. It makes me think. About what it is I'll leave behind, because the simple truth is we are only here for such a short time. Some of us much shorter than others, but there is no guarantee."

"My legacy, my hope, has always been in preserving your family. Keeping you safe. Keeping your brother safe."

"That's all? What is it that your parents wanted when they came to Basilia?"

"Safety," he said, his words hard. "They were on the run."

He'd never told her this before. The idea of him being a boy, running away from one danger and sinking in another…it burned.

"They saw Basilia as a potential safe haven," he said. "Though they never reached the shores, it was a safe haven for me. And because of that I fight to preserve the royal family."

"And because you like us," she said.

"Some days more than others," he said, his voice hard.

She was sure that he almost smiled. That the corner of his mouth moved upward just slightly. Just slightly.

"Today?"

"A trial."

"You don't ever plan on getting married? Having children?" It was a perverse question to ask, but she wanted to try and imagine his life without her in it. Wanted to make a picture in her mind of how things would be after she took this husband, after she left her home and him.

Any ghost of a smile disappeared. "No. My line ends with me. I know my father would have wanted me to carry on this line. Survival was paramount to him, as was the carrying on of his…legacy. He didn't succeed, except on one count. I feel sometimes that the sea was trying to take us all, but didn't quite manage. I have a mission, and that is to repay the kindness that your family showed to me, that your country showed to me. But that is all."

She frowned. "Why… What did your father do in Romania?"

He'd never said. Maybe she should have asked before, but she had a sense of Andrei, of certain closed doors in his soul, and she'd always felt like this was one of them. She'd assumed because of how traumatic the wreck and losing his parents had been.

But now she wondered how much more trauma there was in his past.

"There's no purpose to talking about the past. Especially, I don't wish to speak about my family right now." He looked around, and out at the ocean all around them.

"Of course. I'm sorry."

"No need to apologize. Though you are the reason I'm here."

"I know I—"

"I was teasing," he said, very nearly smiling. "I insisted on coming."

"It's a very dark thing to tease about."

"My life has been very dark so far."

She made a scoffing sound, and pushed herself up out of the lounger. "Will you join me for dinner, Andrei?"

He often refused to do that. He was very strange about his protocols. There were times when he would agree to take a meal with her and with Onyx in the palace, but there were other times when he was hard-line about staying with staff.

His eyes met hers, and her breath caught.

You are everything to me.

"Yes. I will take dinner with you tonight."

CHAPTER THREE

IT WAS A foolish thing to agree to. He should've insisted on maintaining his distance from her.

What he should never have done was tell her how much she meant to him. He wasn't entirely sure that she understood what he was saying.

That was for the best.

The cabin he'd been given for the journey was not going to work for him. He was never going to spend time in the lower decks of a yacht. Images of water pouring in from the top haunted him. He would much rather be on the top deck, where he could jump off into the ocean if he needed to escape. Of course, that presented the concern that if there actually was a problem he would have to find and save Emerald. And she had no issues with the ship whatsoever.

They were projected to have smooth sailing the entire way to Alabria, and additionally, the ship was sound and expensive, with many safety features that had been absent from the vessel that his family had stowed away on from Romania while on the run from very bad men.

His father had been a bad man, of course. And so it was the exact sort of justice you earned when you yourself were a monster.

Still, the events of that day haunted him.

Which was how he found himself standing still on the top deck, looking out at the vast, endless expanse of water. It was a kind of blue he hadn't seen anywhere else. The surface rolled in a rhythmic motion, the surf so calm that the only whitecaps in the water came from the boat's wake. It was beautiful. But treacherous.

"Are you ready to eat?"

He turned, and his stomach went tight.

Beautiful. But treacherous.

Emerald was standing in front of him, her red hair free around her shoulders, curling delicately against her pale, bare skin. The dress that she was wearing clung to her generous curves, and the green, like her name, was a glorious foil for all her natural beauty. She had put on red lipstick, highlighting her mouth in a way that made his blood turn to liquid fire.

He was a man of great control. He had been alone with her countless times since that first spark had been ignited in his blood. He'd thought that he had mastered the art of self-denial.

But he feared, then and there, that that control had never *truly* been tested before. Out here in the ocean, surrounded by nothing but water, with Onyx far away on a distant shore, and his time with her running down like sand in an hourglass, his control felt much more tenuous than it ever had before.

Yes. He was ready to eat. But it was not food that he was hungry for. It was her.

If she knew the fantasies that he had about her, she would run away and hide. In spite of all the pain that she had endured, Emerald was an innocent. It was something that made him feel both pride and shame. She had never been able to date, had never been able to bring a man home, because he had always been there. Standing in the way. If he had been a different bodyguard, one who wasn't interested in her body, but only in the guarding, then perhaps he would've made space for her to have romantic entanglements.

As it was, he hadn't allowed it on his watch, and if he had ever observed a man showing interest in her, he had done his level best to scare the man away.

Emerald was untouched, and he knew it. Because no one had ever been given the chance to touch her.

Courtesy of Andrei.

"Andrei?"

He realized that he had lost himself, and the number of times that had happened was negligible. If it ever had before.

Normally, he was supremely in control of himself, and his reaction to her. It was always there, present, lurking beneath the surface like sharks out in the ocean. But he had dominion over it. Not here. Not now.

He couldn't afford it. He was going to have to be hypervigilant once they got to Alabria. King Lucian had the potential to be an enemy, a danger to Emerald, and Andrei had to keep her safe. Above all else.

"Yes," he said. "I'm ready."

"Oh good. I asked to have your favorite made."

"Why did you do that?"

"I don't know. To tell you the truth, I *was* mad at you and my brother."

He snorted. "I noticed."

"But I realized today how much I'm going to miss you both."

"I'm with you," he said. "You can't miss me."

He ignored the way that made him feel. He ignored his feelings with the same ease with which he drew breath.

With her though, it was always harder.

Suddenly her eyes filled with tears. "I know. But it isn't the same."

Why? Why wouldn't it be the same?

He knew why it wouldn't be for him, but suddenly he was desperate to know why that was true for her.

It was a question he couldn't ask. A question that he shouldn't even have.

He had never allowed himself to believe she felt what he did. But now...now he wondered. He shouldn't wonder. He shouldn't ask things like this.

So he shoved it down deep and followed her to where a table was set with white linens, overlooking the sea, almost as if it were a date, which was something neither of them had ever had.

Not with each other, not with anyone.

"Pasta," she said, smiling, making her way to the table and taking a seat that faced the water. He didn't need a view. He only needed to see her.

"I gathered, when you said it was my favorite." It was one of the first meals he had at the palace. A simple pasta dish with red sauce, and after everything he'd been through it had felt like salvation. It still did in many ways.

And she knew it. Of course she did. Because Emerald could never be accused of being a spoiled princess. Her actions, even now, were evidence of that. He might not agree, he might wish to kidnap her, take her far away from all of this, but he knew that what she was doing was for the greater good.

It was just that he didn't care much about the greater good. Not in the face of her safety.

He moved slowly to the table, taking his position across from her, and putting his napkin in his lap. He had a vague memory of when he had first come to the palace. Slightly feral, and uncertain of how exactly table manners worked.

His father never included children at dinners. Which would always have colleagues—people he had discovered later were from crime syndicates.

The kids had always eaten in the playroom. When he'd been young, he'd found aspects of his childhood to be truly wonderful. But he'd been in danger, and he'd never known it.

Not until they'd had to run away.

Not until it had been too late.

The king and queen and Basilia had taught him. How to be civilized. How to be less feral. At least in appearance. The truth was, his foundation would always be what it was. He would always be the son of a crime lord. He'd thought his childhood was fine, because he didn't know better. He did now. There were things his father had instilled in him, shown him, encouraged him to do, that had been twisted, wrong and vile. They were baked into him, part of the formation of his being. And he would always be a product of a childhood that had encouraged him to embrace his baser instincts.

He kept it on a leash with her. That leash felt dangerously close to breaking now.

"I remember the first time I saw you," she said. They never talked about this. The truth was, they were in each other's lives every day, and they didn't often discuss the past or memories. They had lived through many of them together. He had spent the first twelve years of his life in Romania, and after that he had been with the royal family. He had been with Emerald. The boat, the water, the fact that everything was about to change, that, he assumed was driving these conversations.

He wasn't sure what to make of that.

Or if he should indulge her.

But he decided to. Because there were other things he could not indulge, and so he would indulge in conversation.

"And what did you think?"

"I thought you were amazing. And quite possibly a merman."

That almost made him laugh. The sensation was so foreign, he didn't quite know what to do with it. "A merman?"

"Yes. You came right out of the sea. I know you don't remember when we found you. We were walking on the beach near the palace, and there you were, washed up on shore. Mother picked me up and tried to hide my eyes, because she thought you were dead. Onyx ran to you. Before my mother or father could stop him. He found that you were alive."

He had heard the story recounted to him before, but never by Emerald. He found himself fascinated. He wished that he had the memory, truly. Of that first moment when they found him. When he had been saved.

But it was lost to him.

"When they discovered that you were breathing, my father picked you up, and they began to run back to the palace. We had doctors there, and they immediately called for emergency equipment, more medical people to come and check you out."

"I remember waking up in bed," he said.

He wouldn't speak of the shipwreck itself. "Warm and safe. I was sure that I had died. That I was in heaven, though I did not expect heaven to have bedrooms."

"You didn't?"

"I thought you just sat on clouds."

Emerald and Onyx had been sitting on the foot of his bed when he woke up. Onyx looking grave, Emerald excited, her eyes shining brightly. "You're awake!" Hers had been the first voice that he'd heard in his new life.

"We brought you spaghetti, with marinara sauce and meatballs. And you ate it like you hadn't eaten for months."

"It's funny to me that you remember that."

"How could I forget?"

He refused to put weight to that. Refused to apply significance.

They ate their dinner as the sun set into the sea, and Andrei did his best to ignore her beauty, his reaction to it, how sore his chest felt.

He was not a man given to rumination. He knew his mission, he knew what he had to do. He had accepted a long time ago that there would be no love for him. No happy ending. No wife, no children. It was better that way. Better that he not continue with a poisonous bloodline. Better that he simply focus on serving Onyx and Emerald, being their protector, being everything that they needed him to be.

That was what he had chosen. It was the path that he walked. He couldn't deviate from it now that Emerald was getting married.

He had always known this day would come. He hadn't anticipated that he would have to watch it happen. That he would have to stand by and attend to her new life with her new husband. But he hadn't anticipated her selling herself to a man who might be dangerous.

"I know you think you don't want to meet anybody, but you might," she said.

"I won't," he said, his voice flat. He looked at her profile, graceful and elegant. The swoop of her nose, the curve of those red lips. He had met someone. She was the only person that he would ever meet who did this to him. He had read once about courtly love. About knights who devoted themselves to ladies and accepted the fact that it would never be physical. That it would never be anything other than honor and protection. That was how this would be. Always.

"We're going to go to Alabria, and who knows? The court might be filled with beautiful women."

"I will not be part of the court. You and your brother do not observe protocol the way that everyone else in the world does. A bodyguard, even if he is the head of security, is not part of the royal family. Nor will he ever be."

"I will insist that you are included."

"And I am not asking that of you."

"Well, I want you to be included. When there is a

party, when our wedding celebration happens, I want you to be there as a guest."

"I will be guarding the proceedings to make sure it isn't a red wedding, so to speak."

"You are so grim."

"I'm paid to be grim. It is my job to be grim, and to be distrustful of the world."

"Will you at least dance with me at my wedding?"

He felt like he had been punched in the stomach. "You know full well a queen cannot dance with a commoner. Ever. Least of all at her own wedding."

"We danced before," she said softly.

He looked at her, their eyes meeting, holding. The impossibility of her request revealing in so many ways. Revealing things he'd never allowed him to see. A mirror of his own heart.

Yes. He remembered that ill-fated event. Far too clearly. He chose never to think about it. Chose to keep that firmly locked away in the deep, dark recesses of his memory. It had been a mistake. She had been just eighteen, and it had been her birthday party. She'd asked him to dance, and then she'd taken his hand in hers. She was so soft. Her fingers slim, her frame petite, and as he pulled her body against his he had felt desire like he'd never known before.

Need that went beyond the physical.

He wanted her. He wanted to cup her face in his hands and kiss her, but he wanted more than that. He wanted to be close to her, not just skin to skin, but something deeper.

Something he wasn't able to articulate or explain.

He could feel it echo inside him now.

"I don't think we will dance at your wedding."

"Then you should dance with me now," she said.

She was pushing. There was an edge to her now, and it was cutting deeply into him.

He wanted to tell her no. He wanted to scold her. Why? The only reason to do that would be... For the shameful, secret reasons that he kept buried inside himself. As far as she was concerned, the dance on her eighteenth birthday had been innocent. He was the only one who knew that it wasn't, and he would take that to his grave.

Why not? Why not take this one last chance to touch her? To hold her. Why not dance with her one last time?

He would not do it at her wedding. He would not do it when she was married to another man. He refused.

He stood up, and extended his hand to her. "All right, Princess, show me how you've improved these past years."

CHAPTER FOUR

SHE DIDN'T KNOW what she was doing, pushing him recklessly like this. She had been doing that ever since they boarded the ship. Trying to make him angry, trying to make him smile, trying to get some emotion out of him. Trying to see if he felt what she did. And now, pushing him into a dance... She was playing a dangerous game, except she didn't know if it was the kind of danger she was hoping to find herself in.

Andrei had never once demonstrated attraction toward her. He had never expressed interest in her body. Only in her protection. She was a duty to him, and she understood that. But she was also a woman, and he was a man. Of course, he had known her since she was a child, and it was possible that he would never truly see her as she was.

But now his hand was in hers, rough and big and warm, and he was drawing her toward his body, and she chose to forget everything but this. If this was the last time Andrei would ever hold her, then she would revel in it. Relish it. Then she would live and love only this moment for as long as she could.

She wrapped her arms around his neck, and he put

his on her lower back. There was no music; his gaze was intense.

You mean everything to me.

Those words flashed through her mind, and she felt electricity skitter down her spine. She was everything to him. Did that mean what she hoped it did? Did it mean that he wanted her?

There would never be another chance for this.

This was why she'd wanted to get away from him, so she didn't...so she didn't do this. But God, how was she supposed to deny it? How was she supposed to be given this time with him and do nothing with it?

She angled her face upward, bringing her mouth perilously close to his, and if it created any feelings inside him, he didn't show it.

Her own heart was beating so fast she thought she might pass out. His hands were hot against her lower back, and then he moved them, so that he was holding her hips. She couldn't stop the feminine sounds that caught in her throat, and she closed her eyes, willing herself to keep standing even though her knees had gone weak.

She opened her eyes again, and he was right there, all that molten heat directed at her. His expression was stern, and hard, and she knew looking for anything soft or welcoming in that face was a losing proposition. Except she could see the heat in his eyes.

He wanted her.

Andrei *did* want her.

A blessing, a curse. A total upending of everything she'd allowed herself to believe. If she'd known he wanted her...

She would never have been able to resist touching him. Tempting him. Tempting them both. She couldn't resist now.

Not now, when they were sand in an hourglass.

"Andrei." She whispered his name, and reached up and touched his face.

He drew back as though she had slashed him with a knife. "Princess," he said. "I would advise you not to step outside protocol."

"There is no protocol for us. There never has been."

"Do you or do you not have a marriage arrangement with King Lucian?"

"I do, but..."

"But?"

"He is not on this boat."

"I see. And so you think a man like me, a peasant, should be happy to be your entertainment for the ride before you marry the man who is worthy of you?"

Her thoughts were racing. What he was saying wasn't fair, and it definitely wasn't true. She didn't have any experience. Wanting to touch him, wanting to kiss him, wanting... That was the momentous thing. It was not some throwaway, it was everything. He'd had lovers before, she knew that.

One time, when she'd been in a bar in university, and he had been in the back of it, brooding against the wall, there had been a woman who had sat down next to her and her college friends, and she had told the story of how the man in the back had taken her to bed and blown her mind, but then never called.

She was the one who apparently wasn't *special* enough for that.

Or common enough.

But she was too wounded to say that. Because what he'd said wasn't fair at all. She had never treated him that way. Not ever. She had never treated him as anything other than special. As anything other than one of the most important people in her life. And him trying to make this about snobbery, trying to make her marriage to Lucian about anything other than benefiting Basilia was utterly and completely unfair.

She'd been brave now. She'd been the first one to speak the truth of the thing that burned between them, and he'd humiliated her for it.

All while being a coward.

"If you don't want me, then just say so."

She turned, and left him standing there, and she didn't look back.

If he didn't want her?

He was plagued that night as he lay out on the lounger on the top deck, trying to sleep.

Of course he wanted her. He had wanted her all this time, and she dared to say that to him?

It didn't benefit either of them for her to know how much he wanted her. So he had not gone after her, and he had not sought to close any of the distance between them because that could only end in disaster.

It nearly had.

The way that she had looked at him, the way that she had touched him? God. He had been undone. All these years of practicing discipline. Of turning himself into a good guy. A man who could be trusted. A man who could not be called a villain, not the way that his father had been, and he was ready to destroy it all for her.

To burn the world down to touch her lips to his.

I would very cheerfully kill him.

Because there was no good end to it. There was nothing that could come of it.

She had run away from him, and it was for the best.

His phone lit up in the dark. There was Wi-Fi on the boat that allowed for messaging even out in the middle of the sea. It was Onyx.

How is everything?

As good as it can be.

Meaning?

Your sister is still marrying a man who might kill her, and I am taking her to her doom.

But everything is going according to plan.

According to plan. Yes, the plan where he sent Emerald to another man's bed.

Fuck.

He threw his phone down on the deck, and it made a loud clatter.

He heard a gasp. "What are you doing out here?"

"Sleeping," he responded, annoyed that yet again, it was Emerald. Yet again, he could not escape her.

"Don't you have a cabin?"

"Yes. I don't wish to make use of it."

"Why not?"

"Go to bed, Emerald."

She came into the dim light glowing from the deck above. She was dressed in pajamas now, her face scrubbed clean, and she was no less beautiful for it. Brave for standing there, facing him in spite of what he'd said. "I don't want to fight with you," she said.

"There may be no other option for us," he said.

"But why? We've always been important to each other, and everything is going to change. So why can't we be like we've always been to each other now."

"You do not always touch me," he said.

"No," she agreed, sounding subdued. "I don't have to do that again."

"I will need you to *not* do it again." His voice was hard, and he was aware of what he'd done here. That with this statement he'd exposed himself. His desire for her.

"Okay." She came and sat down in the chair next to his, her hands folded in her lap. "Look. I'm behaving myself." Her smile was almost impish, and it made the desire inside him rage.

He did his best to keep it on the inside, to not let it show. A memory rose to the surface, and he decided to speak it aloud. Anything to crush the desire that was threatening to stage an uprising inside him.

"I was on a lower deck when the ship began to sink when I was a child. And I remember the water coming in from above. Beginning to fill up the room. If we hadn't been able to get to higher ground, we would've drowned then and there. I don't like the feeling of being trapped in small spaces, and I particularly don't like it when there is water all around. I am happy to sleep up here."

"Oh. I'm so… Sorry. I don't think we've ever talked about what you remember from that day."

"Because none of the memories are good."

"I know. But have you ever talked about it with anybody?"

"No. I remember everything about the shipwreck, until I passed out from not being able to breathe in the water. But I remember fighting with the water. I remember being certain that I was going to die, that the ocean was going to swallow me whole. I could hear the crew, my parents, other passengers, screaming before they went under." She had asked, and so he was telling her, though there was no purpose to any of it. To either being cold to her or kind to her, because none of it would change anything.

None of it would change what he had to be to her, what she was intent on doing.

"I'm so sorry. I would touch you, but I'm forbidden from doing that."

"Yes," he said, his voice rough. "You are."

"I think that if you weren't here I would be very scared," she said. "I think if I were doing this on my own… I would do it. I'm the one who signed the papers. I'm the one who made the agreement. I would do it. But you don't know how much you being here matters to me. To think that all those years ago I could have lost you in the bottom of the sea…"

"You have to have me to lose me, Emerald. And it isn't like that between us."

He was being cruel to be kind.

Perhaps he was just being cruel to protect himself. As deadly as it was to want her, the deeper, emotional need for her was almost worse. He needed her to not touch him.

It would shatter him. Everything that he was, everything that he had styled himself to be.

"I don't have you?" She squinted, looking at him as though she were trying to see him from a great distance. As though he were difficult to see clearly. "Yes, I do. You are with me all the time. Every day. You are my silent shadow, standing behind me, ready to put your life on the line for me."

"For the Crown."

"So, is it only my brother that you care about? Or is it the position. Your loyalty and allegiance to my parents, even in death."

"All of those things."

"But not me?"

"Not in the way that you are asking."

He stood, but so did she. "Andrei," she said. "I'm doing this for the country. Because this has always been my fate. There has never been another path for me. Just like Onyx."

"I know that," he said. "I know that. You must marry royalty, you must marry for the good of the Crown. Just as I must not marry, also for the good of the Crown."

"And is that all we are?"

"Duty and honor? Yes. It is all we are. It is all we can be."

She looked ahead sightlessly at the black horizon. "I thought it would feel better. I thought it would feel like something triumphant."

"Does it not?"

She shook her head. "I wonder what my mother felt.

When she came down from her village, the only place she ever knew, and married a man she had never seen before. I wish that I could ask her."

"That is one of the terrible things about loss. It echoes, continuously. There are always questions you want to ask, always things you want to tell them. But you can't."

They'd never spoken of such deep things. But everything felt different now, now that their time together would end. It felt like it all might as well be said.

She looked at him, her eyes glossy. "I don't know that I will ever feel like the fullest version of myself. Because somewhere out there perhaps there is a version of me who got to learn all of her mother's wisdom. But I didn't. All I can do is study about her in history books just the same as everyone else who lives in Basilia. All I can do is know her in writing."

"But you did know her," he said.

"I didn't know what to ask. Not then. I didn't know how to ask what I wish, so desperately, I knew now. I only ever asked her to do things for me. To read to me, to watch me dance. I wish I'd asked her how I should live. What makes a person brave? What made her brave?"

"I think that is the burden of growing older. You lose people, and realize all that you didn't say. When you were a child, your mother was only your mother. But now you see her as the queen. As a woman who made difficult decisions."

"Do you wish that you could ask your parents questions?"

"Yes," he said, standing up and moving away from her. "But I do not think that I would like any of the answers. You should go to sleep, Emerald. We have another full day and night of sailing yet."

"You say that like this is taxing." Perhaps it was only taxing for him.

"Either way, they are your last days of freedom."

He hadn't intended to say it. But he had, and neither of them could fully argue with the sentiment.

CHAPTER FIVE

THESE ARE YOUR last days of freedom.

His words echoed inside her head all night. She couldn't sleep.

When she woke up, she felt wretched and grotty, and completely unable to control her emotions. It took a pot of coffee in a lovely silver service for her to even feel remotely civil. She didn't seek Andrei out until after that. She was sure that he had slept up on the deck, just as he said. She castigated herself for putting him in the position where he had to be on this journey.

She had been angry at him, and at her brother, but the closer she got to Alabria, the more grateful she was for the protection. The more she questioned herself, even if she wouldn't let Andrei know that she did.

Though their attraction—mutual!—was now out in the open, and it made everything feel electrified. It made breathing feel painful.

She didn't see him at the front of the boat, and wandered around the starboard side, taking in the view of the glorious Mediterranean before she went aft and stopped. Because there was an even more glorious view there.

Andrei. Swimming in the pool. He was shirtless, his dark skin glistening in the sun. He leveraged himself up out of the pool, the muscles on his body shifting with the motion, water droplets sliding down the hollows in his chest, his abs. He was wearing tight black swim shorts that did not cover his magnificent thighs.

He was a work of art. She had never painted a damn thing in her life, but suddenly she wanted to take it up. Or maybe sculpt him out of something. If it was the only way she would ever know what it was like to touch his body, she would take a hunk of clay right now and try to shape it into him.

Because at least then maybe she could caress the fine lines of his body. Wow, that was an incredibly weird thought. But she was in an incredibly strange state. The door on her self-imposed prison was about to close, and then Andrei would be out of her reach forever.

He's always been out of your reach.

Maybe.

"Good morning," he said, his dark eyes flickering over her dispassionately. She looked down at her loose pajamas, and felt annoyed. If she were in her underwear, he probably wouldn't be able to look so disinterested. It wasn't fair. He was basically naked.

"Good morning," she said.

"How did you sleep?"

She huffed a laugh. "Not well. Though I don't suppose that would surprise you."

"Because I don't like boats?"

"Because of my looming marriage," she said.

Manacles. Chains. A total loss of freedom.

How ridiculous to be so angry about something she had engineered. It wasn't like anyone was forcing her hand. Nothing other than her own desire to positively impact her country. Her own obsession with legacy.

But sometimes she did feel trapped by that. By her own impossibly high standards for herself and her life.

Now, see where it had led her.

He began to walk toward her, her stomach clenching tight, her... She could feel the echo of each and every footstep between her legs. Could feel herself getting sensitive, getting wet.

He was such a hazard. This wasn't the first time her body had gone completely rogue around him.

One time he had tried to show her some basic self-defense moves, and his hands on her body had given her fantasy fuel for weeks. She was absolutely sure that if he had any idea what she'd done to herself in her room after that he would be horrified.

Or maybe he wouldn't be. Because however he had reacted afterward, he did want her. At least, he had in the moment. But he was a man, so it could be that simple. He had a woman's body pressed against him, and maybe that was all it took. Maybe it wasn't about her at all, but just his sex drive.

He walked by her, his shoulder brushing against the side of her arm as he reached down and picked up a towel from one of the lounge chairs. He began to towel off his hair, his chest, and she found herself held captive by the motion. His chest, his washboard flat abs. His hip bones. Oh God, don't look there. Right at the center of those very tight swim trunks. The mysteries of the male form in all its glory were beneath those shorts, and she found herself very curious indeed.

Not that she'd never seen a naked man in pictures, but

she hadn't actually seen one in the flesh. And anyway, he was the only one she wanted to see.

Lucky you. In a few weeks, you'll be seeing Lucian.

A stranger. A man she'd never even met. The idea was like a bucket of cold water poured over her head.

It wasn't that he was a stranger, if she was being honest. It was that he wasn't Andrei.

"What do you want?"

He sounded put out, his temper short.

"I don't know. I thought that I might seek the company of the person on this vessel that I know best?"

"You are staring," he said.

"You're a sight to behold," she said, not seeing the point in lying. He must know that he was beautiful.

"Stop," he said, his words short. Clipped.

"What?"

"You *know*."

He wasn't doing any better than she was. It made her feel strangely powerful. She'd felt alone in her need for him for so long. Discovering that he was tortured by it too? It was a heady drug.

"Maybe. But if you keep denying it then how will I really know?"

"I'm not playing games with you," he said. "Not for the entirety of this journey."

"Who said that I was playing a game?"

"You know how things are. A game is all it could ever be."

He turned and walked away from her, and she stood, mesmerized by the muscles in his broad back, immobilized by the pain in her heart.

The problem was her. She'd had to decide what she

wanted. What she was going to do. This had been her decision, and she had regrets now. Maybe there was a way that she could have fewer regrets.

But he was right about one thing. She couldn't play games. She had to be certain.

He had been cruel to her earlier and he regretted it. But he needed his distance. What would she have done if he had grabbed her? Kissed her? Shown her exactly what he wanted to do with her. Shown her exactly how he wanted her.

She thought she wanted him, but what she wanted was a fantasy. She thought she could poke and provoke him as she might do some frat boy who approached her at university.

If she got a taste of his real need she would run, terrified, and she would have every right to. Because she didn't *really* know.

And instead, you'll let Lucian, the Sea Serpent of the Mediterranean, introduce her to pleasure?

The idea made him feel homicidal. And that wasn't beneficial for anyone. He had to be able to walk into that palace as her bodyguard, and not present as a threat to the ruler of the country, or he would find himself executed and quickly.

It was perhaps not a ringing endorsement for his mental state that the only thing that bothered him about that was the possibility that he wouldn't be there to protect her.

But in many ways, life for him would end after she married another.

Nothing has to change. She can still be yours in all

the ways that matter. You will sacrifice yourself for her. Devote yourself to her.

Yes. That was true.

Without ever corrupting her, or violating Onyx's trust.

Yes. Lucian will get to violate her instead.

He growled furiously, angry, yet again, that he was trapped on this boat. If he didn't hate the ocean so damned much he might've thrown himself in to swim for a few laps. He was a good swimmer, and had become a better one in the years since the shipwreck. But he did not swim in the ocean recreationally. For obvious reasons.

It was growing dark, and they had made no plans to eat together. In fact, he had seen a staff member with a tray of food heading to the lower decks earlier, and he thought that perhaps she had taken dinner in her room. All for the best.

He walked around to the forward deck and saw Emerald, leaning against the railing, her red hair a curtain around her face. Her shoulders were shaking.

"What's the matter?"

She gasped, lifting her head and wiping her cheeks. Then she looked at him, her eyes glittering with sadness, with fierce determination.

"I can't imagine."

"You don't have to go through with this." He would demand that the yacht turn around now and head straight back to Basilia. Hell, he would jump in and swim them both back. His fears about the ocean be damned.

"I *do*." Her stubbornness sounded nearly petulant.

"You can find another husband."

"Is that what you think? That this is about me being

afraid of King Lucian? No. What I'm grappling with is that there's no way for me to marry someone who isn't you without feeling extraordinary pain."

He could say nothing to that. She had said it. She had spoken the invisible thing into existence. She had put into words something that they should never acknowledge. Something that he would never acknowledge, no matter how she changed the rules on them now.

"Emerald," he said. "You are emotional."

She threw herself at him then, as if she was leaping off a cliff, wrapped her arms around his neck and buried her head in the curve of his neck. The warm, soft press of her body against his undid him. He wrapped his arm around her waist, held her there, even though he knew that he should not. "Yes, I'm emotional," she said. "Because I'm never going to know. I'm never going to know what it could have been. I'm never going to know what passion is. Not really. I waited, all this time. I've never been kissed, I've never been touched, I've never—"

He kissed her. He could take it no more. He swallowed her words down like the sweet honey that they were, an elixir that turned his dark soul into sunshine as the sweetness of her mouth flooded him. He kissed her because he could do nothing else.

He kissed her, because he wanted her. Because he had wanted her all this time. She clung to him, her fingers pushed through his hair as she deepened the kiss, as she parted her lips and slid her tongue against his, as she arched her body against him, her breasts firm against his chest.

"Please," she whispered. "I didn't promise him a virgin bride. I don't want to go to his bed untouched. I want to have *you*. One night. Please."

He gripped her hips and growled. "No."

"Andrei—"

"Why should we light ourselves on fire only to burn? Don't you see, this is going to kill us both."

"I don't care," she said. "You're right. I was being frustrating before. Because I was trying to dance around the issue. I was trying to say it without saying it. Hot and cold, acting like your sister, acting like a jealous lover, acting like a spiteful ex. When the truth is I just want you, Andrei. With everything that I have, everything I am, I want you."

"You don't know what you want," he said. "You're far too innocent to know what you're asking for."

"You," she said. "Inside me. I want you to show me what passion is. I want you to show me what desire is. I want you to be the one to take my virginity. I don't want to give it to him. Shouldn't I give it to you? The man that I cared about for most of my life, the man who has protected me for all this time. It belongs to you."

But she could never belong to him, and that was the great and terrible truth. She could never be his, not truly.

But did it matter? Did it matter if she could be his for a moment. For a night. Would he take that and give her a lifetime of suffering?

He felt like he was standing on the edge of a cliff, balancing on the sharp edge of a sword. One wrong move and he would cut himself in half, but he was going to be cut in half anyway. She was going to marry another man. She was going to belong to someone else forever. That man would always have his hands on her. Would always have her body beneath his, because what man wouldn't?

So tonight, tonight she could belong to him. She could belong to him first.

Her kiss had been sweeter than anything he could've possibly imagined, and he wanted more. He wanted all of her.

He could have her.

And ever and always, all the days of her life, of her marriage, her skin would be branded with his hands. Always, she would have the memory of his cock surging inside her. Just thinking of that made his blood run hot. Molten like lava, his need for her as deadly and destructive as any natural disaster.

Nothing would make it better. Nothing. So he could suffer all of his life not knowing what it was to touch her, to taste her, to have her, or he could claim this. Just this once.

It was like drowning. Like dying. Like not knowing if he would ever reach the surface or if he was swimming to his death.

It was like his greatest fear, and his salvation rolled into one.

He growled, wrapped his arm around her neck, pushed his fingers through her hair and pulled her in for a rough kiss. He cupped her chin, holding her face tightly in his hand as he held her mouth open for him, tasting her long and deep, making her stand frozen like that as he gorged himself on her.

She was a revelation. A great and glorious beauty he couldn't get enough of.

He was so hungry for her he couldn't bear it.

His heart was hammering so hard he thought it might go completely through the front of his chest, leaving nothing but a bloody hole behind, and that would be a fitting tribute. For Emerald, he would give up his heart, his soul, his body.

He had already done so.

"We can't," she whispered. "Not out here. Not where someone could see."

He would do that too. Go down below, risk the entire ocean closing in upon them. As long as he was inside her it didn't matter. If they were his last moments on earth, then he would die happy.

He took her hand and led her down the stairs.

Let her lead him the short way to her cabin, her windows vast and open, facing the sea.

What a fitting way for this to end.

The ocean stretched before them. His greatest enemy. How perfect that it would be witness to this. He had gone down with a ship once before.

And now here he would again.

He sat down on the edge of the bed, looked at her. "Strip for me," he said.

This would be her first time, and he would make sure that she was well acquainted with pleasure. He would make sure that this was the best sex she could ever possibly have in her life. No other man would ever be able to please her the way that he did because he had years of fantasies inside him. Years of thinking about her, and her alone. The curves of her body, the way that her face would look when it reached the peak of pleasure, the sounds that she would make. No one would have all that desire inside them for her, and no one would ever be able to make her feel the things that he did. He knew that for sure.

But as for this moment, the one where she unveiled that body to him, he would sit, and he would take that pleasure for his own.

She looked at him, her eyes never leaving his as she stripped off her top, a white, lacy bra underneath. Then she pushed her pants down her legs, kicked them to the side. Bridal white. Innocent white.

His.

She moved toward him, lifted her knee up and pressed it to the mattress next to his thigh. He lifted her up off the floor, bringing her close to him so that she was straddling him, his arm locked tightly around her waist.

Confession was supposed to be good for this, but the words burning in his chest didn't feel like they would be good for either of them. And still. Time felt like a loaded gun pressed to his head, and so he needed to speak. If not now, he never would.

They were doomed either way.

"You know how long I've wanted this?" he growled, looking up at her. There was confidence in her eyes, but also so much… Hope. It was the hope that hurt the worst.

"No," she whispered. "Tell me."

"Always," he said. "For so long. You have been mine from the moment I laid eyes on you, mine to protect. But then, that began to change. As you became a woman, I began to want you as a man. But I knew that I could never touch you. I knew that all I could ever do was protect you."

She shook her head. "Tonight I don't want you to

protect me. I want you to corrupt me." She pressed her thumb against his lips, traced the outline of his mouth, and he closed his eyes, reveling in the sensation. "I want you to do unspeakable things to me. Things that you think might shock me, because I don't think they will. Do you know how long I've fantasized about you? You don't, do you? Oh, Andrei, I have wanted you. For so long. I have hated every woman you've ever taken to your bed. Even if I didn't see them, I knew that it was happening, and I hated them, as much as I envied them. There was a woman. I met her in a bar when I was in university, and she talked about how good you were. She talked about how you ate her. God, do you know how I fantasized about that?"

He tightened his hold on her. "It won't be like that between us."

"Why not?"

"Because I want you more. I don't know who that woman was. I wouldn't be able to remember her face if you tried to describe her to me. I never wanted her. I only wanted sex. But you... I want you. I'm starving for you. And I will remember this for the rest of my life."

She reached behind her back, unhooked her bra, let it fall free, revealing her pale, glorious breasts, her peach-colored nipples, tight with desire.

He had no control left in his body. He pressed his palm between her shoulder blades, brought her toward him, as he lowered his head to feast on her body. Her curves. He sucked one nipple deep into his mouth until she cried out, then he moved to the other, his thumb teasing the first one, using all the slickness he left behind to ease the friction.

She was grinding her hips against him, against his hardness, and it was all he could do not to free himself then and there. But if he did that, it would be over too quickly. And he wanted to savor this.

Because she was perfect. And tonight she was his. There would be nothing in the future. He would close that off ruthlessly at the bedroom door. The only thing there was, was this need between them.

This desperate, unending need that had built over a course of years. As far as the past went, those were the only memories he would allow. The memories of how much they desired each other. How much they wanted each other.

He began to unbutton his shirt, and she moved her hands, hastening the removal of his clothes. She pressed her palms against his chest, her expression one of awe. "You know how badly I wanted to do this earlier? I wanted to touch you so much."

"Do it," he said. "Touch me however you like. Taste me however you like." They had all night. But it was only one night, and so it had to be everything. Every fantasy. They had to gorge themselves on it until they were sick with it. Because it was all they had, so it had to be everything.

She moved away from him, for just a moment, pushed her underwear down her hips and discarded it on the floor, naked and perfect in front of him. Her skin was pale, her curves generous, the red thatch of curls between her thighs the answer to his every prayer.

How long had he stared at all the beautiful copper curls on her head and wondered about the rest of her? For far too long.

He was seized by the same hunger that had claimed him before, and he grabbed her hips, bringing all her luscious glory toward his mouth, lifting her up off the floor and laying back on the bed, bringing her down over his face. She gasped, reaching forward and grabbing hold of the headboard as he parted her thighs ruthlessly and tasted all of her slick heat. "Andrei."

"I will satisfy myself here," he said against her. "And then, there will be more."

He licked her, ate all of her sweetness, tasted her desire, his body so hard it hurt.

He moved his hands around to her glorious ass, holding her tightly against him as he ate even more deeply into her, as he felt her thighs begin to shake, as he felt her stomach contract sharply, as she cried out in sensual agony, as her release claimed her.

But he didn't give any quarter. He didn't stop. He kept going until she was shaking, sobbing, begging for relief. From the onslaught of pleasure that simply wouldn't end.

He was in pain, but he gave thanks for it. If he was going to die, then this was how he wanted to do it.

It was torture he would submit himself to for all of eternity. Pleasuring her while he was left in a state of arousal that wouldn't be satisfied.

It was his version of heaven and hell all at once.

"Please," she whimpered, but this wasn't just asking for him to stop. It was asking for more of him, and he could no longer resist.

He released his hold on her, and saw that he had left red fingerprints in her pale skin, on her thighs, her hips.

Had marked her perfectly.

She brushed her hair out of her face, damp with sweat,

then she licked her lips as she moved forward, undoing his belt, the closure on his pants, and he was too far gone to make a game. He helped her strip the rest of his clothes off, helped her reveal his aching arousal, and when she leaned in and took his cock into her mouth he gripped her hair and surrendered.

She sucked him in deep, before releasing him, sliding her tongue down the length of his shaft, and taking him back in again.

She licked him like he was the finest of sweets, and he arched his hips up hard, forcing her to take him as deep as she could.

He could play this game forever, except his control was too tenuous, and he was afraid that he was going to come down her throat. Something he would've loved to do someday. With more time. With more hours to spare.

But that was for lovers who had the luxury of years. Of recreation. He had nothing beyond a few spare hours to claim her. And he would do it thoroughly.

Irrevocably.

He moved her head away from him, her face confused, dazed and pleasured.

"Mine," he growled, kissing her mouth as he laid her back onto the pillows, kissing her deep and long, pressing his body to hers, her breasts against his chest, her hips against his, the hard ridge of his arousal nestled against her slit. It was a moment that he was going to pause and be in. Her all against him, the scent of her, the taste of her on his tongue.

But then, he could savor no longer. He parted her thighs, guiding himself to the entrance of her body, testing her, and finding her willing but tight.

"Just a moment of pain," he whispered against her mouth before he thrust in deep.

The roar that clouded his vision, his brain, his body was primal.

His. Lucian might marry her, might claim her, might have children with her, but she would never be his. Not in the way that she was Andrei's.

He would always be the first man to have her. It was all he could take. All he could call his own, and so he would.

He began to move, the feel of her slick, tight body all around him enough to make him lose control instantly. But he held on. This wouldn't be the only time tonight. He would have her until they were out of breath. Until their voices were hoarse from screaming out their pleasure, but there would be only one first time.

He wanted it to go on for as long as it could.

His thrusts were measured, slow, all in the interest of drawing it out. Of keeping them suspended in this moment, but then her nails dug into his shoulders, her back arched and she cried out his name. His name. "Andrei," she moaned. And he lost it. Completely. His thrusts became hard, totally uncontrolled, and he began chasing his own release, completely unable to put it off any longer.

And when he shouted out her name, it was both a curse and a prayer.

Because it didn't matter how many times he had her tonight. He was going to be haunted by Princess Emerald for the rest of his life.

And tomorrow he had to deliver her to another man.

CHAPTER SIX

WHEN EMERALD WOKE UP the next morning, her body was sore. There was no place that hadn't been branded by Andrei. His hands, his mouth, his tongue.

She had been made his ten times over, in every way possible.

She was grateful for it.

But she wanted to weep.

She swallowed hard, looking over at the man sleeping next to her. He looked so much younger in sleep, carefree in a way that she had never seen him. He had been marked by trauma from the first moment that she'd met him.

And now they had scarred each other.

She might love him.

He hadn't said that he loved her. She blinked hard, trying to hold her tears back. She really didn't want him to say it.

Because if he's said it…

Better to let it just be sex. Better to let it just be one night. One night that she would never forget, but one night all the same.

She swallowed hard and stood up, and then there was a knock on the door that made her startle. "Yes?"

Andrei stirred, and sat up, the covers falling down to his waist, her attention completely captivated by his half-naked form.

"Princess," came the voice from the other side of the door. "I have breakfast for you."

"You can leave it," she said. "I'll only be a moment."

He looked at her, his mouth a grim line. "I will go back to my quarters and ready myself to be presented at the palace. You should also ready yourself."

There were not going to be any soft words for her. No goodbye. When he got out of her bed, he began to dress in silence. And when he left the room he didn't kiss her goodbye.

She cried. For a few minutes, she cried. Because there was no way to fix this. Not ever. She'd made her decision. She had signed an agreement. She had given herself away.

But last night had been something she'd chosen for herself. She had to be okay with it. She was the one who had set the terms.

Still, she sobbed as she got dressed. Forgot that there was breakfast outside and nearly tripped over it when she opened the door, as the yacht moved into the port.

She wiped her face, but she knew that she looked like she'd been crying. Maybe King Lucian would like it. It was rumored that he was a ruthless bastard.

Maybe it would suit him.

When she looked out at the view of Alabria, she was shocked. It was a rocky, mountainous island, and a large black palace stood on top of the highest peak, like the tower of Barad-dûr in Middle-earth. All that was missing was the Eye of Sauron. If he wanted the world to think of him as a villain, he had certainly done a great job setting up the optics.

Dead wives not required.

She had been so focused on the grief that she felt over losing her chance with Andrei, that she hadn't fully allowed herself to feel grief over the situation she was putting herself in.

Because there's no point. Because you made your bed, and now you have to lie in it.

Hilarious, because the bed in her cabin still wasn't made. It was demolished from letting Andrei have her all night.

As soon as the yacht docked, they lowered the gangway, and as they were preparing to get off, they were boarded instead.

Andrei was immediately beside her, his hands on her as though he were ready to flee with her if necessary. "We are emissaries of the king," said a man dressed in a military uniform.

"What makes you think this is a necessary display? This vessel belongs to King Onyx of Basilia. And it is very easy for us to take this as an act of aggression," Andrei said.

"Of course it is not an act of aggression," the man said. "A treaty is signed between Princess Emerald and the king. There is no aggression here."

Her heart hammered in fear as she allowed the group of emissaries to lead her off the ship and put her in a car. They paused in front of Andrei. "Your services are not required," the man said.

"I am the princess's personal bodyguard. I go with

her wherever she goes. I think you will find the terms of that are nonnegotiable."

The man looked Andrei up and down. "I will leave that for the king to decide." He moved out of the way and allowed Andrei to get into the car next to her, and it was all she could do not to cling to him. She didn't have the right to do that, and he had made it very clear that physical touch, other than him protecting her, was not allowed this side of daylight. The car drove down a long, winding two-lane road that wound around the mountain, bringing them closer to the evil tower.

Reality was setting in very hard.

Warring with memories from last night. His hands on her skin. His body moving inside hers.

Stop this.
Stop this.
Stop this.

Her heart was beating a powerful rhythm, and the words echoing in her head were making it ache.

The car pulled up to the front of the palace, and they were ushered outside the vehicle. Andrei attached to her like a shadow at her back.

The doors to the palace opened, and they were brought inside, into a stark, black antechamber.

"The king awaits in the throne room."

A throne room? They didn't have anything half so prosaic. Onyx had a study where he conducted correspondence, and there was a sitting room where he entertained people. He didn't sit on an actual throne.

But it was clear to her that King Lucian really was stuck in the Dark Ages, just as the rumors said. The double doors to the throne room opened, and she stepped slowly inside, feeling like it was entirely possible that movement might release axes from the ceiling that were waiting to swing across the walkway and cut her to pieces.

She looked ahead and saw a figure sitting on a large, iron throne. Blond, his skin damaged on one side, perfect on the other, his eyes crystal blue, piercing through her from the great distance between them.

Whatever they'd said about his looks...they had underplayed it.

He was, in part, the most beautiful man she'd ever seen.

But where he was scarred, that beauty was ravaged.

"Princess Emerald," he said, his voice low, his accent indefinable. "Welcome to Alabria."

"Thank you," she said. "Your Highness."

She didn't genuflect because she felt that it would set a bad precedent.

"Let me see you."

He didn't move, he only sat there waiting for her to approach him. The way he looked at her made her feel like he was looking into her. "You are as beautiful as it is rumored."

"Thank you."

"You don't have to return the compliment," he said, smiling, the scars on the right side of his face twisting garishly as he did. "I don't like lies."

She had nothing but lies to offer him, and it had nothing to do with his beauty. Because she might have signed this agreement, she might make vows to him, but she would never truly belong to him. She would always be Andrei's.

"You will spend the next month becoming familiar with the palace, our customs and my expectations. Then in four weeks' time, we will have a ball and a wedding. And our nations will be united."

"Of course your plan is best, Your Highness," she said.

She knew that it didn't seem honest. She could also tell that he didn't care.

She didn't know what to expect. She had thought that maybe he would want to spend some time together, but clearly he didn't. He waved his hand. "Show the princess to her room."

"And what about my bodyguard?"

He looked past her, at Andrei, as though he was seeing him for the first time. "The staff will find quarters for him."

"He has to be near to me."

He lifted an eyebrow. "Unusual."

"Is it unusual for royalty to travel with her own trusted protection to a country she's never been to before?"

"You demonstrate a lack of trust in me." He smiled, slowly. "Smart."

"A room. Near mine."

She could tell that it was costing Andrei to be silent. He was not her staff, he was so much more than that. He was a leader, through and through, and to be put in a position where another man held power like this was likely offensive to him.

But it would be foolish for him to behave any other way than he was now. Silent. Waiting. Deadly, she knew.

With very little provocation he would and could leap across the throne room and tear out Lucian's throat. That she knew for certain.

That was how she found herself bundled off to her room high up in a tower, with Andrei put in the one adjoining.

The temptation that she felt to open up the door between their rooms was real. But she knew that she couldn't do that. She knew that it wouldn't be met with welcome, not right now.

Because she was going to marry Lucian. She had made that decision, she had made that bargain, and for the good of her people, she couldn't turn back.

No matter how much she wanted to.

Marriage had never been about her feelings.

And it couldn't be now.

CHAPTER SEVEN

It had been four weeks since they had arrived in Alabria. Andrei hated everything about the place, and he hated the king most of all.

He was mercurial, ruthless and odd. He didn't seem to respect anyone or anything but himself. Andrei also found it dishonoring of Emerald, in a strange way, that the man allowed them to stay in adjoining rooms. Not that either of them had used the door. He was standing in his control. He was here to protect her, to protect the Crown, the throne, and not to pleasure himself.

It was something that simply couldn't be done, and yet she haunted him at night when he tried to sleep.

His every waking moment was taken with his desire for her.

And he did not know how he might combat it.

It didn't matter. At this point, he wore it like a righteous mantle. Accepted it as part of who he was. The cost of protecting her.

He was being a martyr, and he knew it, but both he and Emerald occupied positions in life that demanded they martyr themselves.

What other choice was there?

Onyx was flying to Basilia with his wife, preparing

for the marriage ceremony, and Andrei couldn't say that he was looking forward to seeing his friend face-to-face. But this meeting between the kings would be very important, one last chance for all of the diplomacy to fall apart, he figured.

There would be a rousing party in celebration of the wedding, and Andrei couldn't imagine what sort of party a king like Lucian might throw.

"Not a very fun one," the housekeeper said to him when he'd asked. This was the benefit of the way that he moved between worlds.

He could get information that other people could not.

"In what way?" he asked.

"Lucian likes to display his wealth and power. He doesn't especially like to share it."

"I see. And are the rumors about him true? Has he murdered his other wives?"

"Oh," the housekeeper said. "I think those rumors are greatly exaggerated."

"You *think*?"

"Yes. Lucian is coldhearted, that much is true. He is ruthless, but I don't believe that he's a killer, because it simply wouldn't benefit him. To kill someone implies passion. And I don't believe that he's ever felt passion for anyone, or anything but himself."

"You don't paint a kind picture of him."

"He doesn't paint a kind picture of himself. But then…" Her face softened. "I remember when he was a boy. Before there were troubles in the country. Before the attempted revolution. His own father was a monster, and then he was caught between a monster and a righteous horde bent on ridding this entire nation of a royal family that was corrupt. They tortured him."

Andrei nodded, not shocked at all. These were things that he knew from reading about the country. "Yes. And does he see it as his sworn duty to torture everyone else around him?"

"I think mostly he tortures himself. But again, I cannot imagine him raising a hand to kill anyone, much less a woman. Much less any of his wives, who were simply spoiled and selfish."

He thought the older woman was a bit overly taken with Lucian, but took her commentary to heart.

He carried the story with him to Onyx when Onyx and Circe arrived. "Your Highness," he said.

"Don't stand on ceremony with me," Onyx said. "It bothers me."

"Sorry. I have spent the past month engaging in nothing but protocol. This motherfucker has a throne room."

"Yes, I've been," Onyx said. "I cannot believe that my sister is intent on marrying him."

"She is."

He and Emerald hadn't even spoken privately in the past four weeks. He was there, doing his job, guarding her, as she got acquainted with the palace, and the people in it. He had watched her begin to relax there, had watched as she had found ways to make herself consequential, had found friends. It was wrong of him to find that enraging. That he found it irksome. He should be glad that she was finding her way in this life that she had chosen.

"It is good for the country, and I can't deny it, but I worry about her."

"There is no need to worry." Flashes of his night with her played in his mind. "You know I would die before anything happened to her."

Onyx got a strange look on his face. "Yes. I do know that."

Circe made herself absent during the conversation, as she always did. The tension between her and Onyx was always palpable.

It wasn't sexual tension.

She simply didn't like him.

Onyx could be a difficult bastard, nobody knew that better than Andrei, but he found his wife's dislike of him to be incomprehensible. He was a good man. He didn't deserve her vitriol. And yet he took it.

The night before the wedding was the event, and he could certainly see what the housekeeper meant. Lucian liked to show off his wealth. And it was on full display in the ballroom. The large, cavernous room was decorated with glittering lights, each one made from crystal—so it was rumored. There were twisted tree branches all lit up as well, the whole thing like a dark fairy forest. He wasn't simply demonstrating wealth, he was flaunting it.

The goblets were gilded, every plate studded with gemstones. It was ostentatious to a rather obvious degree, and it was clear that Lucian didn't care. He did what he wanted, and didn't care for the greater good, and yet he was marrying Emerald, which would benefit his country, and hers.

He was a strange man, and Andrei did not quite have the measure of him. It would be easy for him to call him bad and let that be done. In fact, that was what he wanted to do. Find him to be a threat so that he could cut off his head.

And yet it wasn't that simple.

The entire event was designed around Emerald making her debut, and he was positioned at the back of the room, waiting for her when she walked through the double doors and came to the edge of the steps, like Cinderella. But she was wrapped all in gold, as was everything else, and he wouldn't be surprised to learn that the dress was woven with real golden thread.

Her red hair was captured up off her shoulders in an elaborate design.

Her lips were red, tempting, beautiful.

He remembered that mouth being on his body. Knew exactly what those lips could do.

She would do that for him.

The burning hatred at the center of his chest was a living, breathing thing. His envy was a monster, and if it would not create an international incident that would utterly devastate both Emerald and Onyx, Andrei would've been tempted to kill Lucian then and there.

To carry her away like a marauder.

His father would never have allowed this wedding to continue.

His father had been selfish. He had cared only for his own desires. He would've picked a woman up and carried her off whether she wanted to be or not. He would've taken what he wanted, what was his.

He'd always known that about his father. It wasn't until he was older that he'd realized that was wrong.

He had decided that was a weakness. That true strength was giving desire over for the greater good.

He would do that now. Unless Emerald said otherwise.

He could feel a collective breath of the room catch as they saw her. Could feel the impact of her beauty, not just on him. She was ethereal, a creature from another world. Except he had held her body in his hands. Had touched her everywhere. Had experienced the glory of just how earthy she was.

It would haunt him for the rest of his life.

But he would rather be haunted by the memory than by what could've been.

He watched as she floated from person to person, a bee pollinating flowers, leaving sweetness wherever she went. He watched, and felt as if his heart was walking outside his body.

He had never loved anything in this world, anything but her.

The housekeeper was right. The party wasn't fun, but that could be because it felt like engaging in torture.

What a way to die.

He would give himself over to her protection now. To her mission. He would not compromise them, not ever again.

He repeated that mantra the entire evening. And when it finished, it was up to him to accompany Emerald out of the ballroom, down the hall and to her bedroom door.

"Good night, Princess," he said.

He turned away from her. "Andrei," she said.

He turned back to her. "Yes?"

"Is this how it's going to be? You… You're not going to speak to me anymore?"

"There is nothing to say."

"I think that you should leave."

Rage poured through his veins. It was like she had stabbed him through his chest with the sword. And yet he could see the wisdom of it. He shouldn't be here. He shouldn't look upon her every day, and yet he didn't trust anyone else to protect her. There could be no one else but him.

"You're a fool," he said.

"It's right. And you know it."

"Then I will speak to your brother after the wedding tomorrow."

"Good night."

"If it pleases Your Royal Highness. After all, next to you, I am nothing." With that, he bowed with no respect at all, and left her there, along with a piece of his soul.

CHAPTER EIGHT

SHE WENT INTO her room and closed the door firmly behind her. He went into his own, pacing, reaching. He wanted to tear the place apart, brick by brick. He wanted...

He wanted.

Tomorrow she would marry another man. Tomorrow, she would give her body to that prick. Without thinking, he jerked the door open that separated the rooms, the first time it had been opened since they had come here. She gasped, turning around, her hand on her heart.

"If I am to go, then I will leave you with a parting gift," he growled. He crossed the space and pulled her into his arms, kissing her savagely. There was nothing tender about it, it was none of the expression of tender feelings that had happened that night on the yacht. Where they had lived out so many fantasies in a short space of time, where he had devoted himself to the worship of her. No. This was about him claiming one more night. About him branding her one more time, so that she had to go to Lucian's bed with bruises from his hands on her hips.

It was cruel of him, and he knew it, but he would not allow it.

He would not allow her to go so easily. He would not let her be rid of him so easily.

He turned her away from him, so that she was facing the mirror, her back to him, and he began to lower the zipper on her dress slowly. Her breath hitched, her eyes closing. "Your body belongs to me," he said. "Don't you forget that."

Her dress fell away from her curves, and he leaned in and kissed her neck before putting his hand around her throat, tilting her face upward so that she had to look at them full in the mirror. "You belong to me."

She couldn't breathe. This was wrong. But then, all of it was wrong. Nothing was right, and it never could be, but surrendering to Andrei like this the night before her wedding was... It was a mistake. But she couldn't stop herself, any more than she could stop him. She looked in the mirror, at the two of them, at her face, which was like a stranger's. Her eyes were round, dark with need, fear, desire. She looked hungry, starving for him.

Such pointless honesty in a moment where it was too late. It made her want to rage. But all she could do was stand there, staring, looking at the picture they made in the mirror.

"Watch what I do to you," he said, commanding in her ear. "And you can think about it later when he touches you. You can watch yourself in the mirror as his hands move over your body. Watch and see if the pleasure is there, the need. It won't be. You will never want him the way that you want me."

"You're cursing us both," she whispered.

He was. Cursing her to a life that would never feel

quite right. Cursing her to an existence that would always feel like half of what they had experienced together that night on the yacht.

She welcomed it, in a perverse way.

Wanted to sacrifice her sexual desire on the altar of Andrei and let it go up in flames. Wanted to punish herself for doing this to the both of them. For choosing to marry Lucian in the first place.

This was nothing like the first time they'd come together. There had been a joy mixed in with the bitterness. A sweetness.

There was none of that here. He was angry, and she couldn't blame him. She could do nothing but take it. Because she deserved it. She had done this. He tilted her head to the side, and bit her on the neck, then he released the strapless bra she was wearing, exposing her breasts, his dark hands cupping the pale globes before skimming down her stomach, beneath the fabric of her panties, as he roughly pushed his hands between her slick folds. She gasped, moaned as he began to tease her, torment her. She could feel the hard pressure of his arousal against her rear, the insistence of his desire.

"Watch," he commanded.

He pushed her panties down her hips, just above her knees, placed his fingers between her legs, spreading her lips open so that she could see her own slickness, the pink flesh there. Then he began to circle his finger around her clit before thrusting it deep inside her. Watching it felt obscene. And she was powerless to do anything but stare.

Was powerless to do anything but watch as he pushed a second finger inside her before dragging his fingers up toward her lips, and demanding that she open. "Taste yourself," he said.

She parted her lips and let him have entry, licking her own desire from him.

"Good girl," he said. "Would you ever do that for him?" She shook her head. "I hope you *do*. I hope it doesn't taste nearly as sweet."

Erotic confusion assaulted her, and she leaned back against him as he pushed his hand back between her legs, teasing her, toying with her. He had been a generous, wonderful lover their first time together, and there was certainly a physical generosity to the way he pleasured her now, but the emotional connection was gone. This was rage.

And it still felt so good.

He pressed his hands to the back of her neck and pushed her forward, then she could hear him undoing his belt buckle. He positioned himself at the entrance of her body, thrust inside her, and she watched the pleasure build on his face, watched it build on her own. The anguish.

And there was no small amount of anguish as he drove them both to the peak of pleasure. They made a profane work of art, there in the mirror, one hand on the back of her neck, the other on her hip as he thrust deep within her, driving them both to the limit.

Then he threw his head back and growled, pouring himself inside her, and she gasped out her own release, the waves of need rippling inside her endlessly.

When it was finished, she was covered in shame.

She'd given in to him, to his punishment because even that felt good. Even that felt better than not touching him. She'd been willing to accept his disdain, his hatred, on the eve of her wedding to another man, just as joyfully as she'd accepted their goodbye on the yacht.

Her going forward with this wedding had turned his feelings for her, she could see it. It had poisoned his love.

He hated her as much as he'd ever cared.

"Get out," she said.

"As you wish, Princess."

Out of her room. Out of her life.

Then he was gone. She wondered if he would even go to the wedding tomorrow.

Do you even want him there? What kind of sick person are you? There is nothing left for the two of you. Nothing.

She tried to sleep, but it was fitful. It was the night before her wedding, and it felt like a death march. But even more so when early in the morning she realized that for the first time in her life, she was late. And by the time the sun came up she had answered the question about why.

Thanks to the help of a sympathetic nursemaid, she acquired a test, and got her answer. She was pregnant, and it was not with her future husband's baby.

She knew what she had to do. Because King Lucian had said that he hated liars. And if she walked down that aisle carrying Andrei's baby then...

Maybe he'll set you free.

No. He wouldn't. He would kill her. And the baby. At least, if his reputation was to be believed.

Her heart was hammering hard when she entered the throne room. "I need to speak to the king in private."

"It is bad luck for the groom to see the bride on the wedding day," Lucian said. "And you should believe that, because my brides have had very bad luck."

"I will risk it."

He waved his hand and the guards melted away.

"And where is your ominous shadow?"

"I assure you, I don't know."

"I see. And what is it you have to tell me?"

"I'm pregnant."

"I have been told my virility is powerful, but I believe this is pushing the limits even for me," he said.

"Obviously it isn't yours."

He shrugged. "That is of no matter to me. It speeds along the production of an heir, but don't think that it will spare you the wedding night."

"You don't… You don't care?"

"No. I've lost two wives without the benefit of an heir. This is a boon for me."

"But most men—"

"Blood means nothing to me," he said. "You mean nothing to me. I don't care if you fuck your brother's entire guard, or just the one. Am I clear?"

She clenched her teeth together. "You have no interest in calling the wedding off?"

"None. And in fact if you were to do so, the consequences would be disastrous. For you. I would find them enjoyable."

"Then I will see you in a few hours."

The reality of the situation was about to crush her. Her wedding gown was beautiful, but it was for a woman with an entirely different sense of style. Lucian had chosen it, because this was his play, and she was merely one of the players. She was a pawn. Just like her baby was.

Hers and Andrei's baby.

But Andrei was gone, and she had no choice.

She was on the verge of panic. She couldn't think clearly. She felt like she was halfway down death's road, her whole body strung tightly with anxiety and fear. Going forward with the marriage felt impossible. Leaving felt fatal. So all she could do was go through the motions. Go along with the plan already in place.

Before she knew it, it was time for her to walk down the aisle. Onyx took her arm and looked at her, a strange sort of sadness on his face.

"What?"

"I don't know. Something about it doesn't feel right."

"It's too late. I've signed the agreement."

"I support you, Emerald, and whatever it is you need."

She nodded, and she and her brother began to walk down the aisle. At the head of the aisle was Lucian, and behind him a priest, kneeling in prayer, his back turned.

He was wearing blue robes, with a large cross on the back. A symbol of torture and salvation, depending on the context. Right now, it felt like torture.

Stop this.

Stop this.

Stop this.

But she didn't. She couldn't. For the safety of the country. For the safety of her baby.

Her legacy didn't feel like it mattered much anymore.

When she arrived at the head of the aisle, Onyx released his hold on her, and Lucian extended his hand.

She took it, and found herself standing across from him at the altar.

The priest rose slowly, and then he turned.

And her heart dropped into her feet. "Andrei?"

"Oh. The guard," Lucian said, looking at him and then out at the crowd. "This is a bit dramatic."

"It is," Andrei said. "Because I wanted you to know. I wanted everyone here to know, who it is who took your woman. Surprise. She's mine now."

He wrapped his arm around her waist, lifted her up and brought her up against his chest. "I'm taking her somewhere you won't find her."

"Guards," Lucian shouted.

But Andrei was too quick. He had a plan.

There was a clear route, diagonally and through the back door, and then they disappeared suddenly into a side passage that spit them out outside. And somehow, no one followed them that way. "What are you doing?"

"You didn't think that I was going to let you marry him? I'm only shocked that you let yourself get that far."

She looked at his face, and she saw that something was irrevocably broken between them.

Whatever feelings he had for her before, they weren't there now. He was being driven by fury. Possessiveness.

Rage.

He must've found out about the baby.

But she didn't have time to ask him, because suddenly, she was being gathered more tightly against him, and he jumped off the edge of a cliff, taking them both down into the churning sea.

CHAPTER NINE

THEY WERE DROWNING. Together. He didn't know which way was up. He didn't particularly care. For a moment, he just let it all not... Hurt.

And then, his body sprung into action.

He began to swim them both toward the surface of the water. Up and up, to where he had the small boat moored against the side of the rock.

He had given up all his honor for this. For them. He had gone to the darkest place inside him to claim her as his. This might be sharp, hard, she might be angry that he'd thwarted her, but he could not allow her to give herself to another man.

He'd thought he could.

But he was his father's son.

He'd run from that all his life, until he'd needed to run to it. And now he was embracing it. Along with his fury. She should have felt the same way. She shouldn't have been able to go through with it—as he hadn't been able to allow it.

She hadn't, and he was angry about that.

But he had her now. And no matter how angry he was now, he wouldn't let her go.

Not ever.

He hauled them both into the boat, starting up the motor and moving them away from the coastline as quickly as possible.

"Are you *insane*?" she sputtered, her white dress in tatters, her hair a wreck.

"Yes," he said.

"You could've killed us both."

"But I didn't."

"You could have. You could have… And the baby."

He froze. "The baby?"

"That's why you came for me, isn't it?"

"What baby, Emerald?"

She was waxen already, utterly pale, but all the remaining color flooded away from her face as she stared at him. "You didn't know?"

"No. I didn't fucking know. I still don't. Tell me. Now."

"I… Andrei, I'm pregnant."

Rage. Rage and this crushing, relentless pain in his chest was all he knew.

She was pregnant with his baby, and she had been planning on marrying Lucian? Had been planning to give not just herself, but his child to another man.

It changed everything.

This had been about them. He'd been wounded that she'd been able to let it go so far, that she had kept walking toward this inevitability while he had broken.

In the stillness of the night, the ghost of his father had visited him. In the form of his own disgust. And it demanded to know why any son of the Ardelean crime family would behave with such cowardice. Would put the greater good over what he wanted. Needed. Deserved.

But now things had taken an even darker turn. Her willingness to marry another, and now the realization that she'd been trying to pass his child off as another man's, made a mockery of them. Everything they were. Everything they had ever been.

He had been the one to go back on his word by taking her, by not allowing her to do what she felt was right, was her duty. And he had felt weak for that. But knowing now that she was pregnant with his child, knowing now that she had intended to pass that child off as belonging to another man, all of his illusions, and his guilt, shattered.

"I signed an agreement."

"When did you find out?" The salt air was in his face, the spray of the sea lapping up against the boat, and it was not fear he felt now. Rage.

"I…" Her teeth were chattering, and had he been in a different mood, had it been a different moment in time, he would have done everything he could to keep her warm.

But everything had changed in the space of a breath. From the time they had gone beneath the surface, to when they had come up. Nothing was the same, and it never would be again.

"Did you even go to bed with me, say goodbye to me, knowing that you were pregnant with my child, withholding this information from me?"

"No," she protested. "Andrei, of course I didn't know. I found out this morning. I realized that I never had my… I realized that I was late. Ever since the yacht, and I hadn't thought about it because everything has been mixed up since that day. I didn't know. I had very little time to figure out what I was going to do. You were gone."

"I would have answered your call."

"I know that. But I thought that when I told Lucian…"

"He knows?"

"Yes. I told him."

"And he decided to steal my child?"

She nodded. "He needs an heir. He said that it didn't matter to him because… He's been married twice, and neither of his wives has lived long enough to produce heirs. He thought that it was convenient that I was pregnant already."

"Then he is a monster. But so are you."

She said nothing more. Her unwillingness to fight him, her lack of desire to explain herself, spoke volumes. There was no sound, only the motor of the boat, the crash of the waves. They weren't being pursued. It would be a very slow trek to the island of Marake, where he had arranged air transport for them. They had three hours in this boat, and frankly, if Lucian realized that they had taken to the sea, he would be able to overtake them in just about any air-or watercraft he chose.

Andrei had to continue to hope that it didn't occur to him.

And that if Onyx were to give any guidance, even genuine guidance, he would say that Andrei would never take to the sea.

But he didn't know. He did not know the ferocity of his feelings for Emerald, nor the things that had happened on the water in these past weeks.

The way that it had changed him.

"Where are we going?" Her teeth were chattering; she had been silent for what felt like an hour.

"Somewhere warmer than this."

The journey on the water was brutal. Emerald's stomach was churning by the time they got off the boat, and she found herself bundled onto a private jet.

"How do you have… Access to this?"

Andrei turned to her, his expression severe. "You think I do not have money of my own? Do you think I have not taken what your brother has paid me and made investments? You truly do think me common."

"I don't, I…"

She was miserable. She should be ecstatic. Andrei had come for her. She was pregnant with his baby. But this was like being on the other side of the looking glass. As if she had stood there, seen her dream and fallen down into the other side, been presented with a backward, twisted version of the thing that she had always wanted.

Because she had hurt him. She could see it. He was furious in a cold, frightening way. She wasn't sure that they would ever recover from it.

The truth was, what she'd done had been a decision made in shock. Likely, she would've come to her senses at some point, but everything would've been more complicated. It was a narrow escape, this brush with marriage to the wrong man, but now she had fallen out of the frying pan and into the churning waves.

"I really didn't have time to think—"

"I was going to take you. Regardless. I had no idea about the child."

He sat down in a plush, leather chair, forearms rested

on the arms, his legs spread wide. He was wet, and furious. She stood, unwilling to sit down, unable to. Her whole body was trembling.

"If you do not sit when we prepare for takeoff, you will fall over."

She did sit then.

"I could not give you to him. But I had no idea what a treacherous woman you were. Still, all the better that I did take you, or I would have been denied my child. I have lost all of my family, Emerald, and you would take my child from me too."

"I didn't think of that. I didn't... I didn't think."

"No," he said. "You didn't think of anyone but yourself. Your legacy, is that not correct? That is all you think of. The way that you will be written about in the history books. Well, I don't know about the history books, but what happens today will surely be written about in headlines the world over. And our child will be able to read those headlines. What do you think they will make of them?"

She wasn't sure that it mattered, because she didn't know she was going to survive this. She didn't know if she was going to survive any of this. It also wasn't true.

"It isn't about what they write about me. I wanted to do the right thing," she said.

"How could right have ever been *this*?"

She had no idea. But every moment since this morning had been the shortest and longest of her life. She was tongue-tied. She hadn't said half of what she should have said—to him or to Lucian.

Now she had been kidnapped by a man who hated her, she was pregnant with his baby, everything felt like it was imploding and Lucian might start a war. Lucian. "You know there's going to be consequences for Basilia."

"Yes," he bit out. "I do know that. But I have kept your brother out of this. He knows nothing, nor does he know where we're going."

"He's going to find us."

"He won't. We are going to disappear."

"You seem so confident in that."

"I am. I am the head of security for a major nation. Do you think that I don't know how to hide? You think that I do not understand what is at stake? Do you think I did not calculate these risks? Pity that there was one major factor I wasn't aware of. Your faithlessness."

She sat down in the chair, shivered. "That isn't fair. I told you what I would be faithful to. I told you what I was going to do, and why it was essential for me to do it. You knew. You knew what was important to me. You knew that I was fixed on this, that I was doing this for Basilia."

"Everything changed."

But why had he only taken her now? Why hadn't he offered her anything before?

She wanted to cry. Because he was right. Everything had changed. Not just when she had discovered she was pregnant, but from the moment they touched. And now she had fractured them. She was not her mother. She wasn't brave. She made the wrong choice, and she didn't know how they could recover from it.

"Are you going to tell me exactly where this plane is taking us?"

"No," he said.

She didn't have her phone, anyway, to message anyone. And also, there was no way for her to be tracked. She imagined that was a handy side effect of her being kidnapped straight from the altar. How nice for him.

"You should go and get changed," he said.

"I'm fine."

"You are not fine. You're going to catch your death."

She was in a wet wedding dress. It really was quite ridiculous. The fabric was ruined, sodden. Just like everything else.

"I don't have anything with me."

"Foolish woman. You think that I took you without making preparation for you? Do you think that I planned to fling you into the sea without providing you with warm clothes?"

He got up and went to the sideboard, took out a bottle of whiskey and poured himself some. "You cannot have any. Therefore, you will have to warm yourself by getting dressed."

She stood, her hands trembling. "All right. I will."

She tried to keep her head held high, tried to hang on to some semblance of pride. She didn't like that he was giving orders and that she was obeying them, but this was an order that she really quite wanted to obey. All things considered. She was freezing. She went into the bedroom at the back of the plane, and opened a closet in there. Turbulence rocked her and the hangers just slightly, and she cursed that she tripped over the wet, sodden dress.

Then she dug through all the clothes, found a pair of sweats and elected to go with those. She had no one and nothing to impress after all.

It was such a funny thing. She had treasured, obsessed over, and loved Andrei for so many years. And yet he had seen her in sweats, pajamas and now nothing. He knew her better than anyone. And now he hated her.

It was an extremely brutal reality that she found herself living in.

She stripped the dress off, her skin clammy, and tossed it into the bathroom that was next to the bedroom. Then she slipped on the sweatpants, the sweatshirt.

And as she was doing so, she had the full realization of what had happened today.

Of what Andrei had done. He had jumped off a cliff into the water with the two of them. He had taken her across the ocean to another island.

He was afraid of the water, even if he would never have said it that way. But he had violated his own rules about the sea, had taken her in the cabin downstairs so that he could be with her, and then had engineered this rescue that should've gone against everything he'd designed his life around.

The rescue itself violated his life's work. And he had done it anyway.

It made her feel sick with guilt. Regret.

But then... He would've kidnapped her today even if she weren't pregnant. He didn't know about the baby.

She didn't know whether that made her feel a strange sense of joy, or rage. He hadn't put the country first. He hadn't...

He had put her first.

Or just him.

But knowing that he wanted her that much was a

strange sort of intoxicating elixir she had never known had the potential to be quite so powerful.

She came out of the bedroom, and he was getting dressed. He was wearing only a pair of black pants, and just as she came out, he pulled a white T-shirt on over his muscles.

How could he be so familiar to her, but so novel all at the same time? How could he be the man that she had known for most of her life, and also a stranger? The object of her fantasies, but also a fantasy fulfilled, and one pushed even farther out of reach.

She knew him well enough to know that his fury was not something to take lightly. Knew him well enough to know that this was not a small slight in his eyes.

He would make her pay for this. Possibly for years to come. He had made it so that Onyx couldn't save her, and while she knew that for Andrei, protecting her was paramount, she also knew that she was his now.

Whatever that meant.

"We both had the same idea," she said, trying to force a smile.

"Don't," he said. "Don't speak to me like nothing has changed."

"I made the decision that I made," she said. "It was the only one that I could think to make at the time. But you planned to undermine my decision all along. So I'm not certain that you have the right to be quite this angry at me."

"You would deny me my child."

The words were like a knife. He was singular in his feeling on that, and he wasn't going to shift. She couldn't blame him. The truth was, staring at that through his dark, outraged eyes, she saw the flaw in her decision. Immediately. She couldn't justify it. But she wanted to. She wanted him to believe the best of her, even now. It was such a strange, hollow sensation, this need to cling to the choice she'd made while also feeling that her choice had been a cowardly one.

One that she would've regretted. One she regretted now.

"We will land soon," he said. "We're not going far away."

"But how do you expect we're going to hide?"

"Because we're going back to Romania. To my father's house."

"Your father's house? Don't you think that it's certain that we'll be found in that case?"

"No. Nobody knew about the estate. The whereabouts of the property of the Ardelean Crime Family are very secretive. My father told me this when I was a boy. Then I have known ever since."

"You… Crime family?"

"Yes. My father was fleeing persecution of his own making, Princess. My father was not a good man. But, that has its uses for me now. I wanted to be different than him. I didn't wish to treat a woman like a position. I did not wish to put the needs of myself above the needs of a nation. And yet, now I find that I feel differently. Because your wishes have no place here. And nothing matters but that I get what I want. And what I want is you. I would have taken you to be my wife. But now I'm happy to keep you as a prisoner. You are used to seeing me in your brother's kingdom. But in my home, no other man sits on the throne. There, I am your king."

CHAPTER TEN

THE WATER WAS so blue.

She didn't know what she had expected Romania to look like, but in truth, she had imagined something dreary and grim.

A sort of Soviet blockade.

But this was all green mountains wreathed in mist, and the unfiltered light of the sun. It was glorious. But she didn't want to say that. The plane landed at a small airport, and from there they were put in a helicopter, which carried them high over the mountains until they arrived at the top of one, and there, nestled in trees was what could only be described as a fortress. It was made from natural gray stone, blending in with its surroundings. Vines and roses climbed all over the walls, as though nature was trying to draw it back into itself.

She wondered how many years it had been since anyone had occupied this place.

"I had it prepared for you," he said. "I hired people from down in the village to come and make sure that it was ready for habitation."

Since he seemed to be reading her thoughts, his words going directly into her ears, the headphones she wore for the helicopter ride making that possible, she decided she might as well ask the question.

"How long has it been since anyone lived here?"

"Since we left for Basilia. Under cover of darkness. We did not take a helicopter. We hiked through the mountains. Swam through the rivers. Until we arrived at the sea."

"Oh."

She found herself feeling sympathy for him, even as she had been proclaimed his prisoner.

Perverse, perhaps.

Well, definitely.

The helicopter began to descend, and she found herself looking for something to hold on to. The most logical thing would have been Andrei, but she did not want to touch him now.

It seemed wrong.

The helicopter landed in a barren field, and she and Andrei got off. Nobody got off with them. And once the helicopter lifted back up in the sky, the wind howling around them, they were the only ones there, shrouded in the wilderness, enveloped by trees. She could still hear the helicopter rotors in the distance, but otherwise, it was all birds.

He was looking around, marveling at the place with just as much interest as she was.

"Have you been back here at all?"

"No. I was pleased to discover that it was still standing, though the condition will be an interesting thing to discover. I was sent photographs, but I had to act quickly. Now you see why I say you will not be found."

"And you think that we can just stay here forever?"

"I think that we will stay here until I say otherwise. Don't worry, I will contact Onyx."

"I want to talk to him."

"Not now."

She felt a sort of hollow, cascading terror. This was nothing she had ever expected. This was a side of Andrei that she had never seen. But he was right. She had always seen him in a country that wasn't his own. She had always seen him next to her brother, to whom he had sworn a level of allegiance and loyalty. But obviously there was a breaking point to that. She had found the breaking point.

He began to walk ahead of her, through the dense trees. And she hurried quickly after him. Whether she felt any symptoms from her pregnancy or not was difficult to say. She felt nauseous, that much was certain. But there were a lot of reasons for her to feel nausea right now.

The trail was overgrown, and even though he hadn't been back here since he was a child, she was beginning to suspect that he might not know exactly where they were going. Until they came to an overgrown gate.

He looked up, and she was certain that there must be security cameras. "Andrei Ardelean is here to take his rightful place."

The gates opened, and he went inside. He didn't touch her. Of course he didn't. Of course he didn't.

She went after him and into the garden. It was like an enchanted space. It wasn't only the walls that were overgrown. Here, ivy had taken over everything. It was glorious and wild. Utterly unexpected.

But then, none of this was expected.

They walked through the shaggy hedges, the untamed greenery, until they came to a small door. Not the main entrance of the house. It opened for them without him having to knock.

And there was a small woman standing there, her white hair captured in a bun. "Andrei," she said. "I knew you would return home one day."

His face shifted, shock on his features. "Rebecca?"

"Of course. We kept this place for you. We knew that you were alive. Word of your survival made it back here."

"And why did Ricardo never come for me?"

"With your father dead, there was no point going after you. Particularly not when you were protected by the royal family and Basilia. I heard, as well, that the king there paid him in political favors to leave you alone."

Her father had kept Andrei safe. All this time. Even in death. Emerald was shocked.

"I did not expect to find you here," he said, his voice rough.

"I have nowhere else to go."

"Weren't you all at risk?"

She shook her head. "Your father's death released us all. This place always remained secret outside the scope of the village. He was afraid that would change. But it didn't."

"We could've simply stayed here."

She shook her head. "No. You would've been trapped here for all your days. Your father never could've lived like that. You know he enjoyed…"

"Attention," Andrei said.

"If you wish to call it that." Rebecca's focus turned to Emerald. "And who is the lady?"

"Princess Emerald. Of Basilia. She is pregnant with my child."

Rebecca did not evince a very big reaction to the news. "Babies are good luck," she said.

Emerald wanted to tell her that it very much depended on the circumstances surrounding the pregnancy, but she didn't. She had a feeling that she did not want to be at odds with this woman.

The room they were standing in was a small, cozy kitchen, and the smells were enticing. This was the first time that Emerald had realized she was hungry. But it had now been several hours since her disastrous wedding, and she realized that she was still cold from being thrown into the sea, and now ravenous.

"Take the princess to your quarters. I will serve you both dinner soon."

She had never seen Andrei take orders outside a security capacity with quite such acquiescence.

"Who is she?" Emerald asked when they were out of earshot.

"She was... Our cook. A nanny of sorts. Like a grandmother. Who worked for us."

"You love her," Emerald said.

It came out more of an accusation than she had intended it to be.

"I'm not entirely sure what love is."

His words were a dagger straight to her heart. Andrei should know what love was. Because she'd loved him all this time.

Except you didn't show it to him, because you couldn't. So now it's all broken.

The house was like something out of a storybook. The walls were gilded, with ornate wallpaper. The stairs had luxe, patterned carpet. There were gold details everywhere, not like the palace in Alabria. It was more quaint. But in an opulent way. He pushed open the door and revealed a bedroom that was fitting for a fantasy princess, rather than for her.

Her own room at the palace in Basilia was quite modern. The one in Alabria had felt like a relic, but this was something else besides.

In the room was an ornately carved fourposter bed, with flowing swathes of fabric cascading down each post. An elegant canopy stretched over the top.

"This is lovely."

"I'm glad they fixed it to my specifications." His dark gaze flickered toward the back. "You will find that you have clothing there. If you wish to dress for dinner."

"Are you going to?"

"It is my first night as master in this home. Yes. I will dress for dinner. And I will see you there."

And with that, he walked away and left her, in this bedroom, in an unfamiliar home, in an unfamiliar country.

For the first time in her entire life, Princess Emerald felt stripped of everything. Her power, her status.

And perhaps worst of all, of any certainty in her relationship with the man that she had known for most of her life. The man she had always depended on. Trusted.

She was pregnant with his baby, and right now she had no idea what they were.

Or what would become of them.

Andrei knew he couldn't avoid the phone call when it came through.

He wasn't a coward. And when it came to this, he would face up to what he had done, even though it was going to destroy everything. He had known that it would. From the moment he had taken hold of her and carried her away, he had known it would. Hell, he had made that calculation when he had decided that taking her was the only thing that could be done. After he'd had her in front of the vanity, a punishment for them both, he had decided that they would both end themselves over this.

But that was before.

And now, there was this conversation.

He answered the phone. "Hello?"

"That's what you have to say to me? *Hello*. As if this is a call to discuss the weather, and not you taking my sister at the altar and causing an international incident."

"Is it an incident? We are blessedly free from the news."

"How nice for you. I am slowly boiling to death in the consequences. Lucian wants a war."

"There is nothing I can do," he said, realizing what he was saying. He did not think that Lucian would actually start a war over this. Perhaps a trade war. And he understood that there would be long-term consequences to that, but he had given up on the greater good.

There was only Emerald. Though his heart felt dark and scarred where she was concerned. Perhaps it had always been that way.

"Why did you do that?"

"I had to."

"Andrei, you have never done anything that would put our country at risk. You've never done anything that would put Emerald at risk. And so I am asking you, what insanity overtook you that you would steal her from the altar? Was Lucian a threat to her? Because I can accept that. If Lucian had put her in danger, then you did what you had to do. But there is nothing else short of that which justifies your actions."

"He was not a threat to her," Andrei said. "But she's mine."

"This is what I feared. Are you telling me that you... Did you lay a hand on my sister?"

"I laid more on her than a hand, Onyx, and I will admit that before a firing squad if it comes down to it."

"I trusted you."

"And I was trustworthy. Until I was not."

"This doesn't explain anything to me."

"I can't explain it to you. What happened on the yacht is between Emerald and me. The decisions that were made... You are a good friend, and a good king, Onyx, but you don't know everything. Not about your sister, and not about me. We have our own relationship, and have all these years." It felt disingenuous for him to say that now with all of the acrimony swirling inside him where she was concerned. But that was his business too.

"Are you going to marry her?"

"I haven't decided. There is the complicating factor of her pregnancy."

"What?"

"She's pregnant. The baby is mine. She was going to marry him and keep the child from me. I think you can see where that has put Emerald and me in a difficult position personally."

"If you harm one hair on my sister's head—"

"I won't harm her. But whether or not I marry her remains to be seen. But I will have my child, Onyx, and

I will not let anyone or anything interfere with it. Until the child is born, Emerald stays with me. I will not have another man claim my son or daughter. Do you understand me?"

There was silence on the other end of the phone. "If you were here, I would cut off the offending member myself. I hope that I've made myself clear."

"You have. And I wouldn't blame you for it. In your position I would do the same. At least, I would if I had family. I don't. This child is the only family that I have. The only one I will ever have. She tried to take that from me. She knew that she was pregnant. She was going to allow Lucian to claim my child as his heir."

He knew Onyx enough to know that he was struggling with that. To know that he would find that as much of an affront as Andrei did. To know that he would not let that stand.

Whatever he said.

"You would claim your heir. Whatever the cost, you would claim your heir, and we both know that."

"You're a bastard who should never have gotten my sister pregnant in the first place."

"What happened between she and I is our business, but I will not allow you to labor under any sort of delusion that she was taken advantage of. I would never have touched her." That tasted like a lie. Because as they had gotten closer to Alabria, he had been tested to his breaking point. Emerald had pushed, and he had given in, but what would he have done if that hadn't happened? He couldn't say for sure, not now, not given what had happened in her room at the palace in Alabria, that he would've kept his hands to himself.

"I don't think that you would force yourself on her," Onyx said finally.

"Of course I wouldn't."

"Are you in love with her?"

"Whatever I felt for Emerald is clouded at the moment."

There was another long pause. "Where are you?"

"I cannot tell you that."

"For God's sake, Andrei, is there no trust between us?"

"No," Andrei said. "I can trust no one and nothing. Where we are is none of your concern."

He'd thought he could trust Emerald. He'd given her more of him than he had ever given to anyone. He'd sacrificed his honor at her altar to discover she'd betrayed him in a way he hadn't even fathomed.

"I can have your phone traced."

"You can't, actually, because it is blocked, because I am the head of your security, and not even you will be able to get the permissions to do that."

"Emerald is my world," Onyx said. "You would keep my sister from me, even now? She is pregnant with your baby and if she wants you, and doesn't want Lucian, then of course we can discuss this."

"I cannot. I won't."

"You are dead to me," Onyx said. "There is nothing complex about that."

"Then you can forget that either Emerald or I exist."

He hung the phone up and threw it down onto the floor, crushing it beneath the heel of his shoe. He did not think that Onyx would be able to track it. It was a completely blocked and protected phone. But if he was able to somehow break that, and find a location for it, Andrei wasn't going to assist him.

He buttoned up his black jacket and walked out of the bedroom, heading down to dinner.

His mood was black. And he almost felt sorry for Emerald that she had to deal with him. Except, she had created the situation.

He walked down the stairs, surprised at how much memory of this house was inside him. He hadn't realized. He didn't think about his home in Romania, at least he hadn't done so until he had needed it. Until he had needed to call upon the strength and ruthlessness of his father to save them both, and he'd thought that she would be happy.

He'd thought he would be, but the baby made it a betrayal in a way it hadn't been before.

And now... He knew it had been there all along. He had suppressed it, for honor. For the sake of duty. Because he felt that he owed Onyx fealty. Now? He would owe no one but himself. It was a devil's bargain, this. Embracing the poison of the Ardelean blood. Yes, it was a trap. And now that he had snared himself in it there was no going back. He had chosen this road. This path.

He walked into the dining room, and Emerald was already sitting there, dressed in green. He had specifically requested that they make as much of her clothing as possible green. He loved her and that color. At least he had. When he didn't look at her and see half enemy half lover.

"Your brother called," he said.

Her eyes went wide. "Is he..."

"Furious."

"I want to call him."

"Well, that will be difficult now, because I destroyed my phone. And so the two of us find ourselves here without a means of communication to the outside world."

"You're insane," she said. "I've known you for all these years, and you have never… You have never behaved this way."

"And *you* were going to pass my child off as belonging to another man. So, I suppose these are unprecedented times for us all."

"I didn't know what else to do," she said.

"And what you did was the wrong thing," he said.

"How nice of you to have such a clear view of it, as it affects you."

"And what other view should I have?"

"I asked him if he'd set me free. He said no. And as far as I knew you were gone, so what else was I supposed to do, Andrei? Free myself? Run past a gauntlet of guards?"

Her words affected him, and he didn't want them to. He wanted to stay in this space he'd gone to when he'd decided to capture her. This place that was filled with anger, justification for his actions. For his hurt.

"I've given up on duty. It's done. I burned it all to the ground. I made my choice. So you can sit there, in all your piety, and reflect on the good works that you would've done. And what good works they would have been. Pleasuring King Lucian, standing as his queen, bearing my child for him, and then more children for him besides. And did it make you feel good? Because you might think that you need a sense of satisfaction for your honor to get off, Emerald, but you and I know differently. You were well able to get off just with me. Knowing that it contributed to nothing, no good, greater or otherwise except the explosive desire between us."

"You are the *most difficult man*." Her face was red, her whole body rigid, vibrating with anger.

"And I can be more difficult, if it comes down to it. I would suggest that you don't try me."

"Do you think I'm going to make this easy for you? You don't get to take away my agency, my free will, my choices, and then have me simper at your feet. Is that what you think? That because of all this long-standing history between us I'll get on my knees and give you pleasure, thank you for rescuing me from my own choices?"

"You would, if you had any real idea of what I saved you from."

"Is that going to be what you use to make yourself feel better about all this? You're going to pretend that he's the monster everyone says he is."

"I don't care. He could be the best and kindest king in the history of the world—though we know he isn't—but you don't want him. I know what it's like to sleep with someone and to feel nothing but cold afterward. To feel further away from yourself, and who you are, and from any other person than you ever have. Because when you try to fill the deep, unending hole inside you that wears into you over time from unrequited need, all that you do is fill it with acidity and disappointment. Ask me how I know."

"So you claim you're saving me from a lifetime of bad sex?"

"You've only had good sex, Emerald. See, you don't actually know what a gift I've given you."

"Bastard."

"No. My parents were married when I was born. My mother was forced into it by my father. I won't force you into marriage. So our child very well could be a bastard. I would learn to keep my judgment to myself. Otherwise, look at what you're calling your own child."

"I don't know that I want to have dinner with you," she said, standing.

"Sit," he said. "This is not your brother's palace. It is mine."

She shocked him by obeying. He would've done nothing to her had she not. And she should well know that. But this was the trouble. She was compelled by him, even though she was furious at him. She wanted to be near him, even though she wanted to push him away. He knew that because it was how he felt. He wanted to spit all kinds of venom at her, and then he did want her to kneel before him. He wanted her with him, as much as he wanted to push her away. As much as he wanted her to feel a dagger in her chest, betrayal at his hand, as he had done with her. He wanted her near.

It frightened him how much that reminded him of his own parents. His mother had been forced into marriage. A trade between crime families, and she had loathed his father. But she had been helpless in the face of her desire for him. So much so that even he, as a child, had realized that. That there was a bond between his parents that neither of them seemed to truly want, but they couldn't escape either.

This house, this moment, this woman, reminded him of things best left in the past.

"And what is your plan?"

"To keep you with me until the child is born. Until I can ensure that I have claimed the child, and no one else can."

"And then what do you do with me?"

"Again, that remains to be seen. Perhaps I will return you to your kingdom. And I will keep your child with me."

He was being a villain now, and he knew it. He didn't mean it, either. But he'd wanted to say it because it helped feed the dark, angry thing inside him.

Her face drained of color. "You can't do that. You can't take my baby."

"But you tried to take mine."

She looked down. "That was different. You wouldn't have known. You would never have known."

"And that makes it better?"

She shook her head. "No."

The doors to the dining room opened, and Rebecca came in, carrying a tray with a giant bowl on it, and two smaller bowls beside it, along with some rustic bread. This was not the kind of showy feast that was served in Basilia. But it reminded him very much of meals he'd had in the nursery. With the other children. Other crime lords' children. He wondered if any of them had survived to adulthood. If any of them had been able to decide their own fates. Or if, like his mother, all of the girls had been married off to dangerous, ruthless men. If, like him, the sons had been in danger of being collateral damage in a war, and if some of them had died before ever becoming men.

Likely.

They hadn't known it, not then. They'd had fun, like other children did. Especially when they were able to be with each other. Rebecca set the terrine on the table and dished a helping of soup for him, and another for Emerald. "There is also bread and butter," she said. Then she looked at Andrei for a very long time. "It is good to have you back. You are the image of your father."

Andrei tried to smile. "Thank you."

Then she turned and left them there. Emerald looked angry, but took a bite of soup, which turned into two, and then three, as she ravenously attacked it.

"Hungry?"

"Yes. I was stolen from my wedding and brutally dragged into the sea. It works up an appetite."

"I would imagine."

His own stomach growled, and he reached for the butter and the bread, lathering on a thick layer before dipping it in the soup.

The taste of home was undeniable. Strange. He wouldn't have said that he missed this. That he missed Romania, or anything about the life he had before. But this reached down deep, into corners and memories that he hadn't known existed still. This made him feel... Whatever the feeling was, he couldn't say that he cared for it.

"You grew up here?"

"Partly," he said. "My father had many residences. For many reasons. We would have people here to visit us, but they would have to switch modes of transportation to make it confusing. They would come blindfolded, guarded."

"And they… Were okay with that?"

"I don't think you understand. What Boris Ardelean demanded, would be done. He was a dangerous man. And no one stood against him. Except for Luca Accardi. Leader of one of the largest crime families in Italy. He was the only one who dared go up against my father, and he had decided that it was his mission to kill him. And once he stood up against my father, so did many of the other families that we had called… Friends."

"Friends that were blindfolded."

"There is some honor among thieves, Emerald, but it is not a very nice honor."

"But you were only a boy. How were you aware of all of this?"

"It is part of being one of the children in these sorts of families. Particularly if you are the heir. We knew. We were hardened to the violence, to the danger from an early age. When your life is in danger from the moment you're born, and those around you make it clear, you become accustomed to it. Then, you have no fear. When you have no fear, you can be molded into the kind of man who can run that sort of empire."

"But your father was afraid. He ran."

"Yes, and only then did I realize my father might not be…immortal. But he knew, of course. If you are dead, you cannot continue to amass wealth." He was quiet for a moment, memories, feelings, impressions of a time long gone by filtering through his mind. "I do not think my father would have been proud of his death. I don't think he felt there was a risk in the crossing. Because he would've rather died in a hail of gunfire, that much I do know."

"Even as a twelve-year-old boy, that's your perspective?"

He nodded. "Yes. Even as a boy. Because he instilled a certain sort of bravery inside me. Because he taught me all that I needed to know. And he did that from the cradle."

"I don't want that for our child."

"Don't worry. I have no designs on picking up the reins of his criminal empire. I'm happy to let it die with him."

"Good."

"I do not have a need for power. But I will claim what's mine. That is a promise."

"I know that you... I know that you are angry with me but—"

"This is not a difference of opinion to be solved through a conversation, Emerald. You betrayed me. And I may not have designs on my father's criminal empire, but one thing I have in common with him is that I do not forgive easily. Or perhaps ever."

He was not capable of feeling guilt. He had thought that perhaps he was, but the way he felt in this moment proved to him that he was more like his father than he had previously realized.

A pity for them both. But a reality that he was beginning to embrace.

She finished the soup and pushed the bowl forward. "I find that I have spent as much time in your company as I can bear."

"Good night."

There was no reason for her to stay.

He might want to spend another hour or so in her presence, but why? It was only mutual torture.

The part of him feared that a lifetime filled with the mutual torture of wanting one another was going to be a hallmark of their relationship.

It had always been thus. And when they'd had each other, they'd shattered the world.

So back to this it was.

It was too late to change course now.

CHAPTER ELEVEN

She couldn't sleep. The bed was beautiful, and comfortable, and she was exhausted from everything that had happened in the last twelve hours, but she still couldn't sleep.

She was dressed in a soft gown that had been provided by Andrei, and part of her felt that she should perhaps resist his gifts. Resist wearing the clothing that he had provided for her, resist... The food, everything.

Except she couldn't. She was pregnant, and she needed to take care of herself. And also she just... The dichotomy of her feelings for him was overwhelming.

Because in many ways, he was still the man who she had loved for more than half of her life, and then suddenly he was a stranger.

The son of a crime lord. And he looked ruthless. Capable of doing everything his father had done and then some.

She lived in a world where blood was everything. Royal blood meant that you had a duty to the Crown, to the kingdom, to your people. She had long believed that her blood meant that she was destined to be like her mother. To do what she had done, did that mean that

Andrei was always destined for this? For a sort of ruthlessness that defied morality?

And then, part of it... She had to take some responsibility for.

She padded out of the bedroom and walked silently down the halls, the carpet soft beneath her bare feet as she went back toward where they had eaten their dinner. Then she walked through that room and into the kitchen. She startled when she saw Rebecca, standing there in front of the oven.

"Oh. Hello," she said. "I'm just making raisin bread for tomorrow. It's about to come out of the oven. Would you like a slice?"

Emerald's stomach growled. "I—I would."

"Have a seat, dear."

Emerald did and watched as Rebecca moved efficiently around the kitchen. She took the loaf of bread out of the oven, and turned the loaf pan upside down. Then she busied herself grabbing some butter, putting the kettle on.

"Tea or hot chocolate?"

"I would... I'd like a hot chocolate," she whispered.

"Wonderful. That will be a nice late-night treat."

"Have you been working like this at the house even without Andrei here?"

"No. I received a message that the house was being opened up again, and I hoped it was for him. I came the week before to make sure everything was good for him. He was such a lovely boy."

She couldn't help herself. She laughed. "He is... A slightly different sort of man."

Rebecca made a regretful sound. "I was worried about

that. I always hated that with the children who would visit. Eventually, they would become so hard. By the time they were fifteen almost all of them had killed someone on behalf of their family. An initiation into that life."

"Did you always work for families of organized crime?"

She shrugged. "It was often the most secure work here in this part of the world. I always served the Ardelean family. And so, the money that I have always gotten is blood money. Though, all of that changed when Andrei's father died. But he left us money. His staff was cared for in the end."

"That seems such a contradiction. That someone could be so ruthless, and yet remember the people who worked for him with so much loyalty."

"That is the attraction of it. You make for yourself your own kingdom, your own people, your own laws. And you offer fearsome loyalty in return."

"But it's all dangerous."

She shrugged again. "Life is dangerous. As I said, I think the most tragic part is watching the children lose their softness. Because the men in this world, they are so hard. The women too, some of them. Andrei's mother was a great beauty. He has the look of his father in his eyes, but, his mother's features. They fought bitterly, the two of them. And yet they loved fiercely. Or at least they were obsessed with one another."

Emerald's stomach turned. "That sounds like a terribly brutal way to love."

"I suppose it is," Rebecca said. "But then, I think none of them knew another way to be. I think none of them knew another sort of life. Except this painful, life-

and-death allegiance." She set the cup of hot chocolate in front of Emerald, and then, slipped the loaf from the pan without using an oven mitt, her hands obviously toughened from years of cooking.

"Do you have a family?"

She shook her head. "No. I was devoted to the children who came here. When they left, I lost everything. I helped raise Andrei's father too. Andrei was different. He was kinder from the beginning. When I heard that he had escaped, when I heard the news of him being in your country, I rejoiced. I had hoped that it might make him less feral."

"I thought you said he was lovely?"

"He was. Lovely, and feral."

"Well, some of this is my fault."

"I find with passion it is often just messy." She slid a slice of bread in front of Emerald, who buttered it generously, the butter melting, pooling on the sweet bread, and she picked it up and ate it fiercely.

"Well. It's complicated."

"I'm certain. Something is making you sleepless."

"It could just be the events of the day."

"There is a library, just to the left of the dining room. You might find something to help you while away your sleepless hours."

"Oh. That sounds lovely."

"It is," Rebecca said cheerfully. What life must it have been, to serve generations of mafiosi, to constantly be around the fringes of so much violence, but to be the one providing softness, food for the children.

It was such a strange thing. Emerald hadn't had a life free of struggles. She had lost her parents, and it had affected her deeply. But her life was quite limited in its scope.

There were things she never had to consider, like how she would make money and survive without the aid of the Crown.

It made her wonder about the lives of the people who worked in the palace and Basilia. The people who worked in Alabria. She took a sharp breath, and thanked Rebecca for the sustenance before taking herself out of the room and determining that she would explore the library.

She still wasn't tired. No. In contrast, she was invigorated, her thoughts churning.

She wandered down the hall, past some rooms that were dimly lit, empty. It was interesting how many spaces were in this house that didn't look like they had ever been used. Or perhaps that was simply the result of the cleaning. And certain spaces hadn't found their use yet.

Would she give birth to their child here?

Just thinking about spending nearly nine more months cooped up here, with a man who despised her as much as he had ever wanted her, filled her with the improbable twins of dread and hope. Because on the one hand it was difficult to stand being in the same room as him at the moment. But on the other hand, for many long years he had been the person she cared for most, next to her brother.

It wasn't like it had vanished just because things were difficult between them now.

She was surprised to see light flooding out of the library into the hall, and she paused before entering. Then her heart froze.

Andrei was in there, sitting by the fire in a large armchair, holding a book in one hand.

It was as if he sensed her presence. He looked up, his eyes finding hers unerringly.

Like they always did.

"Sorry. I didn't mean to interrupt."

"You've interrupted nothing," he said, intangible emotion burning in his gaze. She could see it even from across the room. But he was, of course, never going to talk about it. Not going to admit it.

"I couldn't sleep."

"What a strange phenomenon."

"It must be strange," she said. "Being here." She was going to try to be nonconfrontational. She hadn't expected to see him again tonight, but she had. So it seemed like it would be best if she didn't start a row when the two of them were already exhausted.

The simple truth was, putting aside the events of the past few weeks, she had known this man since childhood. She cared for him. And—again forgetting that he was the architect of the current moment—he was back in his childhood home for the first time since before his parents had died. Confronting so many things that he'd never had to before.

She could perhaps find it in herself to simply connect with him. To do for him what she would've done had they not slept together. Had he not kidnapped her. Had they not eroded the foundation of all the care they had for one another in a single night.

"No stranger than anything else," he said. "I have been a man outside myself ever since that ship went down. Basilia was not my home either."

"It was," she said. "My parents cared for you very much. They chose to bring you in and make you part of the family. If they were still alive..."

"What?"

Longing expanded inside her chest. If they were still alive, things would be so different. If they were still alive she would never have sought the marriage with King Lucian. She wouldn't have had to. There would've been other treaties. Other ways that her father handled things.

Why do you think that? Do you really believe that Onyx isn't the king that your father was?

No. She did. But Onyx was young. Not even thirty yet, and he didn't have the time on the throne that her father had. If her father were a king now, fifty and with all that experience behind him, then things would be different.

They would all be different.

She wouldn't have felt so desperate and driven to do this ultimate thing to honor her mother. Everything would be different.

"But it was not my home," he said. "It was not my destiny. This was, but I cannot even return here and find my destiny because it is gone."

"You said that you didn't want it."

"I don't. But it is not a real choice, is it? All of my father's legacies have been burned to the ground, Emerald. There is no less crime in the world. No less pain. Power vacuums are meant to be filled. And when one man falls, another rises. And so, many men have risen in the years since to take my father's place. And they have died and others have been reborn to replace them."

"It's exceedingly grim," Emerald said.

"Life is exceedingly grim. Or have you not come to understand that yet? Your parents were good people. They took in a half-drowned boy and it was not their responsibility to continue to care for me once I healed. But they did. And they are dead, just the same as my father, who never lifted a hand to save anyone or anything but himself."

"But my parents have a legacy," she said. "A legacy of kindness. Of care. Of sacrificing for their people."

He said nothing, but he looked around the room, and then at her. "And what is gained by that? So they can be written about in the history books, but where does that leave you?"

"I will go back and serve my country."

"Do you believe that your parents loved each other?"

She blinked. "Yes. I do."

"So was your mother's act one of self-sacrifice?"

"Yes. She couldn't have known what was waiting for her in the palace."

"It wasn't the Dark Ages. She had seen pictures of your father. Certainly she knew that there was an attraction there."

"Well, I saw pictures of Lucian. And I went anyway."

"You have so romanticized martyrdom. It would do you well to romanticize the martyrdom that you will find here. Martyring yourself for your child."

She gritted her teeth. "You're blaming me for this," she said. "And I don't deserve it. You think that if you hadn't found out I was pregnant, you would've taken me here, and we would've what? Married, been blissfully honeymooning by now? Tangled around one another, saying sweet words to one another? No. Because the only thing that you are equipped to do, Andrei, is *long*. Pining is what you're most comfortable doing. For the things that you can't have. Now that you have me, you don't actually want me. Because there's something… Broken in you," she said, completely losing track of the rule that she had made not to fight with him.

She continued on at him. "You know how to want. Not how to have. You do not know how to experience happiness, joy. Nothing. And it suited you, to make me the object of your desire and have me ever out of your reach. I just tested the limits of your self-control, and I think that's what you're really angry about. Your lack of self-control put you in this situation. Because you would have let me go. If you weren't so jealous, because you had touched me, because you knew you had taken my virginity, then you never would've taken me from that altar. You would have enjoyed your life fantasizing that you love me better than he ever could. Better than he ever did, without ever actually having to do any of the loving. Because now that you have me, you despise me. That isn't just about what I did. That's about your own inability to feel."

She began to turn to walk out of the room, but he was lightning fast, out of his chair, grabbing hold of her arm before she could do so. "You do not speak of me that way."

"What? Don't speak the truth to you?"

"I don't love you," he said. "You are right about that. But I wanted you. I wanted you with such a ferocity that it made my bones ache, and the reason that I didn't take you was that I knew nothing could ever come of it. You speak as though I am afraid, I am not afraid. I did you a favor. I could never have offered you marriage. I could never have offered you what you wanted, not and continue to let you live the life that you had before. Princess Emerald of Basilia could not marry the son of a crime lord. There is no noble blood in my veins, there is only selfishness. But it didn't change because I have you. Lust is not love."

He had succeeded in hurting her, and she despised him for that. It shouldn't hurt. Not when he was lying. "You said that I meant the world to you."

"You have to understand what that means coming from a man like me. My own father never loved anyone or anything more than himself. That is the life I know. I know how to swear allegiance and loyalty to a cause. I am very good at that. You were my cause for so many years. And so, there was no more glorious torture than desiring you. Than desiring to break that vow that I made to protect you. To keep you safe above all else. Yes, that's who I am. A man who only enjoys the sacred because they are forbidden. And perhaps you are right about one thing. I was ill-equipped to *have* the forbidden. And now I do. But don't turn it into something more beautiful than that. Do not adorn it with the flowers of love, when it is only base, common lust."

She slapped him. She didn't even think. Her hand was flying through the air, connecting with his face. She had never committed an act of violence in her life. But she had loved this man. With all of herself. And he was doing his level best to dismantle it. To dismantle everything. Because not only had he taken away her legacy, he had taken away her ability to do the one thing that she had needed to do in order to sit secure in her place in her family tree as one who had done well, but he had taken away the strength of what had happened between them. He was destroying it. Undermining it. Making it into something that she knew full well it was not.

He held the side of his face, glared at her, his dark eyes filled with rage. But he did not make a move toward hurting her.

"What would your father have done?"

"He would've given you as good as you gave," he said. "But I have no appetite for hitting women. Even if they are spoiled brats."

"Yes, because the act of a spoiled brat is to sacrifice herself for the greater good of the country."

"You keep telling yourself that. But you stand there, and you accuse me of not being able to have emotions. Are you any different? You have no idea what it means to be alive. No idea what it means to be human, apart from your sense of honor. And so what do you do now, Princess Emerald, if you have no one to live for but yourself."

"I have my child," she said. "I will live for them."

"So comfortable with a cause. You are but a vessel. For justice for your kingdom, for our child. What else are you?"

"Whatever I am, at least I'm not a monster."

Then she did turn, and he didn't stop her. She put her hand to her chest and tried to still her throbbing heart.

How dare he?

How dare he ask those questions and lead her down roads that she didn't want to go down. Because they were...

Because they were right. Because he was right.

He was her weakness.

She knew it.

He was her weakness, and he was the thing that had caused her to stumble.

And now... She had no honor left. She had been exposed to the entire world by now, she was certain. Because Lucian knew the truth, so undoubtedly he had announced it.

And where did that leave her? Here in this house, with this man, with... Nothing.

No greater good. No cause, no... Nothing.

All she knew how to do was to be of service.

He was right. She was a vessel for the legacy of another person. If she were very, very honest. She was living for the memory of her mother so that she could feel closer to her.

She was living for the memory of her mother so that she wouldn't fade from memory altogether.

And she had no idea what living for herself looked like.

Well, she did. Because she had done it once. That night on the yacht, when she had let Andrei have her. When she had given herself to him. To him and nothing else. He had become her mission for that night.

She laughed, wiping tears away as she went up the stairs to her room.

Look what he had done to her. What he had done to them both.

But there was a point where she had to take responsibility for this. And actually look at herself. At what she wanted. It was a terrifying question.

Andrei had been safe for her too. In much the way that he had been for her.

He had been a man that she could long for, desire, and never reach out and touch. The country was her one true love, and everything else was simply a game.

Except he wasn't.

She lay down on the bed, feeling dizzy with tiredness, and despair.

She was so... So terribly frustrated with herself.

She wished that she could escape her own body, fly about the trees. She wanted Andrei to be her friend again.

Except, he had never been her friend. He had always been a man who felt like he owed the Crown.

Just as she was a woman who had always felt the same.

They were both set pieces, being moved around by the whims of politics and the needs of a kingdom.

And now they found themselves alone, with only their humanity, and they were doing a very bad job of wielding it.

They were lashing out at each other. Hurting each other. Her hand still stung from where she had slapped him.

Why had she done that?

She didn't like this version of herself. This version of herself that felt so out of control. This version of herself that was being driven by emotion, rather than duty.

And yet, with all of that stripped away, with the Crown gone, this was what was left. She couldn't escape it. She had to contend with it.

Nothing had ever been more terrifying.

CHAPTER TWELVE

ANDREI WOKE UP sitting by the fire. The sun was filtering through the sky, and his face was sore from where Emerald had slapped him. Deservedly. He had slept in the library all night, though he hadn't meant to.

Was this to be their life? Their marriage?

He owed her better than that. He was angry, still, but... To what end?

And what was he angry at?

It wasn't her. Not truly. If they were going to raise a child together, then they could not live like this.

He had lost his grip on himself. He might've embraced aspects of his father's ways, but one thing he would not do was raise a child the way he had been raised. He would not raise his daughter to be a pawn. He wouldn't raise his son to be detached and deadly.

Emerald's family was royal, she had treated herself in much the way the mafiosi's daughters did. That grim determination to use what she had available to her to make things better for the family.

In her case, the country. And yet the end result was the same.

He got up and walked into the dining room. There

she was, seated already. Drinking a cup of warm liquid, and eating a pile of toast. "Good morning," she said.

She looked up at him, almost shyly. There was none of the antagonisms from the night before. "I'm very sorry that I hit you."

"It is nothing," he said.

"It wasn't nothing. It was a total failure of maturity on my part."

"I antagonized you."

"Yes. You did. But that doesn't mean that I get to behave that badly."

"Sleep seems to have restored some of your civility."

She nodded. "We've known each other too long to fall apart."

He made a short noise in the back of his throat. "I suppose so."

"I realized something. I don't know how to live when it isn't for the greater good. You are right about that. I am ill-equipped to handle my emotions because I have never allowed them to take center stage. That is... It's very difficult. And I don't know how to do this. So, I'm going to make mistakes. And occasionally be deeply unpleasant."

"I am always deeply unpleasant."

"You didn't used to be."

"I was doing my job."

"Yes. And part of your job was suppressing yourself, as a man."

He nodded. "I have long thought that it kept the world safe for me. Because if I carry elements of my father with me—and these last days have proven I do—it is best to keep it under wraps. But I will not be like my father with our child. And to that end, we must find a different way of being, you and I."

She put her elbows on the table, put her head in her hands. "This is so complicated. Because even if we make peace with each other, we might have plunged my country into war."

"Trust Onyx. He'll figure out a way out of this. You and I must focus on each other. On our child."

"You very casually put all this on my brother."

"Only because I devoted so much of my life to him. Asking him to devote a small portion of his to me, to you, is not entirely unreasonable."

She looked like she was considering that.

"All right. So what are we… What are we to do then? We are just in hiding?"

"We have all of these grounds. We can do anything you like."

"I just need to rest right now."

"Fair enough."

He sat down at the table. "Have you experienced symptoms of pregnancy?" The question felt stilted and stiff, but that was fair enough, because so did he.

"Not really. Though, I might be having a little bit of nausea, extra tiredness. But it's very hard to say. You know, given everything else."

"Yes. I suppose so."

"I don't know what to do," she said.

"What do you mean?"

"Even when I went to university, I got a degree that was about making me the best leader that I could be for the country. It was never about what I wanted. Because there has only ever been one real thing that I thought I could do. I was destined to be a political leader."

"And is that what you want?"

"Well, I think I would enjoy being a diplomat more than a queen."

"I'm going to say this to you gently. You have done a terrible job with diplomacy between the two of us."

She laughed. The humor in the moment deeply unexpected.

"Well. Yes. I suppose I have."

"But that is what you would prefer to do."

"Yes. I got such a thrill organizing the marriage deal. And if it had just been a trade deal, I think it would've been such a triumph. I probably could have enjoyed playing games on Wall Street. Rogue trading deals and that sort of thing. I love it. The strategy. But, what I've loved always had to be within the confines of where I was headed."

He nodded. "Yes. Well. Becoming someone who guarded others was a stark contrast to what my destiny would've been had I simply stayed at my father's house."

"You would've taken over the crime empire."

He nodded. "A certain amount of brute strength, hypervigilance, all of that, was required. I suppose I've always used elements of that with security detail. But there has never been a thought given to what I wanted. It has always been about what is right."

"I feel the same. Neither of us knows how to be people, you know. We are just symbols." Symbols that had finally reached their breaking point, given in to their desire for each other, even though it had been a very bad idea. Imperfect, broken symbols, who now found themselves without a mission.

"I couldn't deviate from the mission," she whispered. "Don't you understand? I was so terrified in that moment, and so sad, and I just couldn't make a different choice. I could only do what I knew to do. Part of me felt like you would understand." Her throat went tight. "Because what am I doing anything for if I'm not doing it for Basilia?"

"I know that," he said, the admission heavy because he had been clinging so desperately to his anger and now he knew he needed to let it go. To listen to her. "I know you did not act with maliciousness. I know you didn't intend to hurt me."

"But I did. I hurt you. I'm very sorry. I didn't intend to. I didn't mean... It doesn't matter. I was thinking of everything in terms of the cause. Not the personal. And now that I've pulled away from it all, I can see that what I was doing was shortsighted. I would've left him."

"But not until he had you."

She nodded slowly. "I would've tried. But I know that I would've regretted it. I know that I would've called for you. Because you are right. I have idealized this. This idea of living for duty and honor. But I don't know how to live."

"These things that you love about your mother. You love them in hindsight. What did you love about her as a child? Surely it wasn't the things that she did for duty and honor."

"No," she said. "I loved her softness. Her laughter. I loved it when she read me bedtime stories."

"Your mother is not only a symbol."

"I know." Her eyes filled with tears. "But it's so hard to… You might remember her even better than I do."

"It is possible. My memory of her is that she was extremely kind. Extremely soft. If I'm honest, Emerald, you remind me more of your father. He was very determined. Always excited about another plan, a diplomatic gain. He enjoyed the game of it, but in a way that was always generous, and considerate of others. He was a very good man."

"Yes," she whispered. "He was."

"But they did live. They did have lives that weren't simply symbolism."

She nodded. "I do know that."

"Why don't you rest?"

The idea of rest was foreign to her. She was always doing things. Always spearheading a committee, starting another project.

"It feels… It feels wrong."

"It is not," he said. "You are having my baby, and I have thoroughly antagonized you. I would prefer that you took your rest."

It was his form of an apology. He had never truly had to admit that he was wrong before. And with her, he knew he had been. His treatment of her had been unfair. And had been about his own feelings. Not about her.

"Rest," he insisted. "And maybe, for the first time, try and figure out what it is you want."

She was beginning to feel lazy.

She had spent days lying in bed since that strange, conversation she had with Andrei. She felt tender, thinking about her mom as a human. As her mother. Especially thinking about becoming a mother herself. It made her think about legacy in a very different way. She'd made it less of a personal thing because really remembering her mother hurt.

Andrei had offered her so much insight into her parents, and he had been so kind and... She didn't know where it had come from.

She also didn't really know how to get deeper than that.

He was such a strange brick wall.

There was an inherent goodness to him, she was sure of that. But there was also difficulty.

The man was difficult.

Her feelings for him were no less difficult. The trouble was lying around like this, with no royal duties, with nothing, was that she had the opportunity to examine images of different kinds of futures. And there was one that she had never let herself hope for. Not really. One where she married Andrei. Where she had love. And maybe she wouldn't be written about. A princess who married her bodyguard. Maybe it was no kind of legacy. Maybe it would make headlines, but nothing deeper than that.

She had lived her entire life for what would happen after she died.

She had no idea how to live.

It was that thought that finally got her out of bed on a supremely sunny day, and outside. Rebecca told her that there were berries along the trail, and if she wanted a cake, she could go and pick some. So, she found herself out on a sun-drenched trail that wound through a field, picking fat, red berries and putting them in a basket.

It was a delightfully slow, rustic thing to do, and she had never lived a slow or rustic life.

It was strange to think that only a month and a half ago she had been boarding a beautiful yacht with every amenity she could want, and now she was in a crumbling manor without access to the internet.

Picking berries.

But without the input from the rest of the world, it was like she could finally hear herself.

"What are you doing out here?"

She turned sharply, startling for a moment, because that there would be anyone out here was a shock, and her first thought was that Onyx or Lucian had found her. But it was Andrei. Thank God.

"You scared me," she said.

"Sorry. I didn't expect to see you out and about."

"I'm tired of myself," she said.

He laughed. "It's a common malady these days, I fear."

"Are you tired of yourself, Andrei?"

"Yes. One thing that living for a cause gives you is the relief of the weight of your own humanity."

She had to laugh about that, because it was true.

All she was left with now were her own petty fears and discomforts. Her desires, the things that she wanted, even if she shouldn't or couldn't.

It was exhausting. It was better, actually, to worry about things on a global scale, because her personal economy was far more troubling, and also, it felt even more out of her control.

"I'm picking berries for a cake, because that at least feels like something."

"Can I join you?"

"I would like that."

"We used to come out here all the time when I was a child. Pick berries."

"You and who else?"

"There were often children. Of associates of my father. It was such a strange childhood. There were times when we were left to our own devices, left to run wild. And other times…"

She looked at him. "What?"

"I don't want to spoil a beautiful day with things about my childhood."

"Tell me."

"My father saw it as his duty to prepare me to take over the family business. That meant that when there were people who needed to be… When violence had to be dealt out, he would ask that I watch. You get used to it. You learn to stop thinking about how much it must hurt the other person. Slowly, over time, it begins to kill your empathy. That's the idea behind it. He didn't want me to have empathy. He didn't want me to care what happened to other people. He wanted me to care only about the mission. And so I am very good at that."

It was such a strange thing to realize, that he had been shaped by something so dark and sinister, and yet it had turned him into a very similar person to her.

Her own parents had been sweet, lovely. Well-intentioned.

She wanted to honor them, and that was where all of her feelings came from.

His father had simply bent and twisted him into a

vessel. One that could contain all the violence his family required.

And then he had transferred that, that loyalty, to her and Onyx.

"It must be really hard to be back here, actually."

He shook his head. "I have some of the nicest times of my life here. I cared very much about all of my friends. I think that is actually the difficult part. It was not a miserable childhood entirely. I suppose children are resilient and they are determined to create fun no matter what. But there were things that... There were things that were quite miserable."

"I wish I had known this about you."

"Why? It wouldn't have changed anything. You and I were always going to be bound by the rules we made for ourselves."

He was right. Only in childhood had there ever been any lightness for either of them. When she was a little girl, she hadn't thought about her legacy. It was only after her mother had died. Before that, she'd known what fun was. What dreams were. She had imagined a family like her own.

"If I'm honest," she said, "I suppose I probably did romanticize the idea of marrying a stranger. Especially as I got older, because I did know that I would probably have to do a diplomatic union. Knowing that my parents had done it, it just made it seem like there was the possibility for it to be wonderful. Like there was the possibility for it to work out."

His eyes burned into her. "And your feelings for me?"

She took a breath, looked away, tried to ignore the soreness in her chest. "I learned to ignore them. Sort of.

It was a separate thing. I wanted you, but I knew that I could never have you, so it was sort of... Its own kind of beautiful tragedy, I guess. But please don't call it lust. It isn't. It isn't just lust."

He nodded slowly. "I won't."

"Good."

They finished picking berries in silence, and then she was surprised when it turned out that the offer from Rebecca for cake meant that she had to bake it. She had never baked a cake in her life. "She tricked you," Andrei said. "She's done the same for me."

"You will help her," Rebecca said, which was how she found herself in the kitchen with Andrei, baking a berry cake, which was far less disastrous than it might've been, but perhaps a little more disastrous than it should have been. Especially given that they were two adults with decent educations and a fair amount of competency between them in other areas.

But the cake turned out lovely, and the lemon drizzle on top only made it that much better.

They had that instead of a proper dinner, and afterward, he asked if she wanted to go for a walk in the moonlight.

Was this what being a person was? Eating and baking and laughing. Going for walks because you could.

Not sitting at a table for ages, doing multiple courses, and observing formalities. Working on royal administration at all hours of the day. Not that there was anything wrong with that. With being busy.

But this, this slow slide into humanity was lovely.

The moon was full, and cast a glow on the overgrown

garden, and she followed Andrei through the maze of paths.

"I bet you had a lot of fun in here when you were a child."

"Yes," he said.

He didn't elaborate. It seemed like the happy memories were almost as difficult for him as the painful ones. But then, she could understand how that was difficult. How it would pull you in multiple directions. Because it wasn't all bad. And it was so much easier when things could be absolute. So much easier when they could be clean. So bad that you wanted to wash your hands of them. So good that you wanted it to go on forever.

Maybe that was part of what she was looking for, living a life of duty and destiny. A cleaner, simpler life that didn't have all of this complexity. All of this potential for heartbreak.

And in a way, it kept her mother with her. But only as this simplified version of herself.

But it helped alleviate the grief that she felt over the way she hadn't gotten to know her through the years. As an adult. As a woman.

Now she was going to be a mother herself.

She put her hand on her stomach. It still felt unbelievable.

She looked up at Andrei, the moon casting a glow on his features. Why was this so hard?

Why did neither of them know how to be together?

"This tree," he said, gesturing to it. "We used to climb up to the top, see how far we could see. Until my father put a stop to that. He thought it would help the other kids figure out the location of the house."

"You're kidding me."

He shook his head. "No. I'm not. He was an extremely paranoid man. As you must be when you sow the seeds of violence."

"You loved him, didn't you?"

"I…think so. Though I am not certain what love meant to me then, as I'm not certain what it means now, not inside me. I depended on them. I knew I was supposed to be like my father. I was in awe of him. My mother was beautiful, and volatile. I still carry grief for them, even though they were very flawed."

He reached up and grabbed the lowest branch on the tree. And then he hoisted himself upward.

"What are you doing?"

"Climbing. Because I can."

"I'm going after you," she said.

"No," he said. "You're pregnant."

"I'm pregnant," she muttered. "Not made of glass. I don't intend to fall out of the tree. You know full well we climbed our fair share when we were kids too."

He kept on going, and she went after him. Until he stopped at a very wide branch that sloped out from the tree and neatly made a basket to sit in. She joined him there, their hips touching. It had been far too long since they had touched. Other than her slapping him, which really didn't count. And hadn't been good. What if they had met just like this?

Just as Andrei and Emerald. If he didn't have a crime empire in his lineage and loyalty to the throne, and she weren't a princess. It had never even occurred to her to imagine a different life. Her life was exceedingly privileged, and she did her best to live it with the knowledge of that. With gratitude. But right now, she resented it. Because what would life have been like if she could just be her?

No other baggage, no other responsibilities.

She leaned in and kissed him on the cheek. He turned to her sharply, surprise on his handsome face.

"That was an apology for the slap," she said.

"You already apologized for that," he said.

"I know. But… It was more than that. I imagine being up here with you all those years ago. If we were just kids, and we met, and there was nothing else."

"But there is something else. So many other things, and that will always be true."

"I know, but I just…"

"I don't want to be my father," he said, his voice stern. "Being here, being in this house it is…haunted. By memories that are both good and bad. I find myself burdened by them."

"Why?"

"Because I loved him. And loving him was toxic. I won't be that for my child. We can find a way to fix this. A way to serve the greater good. We are good at that, Emerald, aren't we?"

"You just accused me of having no idea who I am if I don't have a cause."

"Perhaps…perhaps that is a good thing." He turned away from her. "Emotion in all its many forms is messy. Love is a liar. But we could unite and make this better. We could…we can fix all this. For us. For our child."

"I agree," she said, moving away from him, just slightly.

She did agree. But it hurt her. She'd been so happy

with him a moment ago. So carefree and now she felt like she was losing her grip on that happiness. This felt more normal. More what she was used to. This distance. This need for a wall between them.

But what he said was true.

"We have known each other all our lives, and yet we don't know each other. We need to disentangle the difficult feelings between us. My father and mother's version of marriage was toxic. Twisted up in their lust, in all the sharp feelings. When I took you as I did in Alabria…"

"I wanted you."

He let out a rough sigh. "That isn't better."

Maybe it wasn't. Maybe her desire was sick. Maybe it was as damaged as they were.

She wished she knew how her parents had come to love each other. What they'd shared. But she didn't know because she'd been so young when they died. She had no blueprint. She had nothing.

Nothing except this ache inside her that she wanted so badly to make smaller. This ache that only ever seemed manageable when she was doing something. When she felt like she was fixing something.

These past few days here in the estate had been lovely, but she couldn't live like this. She had to keep moving. They had to make a decision about their relationship, because they couldn't stay here forever.

It wasn't what she'd wanted him to say. But she'd… slapped him. It had been wrong of her. It had been because of the way things were between them—so disordered and filled with…

Emotion.

He was right. They had a common duty. One to their child. That had to be the mission.

"We must call a truce," he said. "We are not enemies. We are to be parents."

She nodded. "A family."

He nodded, uneasy. "A family to me is difficult."

"It doesn't have to be. A family can be like mine. It can be happy. It can be…" She thought of her mother and father, laughing, reading to her and Onyx, holding them. The pain and anguish it created inside her almost took her breath away.

It didn't have to hurt. She would learn from it. Let her change her. Let it make her a good mother. A good…

"Let's take this time," she said. "This time here, to decide what we want to do. Together. As parents. For our child."

Because their child should be able to run wild and climb trees, and pick berries. Because their child should live in a home with parents who loved them. Who didn't fight. A mother who didn't lose her temper and slap their father. A father who didn't look at their mother with so much heat and outrage that it felt like they'd burn the whole house down.

She and Andrei knew how to resist each other. They'd done it for years.

If they could do it for the sake of the throne, surely doing it for their own child would be no more difficult.

Surely.

CHAPTER THIRTEEN

THE LIBRARY BECAME their neutral ground. They spent much of the day separate from one another, and Andrei felt that it was a decent testament to how they would manage everything once the baby was born.

He could imagine, very comfortably, the two of them having a life here. They would be... Friends, he supposed. Something so much less toxic than his parents. Throwing dishes, shouting, disappearing to their room for hours.

His mother crying.

His father had been particularly good at twisting the knife in his mother's ribs when he wanted to get a reaction out of her.

And his own love—as he'd known then, as he knew it now—served as a reminder of how emotions could be twisted and manipulated. He'd been so young. A vine that had been easily twisted around a trellis, to grow around the wrong ideas, feelings and conclusions.

It was only the royal family that had allowed him to understand love, but even then, in himself, he could not trust it. For good reason.

This place was so... Haunted. It held so many memories. Good and bad, and often the good and bad twisted around each other. He didn't want his child to grow up that way.

And that made him feel all the more resolved in this.

They took meals together occasionally, but tonight Emerald was having dinner in her room. She was having bouts of sickness at all times of the day.

She insisted that it was normal, and all completely fine. She was on a diet of herbal tea and extremely pungent pickled cabbage that made his stomach curl, but that she seemed to enjoy.

Or rather, craved, which she had informed him was slightly different from enjoyment, and had more to do with necessity.

He had been an only child. He had never really been around pregnant women. It was an experience.

He heard her behind him, and he turned. She was wearing a nightgown, barefoot, her red hair swirling around her shoulders. There were circles under her eyes, and he wished he could go to her and wipe them away. But he didn't.

Because that would be to break this spell between them.

Everything was good right now, and he didn't want to break it.

"And how was your day?" she asked, floating into the room and moving to sit in his chair.

A little quirk of hers. Or, she was trying to be annoying. The thing that was really annoying about it was that he found it cute, and he supposed it was okay for him to find her cute. Maybe they would coparent. Maybe they wouldn't even be a couple.

The thought of that made him taste something metallic in the back of his mouth.

***

"Fine. I did some work."

"What work do you do exactly?"

"I have investments. Mainly in companies that make military grade weapons."

"That sounds…"

"Like the most legal way to be adjacent to the kind of work my father did? You would be correct. But I understand it."

"It wasn't a judgment. I help run a country. I understand how these things work. Or I guess, I did run a country. Who knows what will be there when we get back."

"Well, nothing catastrophic has happened so far. Though the headlines about this are hysterical."

She narrowed her gaze. "You have internet access and you've been keeping it from me."

"Not consciously. But, I did figure it might only upset you."

"That's not for you to decide," she said, sniffing.

"I would disagree, Emerald. As I have brought you here to protect you. In all the ways that I can."

"Yes. Well. I do feel quite wrapped in silk."

"Good. You should."

She wrinkled her nose. "It's a bit weird to have you be this nice to me."

"It's better than the alternative."

"I know. I am very sorry that I slapped you."

"You don't need to keep bringing that up."

"No, I just… You're right. Things don't have to be like that between us. And I understand."

"Your parents seemed to have such a nice marriage," he said.

"Yes. And they were strangers when they met. It's so funny, because I know that in the modern world that's a very strange experience. But in the grand context of history, it's not. It's the way things used to work. And they made a lot of happiness out of it."

"My parents didn't. Or rather they had… Excitement. I fear very much that my mother loved my father more than he loved her. But then, I'm not certain my father loved anything more than he loved himself. No, I know he didn't. Because in the end, he held on to his position in the crime family for far longer than he should have. He should have gotten out earlier. He should've done something to save my mother. To save himself. Something more than running as he did."

"It probably wouldn't have changed the outcome."

"Maybe he would've been able to get safer passage if he hadn't been taking the only vessel available."

"And maybe my parents could've taken a different route. Left five minutes later. Not gone out at all. We can't know these things. And the truth is, you probably don't even have a clear view of your parents' marriage. That is the terrible thing about being young when your parents die."

He laughed. "My parents were not the king and queen of a country. I guarantee you I have a distressingly clearer review of who they were than you do of your parents. Also remember how old I was when I realized what they did in their room with the door closed for so many hours. They would have meals delivered and not come out. Marathons. I mean, I knew, but I didn't fully understand."

"Goodness."

"And my father was not soft with her. Or kind. It was… barbs. Coldness. It was… Extremely painful to be around, even as a young child who didn't fully understand."

"I'm sorry."

"It was much like his relationship with me. We would go outside and play catch. He could be warm and fun. And then he would bring me into witness the beating of a man who owed them money. And would tell me that I needed to get used to it, because it was the reality of running a business."

"Oh… Andrei. That is terrible."

"It was my father. Darkness and light. Good and bad. And God help anyone who loved him. Honestly. I don't want to be like him. I told myself that I needed to be. To claim you. I… I cannot subject either of us to that. But most of all, I will not subject our child to that."

"You're not him."

"I can never trust that. What I know is that my feelings cannot be trusted, and cannot lead. I need to…"

He looked at her, his gaze locked firmly on hers. He wanted to stay here because he felt like he had all the power here. Because there was no king but him. He was God in these mountains, and he did not have to deal with Lucian or Onyx, or the responsibilities that Emerald had in her real life. But that wasn't realistic. And it wasn't the right path.

That was the sort of thing his father would do. Consolidate his power. Protect it above all else. Damn his wife, and damn his child.

Damn them all to the same level of hell that he was destined for.

He couldn't do that. He had made the decision to keep things… Platonic with Emerald.

To keep from descending into that madness that had captured both of his parents.

But now he had to answer that dark part of himself. The one that wanted to keep her here. Keep her away from everyone.

His child was royal, even if he was not. Emerald loved her country.

And there was more to life than this compound. That was the life the child of a crime lord had to lead. Locked away, with so many enemies beyond the walls that you were never truly safe. All because of your father's ego.

He was still acting from a place where his ego was making decisions.

Especially with Emerald, and his refusal to marry her.

"This cannot endure," he said.

Emerald looked at Andrei, certain she was misunderstanding him. "What can't?"

"We are in hiding here, and it is sadly far too much like the last couple of years I spent with my parents. I will not do that to my son or daughter."

"What are you…what are you proposing?" she asked, the calm, tranquil feeling she'd had a moment ago turning into something cold, afraid.

"I think we need to go back. Face all of this. Face all of this mess."

"And what if Lucian orders your death?"

"Come now, Emerald. I would not be so easily defeated. I would not be defeated at all. Do you not know me?"

"I do. You're arrogant and difficult and… I don't want the father of my baby to die."

She didn't want him to die. She didn't want to say that. Not now while he was in this space of cold, remote detachment.

"We need to marry," he said.

"I thought you weren't…"

"I don't wish to force you. You will not be my mother. I will not be my father. But I think it is the only way forward."

So logical. And correct, if she was honest. But it hurt all the same.

"Are you proposing a marriage in name only or…"

"For now," he said, his tone rueful. "There is no way for us to manage all the things we must if we let ourselves get lost in lust. That is what harmed us in the first place."

He was taking a lovely moment and turning it into something so cold.

He was right, though.

She didn't know what to do with all the feelings inside her, so big and unwieldy. She didn't know how she was going to be a mother, a princess, a wife. And the idea that they had a problem to solve together—that felt manageable.

Sorting out the issues between them much less so.

"All right, Andrei," she said. "I will marry you."

It had nothing to do with love, passion or desire.

Nothing to do with what they'd felt for each other before everything.

What a strange realization.

He'd cared about her more before they'd ever made love.

Now…

Now there seemed to be nothing there at all. He'd locked it down inside himself, closed it behind him.

Now when she looked at him, she could see nothing but duty and honor. She'd hurt him with hers. Now he was killing her with his own.

"Good. We will travel back to Basilia tomorrow. You will speak to your brother. Leave Lucian to me."

CHAPTER FOURTEEN

WITH EMERALD SAFELY deposited in Basilia, he decided to make the journey to Alabria. She was resistant to the idea, and she was angry. But she needed to deal with Onyx, and her position in the country in her own time. He would not allow her to face Lucian.

Ever.

If the man were any kind of threat to her, then Andrei would kill him with his bare hands. Given the situation they were already in, that was probably only going to make things worse.

And he had to fix this. For their future. For their child.

They had found a way to be together back in Romania. He could imagine long, happy days, and no, perhaps they couldn't have everything.

Because of who he was. Because of the blood that flowed through his veins. Because of the way he was shaped by the cloistered world his father had raised him in. But they could have this.

They could have a family.

A better version of it than he'd ever had.

He could make peace with Onyx. And he was determined to do so.

But everything had begun to unravel when they had

introduced sex, their own desires, their messy feelings. And in the time since then, they had found something more.

Something deeper.

Something that existed beyond the pining and longing the two of them had managed to make their entire identity.

He'd suppressed his need for her for years, and though he'd let it out, allowed himself to get swept away by it for a time, he could suppress it again. It would be better if they could go back to that neater, simpler way of being.

He took a small, faster ship to Alabria, cutting the journey down to one day, and by the time he set foot on the island, he was prepared for whatever met him.

If he died, it would be in the interest of keeping Emerald safe. And she was ensconced with Onyx, so she would be protected.

He walked up to the front doors of the palace and was greeted by the guard.

"King Lucian is expecting you."

"As he should be. Is there an executioner with him as well?"

"He's interested in what you have to say. He thinks you're brave. And mad."

"Perhaps," he said.

He allowed himself to be escorted into the throne room. They searched him for weapons. He wasn't that foolish. If need be, he would fight for his life with his bare hands.

He himself was a weapon. He didn't need to carry one.

If they had known this, perhaps they would've bound his hands. But they did not.

The king was sitting on the throne much as he had been the first time Andrei had laid eyes on him. With the sort of lazy indolence that many would see as nonthreatening. But he saw it for what it was.

Lucian himself was also deadly. And there was no disinterest in him whatsoever.

He was languid. Like a cat ready to strike.

"My bride thief. Here you are. I didn't expect for you to return to me of your own free will. Do you have my chosen queen with you?"

"No. That is what I have come to discuss with you. I intend to marry Princess Emerald."

"That is a problem for me. Given that I've planned an entire wedding for the two of us. Once you monogram things, they don't let you return them."

"I feel that with the treasury as great as yours, whatever is monogrammed on your linens is not truly your main concern."

"Perhaps not. But I don't like to lose."

"What I propose to you is not a losing proposition. We can make something work."

"So say you. But what if I do not like what you have to offer."

"Reject it. Cut off my head. Promise me, whatever you do, you will leave Emerald out of it."

"I can make you a promise, Andrei Ardelean. But there is no guarantee that I will keep it. I am not a man of my word, nor am I a man of honor. Though, neither are you. I have done an extensive amount of research into your background since you took my bride. You are the son of a criminal."

"That is like calling a battleship a rowboat. My father was *the* criminal."

"Yes. So I read." He leaned forward in his throne, suddenly keen. "It was brave of you to take her like you did. And the spectacle. I enjoy a spectacle. I do not like finding myself without a bride, though. And I was publicly humiliated."

Andrei lifted an eyebrow. "You did not think that you would be publicly humiliated if people found out that she was carrying another man's baby?"

"No one would've ever discovered that."

"Really?" He snorted. "Can you be that naive? I heard that you were a great terror. And yet, your perspective on this is giving… Babe in the woods. Do you not think there would be speculation? Do not think that somebody would try to sneak a DNA test? Anything to undermine you in your power?"

"Why would anyone do that?"

"You are hated. Reviled. You are also blond, and Emerald is extremely pale herself. The chances of the child coming out looking very much my coloring should be a concern for you."

"A good point."

"Besides, you strike me as a despoiler of virgins. And Emerald is not that."

"I do enjoy a good despoiling." He looked thoughtful. Andrei was mindful of the fact that he could not make any of this too much his idea. King Lucian was the sort of man who liked to believe that everything was his own decision. Andrei didn't have to know him to know that.

"Find yourself a new bride. Get her with your own child, avoid the incident."

"I do suppose this adds to my lore. I also like that. As much as I enjoy spectacle."

"Did you murder your wives?"

He smiled. Just slightly. "No."

"Why is it you allow the rumors to persist?"

"I told you. I like a spectacle. And I like for people to not know which direction I'm going to come from. It suits me. I don't give a shit about my reputation, honestly. But I do care about somebody making a threat to my throne. And its sovereignty. And you present a good point about the heir. What will you offer me in return? For you have cost me a lot of money and trouble."

"Military alliance. Trade alliance. Everything that Emerald promised you. In addition to that, one of the things that I do in my own time is invest in new military technologies. If you would like to have access to the newest and latest advancements… They can be yours. For significantly reduced rates."

"Free," he said.

"If it pleases the king."

"Very little pleases the king. I am bored. And one thing I will say about the most recent events, is that they were not boring. I have no taste for killing you, Andrei Ardelean. You will make a good ally, and an even better enemy. So, I would prefer that you stay on this side of the ground."

"Don't expect an invitation to my wedding."

"I wouldn't go anyway. It would be a terrible black mark on my reputation if I were seen as being the bigger person. I'll send a gift."

It rather felt more like a threat than an offer, but then most things of King Lucian did.

"I'll look forward to receiving it."

He was done. And now, all that was left was to plan the wedding.

"I was worried about you."

Emerald was awash in anxiety waiting to hear what had happened with Lucian and Andrei. She was worried for his safety. She…

When she had arrived back at Basilia, Onyx had given her some reprieve. He hadn't demanded an explanation immediately, but today, all bets were off.

"I'm sorry," she said. "I wasn't the one who spirited me off to Romania with no means to contact you."

"What were you thinking? Why would you decide to marry Lucian when you wanted Andrei?"

"Because I had decided that I couldn't have him."

"Why?"

"He isn't royal."

"That is high level bullshit, Emerald. I certainly never told you that you had to marry a man with royal blood. I never even suggested it. Andrei is my best friend. He is the most trusted man—he was the most trusted man—in my employ. I would have given you to him happily."

This was what she had been afraid of. This conversation.

She realized that now, as her brother looked at her with confusion and ferocity in his eyes. He would have allowed them to be together. Of course he would have. He didn't demand that she make something more of herself. He wanted her to be happy.

She was the one who hadn't been able to accept it. She was the one who had been fleeing these feelings for

Andrei, and now she was stuck in this great and terrible middle ground with him, where there was something of a truce, but no more passion.

It was her own fault. It was her own fault because…

She tried to take a breath.

"But I wanted something more. I wanted to make something out of myself. I wanted…" She closed her eyes. "It made me feel close to Mom. This idea that I was going to have a dynastic marriage. One that changed something. I just… I wanted to be like her. Because I can't know her. I can't be with her. And if I have to accept that, that I just have to accept the grief. It's just so horrible. It's endless. And I…"

"The past is undeniably tragic," Onyx said. "For all of us."

"Yes." She looked at her brother, who had a remote expression on his face. She knew he missed their parents. She knew he loved her. But he could be so detached sometimes, like it was what he had to do in order to be king.

But she wished sometimes it wasn't that way.

"I do not give this my blessing," Onyx said. "He kidnapped you. He forced you down the aisle. You are clearly in a state."

"I'm not asking for your blessing. I'm just asking you to… Be my brother. While I try to figure out the situation that I've gotten myself into."

"I am always your brother. You always have me."

"And Andrei?"

"He and I will take some time before we repair our relationship. He took you away from me. He put you in danger. He didn't tell me where you were. He didn't trust me. It will take time for me to get over that."

"And fair enough. But he is the father of my baby."

"And he is that simply through donation of genetic material. To be called a friend is something he will have to earn his way back to."

The doors to his study opened, and Andrei came in. She had to fight the joy in her chest, fight to keep from flying out of her chair and into his arms. That wasn't the relationship that they had. They decided. It was for the best.

"It is done. He has agreed not to pursue any type of retaliation. I've made military alliances with him in exchange. And offered him technology."

"You don't have the authority to make those deals," Onyx said.

Andrei looked at him, hard. "Would you like to make this more difficult than it needs to be?"

"You need to remember who you are," Onyx said.

"I know who I am," Andrei returned. "I know who I am, and I have taken steps to ensure that I will behave with honor either way. I am going to marry your sister. Whether we receive your blessing or not."

"She and I just covered that. I do not extend my blessing, but I will not stop it from happening."

She hated this. The feeling of the rift between them. He was a mess, and she knew that, but she shared the blame. She'd been a coward when he'd needed her to be brave. She had been resisting her feelings for Andrei to protect herself.

And now... All this had happened. It was such a huge mess that needed cleaning up.

But at least they had started. As for the issues between the two of them? She didn't know that it would be so easy.

"How quickly do you suppose we can plan the wedding?"

"It should be easy enough," she said.

"With my money?" Onyx asked.

Andrei turned to him sharply. "I will pay. It does not have to be a royal wedding. We can have it anywhere."

"Don't be a fool. I will pay for it. She's my sister. It is a royal wedding. And it will be here. I may not be giving this union my blessing, but one thing I will not tolerate is you being an idiot."

Andrei almost laughed. "Then you see it done how you wish, Your Highness."

"I have moved your quarters," Onyx said. "You will be in the same wing of the palace as Emerald. A suite of rooms is my gift to you."

"We won't be living here full-time," Emerald said softly.

"Of course not," said Onyx. "But still, that is my wedding gift to you. Not that you'll be needing it."

It was Onyx who stormed out of his own office, leaving her there with Andrei.

The tension stretched between them, her desire to close the gap between them increasing. But she couldn't. She had made vows to him in Romania. About how this would be.

"I'm glad that you're all right."

"I'm quite relieved."

"Onyx is going to be a little bit more difficult."

"I'm not worried about him."

She was. She hated this. Hated the distance between them. Hated the distance between herself and her brother.

"I hope so."

"We have a mission, Emerald. And we are most of the way to completing it. Do not lose hope now."

She shook her head. "I won't."

"Good. This is why we will succeed."

"Of course. This is why we will succeed."

He nodded his head and left the study, and Emerald found herself sitting there by herself. The same room where she had first told her brother that she was going to marry Lucian. The same room where all of this had begun.

She did not feel determined at all right now. She felt defeated.

She had created this problem. Fixing it would be ugly, and Andrei wouldn't like it, That much she knew.

But one thing she also knew about herself was that she was strong enough to do it.

She had loved Andrei Ardelean for all these years. She wouldn't give up on them now.

CHAPTER FIFTEEN

THEY MANAGED TO mostly avoid each other in the lead-up to the wedding. It was for the best.

Andrei found that the ache he felt for Emerald never fully went away. He would learn to live with it. To make the pain part of breathing. The ache a part of himself.

They had made their decisions, and they were the right ones.

There was difficulty between himself and Onyx, and that was all the challenging emotion he could handle right now.

The truth was, he had to figure out how to be a father, when the one thing he knew was that he couldn't be his own. His own feelings for his father were so complicated, so tinged by trauma and loss, by who his father was, that it was difficult for him to figure out exactly what that meant.

If he hated his father it would be so much easier.

He was trying to find his way to that.

The door opened behind him, and he turned. Emerald was standing there, looking at him, her expression tentative. "Can I come in?"

"Of course. This is your room as much as it is mine."

Except they were like that. They didn't have that intimacy.

"It can't be like this for our entire marriage," she said.

"What exactly do you mean?"

"You know that it can't be. We aren't going to be able to resist each other. Not for the rest of our lives. It simply... It's going to end up making more problems than solutions. That's all."

"Emerald, this is dangerous." Everything in him was shouting to run away. After what had happened between them the last time they were together, the monster that had been awakened inside him...

"No," she said. "What's dangerous is us denying ourselves. Look where it got us. It almost started a war, and it certainly started one between the two of us. But we've...we've created a friendship since then. We need to trust ourselves."

Her hands were shaking, her eyes hopeful. If he denied her now, he would hurt her.

And the truth was, he didn't want to deny her.

He burned for her. His entire body shook with the need to touch her, hold her, take her, whenever she was near, and yet he knew he couldn't risk it.

This was a war he'd wage all his life, but the resistance of it would be the proof that he could be better.

Stronger.

"I can't see a future where neither of us ever wants a lover," she said.

Never.

There would never be anyone but her.

"And we may want more children," she said. "Besides, as unhealthy as your parents were, won't we be just as dysfunctional? Denying what we want and..."

His strength ran out. Was there another way? His mind and body were working as quickly as possible to try and make a new bargain. To try and find a new way to be.

A way that would allow something. Just a touch, perhaps. A taste.

He wouldn't lose himself.

He reached out, taking her chin between his thumb and forefinger, holding her steady as he leaned in to kiss her. Different than any other kiss they'd ever shared. It was slow. Methodical. There was no desperation. It wasn't like they were trying to outrun a clock. It wasn't because he was trying to punish her.

It was just a kiss. And there was something beautiful about that. It was a kiss, because they both wanted it. And who knew what it would mean later. It felt good now.

Emerald, and Andrei.

There was no Basilia. There was no Alabria. There was only this.

He picked her up and laid her down on the bed, glorying in the need that was building inside him.

This felt different from what had happened before.

Where the first time had been glorious and painful, aching because it was going to be all they had, and that night at the castle had been her punishment. This was an attempt to rebuild. Not tear down.

This was who they might have been if they'd been free from the beginning to choose who they wanted to be.

He kissed her. This wasn't hurried. It was a slow exploration. His lips over hers, his tongue thrusting deep, sliding against hers, a leisurely tasting.

His heart was beating fast, and he reached down between her legs and pushed his fingers beneath her underwear, feeling how slick she was between her thighs. Oh she wanted him.

He wanted her more than he could possibly say. More than sanity. More than keeping his word. He wanted to go faster, and he wanted to linger in this moment forever.

She pulled at his shirt, and he let her draw it up over his head. Then he reached around and unzipped her dress, tugging it down, exposing her body. She wasn't wearing a bra, only a pair of very brief underwear, and he dispensed of those two quickly.

Still, he just held his body against hers, kissing her. Indulging himself.

She moved her hands over his shoulders, his muscles, helped him take off his pants, everything else. She explored him, kissing her way over the acres of muscle, all of his skin.

And he returned the favor.

Committed the taste of her, the shape of her, to memory.

What if they could have this?

He was on fire with that realization that they could. They had already abandoned everything. They had already burned it all to the ground. They'd rebuilt into this, so why not have this? Why not have each other?

Why not try?

Maybe they didn't know how. But they could learn. They could learn, and then they could always, always have *this*.

She gasped as he kissed her neck, moved down to her breasts, down her stomach, between her thighs, where he feasted on her. She was the most glorious dessert he'd ever had. All slick and sweet like honey. He wanted to gorge himself on her forever.

He wrapped his arms around her, pulled her up into a sitting position, her knees on either side of him. She lowered herself down onto his stiff, aching staff, taking him in slowly, inch by excruciating inch. She gripped the back of the headboard, their eyes locked on one another's. As she rode them both toward oblivion.

She flexed her hips back and forth, then rose up slightly, the feel of her tight wet body around him almost sending him over the edge into oblivion.

She established a rhythm that carried them both over the edge, and when he tightened his hold on her hips, and thrust up inside her, shouting her name…

She was his.

His.

No. He couldn't throw himself into this. He couldn't lose himself.

He couldn't.

He wouldn't deny them this. Wouldn't deny their desire for one another, but it would never be more than that.

It was a good thing.

Because he would never be a father like his own. A father who chose to hurt his son in service to power. A father who would choose wealth above all else, including the safety of his family.

It could never only be the two of them. It would always be the weight of her crown—a weight she had chosen. And the weight of his past.

No amount of desire could overcome it.

He had surrendered to her here. Solidified his own weakness.

He pushed her away from him, his blood raging. "This cannot happen."

"Andrei...we can't..."

There was something wild inside him, a need to push her away he couldn't articulate or fully understand. He wanted her gone, away from him. He didn't want her testing him, he didn't want to face his own weakness.

His own vulnerability.

"This is nothing but part of a plan for you," he growled, the lie on his tongue tasting like acid. "Carefully plotted to make your legacy, your life, look better. Get out."

She stumbled off the bed, naked, beautiful.

Wounded.

She was the promise of something he wanted. Something he'd always desperately wanted.

But it would never be his.

"We will marry tomorrow," he said, his grip on his control slipping. "And we will kiss at the altar. But I will not touch you again."

CHAPTER SIXTEEN

HER BROTHER TOOK her arm just outside the church. It was an echo of her aborted wedding two months ago, and it was painful now to think of how different things might have been if...

And Andrei had the power to destroy her. He always had.

He had nearly done it last night. Her attempt at finding a way to make things easier. To make them better.

Because you still haven't told him the truth.
You haven't told yourself the truth.

What she felt for him was so big that it had always felt like the right thing to run away from it. It had always felt safer and better to turn toward duty, rather than surrendering to what she felt for him.

And now it was too late. Because the fire between them had turned into something uncontrollable, unbearable, kerosene on a little match when she had decided to marry Lucian after being with him.

He had sacrificed everything for her. To be with her. He had given up on his duty. He had embraced the thing inside himself that scared him the most, and she hadn't. She hadn't offered him anything.

She had chosen duty over the desire that existed between them, but not because it wasn't strong for her, but because she was afraid of it.

Scared enough that the idea of marrying a man she didn't love, a man who was potentially cruel, a man who was potentially a murderer, seemed less frightening than submitting herself to a future loving Andrei. Needing Andrei.

Because when you needed people, they died.

And all that was left was their memory.

All that you could cling to was… Grief.

Unless you could make it a mission. She was so good at making a mission.

And so bad at living. At feeling. At being a whole person.

"What is it?"

"It's too painful. I can't bear it, Onyx. I can't bear how much I love him. I haven't been able to bear it or stand it or admit it since I was fifteen. If I were to lose him, I would lose everything. Love is terrible. I pretty much went to the ends of the earth to outrun it, and it came after me."

"Then why do you look so sad? If the two of you love each other…"

"Because we don't. Because it… I love him. I do. But I don't know how to reach him. I don't even know how to reach myself. It sounds so stupid, but I only know how to be a princess. In Romania, it was different. I was… Angry, and sometimes unstable. I was his friend. Then we decided that we would do this, for the good of our child. We are better when we're on a mission, don't you get it?"

"I don't. I've never been in love."

It spoke volumes about his marriage. He wasn't even trying to hide it. She wondered how things had been in the months since she and Andrei had left. The answer was likely, not good. Not good at all.

"Well, it's terrible. I… I hurt him. I think he did love me. I don't think he ever will again. Our relationship is now in name only."

"That is the most foolish thing I've ever heard," Onyx said. "And guaranteed to end in destruction."

"It won't. We're both very good at this."

"Let's not discuss the severe implosion the two of you had right before your wedding."

"I'm sorry. That's really what I'm trying to say. I'm sorry. I am going to marry him. Our child will be legitimate." Since she was making demands now, she would go ahead and make more. She still wanted to do something of importance for her country, and she would. "And I would like a job in your cabinet. I would like to take on foreign affairs. I know that I can negotiate different trade deals, different alliances. I'm good at that."

"You are. You know you could've always had this, if only you would've asked."

"But I was being the architect of my own impossible love story," she said. "I couldn't ask you for this, I couldn't take it, because then… I wouldn't have any excuses, and how can I keep myself safe?"

"And how will you do it now, sister? How? Because you will have everything you want, and still deny yourself? You will have the man of your dreams, be married to him, have a child with him, and deny yourself everything?"

"I'll have him. With me. That's not denying myself

everything. The worst thing is to miss somebody like you've lost a limb. At least to have him with me."

"Hear me when I tell you this. There are worse things than that. Having somebody with you and not being able to reach them, that is the loneliness that you are not prepared for."

It felt like such a deep, dark warning, and it left her feeling shaken.

"Well, it's something I'm going to have to get used to, I fear."

"You don't have to get used to it, Emerald. You can still turn back from this. I don't care if there are two thousand people out there and millions on a live stream. Nothing has ever mattered but your happiness."

It wasn't a shock to hear that from her brother. He had always behaved that way. It seemed like she was the only person who had a difficult time wanting to be happy. Because happiness on a grand scale felt so risky. It felt like something that could be taken away. Felt like something awful, painful and terrible.

"You can turn back."

She was in a terrible position now. Because the truth was, she could never fully be happy without Andrei. He was her person. In so many ways. But now that she was looking straight down the barrel of her own cowardice, she realized that there was one thing she hadn't offered him. Her heart.

She had offered her body, she had offered her hand in marriage, but she hadn't truly made herself vulnerable to him.

He had done it for her.

He had risked everything to take her from that wedding. He had shown his heart. Because he hadn't been claiming the baby. All of his anger and his rage after that had been because he had broken his own moral code, his own vows, for her.

Why would he say that he loved her after that?

He had been willing to break himself in half. And then, he hadn't been.

But if he understood that it came from a place of fear... Because her feelings were so strong, not because they weren't strong enough.

She gripped her bouquet of flowers tightly, and held on to her brother's arm.

"You love him."

"Yes."

"And you don't think he loves you."

"Not anymore. I feel like everything inside him retreated. And why wouldn't it? You don't know everything about him. His father was a horrible crime lord, and his whole life with him was difficult. It's made love such a complicated thing for him."

"Don't be too hard on yourself. I think he does love you. I also think you are right. And it's a difficult thing for him. I think that he hasn't given you the words either."

"He gave me the gesture."

"Trust me, the man is much more likely to jump off a cliff into the sea than admit his feelings. Don't let him off the hook that easily."

With that, the music changed, and it was their cue to go down the aisle. Andrei was there, standing, his dark eyes glistening with something she couldn't quite discern.

Emotion, maybe. If it were somebody else. But it was Andrei.

And so it was impossible to say.

Did he feel the same way about her?

Would she be able to get it back? If she risked everything. If she tore herself open and bared her heart to him.

She'd already tried. She tried to do it softly. With sweet sex, and he had pushed her away.

So she had to give him the words. She had to.

"And who gives this woman to this man?"

"I do not give her," Onyx said to the priest. "I stand with her, because she is my sister, and I love her. But the choice she makes today is hers. She does not belong to me, nor will she belong to her husband. Princess Emerald will always belong to herself. She stands alone. The most selfless. And I only hope that Andrei understands what he has in her."

Her brother's words were wholly unexpected. They shocked her and brought tears to her eyes.

"Onyx," she said, throwing her arms around his neck and giving him a kiss on the cheek.

She pulled away from him and looked at the front row, where her sister-in-law sat, looking at herself in her front-facing camera.

She wasn't even paying attention to the wedding. Or to the beautiful gesture that her husband had just made.

Circe did not see Onyx. Not for who he really was. Or in any way whatsoever.

She just wanted the crown.

She was a good queen, Emerald could grant her that. She was well loved by the people, and went out of her way to treat everyone with kindness. Except her husband.

But she couldn't fix Onyx's wedding. She also would never be able to forget what he'd said about isolation and loneliness in a marriage.

All she wanted was for her brother to have love.

Worry about yourself.

She found herself being captured by Andrei, his hands large and firm around hers as they stood there in front of the priests. Her whole body was on fire from his touch. Even just last night, he had her. And yet, it would never be enough. But the sex was only a physical expression of the emotion that was already there. It always had been.

Of their desire, of his anger and desperation, of her wordless need for reconciliation and his desperation to take that, even though in the end he had pushed her away.

She needed to add real words to it.

Somehow, she had to show him that they weren't destined to be broken. He was afraid, she thought, not of being his father. But being his mother. Lost in a toxic relationship with a person who didn't care as much as he did. And that was partly her own fault. Or maybe, they were both his mother in a strange way. And somebody had to make the first move.

She already had. It was true. But she would make the first move again and again for him.

Because it had always been him. From the beginning. It would only ever be him.

The words that they spoke in their vows were written by other people, hundreds of years ago, but she did her best to convey everything that they meant to her. To them. This was the one chance she had. This kiss.

He had promised her this kiss, and nothing more. So when it was time, she leaned in, and kissed him with everything she had.

She only hoped that he felt it.

What was he? What manner of man, and what father would he be? What manner of husband?

Toxicity? Was that his story. Or was he just resisting vulnerability.

The very idea of it made him choke. She was kissing him, and there was very little else that he wanted in all the world but for Emerald to kiss him. What insanity was he indulging? He had her. She was his wife, and he was holding her at arm's length.

She was right. She had been right all this time. He knew how to want, and he didn't know how to have. And whatever the host of excuses he gave for that, it all came down to fear.

Because love was confusing and terrifying. Because it was both good and bad. Because it hurt, as much as it had ever healed. Because loss was brutal, and when you lost an imperfect person that you loved, you spent all the years after contending with the messy pain of it all.

But he had her. He had her.

So there was nothing left to resist.

He put his hand on her face and he kissed her, poured everything he had into that kiss. Accepted everything she was giving him. It didn't matter what she said. It didn't matter if he loved her more. It didn't matter. Because what was martyrdom, sacrifice, any of it, if it wasn't met with declaration. If it wasn't met with absolute devotion.

His own had been contingent on her actions, and that was weak.

It was the act of a man desperately protecting himself. Maybe she would've chosen another man. Another fate. And so it was up to him to spend the rest of his life proving to her that this was the better path. That this was what they both wanted. He would not do that by shutting her out.

When they parted, she looked dazed, and he felt the same. Their perception was a study in endurance.

He didn't want to be there. He wanted to be alone with her. There were things that needed to be said. But first, he needed to show her that he'd been wrong. About their passion, about their desire. It was so strong that it had the power to encapsulate his rage, his betrayal, and in that moment it had been sharp. But it wasn't toxic. That need between them never could be.

Because he loved her. And if he had to spend the rest of his life working to make her love him in return, then he would.

He would lay it all at her feet.

And finally, when they were able to go back to their suite of rooms, he didn't wait for her to speak. He captured her face in his hands and he kissed her.

"Andrei," she whispered.

"Let me show you," he said.

He would worship her. Her body, her soul. Everything that she was.

He unzipped the back of her dress, and that beautiful creation fell free. He couldn't remember what that ruined wedding dress for her aborted wedding had looked like. Because she had been a bride for him today, and that was all that mattered. Lucian didn't matter. The only way that he mattered was that he had been the catalyst for the two of them finally giving in. For the two of them finally claiming what they actually wanted. For that, he almost had to give thanks for him. Almost.

He would not give the man that much credit.

Underneath the wedding dress was the most beautiful lingerie set he'd ever seen. White, pushing her glorious breasts up, revealing the shadow of her peach-colored nipples beneath. She had white stockings with garters on, and he could see the dusky patch of curls between her thighs, just barely covered by a web of lace.

She was worthy of praise.

She was worthy of everything.

He had thought that fixing his gaze upon a mission would keep his pride intact.

His pride could be damned.

It was nothing. It meant nothing.

"My princess," he said, kneeling before her, an expression of fealty, but so much more. He gripped her hips and pressed his face to that patch of curls between her legs, swept her underwear to the side and began to taste her, lick her. For she was as addictive as any sweet ever could be, and he would never get enough.

She gasped, gripping hold of the back of his head, using it to steady herself. He looked up and saw that her expression was filled with wonder, shock.

Was it love?

In the end, he would make her call out his name, and his alone.

Tonight that might have to be enough.

She came hard, her desire flooding his mouth, and

then he kissed his way up her thigh, her hip, her stomach, and kissed her, letting her taste herself on his lips.

When he pulled away, she looked nearly drunk on her own desire.

He knew what had to happen next.

He walked her across the room, brought her to the vanity and bent her over, a repetition of what had happened that night in Alabria.

That night when he had decided to embrace his selfishness.

Affront. That's what it had been. He had been undone by his love for her. Brought to the brink by it. And it was so much easier, so much more comfortable for him to say that he was like his father. Selfish through and through. Because admitting that he loved her, that unmanned him.

And so unmanned was what he would have to be. He wanted her to see this differently. He gripped her chin, forced her to look straight ahead. "Look at us," he said, his voice tender. He held her throat, softly, letting her feel the care. The strength restrained.

Her breathing was rapid, her pulse fluttering at the base of her throat. He curved his head around and pressed his mouth over it. Kissed her.

And then he unhooked her bra, let her breasts spill free, into his hands, pinched her nipples between his fingers before moving his hands down her hips and tugging her panties down as best he could around the garter belt.

He bent her over, his hand not forceful, but firm. He wanted her to feel the way that he cared about her. The way that he held her.

He wanted her to feel the shift, the promise.

"Look at us," he whispered.

He wrapped her hair around his hand and breathed in deeply, the scent of lilacs and summertime. Of Emerald.

He freed himself from his briefs, and pushed deep inside her. He held them both there, like that, an expression of awe and wonder on her face, one that was matched on his own. "I love you," he growled.

He thrust forward, claiming her, over and over again, driving them both to the brink. "I love you," he said.

"I love you."

He said it with each thrust. Like a prayer, like a promise. He said it from the very depths of himself. Because it was true, whether she ever said it to him or not. Because that was what it had always been. And yes, he had loved her with the promise of never having her in return, and there was something about that that had comforted him. Because he had been a boy, scared, of his own memories, of himself, but he wasn't afraid anymore. He had thought that this was being unmanned. That wasn't true.

His father was not a man. Because he had never truly been able to love those around him more than he loved his own pride, his own comfort, himself.

But Andrei loved her. More than anything.

He lost his control then, on a shout, pouring himself into her as she lost her own control, gripping the edge of the vanity, trembling and shaking.

"Andrei," she whispered, his name a sob, and when she looked back up at him in the mirror, their body still joined, there were tears on her face.

He withdrew from her, turning her to face him and cupping her. "Did I hurt you?"

"No. You love me?"

"Yes. I love you. And I am sorry that I didn't tell you before. I was afraid. I was afraid of what it meant to be in love with you alone."

"You're not," she said. "I promise you that you're not. I love you. I… I was going to tell you this tonight. I wanted us to have a wedding night too. I swear it. I was going to keep giving myself to you, throwing myself at you until you believed it. But I knew that I needed to give you the words. The reason that I went ahead with the wedding to Lucian was because I was scared. Not of what he would do, but of my feelings for you. What I accused you of, that was me. I was so comfortable pining for you." She swallowed hard. "I told my brother that the reason I couldn't be with you because you weren't royal. He reminded me that he never would've cared. I knew that." She choked on a sob. "I knew that. It was never why. It was always because I feared that if I had you, I would love you in such a way that I would lose myself, and Andrei, I struggle… Even with the memory of my mother."

She buried her face in his neck, crying in earnest now, and he simply held her. "The reason that it has to be a mission is because if it's not, then she's just someone that I miss. And I miss her so much. Every day. I remember when she died, and she'd been gone a week, that it was the longest I'd ever been away from her. And every day… It's the longest I've ever been away from her. And time just keeps going on, but the pain doesn't go away. So it's better to turn it into action. And then there was you." She looked up at him. "I loved you from the first moment I saw you. And it was a relief, because

I knew that I couldn't marry someone who wasn't a king or prince. Don't you see, it protected me from everything. Making my mother's memory a crusade. It kept me from grieving her, and it kept me from being hurt by you. But what I didn't anticipate was that our feelings were just too strong for that. It broke down my walls. It broke down all of my defenses."

"Emerald," he whispered. "My princess. You broke down all of mine. I have never wanted anyone else. Not really. I've never loved another. And you are right. There was something deeply comforting in that. But I think we know how to love each other. We have worked together, helped each other. We have passion. We have friendship. Over every stage in our relationship, we have found these things, and now all that is left for us is to put them together. As husband and wife. As parents. Lovers. Friends."

"Yes," she whispered.

Here they were, newly married, half naked, and filled with love for one another. "I can't wait to tell Onyx."

He laughed. "Maybe he will be my friend again."

"He better be. You are, after all, going to be the father of his very first niece or nephew. And you are his brother-in-law now."

"And we are family," he whispered.

"Yes. Forever."

EPILOGUE

When Honora Rose was born, named for her two grandmothers that she would never know, no one was happier than her mother and father.

Though her uncle was close behind them.

Onyx held his precious niece, and smiled up at Emerald. "Thank God she favors you. If she had looked like Andrei…"

"A pity," Andrei said. "That she is so brilliantly ginger like her mother, only because that is part of how I convinced Lucian to extricate himself from the situation."

Onyx laughed. It was all funny now.

His relationship with Andrei had repaired itself fairly quickly after the wedding. He had seen how happy Andrei and Emerald were together, and he couldn't stay angry.

The issue really had always been the violation of his trust, but once he realized how wrecked Andrei and Emerald had been over the whole thing, how much they had hurt each other in the process, he hadn't felt like he had the right to stay angry.

"You are ready to be a father," Emerald said.

"Yes," Onyx agreed. "It is time for me to have an heir. I… Circe and I have been discussing it. I… It's time."

She felt bad, but the idea of her brother being even more tied to his wife than he already was made her feel sick for him. That was silly, she supposed. They were married.

But he wasn't happy.

She could only hope that the addition of a child to her brother's marriage would do something to break the wall of ice between the spouses. But she had her doubts.

Then again, she and Andrei had found their way to each other. After everything.

After Onyx left their quarters, it was time for Honora to have her nap, and Emerald lay down in the bed holding the baby, with Andrei beside her. This was what she had always imagined was impossible. This happiness. The simple joy.

This was what Emerald, the woman, not the princess, not the symbol, had always wanted. This sweet, simple happiness with the man she loved.

She smiled.

"What?"

"Oh, I was just thinking. Love is so simple. When you can heal from all the things that kept you captive all your life."

Andrei laughed. "Yes. Such a simple thing. And a miracle."

He leaned in and kissed her, and she had never been so grateful. For everything. Even the pain. Because it had brought them here.

And there was nowhere else she would rather be.

* * * * *

If you just couldn't get enough of
Princess, Pregnant, Prisoner,
then be sure to check out King's Captive Bride,
the next installment in the
Young, Hot and Royal trilogy by Millie Adams!

And why not explore these other stories
by Millie Adams?

His Highness's Diamond Decree
After-Hours Heir
Dragos's Broken Vows
Promoted to Boss's Wife
Heir of Scandal

Available now!

HIS FORCED SICILIAN BRIDE

JACKIE ASHENDEN

MILLS & BOON

To my Oregon family
(and that little trailer in particular).
Love you guys. <3

CHAPTER ONE

Caterina

I CLUTCH MY bouquet of calla lilies in sweaty hands, my stomach in knots. I'm in full bridal meringue, standing before the altar in a flouncy strapless gown of white silk, with a long gauzy veil held in place by a jewelled diadem. My father was grudging, saying at least I look the part, not that I care what he thinks.

Myself, I hate it. I hate all of it. I've never been the good, quiet Salvatore princess he wanted me to be. I'm too argumentative, too hot-tempered, too impulsive, and I hate being told what to do, all of which are terrible flaws in a daughter, according to my father.

But today is my wedding day and I have a part to play, no matter how much I hate it. As my father has impressed on me many times, I have to make up for the deaths of my mother and brother somehow, and all of this is for the good of the family.

The Roman cathedral where the marriage is taking place is full of people. My own family, the Salvatores, but also the families of our allies and naturally the family of my groom, Carlo Bianchi.

Our union was arranged years ago, by my father and

Carlo's, while I was still under-age, and for the longest time I forgot I was Dad's most valuable pawn in his games of power. I was too busy completing my history degree via an online university and thinking about getting a job.

But naturally my father had other ideas. It was time I was married, he told me. Our hated enemy, the Wolf of Sicily, aka Vincenzo Argenti, head of the Argenti family, was growing ever more powerful and if we wanted to survive we had to ally with as many other families as we could. Marriage being the best way to do that.

I've got nothing against my groom, Carlo, but I barely know him and I suspect he feels the same about me. We both have no choice, though. In our families, in the *cosa nostra*, duty comes first and refusal is not an option. This is the way it's always been and my personal feelings about it matter not at all.

Behind me, in the pews, I hear people shuffle and whisper then quieten. My stomach tightens as the priest looks at me. He can probably see how white I am behind my veil, but there's nothing he can do for me. There's nothing anyone can do for me. My family, the Salvatores, were powerful once, but years ago, when I was a child, my mother and older brother were killed in an Argenti hit that left my father badly injured. It was a blow against our family that we've been trying to recover from ever since, and consequently that meant finding allies however and wherever we could. Being seen to be weak is not something we can afford, not if we want to survive.

I did try to get out of the marriage. In fact, I've spent the last month arguing with Dad about the necessity of it, but he insisted. The old ways of bonding allies, by blood, were the strongest and I would do this for the family whether I liked it or not. Dad's not big on choices.

Going against the head of the family isn't done, especially if you're a woman and the only child left. And most especially when your father has impressed upon you that if you don't do this, the deaths of your mother and brother would have been for nothing.

The priest intones the beginning of the ceremony and I feel the combined attention of thousands of eyes on me. A family wedding is always a big deal.

Carlo shifts on his feet—he's as excited as I am about this marriage, which is not at all—but he, at least, is present in the moment. I, on the other hand, am mourning the ending of my freedom, since once I'm his wife, I'll be his property. I'll be denied a career. My only value is my name and the protection it brings the Bianchis. Oh yes, I'll also be an acceptable vessel for children, because how else to breed the next generation of family soldiers?

This was never the life I wanted—I wanted to study more, and maybe teach or get a job in a museum—but it's the life I was born into and I have no choice. The silver lining is that at least as Carlo's wife I'll be out of my father's house in Rome, where I'm guarded and protected like a princess out of a fairy tale. Being the sole remaining child of a family is dangerous, since my destruction would also ensure the destruction of the Salvatore family.

Another reason I can't refuse my duty. I can't be responsible for the death of the Salvatores, that's a burden too heavy to bear, especially when I'm already carrying the deaths of my mother and brother. All I can do is marry Carlo and hope against hope that he'll allow me some semblance of freedom, at least as much freedom as the wife of one of the *cosa nostra* families can have. Ha.

I stare down at my feet in my white wedding slippers, trying to calm the frantic beat of my heart. It'll be okay, I tell myself. Being married to Carlo won't be so bad. It'll make my father happy, ensure our family's survival, and if I'm lucky, I'll be able to build some kind of life for myself that isn't just shopping and lunching, minding children and drinking cocktails with the other wives. I mean, really, it could be worse.

Except no matter how many times I tell myself that, I know it won't be okay, and the dread sits heavy and cold in my gut. Shopping and drinking cocktails is all very well, but the risk of death is ever-present. You'll always be a target and so will your children, and that's not the kind of life I want for either myself or any kids I have. To be always looking over your shoulder in case of car bombs or ambushes, or any one of the thousands of ways you can die.

I'm in the middle of these depressing thoughts and spiralling, when I hear more shuffling and whispering behind me. The priest is still speaking but gradually he slows down and stops, a frown appearing on his face.

I glance at Carlo, who is also looking over his shoulder and frowning, so I do too, turning to see what or who is creating all the fuss. And just as I do, the big double doors of the cathedral burst open and suddenly the entire nave is full of men carrying guns.

Chaos erupts. There are screams and shouts, people leaping up from the pews and calling for bodyguards, weapons being drawn, but a man is striding down the aisle. He's dressed in black, moving with a panther's grace, an apex predator in a room full of prey.

Everything about him is dark, including the wave of violent energy that seems to emanate from him. He's very tall, with black hair and sharp, sculpted features. Ink-black brows. A hard jaw. And eyes that burn like molten silver.

Those eyes are looking nowhere except straight at me.

I freeze, rooted to the spot as a wave of pure fear washes through me.

I know him. Everyone in the entire room knows him. It's the Sicilian Wolf himself, Vincenzo Argenti, and he's been slowly but surely amassing power and collecting allies for years. I've overheard Dad say that the Wolf wants all the families under his thumb and he'll stop at nothing to do that, though no one knows the truth for sure.

What is true that is that anyone who resists him ends up dead.

He's also the man who murdered my mother, Claudia, and my brother, Alessio.

'Nobody move,' the Sicilian Wolf says to the cathedral at large, his dark, deep voice echoing in the vaulted space. 'No one wants a bloodbath in a church. Though I assure you, if anyone lifts so much as a finger, I will not hesitate to start one.'

His men are everywhere, standing sentinel around the walls, semi-automatics pointed at the gathered wedding guests. I have no idea how they managed to get past the heavy security my father personally oversaw, but they have. Then again, I've heard all the stories about Vincenzo Argenti, how he can walk through walls and turn invisible at will, so who knows? Perhaps he and his men did exactly that.

A deafening silence has fallen as he strolls calmly towards me, ignoring Carlo, the priest and the rest of the gathered guests as if they don't exist.

'Caterina Salvatore,' he drawls, my name rolling off his tongue like fine wine. There's a rough timbre to his voice and a chill that ices my blood. 'A pretty name. But I think Caterina Argenti is even prettier.'

Caterina Argenti? What is he even talking about?

My thoughts reel about drunkenly then reality slowly adjusts itself. Vincenzo Argenti, the demon in the dark from the night Mama and Alessio died, is here, at my wedding. I remember him. He was with all the men with guns who came into our house, and he shoved me into a closet and locked the door. Then I heard the gunshots outside that killed my family. I was five.

To this day I don't know why he didn't kill me along with Mama and Alessio, but I was shut in that closet for a long time until someone found me. For years afterwards, I used to have nightmares about that closet, about him, and now he's here, holding up my wedding at gunpoint. Is he back to finish the job? To wipe out the Salvatores once and for all? Gun me down in front of the altar and then kill all the guests too?

Beside me Carlos makes a soft sound, then backs away rapidly. The priest begins to say something, but the Wolf lifts one long-fingered, commanding hand and the priest decides not to say something after all.

My bouquet of calla lilies falls out of my nerveless fingers and onto the stone floor, scattering petals everywhere.

The Wolf doesn't hesitate, walking straight up to me. Then he extends a hand. 'Shall we?' His silver eyes glitter and even the dusting of white at his temples doesn't detract from the impact of his physical presence. He's more frightening than anyone I have ever met, and I want to close my eyes, shut him out of my field of vision, pretend he's not there.

But he is there. He most definitely is.

'To be clear,' he goes on, steel in the words. 'That was not a request. That was an order.'

I'm too shocked to move, but this is happening, and slowly it penetrates what exactly 'this' is. His men are merely standing guard, not firing into the crowd, and he himself looks to be unarmed. He's certainly not pointing a weapon in my direction. Which means…

It's not a hit. It's a kidnapping. And he's kidnapping me.

When I don't move immediately, he makes a gesture and abruptly two gunmen appear beside me as Carlo and the priest back frantically away. My father is on his feet and so are his allies and they're all beginning to shout.

'Silence!' the Wolf thunders and a deathly quiet falls in the cathedral. He's still looking directly at me.

And deep down inside me, a small flicker of anger ignites.

I already didn't want to be here, and now the man of my nightmares is standing right there, making this terrible day even more terrible, and ordering me to do his bidding at gunpoint.

I've been ordered around by men my entire life and right now, right here, is the last straw. I'm tired of it. I'm tired of being my father's pawn in his relentless quest for allies. I'm tired of having my duty explained to me every goddamn day. I'm tired of having the deaths of Mama and Alessio flung in my face and used to manipulate me.

Tired of never having choices of my own.

So I don't move, merely lifting my chin instead, because at this point, I have nothing left to lose. 'So you're kidnapping me? Is that it?'

'You catch on quick.'

'Well,' I say, scraping together the dregs of my courage and lifting my chin even higher. 'Respectfully, I decline.'

His eyes glitter, and one side of his cruel mouth curves. 'Respectfully or otherwise, your consent is not required.' He lifts his hand again and the man beside me shoulders his gun, puts his hands on my waist.

I tense, cold with fear but unwilling to let the Wolf see that. 'I see,' I say, forcing as much disdain as I can into my voice. 'Not strong enough to lift me yourself? Or are you not man enough? Which is it?' Either way, I'm going to be some man's property, so I might as well make it as hard for this particular man as possible.

Vincenzo Argenti's smile doesn't waver, but something leaps in his sharp silver eyes and it looks like amusement. 'Interesting,' he murmurs. 'Well, I've never been one to resist a challenge.'

Then before I can move, he motions his soldier aside, puts his own hands on my waist, before hauling me up and over his shoulder. Then he turns around and stalks out of the church, with me screaming obscenities in his ear.

CHAPTER TWO

Vincenzo

SHE'S A FIRECRACKER, I'll give her that, squirming and wriggling about on my shoulder while she screams in my ear. I have to tighten my grip on her to stop her from falling, which would very much ruin the performance I've just given back there in the cathedral.

Kidnapping isn't normally something I take a personal hand in—I leave that to my men—but this one was a special case and it required my presence.

I timed it perfectly, even if I do say so myself. I entered just as the ceremony was starting and everyone's attention was on the bride and groom. With the crowd distracted and the Salvatores' security poor, it was comparatively easy to get into the cathedral, though I have to admit that I didn't intend to put hands on Caterina Salvatore myself.

She stood at the altar, very tall and straight in a strapless, ivory silk gown that billowed around her like a cloud. Her long black hair had been piled on top her head in complicated curls, with a jewelled tiara crowning her, green eyes glinting at me from behind the silk of her veil.

The little girl I remembered from all those years ago was now a woman, and one who held herself like an empress.

I was expecting her to scream or at least to cower as I strode down the aisle towards her, yet she did neither. She was, in fact, furious, which I hadn't anticipated, since her wedding was one of necessity, or so my intel had informed me. Yet there was no denying the glitter of rage in her eyes, which made me wonder if she actually had feelings for the Bianchi boy.

Not that it matters. I would have taken her even if she was madly in love with him.

Still, it's interesting that he was the one cowering before me in fear, not her. No, she basically flung my lack of manhood in my face, and while I'm very much secure in that manhood, the one thing I can't resist is a challenge from a pretty woman. It added to the theatre of the moment, so I wasn't averse to flinging her over my shoulder—except I'm regretting that now as she screams curses in my ear. Clearly she didn't expect me to take her up on that challenge.

I stride down the steps to the waiting car, deafened by her continued shouting. She's certainly not the good, quiet Salvatore princess I was led to expect by my sources, nor does she bear much of a resemblance to the terrified little girl I shoved in a closet all those years ago. No, she's more a wildcat not wanting to be caught, which is unfortunate since I've now caught her.

By the end of the day, she'll be my wife and then I'll have the perfect hostage to the Salvatores' good behaviour and that of their allies.

After my mother, Elena, died in a car bomb set by

Salvatore soldiers, my father, Stefano, wanted the entire Salvatore family dead in revenge. But he failed. Now he's gone and I'm head of the family, my goal is to get rid of them in a different way. By marrying their last heir and making her an Argenti.

The Salvatores and their friends are the last holdouts, the last few families I have yet to bring under my control, and once Caterina is wearing my ring, they'll at last be brought to heel, making the Argenti clan the most powerful of the *cosa nostra* families in Sicily and Italy, if not all of Europe.

I have a reason for that, naturally enough, and it's not just about power. It's about the stain on the Argenti family honour, the stain put there by my father and his brutal killings of innocents. A stain I partially erased when I took him down myself, but there's more still to do. It's not enough that he's dead. I have to change things completely, end the violence. Unite the families, stop the feuding and the vendettas, stop the killings of family by family, and to do that I need them brought under my rule.

Whether they want to be there or not.

I'm tired of the constant march of death and violence, and I will not have it, even if I have to perpetuate a little death and violence myself. The end will ultimately justify the means.

Though, ironically, it was the death of my mother and the Salvatores themselves that began this crusade of mine.

I was my father's good little soldier back then, and when he ordered me to take some men and hit the Salvatore family, avenge my mother's death and the stain on our family's honour, I obeyed without question.

She'd once been bright and beautiful, a loving mother to me, but over the years, marriage to my father drained the life out of her, turned her into a husk of the woman she'd once been. A woman who preferred lying in a darkened bedroom with her pills to being with me. Even so, her death was a shock and I was desperate to make someone suffer for her loss.

Yet once I got to the Salvatores' villa, everything changed.

Giovanni Salvatore must have had a warning that we were coming, because he was in the middle of escaping when we arrived. I got a shot at him, but it wasn't a kill shot, and he unfortunately got away. Some of my men went after him, while I took the rest into the villa to get rid of any remaining Salvatores.

The men took the downstairs, while I went upstairs, and that's when I found her. A little girl of no more than five. The Salvatore daughter, Caterina.

I was young, only twenty, yet already battle-hardened. Already wrought into the hard-line successor my father wanted and needed me to be, and I didn't expect this to be a hard task—I'd killed men before, after all.

But this wasn't a man, this was a child, and a child, it turned out, was different. She'd had a doll in her hand and the biggest green eyes I'd ever seen, her long black hair in braids. And she was terrified of me. Up until that point in my life, my father had taught me to have no morals and no boundaries except obedience to his will. Yet looking into the little girl's terrified eyes, I found I did, in fact, have morals and boundaries.

I could not kill a child. She was blameless, an innocent, and while my mother had been innocent and blameless, too, killing this girl wasn't going to bring her back. Even at twenty I didn't have much of a soul left, not after my father took over my upbringing. Still, I had enough of one to understand that if I killed this girl, there would be no going back, not for me. I would become my father entirely. It was in that moment I knew that I didn't want to be. I didn't *ever* want to be a man who put his own revenge above a child's life.

So I shoved her into a closet, ordered her not to make a sound, then I locked the door.

I went back downstairs, fully intending to stop the killing of Claudia and her son Alessio, my father be damned, but by the time I got down there, the rest of my men had already carried out my father's plan. Both were dead.

Stefano punished me for my 'failure' and I still bear the scars, but even so, it was then that I'd decided. Those scars would serve as my vow to end the killing of innocents. End the violence of family against family.

Caterina Salvatore was the catalyst for that vow, and it's fate that delivers her into my hands now. She's the last piece I need to bring the families into line and once that is done the jigsaw will finally be complete. The families united under one law: mine.

Satisfaction settles in me, the way it always does when a plan goes completely to my design, though it would have been more ideal had she not been screeching in my ear like a banshee. To make matters even more uncomfortable, I can feel the softness and heat of her body draped over my shoulder, the warm scent of jasmine releasing as she struggles.

I've always liked the smell of flowers, yet it's disturbing how much I like hers, mixed as it is with a musky, feminine note uniquely her own. I almost regret making her my wife in name only, but it's merely a passing thought and not enough to change my mind. I have no patience for seduction these days, let alone seducing a woman I once rescued as a child and who sees me as the enemy. It's not as if I don't have many lovers anyway.

She lands yet another fist on my back as I approach the car, striking me as if she has no conception of who I am and what happened to the last person who laid a hand on me in anger. What she should be is grateful that I decided on marriage as the way to bring the Salvatores and their allies to me, instead of gunning everyone in that cathedral down. That's what my father would have done. My *consiglieri* was doubtful of the plan, since leaving anyone alive is not without its risks, but I wanted to do it without bloodshed.

Dio, I'm in danger of fucking growing a halo.

My driver has the door open for me and as I'm stuffing the wildcat inside, she manages to land a glancing blow to my temple with one flailing hand. My driver goes for his gun, but I shake my head and wave him away. She's no threat to me, lucky blow or otherwise.

She inhales sharply as I shove her into the seat then jerk the seat belt across her, buckling her up even as she tenses, ready for another round. Safety first for my future wife.

'You were a lot less trouble when you were five, *gattina,*' I tell her.

'Bastard,' she spits as the car pulls away from the kerb, the rest of my men following in other cars behind us. 'I'm not a little cat. And you didn't need to throw me over your shoulder like a sack of bloody potatoes! I would have come quietly.'

'Would you?' I give my temple a theatrical rub. 'I've killed men for less than that blow you just gave me.'

She glances at my forehead then back at me, not an ounce of contrition in her emerald gaze. 'Kill me then. I should have hit you harder.'

'My,' I murmur, amused by her fire. 'So bloodthirsty.' And it's strangely refreshing. I can't remember the last time a woman was so furious with me, or at least not so openly. People tend to tread lightly whenever I'm around.

I sit back in my seat and take a moment to study her.

She's radiating anger, glowering at me like I'm not the most feared man in all of Europe, though I suspect that beneath that fury, she's afraid. But she's not giving in to it and that takes a certain amount of courage.

Interesting. It seems my bride-to-be is a little warrior, though she doesn't look like one, dressed as she is in a flamboyant white wedding gown and veil. Her tiara is slightly askew and some of her glossy black hair has come out of its pins, and her pale skin is flushed with temper.

The little girl I protected has blossomed into a very pretty woman, it seems. Not that I require her to be pretty or indeed anything other than being a Salvatore. Her name and her value as a hostage are the most important things.

'I could in fact kill you,' I say. 'Would you like that?'

'That's why you took me, isn't it?' Her pointed chin lifts, her expression half defiant, half imperious. 'So you could finish the job you started twenty years ago?'

So, the little *gattina* remembers me. I wasn't sure if she did.

'If I wanted to do that, you'd be dead already,' I observe. 'But you were right back there in the cathedral.'

Her long, thick black lashes flutter as she blinks rapidly. 'You kidnapping me, you mean? Oh…' Understanding dawns. 'I'm a hostage.'

I give her a slow smile, because I do like an intelligent woman. 'Excellent answer. Ten points to you.'

'My father will—'

'Your father,' I interrupt, 'is irrelevant, no matter what he will or won't do. I'm afraid, *gattina*, no one is going to save you this time.'

The delicate bow of her mouth, highlighted by some kind of shimmery pink lipstick, compresses into a line and fear flickers briefly in her eyes.

I expect her to cower in her seat, but she doesn't. Instead, she stares back at me, undaunted despite her fear. 'So? I'm going to be your prisoner?'

'No, *gattina*,' I correct her gently. 'You're going to be my wife.'

CHAPTER THREE

Caterina

THE AIR IN the car feels as if all the oxygen has been replaced by something else, something sparking and electric and tense. I'm already breathless from being thrown over this despicable man's shoulder and carried ignominiously from the cathedral—admittedly, I have only myself to blame for that—but what he's said just now has taken away what little breath I have left.

His wife? His *wife?*

He's leaning back in his seat as if he's at home, lounging in a favourite chair, one foot propped on the opposite knee, his large, long-fingered hands loose on his thighs. He's overwhelming close up, his kinetic, violent presence filling the car, while his intense silver gaze burns into me.

The man of my nightmares is right here and not only has he taken me hostage, now he's telling me he's going to make me his wife.

I almost can't take it in.

'It's a shock, I know,' he says, his voice deep and lazy, a thread of dark amusement winding through it. 'Luckily though, you're already dressed for the occasion.'

'I'm not marrying you,' I say, my temper running away with my tongue before I can stop myself. 'You can take your damn proposal and shove it up your arse.'

The smile that plays around his mouth makes it curve into something like a sneer, while his eyes glitter like diamonds, hard and sharp. 'Such language,' he murmurs, chiding. 'Also, you're incorrect. I did not propose. I merely told you what is going to happen irrespective of where you wish to shove it.'

His measured response is disconcerting. I'm expecting him to be angry, because every man in the families gets angry when a woman talks back. We're expected to be pretty and decorative, to have no opinions except about child-rearing, household management, cocktails and shopping. And we're definitely not allowed to swear. My father would have had fifty fits listening to me shout the moment Vincenzo Argenti flung me over his shoulder.

I really *wasn't* expecting him to do that, no matter how stoutly I dared him to, so I got the shock of my life when he picked me up as if I weighed nothing. Then shock was replaced by fury. The ignominy of being carried out of my own wedding like a naughty child was too much, and yes, I lost my temper. It's never too far from the surface, no matter how hard I try to push it down, and it overcame my fear, spilling out inside me like lava.

Not that hitting or shouting made any difference to the Wolf of Sicily.

His shoulder beneath my stomach felt like stone, his arm wrapped around my thighs an iron band. My fists on his strong back made no impact and I felt every bit of my powerlessness and fragility in that moment.

He could have done whatever he wanted with me and I wouldn't have been able to do a single thing to stop him. Now, he wants to marry me and I can't stop him from doing that either.

I can't stop him from doing anything at all.

His manner is lazy, but I don't make the mistake of thinking he's anything but lethal, no matter how casually he lounges in the seat next to me.

'I won't do it,' I say, even though it doesn't matter and it's going to happen whether I want it to or not. 'I won't say "I do".'

'Yes, you will.' His head tilts, the afternoon sun glossing his black hair. 'Because if you don't, your father won't live to see another sunrise.'

I go cold. My issues with my father are many and varied, but even so, I don't want him to die. And I certainly don't want his death on my conscience, not when the deaths of Mama and Alessio weigh so heavily on me already.

I wish I could tell myself that this man wouldn't kill my father, but he would. Of course he would. Without a second thought. There's no mercy in those silver eyes, no kindness. No gentleness. I'll never know why he spared me all those years ago, but I don't want to know. These are the eyes of the killer who pushed me into a closet and locked the door, before walking away to murder the rest of my family.

'You can't force someone into marriage,' I shoot back, purely for form's sake, since I'm pretty sure he could force anyone into anything.

'I won't be forcing you, *gattina*,' he says as if my objections are of no moment. 'You'll be choosing to marry me to help your father stay alive.'

I stare daggers at him.

He merely smiles that cruel smile again and adds, 'It's a matter of perspective, you see?'

'You're a bastard,' I repeat, pointlessly.

'You should vary your insults. You've already called me a bastard more than once. Try something new, hmm?'

'Son of a bitch,' I growl through gritted teeth.

He lifts one straight black brow. 'Better. Though not very imaginative. Then again, I don't suppose imagination is encouraged in the Salvatore family.'

Insulting him is futile. Why bother?

Good question. I want to keep arguing with him, which is stupid, because it's not going to get me anywhere. Besides, my anger is just a mask for the fear that lies cold and sharp in my stomach. That fear makes me feel like that helpless little girl again, shoved into the darkness with the door shut in her face. Not being able to get out no matter how hard she kicked at the door, then hearing the gunshots…

I've had claustrophobia ever since and it's sliding its icy fingers around my throat and squeezing tight even now. I fight it though, because I'm not going to have a panic attack in front of this man. Nor am I going to lose my temper again. I need to put on the imperfect mask I managed to develop after my mother and brother died, when I was forced into the part of being a good Salvatore daughter. Where I had to keep my temper locked down and my tongue under control, or else risk punishment from my father.

The Wolf frowns, his focus on me intensifying in a way that makes me even more breathless than I already am. 'You look like you're about to have a panic attack,' he observes almost clinically. 'I have some sedatives if you need to take one.'

My temper rises at his tone, but I have myself under better control now. 'No, thank you,' I say stiffly. 'I prefer to experience my nightmares fully conscious.'

Again, the corner of his mouth lifts and I get the impression that once again I've amused him somehow. 'Don't worry, *gattina*. All I need from you is your physical presence at the ceremony and your name on the marriage certificate. I will not be needing you in my bed.'

For a second I can't process what he's saying, and then abruptly, I do. Sex. He's talking about sex. As soon as the thought occurs to me, I become suddenly and intensely aware of him. Of his powerful, physical presence in the car. Of how near he is to me, one hard muscled thigh brushing the white silk of my wedding gown. Of the way he's looking at me, both lazy and intense at the same time, those sharp silver eyes cutting right through me.

I've been protected all my life, guarded and warded like Rapunzel in her tower. I went to a private girls' school, and when I went to university, it was online. I've never been alone with a man who wasn't either related to me, employed by my father, or been an ally of his. I've certainly never had a boyfriend.

That doesn't mean I don't know how sex works, though. I've seen things online and I know how to give myself pleasure. But I've never met a man I've been attracted to and this man, this nightmare of mine, sitting right next to me should be the last man on earth I'd ever feel the slightest pull of attraction towards.

But now he's mentioned his bed and me being in it, and now my brain is off and running, wondering what it would be like and I don't understand why I'm thinking about that. I don't understand why I'm blushing, either.

'Good,' I snap, pushing those thoughts away. 'Because even if you were the last man on earth I wouldn't sleep with you. I'd rather sleep with a goat.'

'Careful, *gattina*,' he says, amused again. 'I think you're in danger of liking me just a little.'

He's goading me and I know it. But I'm also aware that there's a piece of me, way down deep inside, that is almost…enjoying this. Because for a long time I've struggled with who my father wanted me to be and who I actually am. At first all I wanted was to be his good, obedient girl. I wanted him to notice me, be proud of me, be glad that I hadn't died along with Mama and Alessio.

But no matter how hard I tried to be good, he wasn't proud and he wasn't glad, and when he drank too much at night sometimes, he'd tell me that he wished I'd died instead of Alessio, because then he'd still have an heir.

It hurt. It hurt to know that nothing I did or would ever do, would be enough for him. And the worst part of all was the fact that he was my father and I still loved him.

But I don't love Vincenzo Argenti or care about his feelings, and so there's a bit of me that doesn't want to keep the mask on. A bit of me that wants to argue and shout, and unleash myself on him. Cut the man of my nightmares down to size, because he is, after all, just a man, even if he is the head of the most powerful clan in Europe.

'Oh sure,' I say, my tone dripping with sarcasm. 'Yes, of course I'm in danger of liking the man who killed my family.' I grit my teeth as I hold his gaze, grasping on to my rage for courage. It's a mistake to keep snapping at him, because who knows what he might do? Still, I can't be more afraid than I am already and he said he wouldn't kill me.

The Wolf's brows twitch. 'Your father isn't dead.'

'No, but my mother and brother are.' My fingers curl in the silk of my gown, holding on tight as if I'm trying to stop myself from falling from a great height. 'I heard the gunshots after you shut me in the closet. You shot them both—'

'I did not shoot them,' he interrupts with some patience. 'They were both dead by the time I got downstairs.'

I blink. My father always told me that Vincenzo Argenti gunned them down in cold blood, and I had no reason to disbelieve him. But now he is saying he *wasn't* the one who killed them? 'Why should I believe a single thing you say?' I demand.

'You shouldn't. I don't care whether you believe me or not, but the truth is that I didn't kill your mother and brother, though I was ordered to.' His lazy silver gaze becomes somehow even sharper. 'I was ordered to kill you too.'

A small, cold shock goes through me, though I'm not sure why. I know he was there to kill me. I saw his eyes as he burst into my bedroom while I was playing with my doll. They were like ice, cold and dead. Even at five I knew I was in terrible danger, and I didn't need to see the gun in his hand to know that. Except he didn't shoot me. He shoved me into a closet and locked the door instead.

I've never wanted to know why he saved me. I was happy making him the monster, because it was easier to blame him than blame myself. But now, I'm almost compelled to ask, 'Why didn't you?'

He doesn't answer immediately, his gaze roving over me as if committing me to memory. It makes me uncomfortable, makes me want to shift in my seat, makes my skin feel tight. Makes me want to open the door and leap out onto the traffic, which is a bit overdramatic, even for me.

Then he says, 'I suppose, since you're going to be my wife, you deserve some kind of explanation.'

I open my mouth to tell him that as the man who allegedly killed my family, I don't care what he thinks I deserve or otherwise, but he holds up a peremptory hand. And much to my irritation, I fall silent.

'My father wanted revenge for the death of my mother. We had word the bomb that killed her was set by a Salvatore, and so he ordered the deaths of your family, and I was to carry it out.' The words are cool and there's a slight impatience to them, as if he's annoyed at having to explain. 'I shot your father, but that didn't take, alas. He escaped, so I went upstairs to find the rest of your family, but I only found you in your little pink bedroom.' His gaze is a steady burn of silver. 'You were holding a doll in one hand and all I could see were your big green eyes staring up at me. You must understand, *gattina,* up until that point, I was my father's man through and through. I burned for the revenge he wanted me to take and I was determined to get justice for my mother. But I saw you and… Well, let's just say I discovered a line I didn't know I had.'

I remember that night distinctly and the sight of his cold, dead eyes. 'A…line?' I ask.

'Yes. I found I didn't want to kill a child in revenge for my mother's death.' He's sitting very still, eyeing me like a bird of prey sighting a mouse in the grass. 'So, I shut you in the closet and locked the door so my men wouldn't find you. Then I went downstairs to stop them from killing your mother and brother, only to find that they were already dead.'

CHAPTER FOUR

Vincenzo

THOSE GREEN EYES of hers are wide and I can see shock in them, which is interesting. I don't know why I'm explaining myself to her, but I thought that since she *is* going to be my wife, she should know that her mother and brother didn't die by my hand. Clearly, her father has been feeding her all kinds of bullshit about what happened that night, so I'm happy to give her the truth. It's tedious to explain oneself, yet there's an unexpected pleasure to be had in upending her expectations about me.

I prefer people to be afraid, it makes them much more biddable, and over the years I've accepted that I'll always be the villain of the piece. That's the role I took on when I decided on my crusade, because the people I'm dealing with only understand one thing: violence.

But now I'm discovering that there's satisfaction in seeing the shock in her eyes. Shock that I'm *not* the villain she was expecting, or rather, less of the villain than she was expecting—I'm certainly not ever going to be the hero.

'Don't tell me,' I say, since she says nothing. 'Your

father has been busy laying the deaths of your mother and brother at my feet for years.'

Her hands grip the white silk of her gown as if she wants to tear the fabric apart and for a second the image of me tearing apart the white silk myself to lay her bare flickers in front of my eyes. A kick of unexpected heat goes through me and I'm shifting in my seat before I can stop myself.

What the fuck? It's been years since I've experienced an unanticipated attraction, and I certainly don't want to experience one for Caterina Salvatore. She's pretty, yes, but she's too young and I'm a man of sophisticated appetites. I have lovers who satisfy me, who don't want more, so why I'm currently thinking about ripping her wedding gown off her, I have no idea.

Maybe I'll organise a wedding night after all, but with one of my current mistresses. Annika likes it rough and she's always ready for me.

'You were there, though,' Caterina says. Her voice has a trace of huskiness that I find more attractive than I care to admit. 'And you shot him.'

'I did,' I acknowledge. 'And I was. But the bullets that found your mother and brother did not come from my gun.'

'But…' She trails off, still staring at me.

I lift a brow. 'But what?'

'You just…didn't want to kill a child? That's the only reason you spared me?' She says this with some disbelief, and I don't blame her. Our world is a violent one, where innocents are hurt or killed all the time. Where fathers beat the shit out of their sons and mothers don't lift a finger to help. Having scruples is unusual.

'Yes,' I say dryly. 'Did you know that outside the families, that's actually considered a normal reaction?'

The flush in her cheeks deepens. Sparks of her ready temper glitter in her eyes. Clearly she didn't appreciate my sarcasm and she's still struggling with whether to believe me or not.

I don't care. Her belief or otherwise won't change what's going to happen.

She looks down at her hands for a moment, then abruptly back at me. 'Why do you need my family's good behaviour?'

'Finally,' I murmur. 'That should have been your first question.'

'Apologies. I was too busy screaming in terror when you carried me out of the cathedral to think about the right questions to ask.'

Oh, she's sharp, this one. I like it. I like it very much.

'You weren't screaming with terror, *gattina*.' I smile. 'You were screaming with rage.'

She scowls. 'Answer the damn question.'

No one speaks to me this way. My bodyguards would have a gun to her head if they were in the car with us right now and she should know that, having been brought up in the *cosa nostra*. I'm not offended, though. As I've already thought, she's no threat to me. Still, if she continues to push, she'll find I have a line and once she hits it, I'll push back. Hard.

'Ask me nicely,' I say lazily. 'And I might consider explaining myself.'

Her chin juts, gaze mutinous. 'Please.' She spits the word out like poison.

I'm entertained by her temper. 'Because I want them under my control, of course.'

'What for?'

'Demanding, *gattina*. You do realise that I am probably the most feared and powerful man in all the families, don't you?'

'I don't care what or who you are,' she snaps. 'I'm not asking for my freedom. All I'm asking for is a reason.'

Well, I certainly can't fault her courage. In fact, it makes me want to give her that reason and for free. Revealing one's plans, though, is a risk and one I never take if I can help it. Because once people discover what you're trying to do, they'll use that knowledge to stop you any way they can, and I know the families. Information is a precious commodity. If this one knows about my crusade, then she could pass that onto her father. Then again, as my wife she'll be under my complete control and I'm certainly not going to give her any opportunity to speak to her father or ever let her see him again. So, what could it hurt?

'The reason?' I echo. 'I'm bringing all the families under my control so the in-fighting and the feuds stop. So the killing of innocents stops.'

Her eyes widen. 'That's it? That's the reason?'

There's something about the way she says it that gets under my skin, as if she's shocked that I should want the violence to end. I understand why—my reputation isn't exactly snow-white—but she has no concept of what it is to be brought up as a family's heir. How, at twelve years old, my father forced me to attend the torture session of a suspected mole, and at fifteen, handed me a gun and made me shoot a family soldier who'd betrayed us. 'It's either you or him,' my father had said when I'd showed reluctance. 'And if you can't do it, I'll shoot you myself.'

'Yes,' I say, allowing a note of anger to show in my voice. 'Do you have a problem with that?'

She flushes and I find my gaze drawn to how the pink extends down her elegant throat and down below the neckline of her gown, where the fabric is pulled tight over a pair of small, high, beautifully shaped breasts.

'No,' she says quickly. 'No. I just...'

'Didn't expect the Sicilian Wolf to care about anyone's life?'

She looks away and once again I feel a wave of satisfaction that I've surprised her, which is puzzling.

Before I can interrogate the feeling though, my phone goes off and I answer it. There are a few logistical issues that need attention, so I spend the rest of the ride to my Roman villa, where the helipad is located, dealing with them.

Once we arrive at the villa, we go straight to the chopper and my wife-to-be says nothing as she is bundled into it. I have a few more business calls to make, so I spend the flight to Sicily making them and putting out the fires that my bride stealing has ignited. I order Elio, my *consiglieri*, to get Giovanni Salvatore's vow of loyalty to me by sundown in return for the life of his daughter, and then I double-check my security.

An hour or so later, we're coming down onto the rolling green lawn of the Argenti family villa. It's built on the clifftops overlooking the Aegean, with stone terraces descending amid cliffs and greenery, all the way down to the sea. A deep blue-green infinity pool reaches the edge of one terrace, shaded by olive trees and white outdoor umbrellas.

The villa itself is two storied and made of whitewashed stone, surrounded by lawns and beautifully manicured gardens. It was my mother's pride and joy, and so I employ a couple of expert gardeners to keep it looking as she would have wanted it.

Caterina stares out the window as we land, her expression guarded. She didn't say a word on the way over and I find myself wondering what she thinks of the villa, though why I care I have no idea. I love the place myself, but my little crusade doesn't leave me with as much time to spend here as I'd like.

The helicopter touches down, my various staff all lined up, waiting for me to disembark so we can get the ceremony started immediately. The Argenti family priest, Father Giuseppe, is also waiting.

I open the door, get out, then extend a hand to Caterina. She glances at it, and with that same mutinous expression I saw in the car back in Rome, she ignores it and slips from the helicopter without help.

Stubborn *gattina*.

Again, I'm amused, though I will be less so if she's going to be this stubborn during our marriage ceremony.

I stride over the grass to greet my staff and Father Giuseppe. Caterina follows me, looking around her warily.

'Come, *gattina*.' I indicate for her to stand beside me.

A ripple of shock crosses her face as she looks at me, then the priest, then back again. 'What?' Her voice has risen. 'You want to get married here? *Now?*'

'Of course. I kidnapped you already dressed for a reason.'

She's standing there as stiff as a post, her back rigid, yet there's something oddly commanding about her. Something proud. And a part of me, the darkness that lives inside me, the wolf, finds that impressive. That even though she's been kidnapped from her wedding by the man she thought killed her family, here she is, standing brave and strong rather than cowering in fear.

She will make an excellent Argenti wife.

The thought snakes through my head, despite having never given much thought as to what kind of wife I wanted. I knew I would marry one day, but I didn't want to do that until I'd consolidated my power base, and that has taken me longer than I thought it would.

So when I received intel that Caterina Salvatore would be marrying Carlo Bianchi in a bid to bolster Salvatore alliances, it was clear what I needed to do and quickly. Too quickly to think about what kind of wife she'd make for me.

But now I've been in her company a few hours, I'm coming round to the idea that yes, she *would* make an excellent Argenti wife. She certainly has the force of will to be one.

She will make an excellent mother, too.

Oh yes, she will indeed. She's fiery and brave, at least what little I've seen of her has been, and those are excellent qualities in a mother. My own, for example, was both before my father's treatment of her crushed the life out of her. He'd wanted another child, but after three miscarriages, he lost patience with her and abandoned her here at the estate.

I won't do that to Caterina, though. I'll need heirs— someone has to carry on my legacy after I'm gone—but if we can't conceive naturally there's always adoption. I'm not as wedded to blood ties as my father was.

'Your father's life depends on your cooperation,' I remind her gently. 'It won't take long, I promise.'

She glares at me then moves, coming to stand beside me, regal as a queen. She very determinedly does not look at me and as the priest begins the ceremony, I find myself staring at her profile, noting the soft curve of her cheek and the lush fullness of her mouth. Her silky black brows and the slight tilt of her nose.

Pretty *gattina*.

When the time comes for her to face me and say her vows, she does so even though her whole body radiates negation and reluctance and fury. Her green eyes burn with rage, and her voice is full of venom as she spits the vows at me. With her tiara askew and her hair half down, she should look ridiculous, yet she doesn't. She looks like a murderous goddess, and I'm confounded by my growing interest in her.

When I planned this, I didn't think of her as a person—or at least, if I did, it was the five-year-old girl I was thinking of, not the woman. But it's the woman I'm marrying now and she's forcibly bringing me face-to-face with the fact that she's not a puzzle piece or a pawn. First with the screaming, then with her flailing hands. Then her quick-fire sarcasm and obvious fury.

She's intriguing, nothing like the women I bed who tend to fawn on me, or the wives of my men and those in other families, who smile sweetly and make no fuss, embracing their roles as adjuncts to their husbands.

You didn't want that kind of wife anyway.

No, I didn't.

She puts out her hand for a ring to put on my finger, but I don't have one for myself. The only ring I wear is my father's heavy gold signet with the Argenti crest, so I take that off and put it in her hand.

It looks huge in her small palm and when she looks up at me, I can see her battle the overwhelming urge to fling the ring in my face. I dare her to silently, but she only sniffs and pushes the ring back onto my finger.

Then it's my turn with the vows, and as I repeat the words, I can't help but reach out and adjust the tiara on her head, before pushing a strand of silky black hair back behind her ear. Her eyes widen as my fingertip brushes the tip of her ear, and she goes very still, electricity sparking between us at my touch.

The surprise of it jolts me, because while I enjoyed her scent and found her interesting, I hadn't planned on seducing a very clearly unwilling woman. But…perhaps she's not so unwilling after all?

Her lashes lower, hiding her gaze, yet it's too late. We were both caught off-guard by that spark of chemistry, and now we both know it's there. Or rather, *I* know it's there.

I was expecting to have an on-paper wife, while still seeing my usual lovers, but perhaps it's worth revising that decision. What would all that fire and fury look like turned into passion? Would she be as fierce in bed as she is out of it?

Something inside me shifts, a thread of desire winding tight, but it's not the time, so I push it aside, taking the ring out of my trouser pocket instead. Then I take her hand and slide it onto her finger as I repeat the vows. It's a simple band of white gold I bought on the way to the cathedral, but a stray thought tells me I should have had emeralds inlaid on it somewhere, to match her eyes.

Ridiculous. I buy jewels to match the eyes of my mistresses, not my wife.

'You may kiss the bride,' the priest says.

Caterina lifts her lashes and looks up at me, her green gaze silently challenging me the way I challenged her to throw my ring at my head.

I dare you to kiss me, she's saying, and not because she doesn't want it, she does. I can see it in her eyes, the curiosity and the heat. She wants to know if that spark between us was real or if she was imagining it, and I'm tempted to show her exactly how real it was.

But she's expecting me to do that, so instead I reach out to cup her face between my palms. Then I bend my head, kiss her chastely on the forehead, before turning and striding into the house.

CHAPTER FIVE

Caterina

I STARE AT the Wolf's back as he disappears into the villa, my heart racing, and I don't know whether to be furious that he kissed me on the forehead like a child, or relieved.

No, I know. I'm relieved. I'm definitely very relieved. Because that would be my first kiss and there's no way I want that kiss to be from him. Ugh, the very thought of it…

You couldn't breathe at the very thought of it.

I ignore the voice in my head, because it's not true, absolutely not. Yet, I can't deny that when he lifted his long-fingered hands to adjust my tiara, and the tip of his finger brushed my ear as he pushed a lock of hair behind it, a bolt of electricity went through me. Part of me wanted to believe it was only static, but the rest of me knows that's not what it was. I saw the way his eyes flared. He felt that electricity, too.

And yes, as much as I don't want to admit it, when he cupped my face between his warm palms and I thought he was going to kiss me, I felt as if I might faint. All I could see was his silver gaze and the heat burning in the depths, and something hot in me stirring and waking up, wanting to play…

But I can't think about that. I don't want to. He's the enemy and the ring on my finger feels heavy, and I still can't believe that I'm here, at the Argenti villa in Sicily, married to the Sicilian Wolf.

On the helicopter ride over here, I tried thinking through plans on how I could escape or maybe get the information he told me about his intentions to my father, but none of them seemed viable. I don't have anything with me, not even my phone, and now I'm here at the Argenti villa, my options for escape or at least getting word to Dad, have narrowed considerably.

The late afternoon sun is beating down and the emotional fallout from the last couple of hours is catching up with me. I feel lost, cut adrift, alone in a forest of enemies with no one to turn to and nowhere to go, and married to a complete stranger.

As I'm standing there wondering what the hell to do next, a woman comes over to me and takes my arm, murmuring that she is Maria, the housekeeper, and she will take me to my room. I let her lead me into the villa, all the energy I had to fight with now gone.

Though my temper rouses slightly on the brief tour of the villa, mainly because it's beautiful, and I don't want to it to be beautiful, with its whitewashed walls and stone floors. Lots of light streams through tall windows with deep sills, silken carpets creating splashes of colour and softness. The furniture is very old, of dark wood, which contrasts with some of the abstract art on the walls.

Maria takes me upstairs and shows me into a beautiful room that faces the sea. The ivory linen curtains are pulled back from the windows while beneath them sits a squashy couch upholstered in faded pink velvet.

Against the opposite wall is a huge four-poster bed hung with white gauze, an antique dresser standing nearby. Bright cushions that carry the same pink as the couch are scattered on the seats and on the bed. Another silk carpet covers the stone floor, the same faded pink in amongst subtle hues of dusty blue and purple.

Maria gestures to the door on the other side of the room, which apparently leads to the en suite bathroom, and then at the sliding mirrored doors that hide a closet. The master has bought me everything I might need, or so she says, and I'm very tempted to ask if that includes a private plane to take me far away from here, because that's what I need most of all. But I keep my mouth shut. There's no point being rude to Maria. None of this is her fault.

Once she leaves me alone, I tear off my tiara and veil, and fling them on the bed. Then I claw at the fastenings of my stupid wedding gown. It feels as if it's suffocating me and I can't get it off fast enough. Beneath it I'm wearing a white silk strapless bra and white silk knickers, all lacy and transparent, because I thought Carlo would like them. But they, too, seem ridiculous now, so I claw them off as well until I'm wearing nothing except Vincenzo Argenti's ring.

I want to pull that off too, and hurl it into the sea, but I have a feeling that he wouldn't care, which makes hurling it anywhere far less satisfying. In the end, I keep it on as I fling open the closet doors to see if he really did buy me everything I might need.

Looks like Maria wasn't wrong since it's full of newly bought clothes, all of them giving off major *cosa nostra* wife vibes. I ignore them and instead go to the dresser, pulling open all the drawers to see what else is in there. Sadly, at first glance, there are no practical underwear. It's all silk and lace, with tiny straps that look incredibly uncomfortable. I finally settle on a pair of purple silk knickers, with a sports bra I manage to unearth in the bottom drawer. There are also some loose black lounge pants in a soft, stretchy fabric that look comfy, so I put them on with an oversized sweatshirt in deep forest green.

They're familiar, these kinds of clothes. They're the opposite of dressed-up and put-together, which my father always wanted me to be since it showed me off as a trophy better, and once they're on, I feel less like a stolen bride, and more like myself.

On top of the dresser are pots and bottles of make-up, along with hairbrushes, eyelash curlers and all kinds of beauty products that I don't want or need. He's bought them for the wife he wants, not the woman I am, which is a familiar feeling, and so I ignore them all.

Instead, finding a black hair tie, I put my hair into a low ponytail so it's out of the way, then I go over to one of the French doors and open them so I can step out onto the terrace. The air is warm and scented with salt from the sea and rosemary from the pots that sit near the stone balustrade.

Below me I can see the green lawn roll to the edge of the cliffs and the deep blue of the Aegean beyond that. It's a beautiful view, but no amount of inhaling the scented air and gazing out at the ocean will change the fact that this villa is a prison, and I know it is because there are men in dark suits everywhere, patrolling the grounds. Argenti security no doubt.

The helicopter on the lawn takes off in a roar and a press of air, soaring up into the blue sky, and I wish I was on it. I wish I could fly away too, but I'm stuck down here, married to my family's hated enemy. Really, marrying Carlo would have been a walk in the park compared to this, because while we didn't know each other well, I didn't think he was all that bad. Certainly, I could have done worse.

You did do worse.

Anger wells up again at the thought, so I turn away from the beautiful view and the lie of freedom it represents, and go back into the bedroom. I try the bedroom door to see if it's locked, and I'm almost shocked to find that it isn't. I guess I shouldn't be surprised. It's not as if I can go anywhere given the level of security in the villa and grounds.

I open the door and step into the hallway outside. There's no one there, but a lovely stained glass window at one end casts colours on the stone floor.

Gathering my determination to at least check out the prison I find myself in, I spend time opening the doors on the top floor, finding more bedrooms, a couple of bathrooms and an elegant salon. Most of the bedrooms look as if they're not used frequently, which means they're probably for guests.

But there's one that *is* clearly in use, its door opposite mine in the hallway, and it's large, with another four-poster bed against one wall, an antique dresser against another. It's very plain, with no couch beneath the windows or silken carpet on the floor, but all the bottles on the dresser are arranged neatly, and everything is very tidy.

The room smells pleasantly of smoke and cedar, the scent sadly familiar. It smells of him, which means this must be *his* bedroom.

Vincenzo Argenti's bedroom.

I freeze in the doorway, listening for any noise, because I don't want to be found lurking creepily around. Yet I also don't want to leave. Maybe somewhere in here is a key or a phone or something I could use to get word to my father. Or maybe even to get out of the villa entirely.

Hearing nothing, I take a little breath and begin to explore.

On top of the dresser are various aftershave bottles, a hairbrush and comb, but nothing else. The drawers themselves reveal only clothes, and nothing much else of interest. After I've exhausted the dresser, I go over to the closet doors and slide them open, seeing only a line of perfectly tailored suits, all in various shades of grey, black and blue. Shirts, neatly pressed, hang next to them, all without exception either white or black.

Clearly, he doesn't like colour or mess, and it's very irritating that there isn't anything immediately obvious lying around that I can use to escape with.

Turning from the closet, I go over to one of the bedside tables. There's nothing on top of it, but when I pull open the drawer I find boxes of condoms and, lying next to them, a gun.

A rush of adrenaline hits me and I reach for it, sliding my fingers around the cold metal. I know how to use one—my father insisted I learn because even though it wasn't expected that a woman would have one, she should at least know how to defend herself. About the only thing he and I agreed on.

'Tsk, tsk, *gattina*,' a dark male voice says from the doorway. 'Don't you know it's rude to go snooping about in other people's bedrooms?'

CHAPTER SIX

Vincenzo

CATERINA IS STANDING next to my bed with a gun in her hand, and I can see immediately from the way she's holding it, with the safety off, that she knows how to use it. Good. A wife who can't defend herself is a sitting duck. What is less good is that the instant I spoke, she lifted her hand and now the muzzle of the gun is pointing directly at me.

I fold my arms and lean against the door-frame, unbothered. She's not going to shoot me, I'm sure of it. She has a fiery temper but I know a killer when I see one and a killer she is not.

No, she's your wife, remember?

Oh, I've not forgotten. I might have spent the last hour or so organising for Annika to attend me tonight, as well as fielding more calls from my head of security to keep me updated on the Salvatores' response, but I'm well aware that I now have a wife.

Giovanni Salvatore has not given any answer to my ultimatum yet, but considering his daughter's life will be forfeit, I'm sure he will. I didn't give him much time, but that was intentional. I don't want him to think, I only want him to act on his paternal instincts.

Naturally, I'm not going kill Caterina—murdering one's wife only hours after marrying her is generally frowned upon, even among the families, not to mention rendering my little crusade utterly pointless—but Salvatore doesn't know that. All he knows is that one of the *cosa nostra's* most powerful bosses has his daughter and will kill her if he doesn't pledge his allegiance to me.

'Put the gun down, *gattina*,' I say. 'You're not going to shoot me.'

Her chin lifts, the gun still resolutely pointed at me. 'You don't know that.'

'Sadly, I do. I'm a killer, but you are not.'

She's out of her wedding finery now, wearing some loose black trousers and a green sweatshirt. Her glossy black hair has been put into a ponytail, long tendrils like black smoke clustering around her ears.

In the loose, shapeless clothes, she looks small and fragile, yet also beautiful, which I find odd. There's no hint of her figure and yet the green of the sweatshirt enhances the colour of her eyes, and the neck is wide enough to have fallen off one shoulder, revealing the line of a black bra strap and some smooth light-olive skin beneath it.

'No, I'm not,' she agrees. 'But it's never too late to start being one, right?'

'You could pull that trigger, it's true,' I say. 'But you wouldn't live long enough to enjoy your widowhood, alas. My security is…how shall I put it? Enthusiastic.'

Her hand is shaking a little, the muzzle wobbling, but she doesn't lower the gun. 'So what then? I'm just your prisoner forever? Is that what you're going to do with me?'

'Correction. You're my wife forever.'

She snorts. 'Is there a difference?'

I decide to ignore this, since I've yet to make specific plans about what to do with her. 'What are you doing in here, *gattina*?' I ask instead.

'What does it look like?' she snaps. 'I'm trying to get away from you.'

'By exploring my bedroom?'

She flushes even as green sparks of anger glitter in her eyes. Interesting. Is she blushing because I said the words 'my bedroom'? How delightful, if so. It's been a while since I've encountered such innocence in a woman.

'I thought I might find something useful,' she says. 'And as it turns out, I did.'

The gun, supposedly, which won't help her, as I've already pointed out. Even if she manages to get a shot at me, she'll then have to contend with all the guards in the villa, and there are a lot of them.

'Well,' I say calmly, 'as refreshing as it is to be held at gunpoint by my own wife, you're going to have to let me go at some stage.' I pause and then decide to mention it, since she'll find out anyway. 'At least before Annika arrives.'

Her eyes narrow. 'Annika? Who is Annika?'

I shift against the door-frame, oddly discomforted, though why I'm not sure. Caterina and I are married, it's true, but those vows of fidelity we swore were only words with no meaning behind them. I don't love her and she doesn't love me, and I'm going to make sure it stays that way, since love is a cruelty I wouldn't wish on my worst enemy. At some stage, though, I might want to explore that moment of chemistry we had during our wedding ceremony, but not now.

I ignore my discomfort. 'She's my mistress,' I say bluntly. 'I'm expecting a wedding night, after all.'

'Mistress?' She says the word as if it's foreign to her and she's unsure of the pronunciation. 'What are you? Seventy? Who has mistresses these days?'

I can't help but smile at the disbelief in her voice. '*I* have mistresses. Don't you think the term is more romantic than, say, "lover"?'

'Romantic?' Again, she says it as if she's never heard the word before. 'Are you serious? You've just married me and you're already talking about lovers?'

I study her a moment, because the shock on her face looks genuine. How strange. Why should she care how many lovers I take? Shouldn't she be pleased that I'm not going to take advantage of her? That I'm seeking pleasure elsewhere?

'What does that matter?' I ask. 'I already told you I'm not expecting you in my bed. All I want from you is your name and your father's obedience.'

Expressions move over her face like clouds, moving so fast I can't read them all. 'So…what do you expect from me? I mean, are you going to get an annulment in six months or what?'

I haven't told her my plans. I'm waiting for her father's capitulation first, but it won't hurt to tell her now. Perhaps it will make her lower that fucking gun.

'I expect you to be my wife,' I say simply. 'As I said, it has to be you to ensure your father's obedience. But

I also need a wife to start a family with, building my dynasty, etc., etc.'

'That might be difficult if we're not sharing a bed.' She goes pink as she says this, which again, I find strangely delightful.

'I presume you've heard of the existence of fertility clinics?' I murmur, then add, unable to help myself, 'Or of course there is the old-fashioned way.'

Her cheeks flush an even deeper rose, but her mouth firms. 'No. My statement about the goat still stands.'

'Pity.' I sigh theatrically, enjoying myself more than I care to admit. 'I could wear a goat costume at a pinch.'

I'm hoping to get a smile out of her since she's managed to get so many out of me, but her mouth remains in a firm line. 'So, I'm what? Just a figurehead? What about me? What about what I want?'

Unfortunately, the answer is that I didn't care what she wanted. But again she's forcing me to contend with the fact that she's a person. It's inconvenient. I don't want her thoughts and feelings getting in the way of my crusade, because nothing can get in the way of my crusade.

I will stop the murders of blameless women and children, stop the inter-family killings. I will stop the men who think violence is the answer, men like my father, and I will not be turned from my path. I will not be stopped, not by anyone, and she needs to understand that.

'What about you?' I ask, allowing a chill to enter my voice. 'What you want doesn't concern me.'

Her gaze narrows even further, turning calculating, which is fascinating, though I'm not sure why. Perhaps it's because while I can read most of her emotions, I can't tell what she's actually thinking, and it's strange to realise that I want to know. 'So, if I wanted to take a lover myself you wouldn't care?' she asks, the gun still firmly pointed at me.

A sharp feeling knifes through me and it takes me a second to process what it is. Jealousy. But no, surely not? I'm territorial, it's true, but as long as she's discreet, what does it matter if she takes a lover? I don't care. My father was a jealous man, but I am not.

Yet a part of me, the wolf, cares and it's insisting that she's mine. It won't tolerate another male anywhere near her.

Her sharp green eyes glitter and I know she's spotted my hesitation, and before I can speak, she says, 'As per usual, a man is free to do whatever he wants, but not a woman.' The muzzle of the gun lowers slowly from my face, tracking a line right down to...*fuck*. 'How would you feel if I shot off your dick?' She's all determination now. 'Not so manly now, hmmm?'

The wolf in me growls in approval at her bravado, but the man is not amused. In fact, the man is now actively pissed off, because this ridiculous conversation has been going on much longer than he wanted, and he has things to do.

'You can have lovers,' I say impatiently, crushing my strange jealous feelings. 'You can have as many as you want, I don't give a fuck.'

'Yes, you do,' she disagrees. 'Don't deny it, I saw you hesitate.'

'Caterina,' I begin.

'I don't trust you,' she says, ignoring me. 'So, know

this. If you don't want me to have lovers, then you can't have any either.'

I give a short laugh and take a step into the room, my patience rapidly thinning. 'I'm not a monk, *gattina,* and I have no intention of living like one.'

She doesn't move, the gun still pointed in the direction of my fly. 'Well, you'll have to figure out how, won't you?'

My anger flares and holding her gaze with mine, I take another step. 'Are you sure that's a good idea?' I ask silkily. 'That would mean living under the same roof as a very hungry wolf. Who sees you as prey.'

Her eyes widen as she understands my meaning. The colour of them is truly astonishing, green as grass and with gold glittering in the heart of them.

I take another step, halfway to her by now, and she doesn't seem to realise that I'm stalking her. Coming slowly closer to grab the gun from her hand. At least, that was my plan, but now I'm fascinated by the colour of her eyes. So green, they can't be real. Pretty, pretty eyes.

The gun shakes slightly, but she doesn't look away. Her pupils are dilating and now I can see the pulse at the base of her throat, just above the neckline of her sweatshirt. It's racing. Is it with fear? Or something else?

She swallows. 'Y-you said you didn't want me in your bed.'

'Perhaps I do.' I take another step. 'In the absence of anyone else, I could be persuaded.'

'Stop,' she says, her voice husky.

But I don't stop, because I'm already there, reaching out to take the gun from her shaking hands as she stares up at me, eyes wide, pupils fully darkened with something that definitely isn't fear.

Except she doesn't let go of the gun. Despite those wide eyes, nothing is going to deter her. 'Cancel your mistress,' she says. 'Do it.'

I could pull the gun from her hands, it wouldn't be difficult. But the safety is off and I'm not fully convinced she wouldn't actually shoot me by accident, so I don't take it. Instead I ask, 'Why?' And it's a genuine question, because I don't understand why this particular thing is important to her.

'You married me,' she says. 'You didn't have to, but you did, so you have to bear the consequences. And those are that you respect me enough not to screw another woman on our wedding night.'

CHAPTER SEVEN

Caterina

HE'S HOLDING ONTO the gun with strong fingers and surely he must know he could pull it out of my grip at any time and with ease. But he's not.

He's a terrifying figure standing so close, towering over me in a way that most men don't since I'm tall for a woman. But it's not just his height, it's the width of his powerful shoulders and the breadth of his chest. He's hard-muscled and strong, and I don't know why any part of me is noticing that, but it is. Just as it's noticing that scent of smoke and cedar too, warm and musky and masculine.

He hypnotised me with his silver gaze, stalking me slowly, and even though I wanted to, I couldn't make my finger pull the trigger.

I don't know what I'm trying to get out of him, because why should I care if he wants to sleep with his mistress tonight? Maybe it's only that with the gun, I can get some power back, because he has it all. I want him to acknowledge me as a person, not just a pawn he's using in his game with my father, because I'm so tired of being that pawn.

I want him to understand what he's doing to me in marrying me. I want him to know that I have opinions and thoughts and dreams, and he's just another man taking them all away from me.

And okay, maybe it's true. Maybe I really don't want him to sleep with his mistress on our wedding night, even though it shouldn't matter.

Still, one thing I do know is that with this gun in my hand, I'm powerful. I can make him do what I want for a change, even if that power is only an illusion since he's right. I'm not a killer. I'm not like him, not in any way.

I only wanted to prove myself and now that I have, I finally lower the gun, click on the safety, and extend it to him.

He blinks in surprise, before looking down at the weapon as if he doesn't know what it is.

'Go on,' I say. 'You wanted it. Take it.'

He doesn't though. Instead he looks at me. 'Why? I thought you wanted to shoot me, *gattina*.'

'I changed my mind.' Oddly, I feel more powerful now the gun has been lowered than when I was holding it. Perhaps that's because I finally did something that surprised him again, made him take notice, and that feels…good. 'Go on.' I shake the weapon at him. 'Take it.'

He takes it from my hand, checks it over with a practiced, reflexive movement. 'What about your deal?' he asks. 'I was about to capitulate, but then you went and gave away your advantage.'

'You were right.' I clasp my hands together so he can't see how they shake. 'I don't care what you do with another woman.'

He glances down at the gun again, a thoughtful expression on his handsome face. 'No, I don't think I was right,' he says slowly. 'I think you were.' His gaze lifts to mine. 'What you said about respect is true. You're my wife and as such, you are worthy of mine. Which means it would be disrespectful to sleep with Annika tonight.'

A small shock goes through me. I'm not expecting him to capitulate, not at all, so all I do is stare at him and ask stupidly, 'What?'

'I'm going to cancel Annika.' He's decisive as he puts the gun down on the bed then gets out his phone. 'Tonight you and I will have dinner instead.'

I open my mouth to tell him I don't want to have dinner with him, but he's already turning away. 'Six thirty,' he says over his shoulder. 'Maria will come and get you.' Then he strides out of the bedroom, the sound of his deep voice echoing in the hallway as he talks to whomever he just called. Annika, presumably.

I'm still trembling, my heart banging against my ribs, and I don't know if I'm afraid or thrilled. Afraid that he changed his mind about Annika and wants dinner with me instead, or thrilled that I managed to change his mind about her and wants dinner with me instead.

Go on, you're thrilled.

I take a deep breath, staring blankly at the gun on the bed. Maybe I *am* thrilled. He's ruthless and single-minded in his goals, and I've had first-hand experience of exactly how single-minded he is. And yet… I got him to change his mind, and I don't think it was just because I'd threatened his manhood. No, he changed it because of what I said about respect.

The families are obsessed with respect and who is

owed it and whether they deserve it, etc., etc. And Vincenzo Argenti is obviously no exception. Then again, he didn't say I was worthy of respect, he said I was worthy of *his* respect.

Which is interesting. Certainly within the families, no one can disrespect another man's wife. But a husband can disrespect his own wife, that's perfectly allowable, and I've seen it happen many times. I was too young to remember what my father's relationship with my mother was like before she died, but whenever he spoke about her, it wasn't with grief that she was dead, it was more about the insult to his and our family's honour.

I can't imagine Vincenzo Argenti actually respecting anyone, let alone the woman he kidnapped and forced into marriage, but when his gaze met mine, I had the feeling he was being genuine.

I don't want to keep thinking about him, though. I don't want him taking up so much space in my head, so I push the thoughts away. Instead I pause over the gun, wondering whether I should take it with me, but in the end I leave it on the bed. He wasn't wrong when he said if I shoot him, I wouldn't last long enough to enjoy my widowhood. His security is insane and I'm certainly not in the mood to die purely for the satisfaction of putting a bullet between his eyes.

Dinner is still a couple of hours away, so I spend time exploring the rest of the villa. It's stunningly beautiful, the gardens, the lawns, the terraces with pots overflowing with herbs and flowers. But through all this beauty it's impossible to see anything but a cage. There are too many men dressed in black and wearing sunglasses, just randomly walking around. Patrolling the grounds.

It makes sense. This plan to unite the families under his rule will have made him many enemies.

I ponder this as I go inside and find a gorgeous little library on the ground floor. It looks over yet another terrace and into some rose gardens, with shelves that are floor to high, vaulted ceiling and a fireplace to warm the room. I wander idly over to the shelves and inspect the spines, thinking about the plan he mentioned in the car in Rome, of bringing the warring factions under one command like he's a medieval king. I would have said that's impossible, but I do know from what my father has said, that he's already brought half the families under his control.

Stop the killings, the Wolf told me. *That's what I want to do.*

It's admirable, I have to admit as I take out another book and examine the cover. But what makes him think the killings would stop under *his* rule? Does he think he's better or more moral than everyone else?

What do you care?

I shove the book back onto the shelf with a little more force than strictly necessary, annoyed by the thought. I *don't* care. I really don't. I want to get *out* of the world I was brought up in. I want to be a normal twenty-five-year-old, with a job and a boyfriend, and live in a flat with a cat.

I don't want to go from one prison to another, to become yet another man's property. I'm tired of it. And I'm tired of feeling powerless, too.

You had some power up in his bedroom.

I turn away from the bookcases, still thinking. It was true, I did. I got him to change his mind, though that might have been the gun. Then again, he changed his mind *after* I gave him the weapon, so maybe it wasn't the gun after all. Maybe it was me. If so, perhaps I can get him to change his mind about other things too, such as letting me go.

I make my way slowly upstairs to my room, because dinner will be soon, and I need to decide what kind of woman I want to be when I meet him again. Do I want to be Cat in sweatpants and sweatshirt? Or Cat in full wifely make-up and dress?

I go over to the closet and slide open the doors, examining the clothes on the rack. Part of me wants to stay in what I'm wearing and he can go to hell with his expensive dresses and stupid lacy underwear. But another part of me is whispering that he might be expecting me *not* to make an effort, so why not surprise him? Or maybe he's expecting full make-up and ball gown, so a sweatshirt is the better surprise?

I stand there looking at the gowns and dresses, paralysed by my own indecision, which is ridiculous, because it's only a dinner.

Remind him again that you're his wife. That you deserve respect.

I blink at the thought. It's true. If I'm demanding his respect I need to look like the wife he's expecting me to be. I need to remind him of the consequences of what he's done by bringing me here and marrying me immediately. If he thought he could put a ring on my finger, legally marry me, then forget about me and lock me away like a trophy in his cabinet, then he'll soon find out he's wrong.

Determination fills me and I reach for a cocktail dress without hesitation. It's emerald green and has so many sequins it's like a disco ball, but when I put it on and look at myself in the mirror, I don't actually look like a disco ball.

The green fabric shimmers and sparkles as it clings to my body, outlining every curve. The neckline is plunging and there is a slit in one side that cuts straight up my thigh to my hip. It's sexy as hell and as much as I hate to admit it, it fits me perfectly.

I take my hair out of its ponytail and shake it out, letting the long straight length of it fall over my shoulders. The treatments the hairdresser put in it in preparation for the wedding have made it look glossy and silky. I've never really bothered with it before, but now I'm bothering and I'm pleased.

Still, if I'm going to go full wife, I need make-up, and since I hate wearing make-up, it's going to be a challenge to get it looking perfect. But half an hour and a few YouTube tutorials later, I've managed to get mascara on my lashes with no clumps, and gold and green eye shadow on my lids without fallout. Then it's a slick of red lip balm on my lips for that freshly bitten look, and some high-heeled golden sandals that make my legs look like they go on forever.

By the time I'm done, it's nearly six thirty, and nerves are gathering in my gut. But I'm not going to wait for Maria to come for me, oh no, I'll be damned if I wait on his order. So, I give myself one last going-over, then I turn from the mirror and head out of the room.

CHAPTER EIGHT

Vincenzo

I'VE ORGANISED FOR Maria to serve us dinner out on the terrace that overlooks the sea, and she's done a fine job. The table is set with a white tablecloth, the finest crystal champagne flutes, heavy silver cutlery and a bottle of Dom Perignon in an ice bucket. Candles in elegant glass holders flicker in the slight sea-breeze, and the bougainvillea that cascades from the terrace above in a riot of pink, hangs picturesquely over the scene.

And as I stand there surveying the scene, a part of me is wondering why the hell I'm fussing around with place settings and candles for my new forced bride, when I could be in bed screwing Annika.

It's a complete fucking mystery.

Everything about my behaviour since I kidnapped Caterina Salvatore seems to be a complete fucking mystery, and I hate mysteries.

I always know what I'm doing and everything is in service to my goal of cleaning the tarnish from the Argenti family's honour. Deciding to cancel my evening with Annika in favour of dinner with my new wife is not cleaning any tarnish from the Argenti family's honour. It's got nothing to do with anyone's honour at all, so I don't know why I did it.

She said I had to bear the consequences of marrying her, that I owe her the respect of at least not screwing another woman on our wedding night, and I…had to admit to myself that she was right.

It was a simple thing she'd asked of me. Nothing to do with giving her freedom or sparing her father's life, only a little respect for one night. Then, of course, without waiting for a response, she gave up her only weapon to me. As if she'd made her point and didn't need it anymore.

Ridiculous creature. In that moment, with her untidy ponytail and her sweatshirt half falling off her shoulder and her loose black trousers, she looked young, vulnerable and fragile. Defenceless. The perfect prey for the predator. And I was the predator. I was the villain. Yet she gave up her weapon without even waiting for an answer, and that made something in me catch and pull, like a fish hook catching on a rock.

A wife in the families is a host, a mediator, she runs the household and takes care of the children. She is guarded and protected, staying out of the business side of things, because that is a job for men.

My mother, Elena, was different, at least at the start. She was fiery, opinionated, fiercely protective and loyal. Yet, over the years, my father slowly ground all those things out of her. He would not tolerate any exceptions to the norm and he would not tolerate those who wouldn't do what he said. His word was law. My mother didn't fit into the box he put her in, so he made her fit by cutting away the pieces of her he didn't like.

I assumed that any wife I eventually had would be exactly like all the rest. A good *cosa nostra* wife who supports her husband, but I knew upstairs in that bedroom, that Caterina Salvatore would not be a wife like all the rest.

She's like my mother, full of fire and spark, and the way she challenged me with the gun and with her wit…

My father didn't respect my mother, not at all. He had mistresses scattered from one end of Italy to the other, and he visited them all while she remained here at the estate, dependent on the drugs the doctors fed her.

I'm supposed to be different. I'm supposed to be better. A more honourable man than he ever was, and so how could I do anything but give her what she wanted?

I suspect there's more to it than that, especially because I didn't feel even the slightest bit of disappointment about cancelling Annika. But I don't want to think about what more there is. Not now. Not when I'm still waiting for Giovanni Salvatore's sworn loyalty.

I can even admit to some…anticipation at the thought of having dinner with my strangely fascinating new wife. She certainly won't be boring, at least.

Turning from my survey of the table, I'm about to find Maria to tell her to summon my wife, when a woman walks through the French doors and out onto the terrace as if she owns it.

She's tall and built like a dancer, long legs, slim hips, small, rounded breasts, each and every curve followed lovingly by the fabric of her green sequinned dress. Her black hair is loose down her back, falling almost to her waist, and her incredible eyes are highlighted with sparkles of gold and green on her lids. She wears high-heeled golden sandals that make her legs even longer, and the basest part of me imagines having those long legs wrapped around my waist as I fuck her. Or maybe flung over my shoulders, the long spike of her heel digging into my back as I make her come.

The woman is unfamiliar at first and I have the passing thought that maybe she's one of my other lovers and if so, what is she doing here? Then, like a blurred scene through a camera lens suddenly springing into focus, I realise who the woman is.

She's my wife. Caterina.

She is cool and self-contained as she stands a moment, studying the terrace, the table, and then me. And when her gaze meets mine I feel the impact, all glittering, sharp-edged challenge.

The wolf in me shifts, hungry, predatory, knowing exactly what it wants to eat now and it's not the food Maria will be serving us. Before in sweatshirt and pants, she looked vulnerable and fragile, and the wolf wanted to protect her.

But right here, right now, in her green sequins and war paint, the wolf wants to fuck her. And so do I.

'I'm early, sorry,' she says, not sounding sorry in the least. 'I didn't want to wait for Maria.'

I move instantly, rounding the table to pull out her chair for her. 'Nor should you. Please. Sit.'

She stalks over to the chair, eyeing me warily, perhaps expecting me to stand back to let her sit down. But I don't. There's a reason she's all dressed up with looks to kill, and there's a reason her make-up is war paint.

She's on a mission, this little *gattina*, that's obvious, and I'm fascinated to discover what kind of mission she's on. Is it to prove she can be the perfect wife like all the others? Or is it to show me exactly what kind of woman I married? Or is it that she knows I want her and is going to use that to get what she wants out of me?

Intriguing woman. The dress and the make-up are pure *cosa nostra* wife, but that look of stubborn determination in her eyes… I've seen that same look in the eyes of my paternal grandmother before she died. All steel, no mercy. The woman who made my father what he was. The look of a warrior.

I hold the sides of her chair as she sits down, and I catch her scent, warm jasmine and musk, and the wolf in me growls, hungry and getting hungrier. I glance down at the top of her glossy black head, noticing that despite her confident entry, her shoulders are tense and there's a stiffness to her movements.

So, this is all an act to hide her nerves. Yet, seeing through her bravado doesn't disappoint me. It only makes me respect her even more. She came to this mission ready, despite being afraid, and she came down to face me. And I am not an easy man to face.

I let go of her chair and walk over to the ice bucket where the bottle of Dom is sitting atop a mound of ice. 'A little of this excellent champagne to celebrate,' I say, opening the foil then popping the cork.

'To celebrate what?' Her voice is sharp. 'My kidnapping?'

'Of course.' I ignore her tone, pouring us out two glasses and then handing one to her. 'And our marriage.'

She takes it, watching me as I sit opposite her. 'To my new wife.' I lift my glass in a toast.

Her eyes glitter in the candlelight, green as the sequins on her dress. 'You'll forgive me if I don't drink to my own imprisonment.'

'A little dramatic, *gattina*,' I chide, mostly for my own amusement. 'You're hardly a prisoner.'

'Aren't I?' She puts her glass down, untouched. 'There are guards on basically every square meter of this entire property.'

'Of course there are guards.' I take a sip of the champagne and it is, indeed, excellent. 'I'm the head of the Argenti family and I have enemies. They're there to keep people out, not in.'

'So, if I wanted to, say, take a helicopter tomorrow and get out of here, I could?'

Oh, she's sharp as the points of her little heels isn't she?

My pulse accelerates as I smile and settle back into my chair, enjoying the challenge she's just thrown at me, and anticipating more. 'Naturally you could. Providing you have adequate security.'

Her gaze narrows. 'And if I didn't want security?'

'Come now, *gattina*. You know how this works. I'm sure your father didn't let you go anywhere without a bodyguard or three, so why would you expect that to change now you're my wife? You're still a target, I'm afraid.'

It's no less than the truth, but it's clear she doesn't like that one bit.

'I've been a prisoner in my father's house all my life,' she says flatly. 'And I refuse to be one here. So if what you said about respecting me is true, then you need to respect my need to feel like I live here, not like I'm trapped here.'

She's so very emphatic, her gaze never wavering from mine, the force of her will measuring itself against my own. It makes my pulse beat even faster. I like it. I like her challenge and her spirit. I like her courage and her ferocity. She's gutsy, this woman, to come downstairs dressed like that, ready to cross swords with me, knowing who and what I am.

But she's right. She is trapped here. Just like your mother was.

Something tightens in my chest, but I ignore the feeling. This is an entirely different situation. Caterina is *not* trapped here. She can leave at any time, as long as she has some security.

Besides, I can't imagine her being anyone's prisoner. How her father even got her to the altar to marry the Bianchi stripling seems like a miracle. Unless she wanted to be there, of course.

It's another question to ask her, but I'm getting distracted. Because the electricity we both felt during that moment of our wedding ceremony is filling the air again. It's making her eyes widen and pupils dilate, her red lips parting.

The wolf in me wants to get rid of the table between us, snatch her up from her chair and rip her dress clean off, put her down on the ground and make her mine completely. But I'm not a teenage boy with no control over himself, and the wolf doesn't control me either, so I fight it.

The wolf is merely an aspect of myself that came into being after I was punished for my failure to kill the entire Salvatore family. In the dank little room in the basement of this villa, my father gave me scars to ensure I never forgot what it was to disappoint him. And in that very same room I became the predator I needed to be in order to take him down eventually. A wolf to protect those who were mine and to hunt down those who were not.

Yet the wolf is not in charge. I am. And I'm not giving into it yet. My new wife clearly has no love for me, though her body might disagree, and I'm not in the mood to change her mind tonight. If I want sex that badly, I can wait and see Annika tomorrow, or maybe the night after. It doesn't have to be now.

'You're very demanding for a kidnapped woman,' I murmur. 'Especially when I'm still waiting for your father to give me his loyalty on pain of your death.'

She says nothing, sitting stiff in her chair, that gaze of hers not letting up.

I take a sip of my champagne and then glance over the terrace at the view of the sun sinking majestically into the sea. 'Sundown is approaching very rapidly.'

Her jaw is tight, every line of her body tense. 'And if he doesn't give it? You'll kill me?'

Surely she can't still think that I would? When I saved her all those years ago? When I told her in the car back in Rome that if I wanted her dead, she would be?

'Of course not, *gattina*,' I say with some impatience. 'I've already made that very clear. But your father doesn't know that.'

Her thick black lashes flutter and abruptly she looks down at the white tablecloth, lovely mouth in a grim line. 'He hasn't given it yet?'

'No,' I confirm, studying her.

She nods and swallows, keeping her gaze on the table.

The flickering of the candlelight betrays her, though. I can see the sheen of tears in her eyes, and it hits me somewhere I wasn't expecting. Somewhere…painful.

A woman's tears have never moved me before, so why they're doing so now, I have no idea. Perhaps it's because I don't like to see a woman with so much spirit and fire in pain. Again, it reminds me of my mother, slowly fading before my eyes as my father kept her trapped here in the villa, using her as his brood mare when it suited him, ignoring her when it didn't.

'You're upset,' I say, not liking her distress.

She doesn't look at me, only blinks furiously. 'No, I'm not.'

I ignore her. 'Are you afraid for him? Or are you afraid for yourself?'

She continues to look at the tablecloth for a long moment. Then, quite abruptly, she looks up at me and I can see pain in her eyes. But also something else.

Fury again. It smoulders in her eyes like a hot, green coal.

'He won't give you his loyalty,' she says. 'He'd rather let me die. I'm a pawn to him, nothing more.'

Her anger colours every word, matching the heat in her eyes, and she throws them at me like spears, each sharp point finding their mark.

I know exactly what it means to be only a pawn to one's father. That's all I was too. After my mother retreated to her bedroom for good, he took charge of me, though *I* didn't matter to him as much as the fact that I was his heir. I had to look like him and talk like him, make the decisions he would make. If I stepped out of line even slightly, I was punished for it.

But isn't that how you've been treating her too? Like a pawn?

A cold current of awareness winds through me. Yes, it's true and I've acknowledged it more than once. But putting my thoughts about her in the context of my own father's behaviour is…disturbing.

Again, I'm *not* him and I never was. Once, perhaps, after my mother died and he was the only family I had left, I wanted to be the perfect son for him. But then he ordered me to kill a child and everything changed. As I took the punishment he doled out, his spiked belt gouging holes in my flesh as he laid it across my back, that's when I decided he was a stain on the honour of the Argentis. A stain that needed to be cleaned, and that I would be the one to clean it. I would be the one to set a new example of what the head of a family could be, a better example.

How is the way you're treating her better?

She sits across the table from me, that fury in her eyes glowing hot, and along with it the pain, and I understand all at once that the way I'm treating her is *not* better. That to actually be a better man and not merely paying lip service to the idea, I need to change my thinking. I need to change how I treat her.

I don't look away. 'What makes you think you're only a pawn?'

'Because he told me so. Basically every day since my mother and brother died. He blamed me for their deaths.'

I frown, puzzled by this. 'How could he do that? You were only a child.'

Caterina's gaze is level. 'Yes. But I was also the only one who survived.'

CHAPTER NINE

Caterina

He's lounging in the chair opposite, his long, muscled body relaxed. Like a panther. He's in black suit trousers and a black shirt with the first couple of buttons undone. He wears no jewellery except the heavy gold signet ring that he took off to give to me so I had a ring to put on his finger.

He's almost monklike in the severity of his clothes, yet no monk looks like he does. The candlelight loves his high carved cheek bones, the straight length of his nose, and that mouth of his that seemed so cruel before, isn't now. No, now it's beautiful. *He*'s beautiful, with his silver-grey eyes and his intense stare.

My heart is beating so damn fast and it won't slow down. I hadn't meant to tell him about my relationship with my father or to fling that confession like a vase at his head. I didn't want him to know how upset I was, but when he reminded me that his deadline for my father's loyalty is sundown tonight, I couldn't seem to find my nice, polite, well-bred Salvatore mask.

Because that sun is going down and if my father hasn't given the Wolf his loyalty by now, he's not going to give it. Which is only confirmation—as if my whole damn life wasn't confirmation enough—that my father doesn't care about me. Not one single iota.

I should have expected it, but expectations and reality seldom meet, and so my own reaction caught me by surprise. The tears mainly, because I didn't want to feel sad about it. I wanted to be angry, since anger is so much more powerful. Dad never had any patience with my anger, said it wasn't becoming in a woman, yet anger is what I cling to, because he can go to hell.

Vincenzo Argenti can go to hell too, though I have to admit, he doesn't seem to have an issue with my fury. No, he's staring back at me as if I've fascinated him in some way.

You like it.

A part of me does. A part of me finds that very powerful.

'He wasn't pleased you survived?' the Wolf asks, his voice cool and detached sounding.

It's wrong to talk to him about my family and our relationships with each other, since technically he's the enemy. But over the years my family loyalty has been steadily worn away by my father's contempt, and besides, this man is my husband now. I'm going to give him my family history whether he wants it or not.

'No,' I say bluntly. 'He wanted my mother and brother to be the ones who lived. My brother, because Alessio was his heir, and my mother because she could make more heirs. I was an afterthought child. A daughter as a sop to my mother.'

'Sounds familiar,' the Wolf murmurs, though he

doesn't elaborate on what exactly sounds familiar. 'He didn't think to make you his heir?'

'Of course not. I'm a woman. My only use was in making alliances.'

Out beyond the terrace, on the horizon, the sun flares as it readies itself to disappear into the sea. My father won't pledge his loyalty to the Wolf. His dream of vengeance against the Argenti threat is more important to him than the life of his one remaining child, and despite myself and my fury, the little girl I used to be feels as if a knife has been plunged into her chest. My mother loved me and so did my brother, and when they died, I lost the only two people who thought I was important. The only people to whom I mattered. And it makes me feel the ache of their loss all over again.

It's his fault. His family's fault.

It would be easy to blame him and the Argentis. That's what my father did. But my father was also the one who ordered the killing of this man's mother for some petty slight lost in the mists of time, so can the fault really lie with the Argentis?

I don't know anymore, but perhaps there's something to the Wolf's aim of stopping the inter-family killings.

He's studying me intently, something in his eyes I can't name. Has my story affected him? It's intrigued him, that's for sure.

'Well,' he murmurs at last, a dark and heated note in his voice that makes me want to shiver. 'Your father's a fool then.'

Surprise ripples through me. 'Why do you say that?'

'Because he missed an opportunity. You have a lot of courage, *gattina*, not to mention determination and spirit, and those are valuable qualities to have in the head of a family, regardless of gender.'

Praise from the Wolf shouldn't make a wave of warmth roll through me, yet it does. I haven't been called anything but disobedient, wilful and a damn nuisance for years, and so a part of me laps up his words like a flower starved of sunlight.

There's a lump in my throat and I don't want him to see how he's touched me, so I reach for my glass and take a healthy sip of champagne instead. The liquid is yeasty and cold, and delicious, so I take another, even though I shouldn't drink it too fast. Getting tipsy here in this literal wolf's den would not be a good idea.

'My father would disagree.' I make myself put down the champagne glass. 'Clearly he's not going to give you his loyalty tonight. Which puts you in the difficult position of having to kill your new wife.' I lift my gaze to his and hold it. 'Good thing we didn't have a proper wedding.'

His handsome features are enigmatic, his gaze glittering. I can't tell what he's thinking. He's been saying he wouldn't kill me all this time, and so far, he hasn't. Perhaps he won't. Still, I can't take his word for anything, can I? He's not only the enemy, he's been my personal nightmare ever since I was a child, and regardless that his bullets didn't kill my mother and brother, he was still sent to our family's door to kill us. Also, he did say to me up in his bedroom that he was a killer.

Fear is a cold snake in my gut, but I don't let it out. I pile anger on instead. Anger is strong and powerful. *Let him try and do it,* I think. *I'll go down fighting him every step of the way.*

'*Gattina,*' he murmurs eventually, putting down his wine glass. 'How many times must I tell you? I am not going to hurt you. I didn't save you only to kill you twenty years later. What would be the point in that?'

'Why should I believe you?' I try to make it sound like a question yet it comes out sounding like a demand instead. 'Your father wanted my entire family dead.'

'That is true,' he concedes. 'But I am not my father. And it's this inter-family violence that I'm trying to stop.' He pauses a moment, his gaze on me intensifying. 'I'm not going to hurt you, Caterina. I give you my word.'

I shouldn't believe him. I shouldn't trust him as far as I could throw him, not when he hasn't given me any reason to. Yet… I see the truth in his eyes now. He means it. He means every word. This is a solemn vow, as binding as an oath.

The tightly coiled snake in my gut relaxes a little, and I let out a breath. 'But you told my father you would. Not following through on a threat isn't going to make you look good.'

'Oh, I'm going to follow through on it.' The corner of his mouth curves. 'At least as far as your father is concerned.'

'What do you mean?'

'You wouldn't be the first woman I've "killed" who then turns up later with a new identity.'

At first I don't understand and then his meaning penetrates. 'You mean you'll…what? Fake my death?'

He lifts one powerful shoulder. 'Yes. And I can usually produce some very convincing evidence, too.'

'So you've done it before?'

He gives a quiet laugh that feels as if it's rolling over my skin like soft, dark velvet. 'Many times. I want to stop the violence, the killing of innocents, but sometimes the so-called deaths of innocents must be staged in order to ensure compliance. Some of those innocents did not appreciate their new lives, but since it's better than actual death, they somehow survived.'

The Wolf of Sicily has had many deaths laid at his door in his ruthless grab for power, that's well-known. Women, children. He's supposed to have no boundaries, which makes this confession so surprising I don't know what to say.

He smiles, a warm and genuine one this time. 'Look at that,' he murmurs. 'I've finally shocked you.'

'But...' I manage. 'Why?'

'I might be many things, *gattina,* but one thing I'm not is a hypocrite.' That beautiful smile slowly fades, the intensity in his eyes burning bright. 'The killing will end if it's the last thing I do.'

The force of his conviction and the almost palpable nature of his will should be frightening, yet I'm not frightened. I'm fascinated by why the head of the most powerful *cosa nostra* family in Europe has suddenly come to value human lives when he never has before, at least not on the face of it.

'Why?' I'm probably too blunt, but who cares? I want to know. 'I mean, that's not what everyone says about you. You're famous for having—'

'No morals or boundaries?' he finishes for me. 'A carefully cultivated lie, once again propagated to ensure compliance.' He shifts in his chair, a wolf settling into his den, studying me from across the white tablecloth. 'Though, once it was true. At least it was until I saw you with your terrified eyes.' Impossibly, his gaze gets even more intense, holding me captive as surely as iron chains. 'Because of you, Caterina, I found my line in the sand. And because of your mother and brother's deaths, I decided that I could not let the pointless killing of people go on. It has to end somewhere and I decided it would end with me.'

I thought I could not possibly get any more shocked, but apparently, I'm wrong. He can't mean that, can he? It seemed ridiculous in the car back in Rome and it seems just as ridiculous here on the terrace now. That me, a five-year-old girl, could change the entire course of a man's life just by looking up at him in fear?

'B-but...' I break off, not able to think of a word to say.

Again, that fascinating mouth of his curves in amusement. He does seem to like shocking me. 'It's true,' he says simply, correctly reading my disbelief. 'My father was very unhappy with me.'

I blink. Oh, of course. There would have been repercussions for him, wouldn't there? Stefano Argenti was not a merciful man, by all accounts.

'What did he do to you?' I ask point-blank.

The Wolf's smile changes, bitterness entering into it now. 'He punished me quite severely for my failure to kill you and your father. But don't worry, I got my own back.' His voice has deepened, roughened and again I can hear the darkness in it. 'My father died as he lived. By the sword.'

A cold shiver ripples over my skin. Even though he hasn't said anything explicitly, I know that somehow he had a hand in his father's death. And all at once, I'm aware that this is a very dangerous conversation to be having and with a very dangerous man. A man who has said he won't kill me, but no matter what he said about staging the deaths of innocents, he's certainly killed others.

The sun has now vanished below the horizon, lighting the sky on fire, and it's beautiful. And here I am on my wedding night, sitting and drinking champagne with my new husband, who perhaps won't kill me after all. Having just been given up by my father who indeed didn't care if I lived or died.

The pain in my heart aches as the light fades, the child in me hurting at the abandonment even as the adult woman is furious for having even a shred of hope that he might care. That the only people who ever loved me are dead and have been dead for years.

'Don't cry for him, *gattina*,' the Wolf says quietly and unexpectedly. 'He's not worth your tears. This isn't abandonment. This is the moment you're set free.'

There's a lump in my throat and I have to swallow more champagne to get rid of it, but he's not wrong. My father doesn't want me. I'm dead to him. Which means I finally have what I've always craved, which is to be free of him.

I look across the table at my husband. 'So, where does that leave you?'

'It leaves me with staging your death and perhaps organising you a new identity.' He shrugs. 'I'd hoped to avoid more bloodshed, but your father has chosen his path. He will come to regret it, I assure you.'

I should feel regret myself at this, but regret is hard to

come by now my father has decided my life isn't worth as much as his pride. 'You'll have to find yourself another wife,' I say.

He tilts his head. 'Do I? A pity. You're starting to grow on me.'

Another wave of warmth rushes through me, and my cheeks heat. I'm not sure why I'm blushing. What do I care if I'm starting to grow on him or not? He kidnapped me and forced me to marry him, and regardless of that strange electricity between us, I shouldn't *like* that he likes me, right?

Except he's beautiful and powerful, and very dangerous, and something wild in me is pleased I've managed to affect him. The girl even her own father abandoned has somehow managed to make this powerful head of a *cosa nostra* family like her.

The air around us thickens, tension gathering, the force of his gaze like a hurricane wind, and my mind blanks. All I can see are his eyes and the silver flames in them, and all I can hear is my heart beating faster and faster.

I remember the light touch of his fingers as he straightened my tiara at our wedding ceremony, and the brush of his fingertip on my ear as he pushed a strand of hair behind it. The prickle of electricity that chased over my skin. The press of his mouth on my forehead, a featherlight kiss that I can still feel burning even now. And I'm looking at his mouth and the fullness of his bottom lip, and how it curves. Cruel and beautiful at the same time.

What would a real kiss from him be like?

The thought blazes in my head and now it's occurred to me, I can't stop thinking about it. That mouth not on my forehead, but on my lips. My first kiss. Would it feel as hot? What would he taste like? I remember the way he picked me up in the church earlier, throwing me over his shoulder like I weighed nothing. He was so hard, like stone, and yet warm, too.

Yet more heat steals through my cheeks, and I can't stop it, and suddenly this all feels too much. The danger in our conversation, my own honesty, the tears in my eyes that I know he saw, and him, sitting there, seeing my blush and knowing why. Because of course he'd know why.

I can't deal with it, not now, so I push myself to my feet, say 'excuse me' in a breathless voice, then I flee the terrace.

CHAPTER TEN

Vincenzo

I'M HALF OUT of my chair to stop her before I know what I'm doing. But when I realise, I force myself to sit back down. I've never chased a woman before and I'm not about to start now, but still, my blood is running hot and my muscles are tense.

I'm disappointed she's gone, though perhaps not surprised.

She's sheltered, clearly a virgin, and that moment of sexual tension between us must have been disturbing for her. Interesting how she displayed nothing but courage up until that point, all bravado as she challenged my threat to kill her if her father didn't swear his loyalty to me before sundown.

She can look death in the face, but the moment our chemistry lights up the night, she blushes and flees.

And there were you, almost going after her.

I shove back my chair and pace over to the stone balustrade that bounds the terrace. Leaning on my hands, I look out over the sea and take a breath, trying to calm myself the fuck down.

Yes, I did want to go after her. I wanted to continue

our conversation. I wanted to hear more about her childhood and how difficult it was. About her father and why there were tears in her eyes when she realised he wasn't going to call me to save her, even though his treatment of her was terrible.

Did she love him? And if so, why? It seemed he didn't give a shit about her and the thought makes me burn with unexpected fury. It drags up old memories I'd thought long buried, of how my own father hated my mother's care of me, telling her it was making me 'weak'. After her death, he took my upbringing in hand to make me stronger. Hardening me to death and violence in the way of the families.

The torture session with a suspected mole that one of the other families had planted in our household, was the first. My father did the torturing along with his *consiglieri* and I was made to watch. If I protested or cried, or turned away, I was struck across the face. In the end, the *consiglieri* held me by the scruff of my neck, my mouth bleeding, one of my eyes swelling shut, and forced me to watch. I was twelve years old.

Before my mother lost herself, I was a boy who rescued baby birds from fallen nests in the garden, and once a kitten that I found on a riverbank, all wrapped up in a pillowcase after someone had tried to drown it. I helped Maria pick herbs from the garden for dinner, and for my mother, I picked roses. I loved my parents wholeheartedly and my favourite thing to do was go for walks on the beach with my mother.

But my father didn't allow such softness. There was no room for mercy as the head of the family and no room for kindness. No room for care. He beat all that care and kindness out of me, leaving me little more than a killing machine.

Until that night I rescued Caterina, and discovered in myself that there were some shreds of kindness and care still there. Scraps of mercy, too.

I'd given up at that stage, thrown myself into my father's world because with my mother gone, it was the only world I knew. But Caterina made me see that parts of the boy I once was still remained, and that I could choose something different.

By then I had no love left for my father, not one iota. And I knew right from the start that if I wanted to keep those scraps of kindness and care, if I wanted to remain at least somewhat whole, he'd have to go. I'd have to end him myself, since I couldn't trust anyone else to do it. So, one night when he called me into his study to issue some order or other, I took my gun with me and shot him in the head.

And I didn't regret it. Not a single fucking shred.

Caterina has more of a conscience than I do, judging from the way her own father's betrayal cut her so deeply. She must care more than she thinks, which is obvious since she's been nothing but furious since she arrived here.

My fingers grip tightly to the stone as I remember the hurt in her eyes as it sunk in that her father hadn't contacted me, and my anger burns hotter at how he discarded his only daughter so carelessly.

I meant it when I told her he'd wasted an opportunity to make her his heir. She would have been the perfect head of any family, with her courage and spirit and steely determination. Her empathy too.

She was made to be a queen. She could be your *queen.*

The thought springs into my head fully formed and once it's there, it's impossible to get rid of. It's so easy to imagine her at my side, helping me to restore the Argenti family honour and to build a new empire that must come out of all this death. It feels like fate, I can't deny it, and I'm not a man who believes in fate.

The same determination I feel pursuing my cause, I see in her eyes when she's challenging me, and I can't help thinking about what we could achieve together. I've yet to meet a woman as stubborn and determined as she is.

She wants freedom, though.

Yes, but there's freedom to be had with me, as my wife. Not the freedom she's possibly imagining, but it's still freedom. And not only that, but power for the taking.

She could be your wife in every way...

That too. In fact, I can see her right now in my bed, all that raging fury turned to passion and all unleashed on me. I would take it and give her back the same, and now all I can see is her on her back, in my bed, her black hair spread out over the pillows, all that delicious golden skin laid bare, and her green eyes glittering with fire as she looks up at me. She's a woman made for physical pleasure, for screaming my name when she comes.

Fuck. I should not be thinking of her like that, because if it's sex I need, I can get that whenever I want. Yes, I made a promise to Caterina tonight, but I could bring Annika here tomorrow. Perhaps a night with her would be just what I need…

Except I don't need the wolf in me to tell me that Annika is not what I want. Any other woman is not what I want, at least not now. Not tonight.

Tonight, I want her.

I grit my teeth, staring at the darkening horizon. She was always going to be my wife in every way at some point, so why not start the seduction now? We have chemistry and I know she wants me. Yes, I didn't have the patience for a seduction earlier, but I can be patient when I want to be. After all, it took me five long years of convincing my father I was his minion completely, before I ended him with a single bullet.

It wouldn't take that long to seduce my little *gattina*. She's too passionate to hold out forever and if she needs more convincing, I can sweeten the deal. If she surrenders to me, I'll give her all the freedom and power she desires.

I think on this as the evening lengthens and I have my wedding dinner alone on the terrace. I tell Maria to take a tray up to Caterina's room, because I can't have my new wife going hungry. After that's done, I retire to my study to consider my next move. There will have to be a response to Salvatore's silence and it needs to be swift. An example will need to be made, because if there's one thing my demon of a father did get right, it's that you can't afford to be weak in this world. Not if you want to survive.

For a moment I debate the manner of Salvatore's death. I keep seeing the pain in Caterina's eyes and the faint gleam of tears when she realised her father wasn't going to save her, and the idea of putting a bullet between his eyes is a pleasurable one. He didn't deserve the daughter he ignored, but his loss will be my gain. He threw away a diamond and I will pick it up and make it the jewel in my crown.

Perhaps though, I won't kill him immediately. Perhaps I'll ask her if she has a preference. It seems right that she should choose since he took all her choices from her.

It takes me some time to put my plans in place, and it's late by the time I finish up.

I resolve to mention the question of Giovanni Salvatore's continued survival tomorrow, since my new bride will be sleeping right now, so I take a glass of brandy out onto the terrace to enjoy the night. It's a rare moment of peace, standing out in the darkness, watching the stars and listening to the waves crash on the beach below.

It reminds me of those walks on the beach with my mother, looking for sea glass and shells, and sand-smoothed stones. She loved the beach. It was the place she'd go to be free of my father, or at least to have the illusion of freedom. We'd sit together on the sand and I'd pretend to be a pirate coming to rescue her in my pirate ship, and then we'd talk about all the places we'd sail to.

I loved those moments with her. But after her third miscarriage, my father moved on to another woman, and Elena took to her bedroom in the afternoons instead of walking by the sea with me. Another thing he took from me.

The darkness is scented with sea and rosemary, and I finish my brandy. I'm about to go inside when a movement catches my eye. It's coming from the pool area, a few steps down onto another terrace from here, so I move over to the stone parapet to see what's going on.

The pool area is floodlit and a woman in a sequinned green dress is standing down one end of the pool. She has her back to me, her long black hair falling almost to her waist.

It appears that my little *gattina* is not sleeping after all.

As I watch, she reaches around to tug down the zip of her dress, before wriggling out of it. Underneath she's wearing a pair of purple silk knickers and a black sports bra, and the mismatch makes me smile. Our wedding night and she's wearing a sports bra. That seems very… her.

She discards the dress on one of the sun loungers, then, moving to the pool's edge, she dives straight in, clean and precise as a knife.

I should tell her I'm here, not stand in the darkness watching like a voyeur, but I say nothing nor do I move away. I want to watch what she'll do when she thinks she's alone, because whatever it is, I think I'll like it.

She surfaces, her hair flowing out behind her like kelp, her body pale beneath the water. There's an elegance to her, precise lines with the most luscious curves, and in my head I'm already stripping away the bra and the knickers, so she's swimming for me naked.

Beautiful. Sheer fucking perfection.

I lean against the parapet, watching her as she begins to swim lazily to the other end of the pool before rolling onto her back and floating like a starfish. She closes her eyes, her hair moving lazily around her head. The purple silk knickers are lacy, giving me tantalising glimpses of the dark curls between her thighs, and all the blood in my veins rushes below my belt and straight to my cock.

I've seen plenty of women swimming and some more naked than she is, and never once have I had an inappropriate hard-on for any of them. But she's different. She's my wife, my little *gattina,* my queen. And right now I want her more than anything I've ever wanted in my entire life.

'I know you're there,' she says, her eyes still closed. 'If you're going to watch me at least have the decency to come out and be a man about it.'

CHAPTER ELEVEN

Caterina

I KNEW SOMEONE was watching me the moment I dove into the pool.

After the abortive dinner, I wanted to go to bed and sleep for a thousand years, and not have to think about anything, especially not Vincenzo Argenti.

But of course, it was too early for sleep and hunger kept me up. Maria left me a tray of food, including another glass of wine, and there wasn't any reason not to eat it so I did. I drank the wine too, since why not? My father left me to die and getting tipsy seemed the least of my problems.

Except, I still wasn't tired, and I was hot, and from my bedroom window I could see the pool. It looked so inviting. I didn't want to hunt around for a swimsuit in that wardrobe full of clothes, bought for a woman who isn't me, and since there appeared to be no armed guards directly near the pool, I went straight there and unzipped my dress. It was only once I was in the water that I felt someone's gaze on me.

I should have been afraid, I suppose, but I knew it couldn't be an intruder since the security at the villa is insane. Which meant it could only be one of the guards and if so, then I wanted him to know that I knew he was there.

The water is cool on my skin and it feels wonderful to float in it weightless, with my eyes closed, free in the darkness. We had a small pool at our house in Rome and I spent a lot of time in it. Floating in the water with my eyes shut was the closest I ever got to actually feeling free, with no expectations pulling me under, nothing tying me down.

But here someone is watching, disturbing my peace, and I don't like it.

I stay in the water with my eyes closed, hoping whoever it is flees in shame, but instead I hear footsteps coming down the stone stairs from the terrace. Unhurried footsteps. Whoever it is, is not at all bothered by the fact that I spotted them.

I keep my eyes firmly shut, showing them I don't care who it is, and I'm not bothered either, but I keep listening until the footsteps come to one end of the pool and stop.

'I should call you *sirena* instead of *gattina*,' a deep, dark male voice says. 'Since you're floating in the water like a mermaid.'

Every muscle in my body tenses, my heartbeat accelerating, and I stop floating, opening my eyes to see Vincenzo Argenti standing down one end of the pool, his arms folded across his broad chest, his silver-grey gaze resting on me.

'What are you doing here?' I demand without thinking.

'I live here,' he says, infuriatingly. 'Where else would I be?'

I experience the ridiculous urge to splash him, get water all over his perfectly tailored black clothes, but that would be childish and I'm not a child, not anymore. 'I mean, why were you watching me?' I glare at him furiously. 'It's creepy.'

He lifts one shoulder, unbothered by the accusation. 'I saw some movement by the pool area so I came to investigate. I didn't want to disturb your swim.'

'And you thought watching me from the safety of a bush was better?'

His expression remains neutral. 'I wanted to make sure you didn't drown.'

Something is in the air between us again, that electricity, that tension. The one that made me leave the dinner table so quickly just before, that makes my mouth dry and my skin tight. In the cool water my nipples are hardening and I'm very aware of a nagging, throbbing ache between my thighs.

I can't pretend I don't know what it is, not now. I know exactly what it is.

You want him.

I do. I don't understand how or why, but the fact remains that I do.

He doesn't move, but his gaze moves over me and there's something in it that makes my breath catch. Something hot. I should feel vulnerable here in the water wearing only my underwear, while he's standing on the side of the pool fully dressed and towering over me, yet I don't.

That glitter in his eyes is definitely heat.

He likes looking at you half-naked.

And I realise that I like him looking. It feels good to

know that while my father might have thrown me away, this man likes what he sees and he wants me.

So I stare back, feeling the tension pull tight, watching the heat in his eyes build higher and higher, and he's letting me see it. He's showing it to me.

A tremor goes through me, like a small earthquake, a key turning in a lock, an understanding I wasn't ready for even a mere few hours ago. But for some reason I'm ready now.

I've been a pawn in Giovanni Salvatore's games for so long, yet in this pool, with the Wolf of Sicily watching me, I don't feel like a pawn. I don't feel like the unloved and unwanted child of an unloving man.

With him watching, I feel like a queen.

A certain power flows through me, a power I've never experienced before, and I realise something else. He's staying right where he is. He's dangerous—so dangerous—yet he's not leaping into the water to grab me. He's not doing anything at all to compel me. He's only standing on the side of the pool, watching.

I lift my hands to my wet hair, pushing it back from my face, knowing that as I do, the wet fabric of the sports bra pulls tight across my breasts. He watches me doing that too, the burn in his eyes getting brighter.

'Well,' I say huskily. 'Here I am. Undrowned.'

'I can see that. Why did you leave our dinner so suddenly?'

The water is cool, but even so, I can feel my cheeks flushing. He knows why, I can see it in his face. 'I think you know the answer already,' I say, not willing to give him the answer quite yet. Wanting to revel in my power a little longer.

He smiles, his beautiful mouth curving, all sensual heat, and my pulse starts to race. 'Come now, *gattina*. Surely you can say it aloud?'

I've never been attracted to anyone before, still less a man like him, and naturally, sex was never a topic of conversation. So I have no experience, none at all. But along with that power, another feeling threads through me, as if a heavy weight is lifting. I'm here in the pool, married to this incredibly dangerous, beautiful man. My father has chosen his pride over me, which makes me officially free of him. I don't have to be a good Salvatore daughter anymore. I don't have to be obedient and quiet, only to be seen and not heard.

Right now, right here, I'm not free—or at least not free the way I want to be—but I'm not bound by my name. I have a different one now. I'm Caterina Argenti, and I can be whoever I want to be.

'Perhaps I don't want to say it first,' I murmur, a heady little thrill going through me as I realise that I'm flirting with him. 'Perhaps I want you to say it.'

The smile that plays around his mouth is intoxicating, as are the silver sparks glittering in his eyes. 'If you come closer, I can show you instead.'

Oh yes, definitely we're flirting, and it's one hell of a rush. Maybe it's the champagne, or maybe it's the relentless pull of his charisma, but I can't help moving slowly through the water towards him, coming closer.

He crouches gracefully at the side of the pool, watching me as my pulse thumps in my head. I'm not afraid, even though this man has stalked my nightmares for years. Even though he kidnapped me and forced me to marry him.

He's not a nightmare anymore. He's a fever dream.

I stop at the edge of the pool, looking up at him. 'Well? I'm here. Show me then.'

For a minute he's still, then he reaches to gently grip my jaw in his strong fingers, lifting my chin. The pressure of his fingertips sends hot little sparks of electricity streaking through me, and in some dim corner of my brain, a part of me shouts a warning. This man is dangerous in ways I can't begin to comprehend, so should I be getting so close to him? Should I let him touch me like this?

But I ignore the warnings, choosing instead to look up into his eyes and seeing the heat there, bright flames of desire, and knowing that I'm the one doing this to him. I'm the one making him want.

'Are you ready?' he asks, still playing the game.

But I'm sick of games, so I put my hands on the side of the pool and push myself up, kissing him full on his beautiful, cruel mouth just as a mermaid would.

I stay there only an instant, feeling the press of his mouth on mine, the warmth and surprising softness of his lips, and I hear the sudden intake of his breath. He wasn't expecting me to do that, was he? I've shocked him, and a surge of adrenaline goes through me.

I push myself back, coming down into the water, moving slowly away, watching him, wanting to see what I did to him.

Perhaps I'm not quite done with proving my power over him after all.

He's still crouching by the side of the pool, motionless, and his smile is gone. His eyes blaze like a magnesium flare, and the raw heat in them is the most intoxicating thing I've ever seen.

'What were you going to show me again?' I ask, taunting him, my voice breathless.

'*Gattina*.' There's a rough note in the word. 'You are very naughty.'

'It's true.' I lift my hands to my hair once again, and give a sensual little stretch. 'I was the despair of my father.'

'Come here,' the Wolf orders softly. 'Or perhaps I'll come there.'

Oh, he's even more dangerous now, issuing orders like he means me to obey them. But I like it. It feels as if I'm playing with a tiger and at any moment he'll turn from a house cat into a predator, and there won't be anything I can do to stop it. It's exhilarating. I can't remember the last time I felt so like…myself.

'You won't,' I tell him, goading. 'You'll spoil all those expensive clothes.'

He rises from his crouch to his full height, all lithe, muscled grace. 'Perhaps I won't,' he agrees. 'I don't chase women as a rule and I never chase them in a pool.'

But he's not going to leave and a deep, feminine part of me knows that. It's his turn to exert his power, and I'm not immune to it. But it's my move now, and I want him to come to me. I want him to chase me. So I do the most logical thing I can think of, and pull the sports bra off over the top of my head, throwing it over the side of the pool where it lands with a wet slap against the stones.

'Suit yourself.' I reach down and slide my purple knickers off, too. 'Because I'm not getting out.' I lift the bundle of wet fabric and send them over to join the bra. 'And I like privacy when I'm swimming naked.'

The water moves like cool silk over my bare skin,

but his gaze is hot and getting hotter as he sees all of me beneath the water. I can see him too, or rather the effect I'm having on him, the long, thick outline of his cock pressing against the fly of his trousers. He's not bothering to hide it either.

'Are you sure you want to keep playing this game?' he asks softly. 'Because I'm considering taking my wedding night right now, right here.'

My mouth is dry and for a moment all I can see is him diving into the pool and catching me in his arms, pushing me against the rough stone side, his mouth on mine as he pushes the hard length of his cock into me.

Desire catches me by the throat and I'm breathless. I want that. I want that *now*.

'What's stopping you then?' I ask, my voice only shaking a little. 'Can't swim?'

He doesn't speak, staring at me. Then, pausing only a moment to get rid of his shoes and socks, he dives headfirst into the pool.

Triumph surges through me. I made him come to me. I made him chase me. But it lasts only a second, because he's surfacing right in front of me, his palms already on my bare hips as he pulls me against him. His hands are hot even under the water, but not as hot as his mouth as it descends on mine.

I tremble as his tongue sweeps inside my mouth, kissing me like he owns me, and in that second he does. He owns me completely. His kiss tastes of darkness and brandy, and it's demanding. I've never experienced anything like it. I don't know what I'm doing, but something inside me is rising, something hungry and hot, and before I understand what it is, I'm kissing him back, just as demanding as he is. He adjusts his grip, one hand on my hip, the other pushing into my hair and closing his fingers into a fist, pulling my head back so he can deepen the kiss. He gives no quarter, no mercy, ravaging me like the wolf he is.

I love the dark alcoholic taste of him, along with something rich and masculine that is all his own. It makes me feel like a starving animal, and I'm pressing myself against his hard, hot body before I know what I'm doing.

He growls deep in his throat and all at once, rough stone is at my back as he pushes me against the side of the pool. Then just as I imagined it, he lifts me, wrapping my legs around his waist. I'm panting, my fingers digging into his shoulders as he feasts on my mouth, one hand beneath the water as he jerks at the buttons of his trousers.

There's nothing but demand in both of us, but even so, when the blunt head of his cock pushes into me, I have to bite down on a cry of pain. He's big, much bigger than I thought a man would be, and he's pushing relentlessly inside me. His kiss is all heat and hunger and teeth, and I'm shivering as I take him. It hurts, but I don't want him to stop, so I curl my legs tighter around him, my nails digging into the wet cotton of his shirt.

Then he's moving and the pain fades, something else replaces it. Hot, liquid pleasure. I shake even harder as he thrusts, deeper, harder, and it's not enough. I want more. I want to take him the way he's taking me, rough and hard. I want to sink my nails into his back, leave scratches on him the way I know I'll have scratches on my back from the stone side of the pool.

I growl into his mouth and he laughs, then his teeth are sinking into my bottom lip, the sharp pain adding to the building pleasure.

'Little wolf,' he murmurs against my throat, his breath warm on my skin. 'That's what you are. Not a cat. A wolf.' Then his teeth close on the delicate cords of my neck in a sharp nip, and I jerk in his grip. He thrusts deep at the same time, and I feel myself begin to come apart.

He snakes one hand down between us, to my clit and then he brushes it lightly and I scream against his mouth as the tight knot of pleasure explodes, making me fall apart completely in his arms. Barely aware of his rough growl as he follows me.

CHAPTER TWELVE

Vincenzo

THE ORGASM THAT hits me is the most intense I've experienced in years—if ever—and for long moments afterwards, all I can do is simply hold Caterina against the side of the pool, my mind blank, mainly with astonishment at myself.

I was supposed to seduce her slowly and with patience, not dive into the water because I couldn't wait, not to mention shoving her up against the side of the pool and taking her roughly. I've never lost control with a woman. Not ever.

But…the way she knew I was there, watching her, even though I was sure I hadn't betrayed myself, had delighted me. She drew me irresistibly to her like a siren on a rock. Pale and lovely in the water with her hair smooth and silky and wet down her back. Her thick black lashes were jewelled with water drops that made her eyes look like sea emeralds, and even though I should have walked away, I didn't. I couldn't.

I wanted to confront her with the reason she left our dinner, to make sure she knew that our attraction was mutual, and when she swam to the side of the pool, her green eyes dark and challenging, I'd only intended to give her a brief kiss, the start of my seduction. Yet I hadn't expected her to be the one to kiss me then swim away, as if this was a game we were playing.

I don't chase women, but I ended up chasing her, because that kiss lit a spark inside me and that spark became a blaze that threatened to consume me whole. I almost dove into the water there and then, but I managed to restrain myself. I wasn't going to dive fully dressed into a pool simply because I wanted one pretty woman.

You goaded her into taking her underwear off.

Yes, I did. But my conscience wasn't working all that well and I wanted to see how far I could push her. How far she would let herself be pushed. She wanted me, I knew that, and it became obvious the moment she took off her bra and knickers, her pale body completely naked beneath the water.

So fucking beautiful. I should have needed more of a push than what she gave me, daring me to swim after her, but it turned out that I didn't. I was barely conscious of anything beyond my own need as I dove into the water, reaching for her and pulling her into my arms. Then she was wet and slippery and her mouth was hot and sweet, and I lost all sense of myself.

There was only her, the soft press of her breasts against my chest and the silk of her hair in my fist, her sweetness on my tongue. I'd had her up against the side of the pool before I knew what I was doing and then the first press inside her… She was hot and tight, and the movement of her hips against mine drove me mad. Then the taste of her as she came, her little screams and growls, the pressure of her thighs clenching around my waist…

You hurt her.

Cold snakes through my post-orgasmic haze. I…think I did, yes. She cried out and tensed, and of course she would, because she's a good, virginal daughter of the families.

I've hurt a good many people in my time, and not felt one flicker of regret, yet the thought of hurting her…

I look down at her dark head resting against my shoulder. She's shivering.

'Caterina.' I cup her chin, tilting her head back so I can look into her eyes. 'Are you all right?'

Her gaze is dark, the brilliant green muted, yet her cheeks are flushed and her mouth looks full and swollen from my kiss. She's so beautifully wrecked by me, I want to growl with satisfaction.

'Yes,' she says, sounding dazed.

'I hurt you.'

'Only for a moment.' She winces. 'My back is sore, though.'

I tug her forward and that's when I see the scrapes down her spine from where I pressed her against the stone side of the pool. And a curiously sharp burst of anger goes through me, at myself and my fucking lack of control. Because I know what happens when I lose it; people tend to die.

You also had sex with her without a condom.

That should make the situation a thousand times worse, yet even as my anger smoulders, a part of me, the wolf, is pleased that I've claimed her for himself. Pleased at the prospect of a child.

It's a primitive thought and one I shouldn't embrace, yet everything in me embraces it all the same. She's mine now. Mine in *every* way, and there can be no letting her go. She'll remain my wife, rule at my side, and bear my children. This will be a marriage in every way there is.

But will that be what she wants?

I don't like the murmurs of my conscience and ignore it as I get us both out of the pool. There are towels on all the sun loungers, so I sit her down on one and start drying her, being careful with the scratches on her back.

She shivers deliciously as I touch her, gazing at me from beneath thick black lashes. 'You look very serious all of a sudden,' she murmurs. 'Was it that bad?'

I'm kneeling on the stone pavers in front of her and the instant after she says the words I grip her chin firmly in my hand and force her to look at me. 'That wasn't bad,' I say, suddenly ferocious. 'That was fucking poetry.'

She blinks, searching my face as if she doesn't quite believe me. 'Oh…' Colour flushes her cheeks. '*Oh…* well. I have nothing to compare it to and I thought that look on your face meant—'

'That look on my face means I've decided you're my wife in every way there is,' I interrupt, forceful now. 'You'll be in my bed every night and once all the families are united, we'll rule over them together. You'll be the mother of my children and—'

'Absolutely the fuck not.' Her ready temper ignites, green and gold sparks glittering in her eyes. 'Are you insane?'

I grip her tighter. I will not be denied, not on this. 'I'm not. Why do you think I married you?'

But her gaze doesn't even flicker. 'To get my father's loyalty. At least that's what you told me.'

'*Gattina*.' I struggle to keep a grip on my temper, since getting angry with her will only make things worse. 'It was always going to be a real marriage at some point, surely you must know that?'

She has no such qualms. 'How would I know?' she demands. 'You didn't tell me what else you were intending beyond having sex with your mistress tonight.'

Ah, *Dio*. She's not going to let me get away with anything, is she?

'Well, I'm telling you now,' I say, refusing to feel any shame about the fact that I wasn't exactly clear when I kidnapped her. 'That's what I intend.'

'In that case, no.' She jerks her chin from my fingers. 'I want freedom, Vincenzo Argenti, not another cage.'

My grip on my temper slips and it flares in response to hers. This isn't going the way I want it to, and I have a feeling that it's my fault.

Of course it's your fault. You're treating her like an object again. The way your father treated your mother.

This time I can't ignore the thought, or the shame that comes with it. I swore to be a better man than that bastard Stefano, and yet here I am, doing exactly what he did to my mother, railroading her, ignoring her wishes in favour of my own. I'm a man who learns from his mistakes and I should be learning from this one.

So I don't move, still looking into her face as I force my temper into submission. 'You think marriage to me would be a cage? Why?'

'Why do you think?' That stubborn little chin of hers juts. 'I'll be relegated to sidelines. Not allowed to do anything but bear children and support my husband for "safety's" sake. Being the little woman looking after the home. That's a cage however you look at it.'

She's right. You know she's right.

I grit my teeth, forcing away the urgent need to press her back against the sun lounger cushion and show her exactly how good this 'cage' can make her feel. 'Then what does freedom look like to you?' I try to make the words sound less reluctant, but no doubt I fail.

She gazes back, all challenge. 'Are you asking me that because you think I need to hear it or because you actually want to know?'

Goddamn. Why had I ever thought this woman would make a good and biddable wife? When she opposes me at every turn? But oddly, when I force myself to think about it, I discover that I actually *do* want to know.

'Tell me,' I growl, getting annoyed with myself now.

Her expression is furious at first, but then that fades, and she glances down at her knees. 'I only want a normal life,' she says, her voice softening. 'I want to have a career and get a flat, have some friends. Maybe have a boyfriend and a cat.' She pauses and then lifts her gaze to mine. 'I don't want to be told what to do anymore. I don't want to be forced into a box I don't fit and never have. I don't want to be surrounded all day every day by guards. I don't want to have to fear for my own life or those of any children I have someday. And I don't want to feel as if…' Another little pause and then she forces herself to go on. 'I don't want to feel like the unloved and unwanted child my father was stuck with after my mother and brother died.'

She's got an uncanny aim when she throws those

spears of hers. They always land directly in my chest, the tips brushing up against my heart, hurting.

Unloved. Unwanted. Those words resonate in a way I don't like at all.

That was how my mother felt just before she died, and I know because she told me one night as the sedatives were kicking in. That's how I felt too, when my father struck me across the face for refusing to look at a torture session. He didn't care about me. He only cared about himself and how much I shamed him.

Elena didn't care about you either.

A sullen anger sits in my gut, an anger I don't want to acknowledge. For how my mother withdrew from me, slowly but surely retreating into herself. Nothing I did made any difference. She might not have left me physically, but she left me emotionally, and she never came back.

But then love does that to a person. It kills them slowly and by degrees, and so before it killed me, I cut it from my soul just like my father cut it away from my mother. He killed her love for him and so I killed mine for both of them, and I never regretted it.

Except I know that love hasn't died for Caterina. I saw it in her tears at dinner just before, the grief that her father hadn't come for her. Grief comes from love, and so no matter how awful her father was, she still feels some kind of love for him.

'You are not unwanted,' I say. 'Know that right now. But love will not be part of our marriage, not ever.'

Surprise flickers across her face. 'I didn't say anything about love.'

'You did. You said you didn't want to feel unloved and unwanted.'

'I didn't mean loved by you,' she snaps back, her anger returning.

'Good.' I ignore what surely can't be a kick of disappointment.

'I was talking about freedom,' Caterina says insistently. 'And love doesn't mean freedom, so why should I want that anyway?'

I narrow my gaze, searching her expression, because this talk of love, when I've only known her an afternoon and evening, is far too premature. 'Forget love,' I say, dismissive. 'I can offer you certain freedoms, but you must understand that your life will be curtailed to some extent purely because you're married to me.'

This does not mollify her. Unsurprisingly.

'You can see why I didn't want to get married, right? But, oh wait, you didn't care about what I wanted, did you?'

Her sarcastic wit amused me before, but it's not amusing me now. It's hitting me in places I thought were well defended and I don't like it one bit.

I rise to my feet, dropping the towel onto the cushions beside her, before getting rid of my wet clothes. Then I hold out my hand. 'Come, *gattina*,' I order peremptorily. 'This conversation is over. It's time for bed.'

CHAPTER THIRTEEN

Caterina

I'M SITTING ON the sun lounger naked, with him towering over me. His hand is extended as if I'm one of his mindless soldiers, ready to obey his every command, and a part of me is actually desperate to obey this command at least.

Because he's beautiful, like a sculpture of an ancient god beaten out of bronze. Every muscle is sharply delineated, the ridged plane of his stomach and the powerful length of his thighs making my mouth go dry. That and his cock, long and thick, and already getting hard.

I've never seen a naked man before in the flesh and while he's gorgeous, I still don't want to give in no matter how beautiful he is. His will is as strong as mine, and I know that if I give him an inch, he'll take a mile, and there's no way I'm going to do that. Not when he's taken so many miles already and so quickly.

I shouldn't have been so honest about what I didn't want, but it slipped out before I could think. His stroking hand was soothing as he dried me off and the warmth of his naked body was so close to mine, I felt almost relaxed. Especially after that incredible orgasm. And naturally I said something I shouldn't, and his reaction…

He'd been so very emphatic about what our marriage would be and then about love, and yes, that had made me angry. Firstly, I'd never wanted to be married at all, let alone to him, and at no point did I agree to any of the nonsense he said about children and ruling at his side. Secondly, I don't know why me saying I didn't want to be unloved and unwanted had made him suddenly go off about not wanting love in our marriage. I hardly know him, let alone love him, and he's not the kind of man I want to fall in love with anyway. He may be hot, but he's everything I *don't* want, no matter how many orgasms he gives me.

You really liked that orgasm, though.

I push the thought away hard. I may know nothing about sex, but an orgasm doesn't mean love, and this is about more than sex anyway. I don't want a man telling me what to do again. I refuse. I won't be his trophy wife, safely locked away behind glass, and I won't be his brood mare, giving him a child whenever he asks.

So, I ignore his outstretched hand, get up off the sun lounger, and walk straight past him, over to where I dumped my underwear. I wring them out then pick them up, before heading to where I left my green dress, and pick that up too. All the while ignoring him completely. Tossing the green dress over my shoulder, I turn my back on him and start walking up the stairs to the villa.

'Caterina,' he says, impatiently.

I keep walking.

'Stop, Caterina.' His voice is harder this time.

But I don't stop.

'*Caterina!*' he roars as I reach the top of the steps.

Again, I ignore him, trying to walk sedately to the villa so he can't tell how furious I am. But my walk has turned into a stalk, so he'll probably guess anyway. My skin prickles and my heart begins to race as I feel his gaze boring into my back, and part of me clenches in anticipation. It wants him to chase me again, catch me again, lose control again, fall apart with me again, because it felt so good and so powerful.

But I don't hear footsteps and the only thing I feel are those prickles, not his hot hands, and the part of me that wanted him is bitterly disappointed.

I push that feeling away too, as I stalk naked past the guards, all studiously looking the other way, because no, I'm not disappointed. He gave me my first taste of sex, and while it was good, I'm sure it's not as good as he said it was.

'*That was fucking poetry...*'

A shiver goes down my spine and something aches inside me, a longing I don't want to feel. His gaze had burned when he'd told me that, gripping my jaw tightly, as if it was important that I understand. And he meant it, I could tell. The way he came after me, the way he kissed me, the way he held me, as if he was starving for me, that was all real.

'*You are not unwanted.*'

I don't want that to touch me, but it does. Since my mother died, I've never felt wanted by anyone, and my father giving up my life as if it meant nothing to him felt like yet more confirmation of my worthlessness. Yet the Wolf wanted me, and that healed a small part of my soul.

But then he'd gone and spoiled it all by raving about

ruling with him and children, and having my freedom curtailed, and how love will never be part of our marriage.

You shouldn't have walked off. You should have stayed and made him discuss it.

How could I? When he'd been very clear he didn't want to talk about it?

I go upstairs and slam the bedroom door hard to get that snide thought out of my head, then I go into the bathroom. Dumping the wet clothes in the vanity sink, I then turn on the water in the huge white marble walk-in shower, and stand under the flow. The heat loosens my muscles, but it doesn't do anything for my fury.

You kind of did this to yourself. If you were the good little girl your father wanted you to be, maybe it wouldn't be so difficult.

I squeeze some shower gel onto my skin and angrily wash myself, even as the truth sits, sharp and cold as ice in the pit of my stomach. Perhaps it's true. Perhaps if I'd been the compliant child Dad wanted, none of this would be a problem. I'd be as happy to be Carlo's wife as I would to be Vincenzo Argenti's, wanting nothing more than to raise children, manage a household, and sit gossiping with the other *cosa nostra* wives. I'd be blind to the bars of the cage. It would only be a villa, protected by guards, nothing more.

Maybe your father was right. None of this would be a problem if you'd died along with your mother and Alessio.

My throat closes, but I swallow hard, refusing to acknowledge the pain that thought brings with it. Plenty of times I'd wished the Wolf hadn't saved me, that Mama or Alessio had been saved instead. If they had, maybe my father would have been kinder, happier... But there's no point thinking about all of that, because that's not what happened. I lived and my father never got over it.

I turn off the water and dry myself, before walking into the bedroom.

I'm suddenly exhausted and it's very late, and now my anger is ebbing, I'm inexplicably on the verge of tears. I need to go to bed and forget about the Wolf and my father for a few hours, and hopefully dream of nothing.

There's only diaphanous, silky nightgowns that are almost transparent in the drawers, so I settle for a new pair of knickers and a T-shirt to wear to bed. And I'm just about to slide under the covers when a note is pushed under my door. I scowl at it for a bit, because no prizes for guessing who pushed it there, but eventually I pick it up. Maybe it's an apology and a good faith offer to give me a new identity and a new life far away from here.

But of course it isn't.

On the white paper, words are scrawled in forceful blank ink: *How would you like your father to die?*

The Wolf is making his move and he's going punish my father for his lack of response. I pretty much expected he would, but I'm shocked that firstly, he's asking me for a method, and secondly, that my instant response is that I don't want my father to die.

He's a terrible father, but I won't stoop to his level. He left me to die without any apparent qualms, but I'm not the same as he is. The Wolf told me I wasn't a killer, and he's right, I'm not. I won't sacrifice a life for pettiness' sake, even the life of a man who doesn't deserve the chance I'm giving him.

I pick up the piece of paper, find a pen in the bedside table drawer, and scrawl on the back: *Don't you dare kill him. I'm not stooping to his level and letting him be murdered because I don't like him. He can live and be alone for the rest of his life.*

Then I shove the piece of paper back under the door.

CHAPTER FOURTEEN

Vincenzo

I'M IN A terrible mood the next morning. I slept badly after Caterina left me standing by the pool, which is not helping, but mainly I'm furious with myself for letting a beautiful, green-eyed banshee get under my skin so badly.

My terrible sleep is her fault entirely. I kept dreaming of diving into pools and reaching for her, only to feel her slippery-smooth body slide out of my hands, over and over again.

That's not her fault. That's yours.

It's a truth that I don't want to acknowledge, yet it burns a hole in my brain all the same. I'd dismissed the conversation because I didn't like the direction it was going, and besides, I was getting hard for her again and wanted her in my bed.

But, of course, my beautiful, oppositional little wife wasn't having a bar of that. She didn't explain when she got to her feet and walked proudly past my outstretched hand. Then again, she didn't need to. I could see the flames in her eyes.

She had a right to be angry.

I didn't handle announcing my intentions to her very well, that's true. I could have worded my statements slightly differently, to make them sound less like proclamations and more like suggestions. An offer of a discussion would have probably been more welcome. After all, I'm trying not to be like my father. Yes, 'trying' being the operative word.

Still, what I'm asking of her wouldn't have been any different to what the Bianchi boy would have asked, so why she got so furious is anyone's guess.

Your dismissal of love, then of the whole conversation, might have had something to do with it.

That particular thought is an uncomfortable one, particularly when I remember what she said about being unloved and unwanted. That had been an unexpected confession and there'd been pain in her eyes when she'd said it, which had made me angry. I'd tried not to be, but in retrospect, I failed badly and been dismissive instead.

She didn't need your anger. She needed your understanding.

I stalk grimly into my office with an espresso, the whispers of my long-dead conscience needling at me. I'm not used to considering other people or even understanding them, because neither consideration nor understanding affects my decisions. Their feelings don't matter in the greater scheme of things, so why I keep thinking about Caterina Salvatore's is anyone's guess.

I down my espresso in one go then sit down at my desk. I have work to do and many things to arrange, and I can't afford to be sitting here thinking about my new wife for hours on end. Yet on the desk in front of me lies the piece of paper she wrote her angry reply on, and it's impossible to think of anything else.

She's relentless in her opposition, even demanding I not issue a hit on her father, because she wants him to live. However, while I understand her qualms and have long let go wanting to avenge my mother's death, I'm still furious at him for his treatment of her. Everything in me is telling me that I need to make an example of him, yet I can't stop reading the words on her note.

I'm not stooping to his level...

She might not stoop, but I've done so many times, and while I see the irony of fighting violence with violence, as I've always believed, the ends justifies the means.

She's not thinking that, though, and now she's got me second-guessing. She doesn't want to be her father—that's what she said in the note—and like her, I don't want to be mine. Yet if I kill Giovanni Salvatore, how am I any different?

Stefano ordered the death of the Salvatore family because of the offence against our family's honour when my mother died. And in killing Giovanni, I'll be doing the same thing. I always thought that allowable, because I'd be taking out our last enemy, and besides it would end with me. Yet…

What if you didn't? What if it ended with Giovanni instead?

No, I can't start thinking like her. I have to take him out or get his loyalty, that's vital to my plans of unification, and there can be no middle ground. There never is in the families.

So why am I still hesitating? Why am I thinking about letting him live? Just because she wants me to?

I'm in the middle of puzzling through this when my door bursts open and Caterina enters the room. She's in a flowing dress the colour of sunflowers and she looks like a ray of sunshine come streaming into my office. But not her eyes. They're sharp chips of emerald mined from the dark side of the moon.

'If you've ordered his death,' she announces without preamble, 'I'll kill you myself.'

The kick of heat that goes through me at the sight of her is a drug and I can't get enough. I want to leap straight over my desk and grab her, devour her, but I can't allow that. I lost control badly last night and it's not going to happen again, so I lean back in my chair and let her fury wash over me instead.

'You have feelings about it, I gather.' I push out my chair and put one foot on the opposite knee. 'At least, judging by that note and your latest threat to my person.'

When people stand before my desk, they're usually white with fear, but not my Caterina. She storms up to the desk itself, puts her hands on the edge and leans forward. Her hair slides over her shoulders, brushing the desktop and the neckline of her dress dips, making it very clear that she's not wearing a bra.

'Damn right, I have feelings,' she says, staring daggers at me. 'He's a terrible father, but that doesn't mean I want him to die. No one should have the power to make life-and-death decisions about another human being.'

Ah, now we're getting into it. Pity. I have no patience for conversations about ethics. 'And yet people make those decisions every day,' I say, trying to keep my gaze from the neckline of her dress. 'Anyway, it's not your decision. It's mine.'

'He's *my* father,' she insists. 'Who decided you get to be judge, jury and executioner anyway?'

It's difficult to concentrate on what she's talking about, especially when she clearly has no concept of what I can see and the fact that I'm already starting to get hard. 'What do you care?' I demand, losing patience. 'I'll be the one taking his life, not you.'

She takes a breath, fury still burning in her eyes. 'Because I'll know I could have stopped you.'

'Oh yes?' I hold her gaze, letting her see what she's up against, the absolute force of my will. 'And how could you have done that, *gattina*?'

At first she's still, just staring at me. Then she takes another breath, pushes herself away from the desk and straightens up. Then before I can move or speak, she's coming around to where I'm sitting and sliding herself up onto the desk in front of me. Then she daintily places one elegant, bare foot on each of the arms of my chair and grips the hem of her dress. 'Let him live and I'll let you do whatever you want with me, Wolf.'

A wolf is what I am and a starving one at that, because I can see a little way up her dress, as she no doubt intended, to the soft, pale skin of her inner thighs, and I can smell in the air the scent of jasmine and aroused woman.

She's using sex against me, and why shouldn't she? After what happened between us last night? I'd admire her guts if I didn't want her so fucking much.

It shouldn't be difficult to refuse, it shouldn't, because this matters to me. This matters to my cause. I can't be seen to be weak, not at this time, and that's exactly what letting Salvatore live would make me seem.

But it *is* difficult to refuse. Because now all I can think about is shoving my chair back, stripping her dress off and laying her back on my desk to taste every inch of her.

'What makes you think I want to do anything at all with you?' I drawl, trying to fight her pull. 'Especially when I've already had you.'

She doesn't speak, but her gaze drops to my lap, where I'm already hard.

'Oh, that?' I don't move. 'I can easily get someone else to see to that. Or I could handle it myself. I have at least one working hand, after all.'

'You don't want your hand.' She's looking straight at me when she says this, as if she knows. As if she can see the truth in my gaze. 'You want me.'

Holy fuck, this woman... She's barely had sex, has no conception of men, yet she's manipulating me with the ease of a practiced flirt. And I'm letting her do it.

She's right. You want her. So take her.

The wolf in me will brook no argument and before I know what I'm doing, I'm shoving back my chair, and stepping between her parted thighs. My hands reach for her hips, feeling the warmth of her body through the thin fabric of her dress.

Her eyes widen and she puts out a hand, her palm landing directly on my chest. 'He lives,' she says insistently. 'Promise me.'

I don't want to. An example needs to be made, yet that's not what I say. 'Yes,' I say instead, barely even thinking about Salvatore and my wretched crusade, everything concentrated on the woman in front of me. 'I promise.'

Her hand slides up my chest, to the back of my head and she pulls my mouth down on hers, and I'm lost. She tastes sweet, like honey and vanilla, and I can't get enough. I devour her, my hands automatically dropping to grab fistfuls of her dress, pulling the hem up to her waist. She gasps against my mouth as I slide a hand between her thighs to find she's not wearing any underwear.

'Naughty, *gattina*,' I murmur as I find her sensitive little clit and stroke her there lightly. 'Using sex to manipulate me.'

She shivers, gasping again as I explore the soft folds between her thighs, stroking her, feeling how incredibly wet she is already for me. 'I… I'm not m-manipulating you,' she whispers. 'I'm only using whatever I can to make sure my father stays alive.'

I slide a finger inside her, then as she moans, another. She's so wet there's no resistance and I'm more than ready to replace those fingers with my cock. But I'm not going to do that now. I'm going to take my time now, explore her completely, undo her the way she's undoing me.

I lift my mouth from hers. 'I'm going to want more than one wedding night,' I say as I trail kisses down the side of her neck, moving my hand to drive her steadily mad. 'I'm going to want you in my bed every night.'

She sighs, her hips shifting against my hand so I withdraw it. 'Promise me,' I say, echoing her as I lift my head and look down into her pleasure-flushed face.

Her eyes are dark, forest green instead of grass, and her mouth is full and red from my kiss. She's delectable, all her anger transmuted into raw desire, and I can't help but think of all the arguments we're going to have and how sweet the making up will be.

'Please,' she says, her voice husky. 'Please…'

'That's not what I asked.' I reach out to cup one side of her face, my thumb tracing the full curve of her bottom lip. It feels so soft I want to bite her. I want to bite all of her, eat her alive. 'You must say "I promise, Vincenzo".'

She shivers, her gaze captured by mine as I ease my thumb between her lips and into the heat of her mouth. Her lashes drift shut as I feel the soft tip of her curious tongue against my skin, and my cock is so hard it's almost painful. But I'm not rushing this, not now, not like last night.

I take my thumb from her mouth, rubbing the pad of it over her lower lip, and her lashes flutter. 'Say it,' I order softly. 'Give me the words, *gattina*, and I'll consider making you come.'

She swallows, the pulse at the base of her throat racing as her lashes lift. 'I…p-promise,' she breathes.

'My name, Caterina,' I remind her as I grip the hem of her dress. 'I want you to say it. I want to hear it.'

She takes a shuddering breath and for a second I think she's not going to give it to me. But then she says, 'I promise, Vincenzo.'

My name sounds like a prayer in her mouth and abruptly, I can't wait any longer. Not that I need to now since I've got what I wanted.

'Lift your arms,' I say and she does, letting me pull the yellow dress up and over her head, and then off.

Beneath it she's naked and just as beautiful sitting on my desk as she was floating in my pool the night before. Her skin light olive and silky. Her breasts perfectly round with hard little pink nipples. Dark curls between her smooth thighs.

She looks up at me, utterly unselfconscious, as if daring me to find fault with her, but I can't. 'My wife, you are flawless,' I tell her. 'And now I'm going to give you what I promised you.'

Then I put my hands between her thighs and spread them wide.

CHAPTER FIFTEEN

Caterina

I'M SITTING NAKED on his desk, my body wound so tight I can hardly breathe. The feel of his big, warm hands spreading my legs wide apart is almost too much. I'm sensitised all over, my mouth throbbing from his kiss, my clit aching from the touch of his fingers, my sex wet and my nipples hard.

This morning I woke up, vividly remembering what had happened between us last night. But I didn't want to think about the sex and what it meant. I was wholly consumed with the idea that he'd ignore what I'd written about leaving my father alive, and issue a hit on him anyway.

In the cold light of day it seemed even more important that he live. No matter what kind of father he'd been to me, he was still my father and no one should get to say who lived and who died. Especially not the Wolf of Sicily.

So I decided that Vincenzo needed to understand that. I had to get a promise from him that he'd leave my father alone, another vow like the one he gave me when he said he wouldn't hurt me, and there was only one way I could think of to do that.

So I got out of bed and had a shower. Used some of the scented body lotion that was sitting on the vanity, smoothing it everywhere. Then I walked determinedly to the closet, leafing through the dresses until I found one that looked good on me, and I put it on. Without underwear.

He wanted me, I knew that. He'd dived straight into the water, still dressed, to get to me the night before and there had been no holding back from him. I'd tested the power of my sexuality on him last night and it had brought him to his knees, and that meant I could do it again.

I could use it to get him to do what I wanted, and since that was the only power I had here, why the hell shouldn't I?

Impetuous of me, but since I didn't want to think about what was going to happen beyond saving my father, I simply headed downstairs and bearded the wolf in his den.

He'd been as intimidatingly beautiful as he had been the night before, lounging there behind his desk. His silver eyes full of flames and a cynical, barbed amusement. He was in a white shirt this morning, the top buttons undone and the cuffs rolled up, and plain black suit trousers. Austere, yet also making him look devastatingly attractive.

I'd known a moment of doubt as I'd stormed over to him, leaning on his desk and making my demands, because he'd appeared so determinedly unmoved. But then I'd caught the dip of his gaze to the neckline of my dress and all my doubts vanished.

If he was so determined to take this path, he'd discover that there was at least one person more determined than he was. Me.

So I'd rounded his desk before he could move, and I pushed myself up on top of it right in front of him. And I'd placed my feet on the arms of his chair so there could be no doubt about what I was offering. Then I'd made my demands.

It had worked beautifully. He'd been up out of the chair, his hands on me before I'd had a moment to think, but I'd at least had the presence of mind to make him give me his promise before anything else happened. And I got that.

But I hadn't expected him to make demands of me in return, to be in his bed every night. There was danger there and I knew it, though with his hands on me, his mouth on mine, my brain was too fogged with desire to know where the danger came from. And when he'd put his thumb in my mouth, shocking me, then electrifying me with the taste of his skin, all I could think about was, yes, that's exactly where I wanted to be every night. In his bed.

I could have refused, I really could have. I hadn't needed to give in. But if I hadn't, I knew what would happen. He'd walk away from me, leaving me aching and wanting and furious the way I'd been last night, and I didn't think I could do that again.

And I know now as he spreads my thighs apart, his gaze fierce and hungry, that I'd been lying to myself last night. I didn't think sex could have the same power over me as it had over him, but it does. His every touch, his every look makes me feel wanted in a way I haven't felt since I was a child, not to mention free. I'd felt it in the pool last night as I'd taken my underwear off, daring him to come and get me, and I want that feeling. I want that freedom.

So, I can't feel any regrets as he kneels before me, spreading me apart with his fingers, and even if I had any, they're lost in a blaze of electric pleasure as he ducks his head between my legs and puts his mouth on me.

I cry out, my head going back, lights exploding behind my eyes. The slow stroke of his tongue everywhere but the place I want him to lick most of all is maddening. He's feasting on me, tasting me like I'm a banquet set before him, but he's not going to gorge. No, he's going to take a bite from every dish and take his time savouring the flavour.

'Look at me,' he growls in a dark, rough voice.

I can't help but obey, looking down into his fierce, quicksilver gaze as he spears his tongue into me. I shudder, another cry bursting from my throat. The sight of him there, with his long fingers gripping my thighs, is the mostly intensely erotic thing I've ever seen.

He licks me and nips me, exploring me, but never quite giving me what I want, and I'm panting, writhing on the desk, unable to stop from begging him. It should be humiliating to beg for anything from him, but in this moment I don't care how I sound. I just want what he promised, which was to make me come.

'Vincenzo,' I pant. 'Wolf…please…oh please.'

This time he answers, giving me the most delicate lick and caress, right on my clit, and the world explodes around me in a burst of colour and unbelievable pleasure.

The room echoes with the sounds of someone's cries,

and dimly I know they're mine. I'm lying back on his desk now, shuddering with the aftershocks, in pieces yet whole at the same time.

He rises to his feet, standing between my spread thighs, arrogantly looking down at my naked body stretched out before him as he undoes his belt. He locks gazes with me, his eyes liquid mercury, and the heat in them makes me burn all over once again.

His movements are lazy as he unbuttons his trousers and pulls down the zip of his fly, but there is nothing lazy in the way he looks at me. I expect him to pull me to him, but he doesn't. Instead, like the wolf he is, he leaps gracefully up onto the desk and looms over me on his hands and knees. He's a predator about to feast on his prey, and I'm shivering with anticipation.

He leans down to take my mouth, his kiss electric, the taste of me on his lips, and I lift my hands, threading my fingers into his black hair, feeling the rough silk of it against my skin.

I arch up, wanting him, and he slides a hand beneath the small of my back, keeping me in position. Then his weight settles on me, and his hands are moving, and I feel the thick, blunt head of his cock pushing into me.

There is no pain this time, only the most incredible pleasure and he sinks deep inside me. I moan as his hand beneath my back slides further down, gripping my butt hard, and then he begins to move. It's slow at first, agonisingly so, making me gasp and moan against him. I pull at his hair, find his mouth, then nip at him, biting at him so he goes harder, faster, but frustratingly, his kisses are as slow and sensual as the movement of his hips.

His lips burns at my throat then move lower, the scattered sparks of hot kisses raining over my breasts, his tongue lazily licking at my nipples. I'm gasping again, arching against him, begging and begging, but he only gives a dark, heated laugh against my skin and carries on driving me insane.

He slides his hands up my thighs, pulling my legs up and around his lean hips, sinking even deeper inside me, and there's nothing I can do to resist the storm of pleasure building inside me. Nothing I can do but surrender to it.

So, I do, my nails digging into his powerful shoulders as he thrusts deeply, lazily into me. And only when I think I can't bear it anymore, does he ease a finger down between us, timing a stroke over my clit with a deep thrust of his cock, and I'm lost as the storm breaks over me.

Dimly I feel him move faster, harder, and then I hear the harsh growl of my name in his ear, and I grip him tighter, holding him to me as the storm breaks in him as well.

Some time passes, I don't know how long, but I'm curiously comfortable, despite the hard wood of the desk against my back and the weight of his hard muscled body pressing down on my front. I've still got my fingers twisted in his hair, and I'm stroking it, looking at the strands of silver threading through all that ink-black. They're beautiful. As beautiful as he is.

After a moment, he lifts his head and looks down at me, his intense gaze searching mine. 'You are a revelation, little *gattina*,' he murmurs. 'I have never met a woman like you.'

He means it, I can see, and a warmth that has nothing to do with sex or physical chemistry fills me. I've never been any kind of revelation to anyone, let alone to a man like him, and I love the way he says it.

'And I've never met a man like you.' I shouldn't give him this truth, I shouldn't give him any part of me at all, and yet I find myself wanting to.

'Is that a good thing?' he asks, his voice wholly empty of the lazy, cynical amusement I'm used to hearing in it.

I stare up at him, meeting his silver gaze. 'Yes,' I say. 'It's a very good thing.'

He smiles that sexy, genuine smile of his, that turns his mouth from cruel to beautiful in seconds flat. 'Well, that's true. I am very special.'

And for the first time since I met him, my own mouth curves in response, giving him back his own smile. 'Not to mention, arrogant as hell,' I say, teasing him a little.

'That shouldn't be a surprise,' he says, his voice full of masculine satisfaction. 'I have a lot to be arrogant about.' He moves off the desk, doing his trousers back up and then, as I sit up, he scoops me up and into his arms. 'Why don't we continue this upstairs, hmmm?'

'That's the best idea I've heard from you yet,' I say as he carries me from his office.

We spend all day in his large, four-poster bed, and he shows me just how much pleasure my body is capable of. Then he lets me experiment on him, telling me what he likes, and I'm thrilled when I have him growling rough demands, before roaring my name as he comes.

But it's not until the late afternoon, when he turns in bed to take a sip of the champagne Maria brought up for us, along with some food for 'sustenance', and the sheet slips down, exposing his back. There are deep, jagged scars marring his smooth deep-olive skin. They're twisted and angry-looking, as if someone has gouged great holes his flesh, and everything in me draws tight with horror.

I must have made some kind of involuntary sound, because he puts down his champagne glass and turns back to look at me, frowning. 'What wrong?'

I'm cold all over, aware all of a sudden of where I am and exactly who he is. The Wolf of Sicily, head of the most infamous and powerful of the families. The man who's ordered hundreds of deaths and forced into submission many other families. And I'm his wife. And I'll be trapped in this cage for the rest of my life.

'Caterina,' he says my name sharp with concern. 'Are you okay?' He gently cups my cheek in his palm, and it doesn't feel like the hand of a monster or a killer. It feels warm and familiar. 'You've gone very pale.'

I don't want to be afraid of him, not now, not when I haven't been before, so I ignore the fear. Instead I say, 'Those scars on your back. What happened?'

A shadow moves in his eyes, but it's gone too fast for me to tell what it was. Then as smoothly as a key turning in a lock, the mask of the Wolf settles over his features. The face of the head of the Argenti family.

'It's not a pretty story, *gattina*,' he says lightly. 'And definitely not one to share when there are other things we could be doing.'

He's trying to distract me and if he was a different sort of man, I'd let him. But he's not a different sort of man. He is who he is and he's my husband, and I have to keep pushing so he doesn't walk all over me.

'Tell me,' I demand.

His mouth thins. He's clearly unhappy with this,

but doesn't attempt another distraction. 'The scars are from a punishment my father gave me. He was from the "spare the rod and spoil the child" school of parenting. So when I didn't obey his orders, he would whip me with his studded belt.' The Wolf says the words as if they mean nothing to him, as if they aren't connected to him at all, but all I feel is cold horror.

I was punished by my father, but he never touched me. All my punishments were psychological, little criticisms here and there, death from a thousand cuts. But this…those terrible, awful, gouges… I can't imagine the pain he must have been in.

'Don't look at me like that,' the Wolf snaps suddenly, anger flickering through his eyes. 'It was a couple of strikes, nothing more. He did much worse to other people. I got off easy, believe me.'

His anger sparks mine and I say heedlessly, 'I wasn't looking at you with pity, Vincenzo. That was horror.'

He stares at me for a long moment and I don't flinch from his gaze. Then the silver flames in his eyes abruptly die away and he says in a milder tone, 'It was twenty years ago, a long time. They don't hurt anymore.'

He's trying to reassure me, I think, but I'm not in the least bit reassured. 'What had you done to deserve it?' I ask. 'Because that seems excessive.'

'If I'd been anyone else but his heir, I would have been killed.' Unexpectedly, he looks down at the white sheet covering him. 'Stefano did love his little punishments.'

'You didn't answer me.' Suddenly it seems important that I know this. 'What was it for?'

He doesn't look up. 'I think you already know what it was for.'

A wave of ice washes over me. Of course I know. That was his punishment for letting me live.

'Vincenzo…' His name comes out hoarse, and I want to go on, but I don't know what to say. The only thing that comes to me that I'm sorry, I'm so sorry you had to bear that. I'm so sorry I was the cause. But I don't think he wants to hear that.

'No,' he says softly, a note of warning in the word. 'That part of my life is over. I ended it myself when I paid him back in kind.' Abruptly, he looks up from the white sheet, his gaze blazing into mine. 'But know this, Caterina. I never *ever* regretted saving you. Not once.'

My throat closes and there are unexpected tears in my eyes, and I have no idea why. I have no idea why my heart aches or why the thought of the pain he had to endure because of me, hurts me too. I shouldn't hurt because of what happened to him as a child, not considering all the lives he's taken and the things he's done, and yet, he doesn't seem a monster sitting here beside me in the bed.

He's only a man who was a boy, a long time ago.

'I blamed you for their deaths for years,' I tell him hoarsely, unable to stop myself. 'You were in my nightmares, always chasing me to kill me. I'm claustrophobic because I spent two days in that closet before anyone thought to check on me. I thought you were a monster.' I swallow, my throat painful. 'But I was wrong.'

More shadows chase themselves over his beautiful face. 'No,' he says softly. 'I'm still a monster, *gattina*. Don't ever think otherwise.' He lifts a hand and brushes away a tear that has escaped with a gentle fingertip. 'But you were so little. No wonder you had nightmares.'

'But those scars…' I swallow again, not sure why I'm still crying. 'What you had to endure because of me—'

'No,' he repeats, softly and yet very firmly. 'I told you. I never regretted saving you and I meant it. I mean it still.' He pauses a moment, then adds, 'You changed my life. It's because of you that I started down this road, to stop the violence. To end the killings. You were the catalyst for all of this, so how could I ever regret it?'

I don't know what to say to that and I don't know how to feel. My heart aches for him, but also for myself. Because this path I somehow sent him down, is as bloody as the path he seems to think he's avoiding. I don't want to say that, though, not now. I don't have the energy to keep pushing, and the way he's looking at me, the way he's touching me, so gently, makes me crave more of it. I don't want to fight in this moment. What I want is tenderness, gentleness, all the things I had as a little girl when my mother was still alive. The things I never got from my father.

I turn my cheek against his palm then press a kiss to the centre of it, watching as his gaze flares. He slides his hand into my hair, drawing me in for a kiss, soft and hot.

'I've never had this,' I whisper against his mouth. 'I've never had gentle or tender, not after Mama died.'

He eases my head back and looks down at me, his gaze searching my face. 'Then let me give you both, my wife. You can have all of it and more.'

He moves, turning me over onto my back. Then he rains kisses down on me, soft and sweet, my eyelids, my mouth, my neck, my throat. Going lower, kisses over my breasts and down over my stomach, before moving even lower. He kisses me gently, softly, his hands moving over me with light touches and caresses, giving me all the care and tenderness I could ever want.

I feel precious when he touches me like this. I feel cared for. I feel like a treasure, a work of art. I relax into his touch and the warmth of his body, the heat of his mouth and when at last, he moves inside me, I reach up and cup his face between my hands. Looking into his eyes as he builds the pleasure inside us both, I see my own passion reflected back at me. We are one in this moment and it feels like being finally whole. As if I've been missing another part of myself and never knew it until now.

He leans forward to kiss me, but I shake my head. 'No,' I murmur. 'I want to watch you come.'

His eyes gleam at that and so he holds my gaze, slowing his movements. But it's not desperate the way it was downstairs in his office. It's a journey we're going on together, building wonder as we go, lingering in each second of pleasure and enjoying the anticipation.

But like every journey, there's an end, I can feel it bearing down on me and I can see it bearing down on him too. But he's a master at this, I already know, and he times it just right, so at the ending of the road we meet and step over the edge together.

The world expands around us, bathing us in light, the silver in his eyes becoming incandescent as he falls with me, his arms gripping me tight.

CHAPTER SIXTEEN

Vincenzo

IT'S A BEAUTIFUL morning as I step out onto the terrace, the little gift I've bought for my beautiful wife safely in my pocket. It was delivered to me late last night and I can't wait to give it to her.

Maria has set a beautiful breakfast table for us with fresh brioche, coffee, jam and honey, fruit and all manner of other delicious breakfast things. There are mimosas also, so we have something to toast with, because I'll certainly be wanting to toast.

The past two days have been... Well, when I told her she was a revelation, I meant it. From the moment I took her dress off in my office, before laying her across my desk, she was flawless. Utterly beautiful. Then how sweetly she fell apart in my arms, saying my name, and the taste of her...

Fucking exquisite.

I *had* to give her my vow not to end her father's life just as she had to give me her vow to stay in my bed, because there simply wasn't another option. Not when her body was made for mine and vice versa. Besides, it's easy enough to make Salvatore disappear, and then I'll crush his allies.

Still, spending the rest of that day in bed with her was the happiest I can ever recall being. Even when she asked me about the scars on my back. I wasn't expecting her to say anything about them, but of course that was foolish of me. They're extremely visible and while I have no hang-ups about them, no one has ever asked me about them before. I didn't want to tell her, not when she was the indirect cause, but when my *gattina* asks me a question, I have to answer.

I didn't mean to make her cry, though, and I certainly didn't want her to either, not for me. It seems that beneath her fiery anger and her sharp claws, my wife has a soft heart, something I should have thought about when she demanded I spare her father. It broke me a little to see her pain, especially when she told me she'd had no tenderness, no gentleness, not since her mother died.

All I'd wanted to do in that moment was to give her everything she wanted. My family was the reason she'd missed out on all the things a mother should have given her, the reason her father had been so awful to her, and she needed some recompense for that.

So, I did give it to her. I worshipped her like the goddess she is, with as much care and tenderness as I was capable of, and I surprised even myself. At the end, when she looked into my eyes as we both came together…

You can never let her go now.

No. Never. I wasn't going to anyway, naturally, but now I'm certain. She's a woman of great worth and she's mine, and I'll keep her at my side and in my bed. I'll give her everything she's ever wanted.

She thought you were a monster, though, remember? And you know she's not wrong...

But I don't want to think about that. Instead, I concentrate on my anticipation as I take the box out of my trouser pocket and place it in the middle of her plate. I left her sleeping this morning, so I could finish up making the necessary arrangements for her father's disappearance. Giovanni's new life will be an uncomfortable one, especially considering the identity I gave him has a record a mile long. They don't like drug dealers in Thailand, but I'm sure he'll agree that life in a Thai jail is better than death.

I go over to my chair and sit down, waiting for my wife to join me, but a couple of minutes pass and she doesn't arrive, so I get up again. I'm strangely restless, so I pace over to the edge of the terrace, to the stone parapet, and pause there a moment, glancing out to sea. Then I turn and pace back to the table, once more checking that everything is in place.

Then I hear a light footstep and when I look up, there she is in the doorway to the terrace. She's wearing a simple dressing gown of peacock-blue silk, with a silk belt loosely tying it closed. Her inky hair riots over her shoulders in the way I love so much, like thunder-clouds I can actually touch and caress.

She blinks at me sleepily, then comes over to where I'm standing and lifts her arms, winding them around my neck as she rises on her toes to press a delicious kiss against my mouth. I take the kiss and deepen it, my hands resting on her hips as I tug her more firmly against me. She feels so good, all hot and silken and female, and I can already feel myself getting hard once again. My hunger for her is relentless. It feels as if I can never get enough.

After a few moments, I lift my head, looking down into her beautiful eyes. 'Breakfast first, *gattina*. You got a healthy workout last night.'

She flushes the colour of roses, the blue in her gown somehow turning her eyes a brilliant turquoise. 'I did. And I blame that solidly on you.'

'I didn't hear any protests.'

Her mouth curves in a smile that makes my chest ache. 'That's fair. There were none.'

I gently untangle her arms from around my neck, pausing to hold her fingers in mine and then turning her palms up and laying a kiss in the centre of each one. 'Sit, my wife. I'll pour you coffee.'

Still flushed, her eyes sparkling like rare gems, she goes to her chair and I insist on pulling it out for her. She sits, her gaze dropping to the little box in the middle of her plate.

'What's this?' she asks.

I round the table and sit down in my own chair, my anticipation building to ridiculous levels. 'A little gift,' I tell her. 'A wedding gift if you like.'

Her forehead creases. 'But I didn't get you anything.'

'Of course you didn't.' I lean forward, my elbows on the table. 'You didn't know you'd be marrying me, remember?'

'True.' She glances down at the box again then picks it up and opens it. Her eyes widen and my pleasure and satisfaction pull tight.

Sitting in a cushion of black velvet are two rings. One a platinum wedding band studded with emeralds, the other a matching engagement ring with a huge emerald in the centre, surrounded by diamonds.

They're beautiful rings and they match her perfectly, making up for my error in getting a simple band when it should have been these all along. And naturally, I couldn't get just a wedding band. She needed an engagement ring too.

Caterina sits there, staring down at them, and I'm waiting for her face to flush with pleasure and her eyes to glitter with happiness. I'm waiting for her to take them out of the box and demand that I put them on her finger. I'm waiting for her to exclaim and hold out her hand, watching the sun catch the light in the jewels and making them sparkle.

But she does none of those things.

Instead she keeps looking at the rings and says nothing at all.

Something in my chest tightens, my muscles tensing. 'Well?' I ask, unable to keep the impatience from my voice. 'Do you like them?'

She doesn't look at me and disappointment kicks hard inside me. Then, hard on its heels, anger. I force them down, because maybe she's simply shocked, maybe that's all it is. Or maybe she doesn't like emeralds, or even rings. Maybe she doesn't wear jewellery at all and she's worried about my response.

'If you don't like the emeralds,' I offer, 'I can get you a different stone. Or maybe even earrings or a necklace if you don't wear rings. If you don't want jewellery at all then I can—'

'What does this mean, Vincenzo?' Finally, she lifts her gaze from her plate. There's no joy in her face, or even pleasure, no, it's anger that glitters in her eyes now.

My disappointment twists hard and part of me is shocked by its intensity. Shocked by how much I wanted her to like these, by how important her opinion has become to me. How important *she* has become and how quickly.

I don't like it. No one should be *that* important to me, no one. There's only one thing of any importance in my life and that's my crusade. Nothing comes before that.

So I shove the feelings aside and force a smile, leaning back in my chair as I clasp my hands together. 'It can mean anything you want it to mean.' My lazy tone has never felt so forced. 'I bought them because I thought you might like a prettier wedding band and an engagement ring to match.'

'Don't do that,' she says unexpectedly, her green gaze seeing right through me. 'Don't do that cynical amusement thing you do.'

A flash of anger hits me, even though I know she's right about the mask I wear, but I'm not happy with her pointing it out. 'I'm not doing anything, *gattina*. I'm merely disappointed that you don't like them.'

She stares at me then picks up her mimosa and takes a long swallow, toasting precisely nothing. 'It's not that I don't like them,' she says at last, putting her glass back down. 'They're beautiful.'

I know better than to let that mollify me. 'Then what's the issue?' I demand. 'If you don't want them, I can—'

'No. The issue is that I never agreed to marry you in the first place.'

'I know you didn't,' I say, my hold on my temper starting to fray. 'We've been through this. But the fact remains that we're husband and wife now.'

'So?' She's sitting rigid in her chair, her whole body looking as tense as mine feels. 'I never wanted that.'

'You were going to marry Bianchi,' I point out, a strange and totally out of proportion anger simmering in my gut. 'Which means you'd have ended up marrying anyway, so aren't you glad you ended up with me instead?'

'You're not listening. I never wanted to marry Carlo. I never wanted to marry *anyone*.'

'It's done now,' I say flatly. 'And it can't be undone.'

'Bullshit.' Her eyes glitter like the emeralds in the box, all sharp edges, anger flickering and leaping like a hot green fire. 'We can get a divorce and you can let me make my own choices.'

My whole body goes tight with negation. Divorce her? Let her go? The wolf in me growls with fury at the thought, but I try to reel it back in. This anger is pointless and why I'm letting it get to me is anyone's guess.

'No,' I say, putting every ounce of will I possess into the word. 'It's too late for that, Caterina.'

'Why?' she demands, her will matching mine strength for strength. 'I want to be free to make my own decisions, Vincenzo. I want a life that isn't…this.' She waves a hand at the villa surrounding us. 'I've already told you that.'

'You did, but my answer is the same. It's too late for you to have that life, not now you're married to me.' I hold her gaze so she understands how serious I am, because it's not just about me and what I want. Now she's married to me, it's an issue of personal safety. 'You're an Argenti and it doesn't matter if you divorce me. You'll always be an Argenti in the eyes of the families, and you'll always be a target. And I'm sorry, but I can't let you go only for someone to hurt you. I'll never agree to that.'

She takes a breath, continuing to stare furiously at me. 'Then give me a new name and a new life, the way you've done for others. That's easy for you to do and no one need ever know.'

For a minute I regret ever telling her about the people I've sent on to a new life elsewhere, because I could arrange that for her as I've arranged it for her father. But as I've told her, it's too late for that. It's too late for her to be free in the way she wants, because now she's mine.

Why is holding onto her so important?

I ignore the thought. 'And what will you do if in three months' time you find yourself pregnant?' I demand instead, which is a low blow even if it's true. She could be pregnant. We didn't use any birth control, and I'll be damned if a child of mine is born outside the Argenti family.

She pales at that. 'If I'm pregnant, I'll let you know, of course. I'd never keep your child from you, Vincenzo.'

'But will you even keep it?' I'm being blunt and forceful, and these questions are difficult ones for her to answer, and I know that. But I don't care. If she's pregnant with my heir, I will take them both.

The rest of the colour leaves her face and she abruptly drops her gaze at the ring boxes again. 'I don't know,' she says more quietly. 'I haven't thought about it. I haven't thought about having children at all.'

'Which is not a risk I'm willing to take.' I don't disguise the iron in my voice. 'If you're pregnant, I'll keep the child and since a child should never grow up without their mother, I'll also keep you.'

She looks up at me again. 'And if I don't want to be kept?'

'You'll survive,' I tell her. 'Somehow, in this beautiful villa with a husband that keeps you well satisfied and where you won't have to worry about money, and you can have everything you've ever wanted.'

CHAPTER SEVENTEEN

Caterina

He's lounging back in his chair with a casual arrogance that's both incredibly sexy and incredibly infuriating at the same time. Anger burns in his silver eyes, the hurricane force of his will howling against me from across the table.

But anger is burning a hole inside me too, along with a sliver of pain I can't identify. It's as if a splinter of glass has caught inside me, cutting me, putting holes in me, and it hurts.

The past two days have been so wonderful, nothing but lying in bed and making love, and talking with the Wolf about everything and nothing. He's a fascinating man, if opinionated, and we've had fun arguing with each other about little things that don't matter. And arguing is fun when you can make up afterwards in the most pleasurable way possible. But it was the tenderness he gave me that changed everything. I asked for it and he gave it to me, making me feel better than I have for years and years.

After I'd woken up this morning, I'd come downstairs to find him, wanting nothing more than to kiss him and lure him back to bed, only to walk onto a beautifully prepared terrace, with breakfast on the table, and a gift on my plate.

I didn't think anything of it initially, only a tight squeeze of pleasure that he'd bought something for me. Then I'd opened it and looked at what was inside and the happy little bubble I'd been inhabiting for the past two days abruptly popped.

I'm his *wife* and how could I have forgotten that? I'm married to a notorious man, whose only goal in life is to build empires and who'll let nothing stop him from doing that. And I can't ever leave, because no one leaves the *cosa nostra*, no one ever.

Being his wife means I'll never be free, and looking down at those rings, I could see that life stretching out before me, hemmed in by guards everywhere I go. I'll never be alone, never have a little flat with maybe a garden, never have a job or career of my own. I'll be relegated to being his trophy, kept safe and secure in that glass cabinet. Taken out to play with on occasion, but mainly being left there. And if we have children... Their lives would be forever at risk.

It's about more than that though, isn't it? None of this is about you.

I shove that thought away though, because why should I care? It doesn't matter what this is really about. I should have considered what he'd told me a couple of days earlier, about how I'd be his wife and rule the families at his side, or some such nonsense, and I'd let him distract me. I'd let myself be distracted by him.

But I can't do that any longer. I'm not staying here. I'm not going back to the life I had as a child, with all the expectations that were placed on me. All the boxes I was forced into or made to fit. I'm not going back to being punished for who I am either, not certainly not for him.

I stare into Vincenzo Argenti's eyes and hold his gaze with mine. 'Everything, except the one thing I actually want,' I say. 'My freedom.'

His anger flickers, the stark planes and angles of his face hardening. 'Freedom,' he echoes, saying the word like it's made of poison. 'What does it even mean? Who is ever free? There'll always be demands on you, always be other people you have to think about. Always things you have to do. No one is ever truly free, Caterina.'

'That's not what I'm talking about.' I'm frustrated now. 'I want to be free of the families. I want to have my own life, a normal life. One where I don't have to worry about being kidnapped or murdered, where I don't have to keep looking over my shoulder. Where I can make my own choices and decisions without someone else making them for me.'

His expression is like granite, the beautiful smile he gave me when I kissed him just before, vanishing as if it never was, and my heart aches at the change. This mask he wears as the head of his family, as the Wolf of Sicily, it's not him. It's not the tender, caring man who stroked me and kissed me as if I was made of glass, who argued with me passionately about something as ridiculous as whether chocolate was better than ice cream, who washed my hair in the shower last night, treating it like it was the most important task he'd ever done. It's not him and I don't like that. I want that other man back.

'That is not possible,' he says. 'And you know why it isn't. I've just told you why.'

My throat is tight but I don't want to cry, so I swallow it back. 'Of course it's possible,' I say sharply. 'You can give me a new identity. But you won't, will you? Because you can't bear to let what's yours go, isn't that right?'

He shifts in his chair as if I've said something uncomfortable, which is strange. He's possessive, all the men in the families are, and I know why. They value respect and honour, and the trophies they earn, not actual people.

'I can give you some freedom,' he says as if I've forced the words out of him. 'I can make sure any bodyguards give you space, and I'll—'

'No.' I don't care that I've interrupted him. 'That's not what I want and you know it. All my life I've been a thing, a pawn for my father, not a person, and I'm tired of it. I was told that if I wanted the deaths of Mama and Alessio to not be in vain, I had to do what he said. He made me responsible for fixing our entire family, and I'm tired of it, Vincenzo. I'm tired of having to do what everyone else wants me to do.'

'You're not a thing or a pawn, Caterina,' he says fiercely, leaning forward all of a sudden. 'And you don't have to fix anything here. You don't have to do anything but what you want here. That freedom I can certainly give you.'

My throat closes entirely, because I can see he wants to give that to me. But while it's something, it's not everything, and that's just not enough for me.

'That might be enough for a while,' I say. 'But what about in a year? Two years? What about in ten years?'

'What about it?' His gaze searches mine. 'What is scaring you so much, *gattina*? Is it only that this wasn't your choice? Or is there something more to it than that?'

I blink and take a breath. Having choices is very important to me since I've been deprived of them for so long, but I know he's right, that it's not only the lack of choices that bothers me. I have to face that thought now, the one I wanted to ignore, about how being his wife and being in his bed isn't really about *me*. Because what will happen as time goes on? When our physical hunger for each other fades? When we have children? When the march of his crusade goes on and on and on? What will our marriage end up being like then?

I take another shaky breath. 'I meant what I said, Vincenzo. Where will we be in five years? In ten? What about this crusade of yours? And if we have children, what about them?'

He frowns, not understanding me. 'The crusade will end eventually and I'll keep our children safe. I'll keep all of us safe, believe me.'

'I'm not talking about safety.' I don't want to have this discussion, but I need to. *We* need to. My feelings are confused because all of this has happened so quickly. He's so much more than I ever imagined he'd be.

You're not falling for him already, are you?

No. No, definitely *not*. Again, he's not what I want in a man. There's too much death around him, too much violence, no matter how kind and caring he's been to me. I have to make him see reason about this marriage of ours, because I don't want to be tied to him forever.

'I'm talking about a relationship. About us being together.' I swallow, my mouth dry as I remember something else he told me. 'You said that love can never have any part in our relationship, and I… I don't want that. I don't want our children looking at us and seeing that we don't love each other.' My eyes prickle. 'I don't want a child of mine to ever look into their father's face and see only anger and resentment staring back.'

Shock crosses his face—he clearly didn't expect that—but just as quickly, his expression is wiped clean. 'Our children will survive,' he says in a hard, flat tone. 'Children can be remarkably resilient.'

'The same way you were resilient when your father laid his belt across your back?' I snap before I can think better of it.

Fury ignites in his gaze. 'I will *never* be like him.'

'No, but children being resilient sounds exactly like the kind of thing he'd say.' As soon as the words leave my mouth, I know I've gone too far.

Vincenzo shoves his chair back violently, the legs scraping on the stone, then rises, his eyes gone molten with anger. He puts his hands on the table and leans in on them, the force of his will battering at me. 'I put a bullet between that man's eyes for what he did to my mother and I. Did you know that?'

I heave in a breath, shock flickering through me. Not that I hadn't heard the rumours about him, and he's alluded to it before. But it's different to hear the truth he's flinging at me now.

My mouth goes even drier. 'I've heard rumours. But what did he do to your mother?'

'He beat her down.' The Wolf's voice is sharp as a knife, his gaze stony. 'She loved him and he cut that love out of her heart and ground it into the dust. She was a beautiful, fiery, amazing woman and by the time she died, she was a broken shell. Because of him.'

I go cold. The only thing I knew about Stefano's wife

as I grew up was that she'd died in a car bombing that my father had engineered. Yet it's clear from the look in Vincenzo's eyes that she was so much more than that. She was his mother and he loved her very much, and he loves her still.

'I'm sorry,' I say huskily, another little piece of my heart turning into glass and cutting me.

'Don't be sorry.' The bitterness in his voice is painful. 'It wasn't your fault, Caterina. Her death can be laid at Giovanni's door, it's true. But she died long before that. And that's no one's fault but my father's. That's why he had to die.' His mouth twists. 'Can you see the irony? I killed my father while you spared the life of yours.'

Oh, I can see it. Just as I see the shadows of grief and guilt and pain in his eyes. It cost him. It cost him to end his father's life and I suspect it costs him to end every life.

'Again, I'm sorry,' I say, my heart hurting for him though I'm not sure why. He shouldn't matter to me, not at all, yet somehow he's become more important to me than I ever thought possible. 'Not that he's dead. I'm sorry that there wasn't another way for you.'

Vincenzo's eyes widen slightly, as if he's not expecting the comment, then I see flashes of other emotions. But they're gone too fast for me to understand. 'Are you worried for my soul, *gattina*?' His voice has fallen back into that dark, cynical amusement again. 'If so, don't be. That's why I have a family priest, after all.'

He shoves himself upright, then rounds the table, pausing by my chair. I'm tense, my heart racing. I want to touch him, tell him it's okay, comfort him in some way. Anything to coax out the man behind that silver-eyed mask.

'Vincenzo,' I say softly. 'Please…'

He ignores me. Instead he reaches down and carefully, with a certain deliberateness, picks up the ring box with the beautiful rings in it. 'If you don't want these, that's fine. Annika might like them instead. She always was very fond of emeralds.'

Then he puts it in his pocket and strides back into the villa.

CHAPTER EIGHTEEN

Vincenzo

I LEAVE THE villa an hour later, heading over the lawn to the helicopter. I have business in Naples and I'm more than ready to forget what just happened between Caterina and I, lose myself in the day-to-day operation of my business.

The meetings I attend run all day and into the evening, ending only at midnight. But I'm too restless to fly back to the villa, not to mention too angry.

The volcanic fury sitting inside me is no one's responsibility but mine, and I need to get a handle on it somehow. After all, people tend to die when I get angry.

So, at three in the morning, I'm sitting in a rooftop bar, drinking vodka, watching the lights of the city spread out beneath me. The associates I was meeting with, and who've been drinking with me, have all left, mainly with women, and there's another woman beside me. She's almost in my lap and has making noises about going somewhere more 'comfortable', but I'm half-drunk and only half listening, because I can't stop thinking about Caterina.

The ring box is still in my pocket, my empty threat

about giving the rings to Annika echoing in my ears. I was never going to give them to Annika. Those were bought for Caterina and Caterina alone. I only said that to her because I was furious and I wasn't sure why.

She told you you sounded like your father.

Fuck. That's true. I was already disappointed because she didn't want the rings or me, that she only wanted her so-called freedom, so that comment only kicked my rage into high gear. I'd built my life these last twenty years on *not* being him, never ever. So to tell me that I sounded just like him was… A red rag to a bull.

But that's not all she did.

I grit my teeth, not wanting to remember the look in her eyes after I told her that I'd shot Stefano. The look of pity that glowed there and her saying sorry that there hadn't been another way for me, as if she'd been concerned about me. About the effect killing my own father had on me.

She was right to be concerned. You're a monster.

My jaw aches and I down the glass of vodka in my hand. The liquid is ice-cold and it burns on the way down, but it does nothing to ease the leaden weight in my gut.

She's right to be concerned, but there's nothing I can do about it now. My hands are so red it doesn't matter whose blood is whose, and I accepted that as my role the day I picked up the gun and shot him with it. What's done is done. There are no second chances, no shots at redemption, and there are none for her either.

Why not though? Why not give her the freedom she wants?

She's right, it would be simple, but I can't do it. I

won't. She wouldn't be safe no matter how many new identities she has, and that's not even considering the fact that she might be pregnant.

The wolf growls a protective warning at the thought of children, and the man is in agreement. My child, out in the world and unprotected is a possibility I can't even think about. Just as I can't think of bringing up any child of mine without their mother, because I know just how painful that is.

So no, she's going nowhere. She's staying at my side and I will consider all the ways and means to give her as much freedom as I can, but that's as far as I'll go. And I'll make sure that what she said about her own father, about looking into his eyes and seeing only anger and resentment, will never happen to our child. I won't let it.

The woman next to me slides a hand up my thigh and leans in to whisper in my ear, promising me all kinds of naughty things. But both her hand and her voice leave me cold. I know the woman I really want and she's not here.

Perhaps I won't stay in Naples after all. Perhaps I'll fly back to the villa. There are many ways I can convince my wife that's she's better off with me. No one else can give her what I can. No one.

Gently but firmly, I take the woman's hand off my thigh. I tell her she's beautiful, but I'm married and I will not be taking her to bed. She pouts a little, then leaves to find another, more receptive man.

I exit the bar, slightly amazed at myself for refusing what she was offering on the grounds that I'm married. Which I am, of course, but I never anticipated that I'd actually be faithful to the wife I kidnapped. And I am.

I don't want another woman, I realise. I don't want anyone else but the woman I married. My Caterina. Now, at the thought of her and the pleasure we shared, my body is waking despite how tired and half-drunk I am. It never woke for that other woman. Not even a flicker.

I organise the helicopter and soon I'm flying through the dark night back to Sicily.

I land just as dawn is breaking. I debate the merits of taking some time to sleep before seeing her, but I can't wait, so I proceed up the stairs to my bedroom—our bedroom—to wake her. But she isn't there.

Discomforted and unreasonably annoyed by her absence, I cross the hallway to her room and push open the door. But she's not there either.

A flicker of alarm goes through me. Where is she? Has she managed to escape somehow? But that's impossible. My security is second-to-none and they would have informed me if she'd somehow left.

I go downstairs and ask one of my guards where my wife is, only to have him inform me that she woke early and wanted to go for a walk on the beach at the base of the cliffs. No, she is not alone. Yes, she has eyes on her.

The relief that sweeps through me is impossible to deny, yet I have no time to think about why that is. Instead, I go quickly to the stone path that zigzags down the steep cliffs to the beach.

It's where I used to walk with my mother, barefoot in the silky golden sand with the waves crashing on the shore. Back before I become the wolf and she became a husk of a woman. Before my father beat the both of us into the shapes he wanted us to be. Me, his perfect heir. Her, his perfect wife.

There are guards at the base of the path and I nod my approval as I go past them. I can see her now, dressed in some kind of billowy, white nightgown that the wind catches, walking slowly along the sand, her back to me. She has her arms wrapped around herself, though the wind isn't cold, and I watch as she pauses and turns to face the sea.

She looks so like my mother, the way she's standing and gazing out at the ocean like a desert island survivor looks for rescue. It sends a spear of ice right through me.

You know what you're doing to her, don't you?

I stop dead in the sand as the realisation comes to me. An unwelcome realisation. Because of course I know what I'm doing to her.

If she's standing here on the beach, looking for rescue just like my mother, then I am my father, keeping her here. I am my father, accepting the parts of her that I like and rejecting the rest. Her need for freedom, her need to have a normal life, her need to feel safe.

I want her passion, her fire and her anger, yet I also want her to obey me, to stay here at my side, to accept the fact that I'm the head of the family and I decide what happens, not her.

The spear of ice twists inside me and a burst of pain radiates out through my chest, squeezing my heart.

It happened gradually to my mother. Stefano slowly crushed the life out of her with his insistence that she never argue with him. He was the head of the family and as his wife she had to obey, and even though he never hit her, his constant belittlements and criticisms took their toll.

Her failure to give him more children incensed him and so he exiled her here to the villa, making her stay so the doctors could examine her and give her special diets, and on occasion sedate her to keep her 'calm'. All so she could conceive.

He didn't stay with her. He kept her like a princess in a tower, his brood mare that he would visit every week to encourage a conception.

She loathed being a prisoner. That's why she and I would walk along the beach every day. As a child I'd thought nothing of it since she'd make each walk an adventure, but in retrospect I knew that she paced the beach like a tiger pacing around the bars of a cage.

Until my father decided that she should join him in Rome for some big family meeting and the car she was in exploded. I was devastated when I learned she'd died. But now, with the benefit of hindsight, I wonder if in that moment of death she felt finally free.

You cannot do that to Caterina.

The world slows and stops as I stare at the tall, slender figure of my wife, standing and looking out to sea. The wind blows her black hair around her face and makes her nightgown billow around her calves, and the spear of ice in my chest begins to melt, filling my veins with ice water.

I try to ignore it, pushing the thoughts away as I make myself continue on to where she stands. She must have seen my approach but she doesn't turn, her attention still on the distant horizon.

Dawn is flaming, the sun rising from the sea, red and

pink shading the dense dark blue of the sky. Another beautiful sunrise, but all she is looking at are the bars of her cage, isn't she?

'My mother and I used to walk along this beach,' I say after a moment. 'We would look for shells and sea glass and pretty stones. Sometimes I'd pretend to be a pirate, and I'd kidnap her in my pirate ship, but then we'd become friends. She'd draw maps in the sand and tell me about all the places we'd sail to, and have adventures there.'

The waves lap against the sand. The tide is coming in. If she's not careful, my wife will get her feet wet, yet she doesn't seem to notice.

'That sounds idyllic,' she says, still looking out over the sea.

'It was.' I pause a moment. 'Until I realised that my mother was trapped here and she came to the beach to feel free.'

Slowly, Caterina turns to me, her hair blowing around her face. Her green eyes are shadowed, and there are dark circles under them. 'Why was your mother trapped here?'

I push my hands into my pockets. 'My father wanted more children and decided that she needed to stay here being looked after by doctors and having her diet monitored. She'd be sedated sometimes too. He thought that would make it more likely for her to conceive. He used to visit her once a week.'

'That's awful.'

'Yes.' I meet her gaze. 'She couldn't leave and nothing she did or said could make my father change his mind. She had three miscarriages and after that, fell into a deep depression. After five years of being trapped here, my father eventually brought her to a family meeting in Rome and that's when she was killed by the car bomb.'

There are flickers of pity and horror in Caterina's eyes, and no wonder. Not considering her own position here and the similarities between my mother and herself.

'Is that how you're going to treat me?' she asks bluntly.

I'm expecting the question, so I don't hesitate. 'No. Of course not. I would never do that to you.'

'And yet that's what you're doing. I'm trapped here. You won't even consider giving me my freedom.'

You know she's right.

I know she is, I know. Yet I can't accept her leaving me. 'You're not trapped here, *gattina*,' I remind her and myself. 'You can leave. With the appropriate security, naturally. You're not a prisoner.'

She turns fully to face me now, her arms still wrapped around herself. I can see goose bumps rising on her skin, so I slip my jacket off and move over to her, putting it around her shoulders.

She doesn't resist, looking up at me. 'I'm just an object to you, aren't I? Just a thing. A wife at your side, a sex toy in your bed and an incubator for your children.'

She's so direct, so blunt, but she's wrong.

'No,' I say, suddenly fierce. 'That's not how I think of you.' Her jaw is tight, her body stiff with anger, but I reach for her, pulling her against me. She's so warm and despite my tiredness, my cock is hard and getting harder. I grip her hips firmly, feeling the softness and heat of her skin beneath her thin nightgown. The fabric is slightly transparent and I can see the pink of her nipples through it, and I feel suddenly feral at the thought of all my guards being able to see them too.

'What you want matters,' I say to her, meaning every word. 'I can work it so that our life will be as normal as possible, I promise. You'll never be a prisoner here. If you like, I can find you an apartment anywhere in the world that can be yours and yours alone. And you can visit it anytime you want.'

Her body is still stiff with resistance, her features set, so I lift my hands from her hips and cup her face between my palms. Emotions move through her green eyes, fury, pain, sadness. They are precious, these emotions of hers, and I want to ease her. Soothe her in any way I can, which is unlike me.

'I can make it easy for you,' I murmur, bending to her mouth and pressing a soft kiss there. 'I can make it so you'll be freer than you've ever felt in your life.' Another kiss. 'There are no bars on this cage, *gattina*.' Another kiss to her jaw. 'There is no cage at all.'

CHAPTER NINETEEN

Caterina

HIS HANDS CUPPING my face are warm and his mouth making its way down the side of my neck is hot. The kisses he presses against my skin burn and my body is starving for him.

After he walked away from our breakfast yesterday morning, I heard the helicopter come and go, and realised he had left the villa. I checked with Maria and indeed, he'd apparently gone to Naples for the day on business. And no, she didn't know when he was coming back.

My disappointment that he'd gone seemed out of all proportion, so I tried to tell myself that I was glad. He'd left in a huff after I hadn't liked his rings, and he'd taken them with him, and if he gave them to his stupid mistress, who cared? Certainly I didn't.

But as the day progressed and I couldn't seem to settle, wandering around the villa restlessly with a pressure in my chest that was starting to turn into pain, I was forced to admit to myself that actually *I* cared.

I cared that I'd upset him. I cared that his father had been such a terrible person, that he'd lost his mother, that he was clearly still grieving her. I cared that he'd been turned into a killer because of an accident of birth, and I was starting to suspect that it wasn't in his nature.

I went in search of Maria in the end, and had a conversation with her about Vincenzo as a boy, since she'd been their housekeeper since he'd been a child. He'd been a kind little boy, she'd told me. He'd rescued a kitten once, and loved his mother. He'd had a puppy for a while until his father took it away to train it into a 'proper' dog, and it came back and killed one of the cats he'd rescued. He'd been inconsolable.

The only time his mother had been happy, Maria told me, was when she was with him, and he was the only one who could make her laugh.

It hurt to hear those stories. It hurt to hear what his father had taken from him and his mother, and it made me so angry too. It was lucky that Stefano Argenti was already dead, because if I'd had a weapon, I'd certainly have taken it, found him and shot him myself.

After that I'd put on a swimming costume and gone down to the pool, swimming laps and then floating on my back the way I remembered from long ago. I kept waiting for his voice to follow me, to see him coming down the steps from the villa, but there were only his guards, keeping watch.

I was disappointed. I was so bitterly disappointed and I didn't know why.

Eventually, after realising he wasn't coming back here anytime soon, I let Maria cook me dinner and I watched TV until late, trying to distract myself. Then I'd gone to bed. I didn't use his bedroom, but the one I'd been given.

My dreams were full of darkness and I was running

down a shadowed hallway, trying to escape from something or someone. And then the dream changed so that I was the one doing the chasing. I'd woken just before dawn, feeling unrested and groggy, so I'd gone down the stone path to visit the beach, needing some fresh air to clear my head. It was such a beautiful beach that I'd stayed to watch the sunrise, trying to ignore the guards that stood on the stone path, looking down at my every move.

And just when I was thinking about going back up to the villa, out of the corner of my eye I could see a man walking towards me. Tall and powerful, moving with that familiar lithe grace.

My heart had jumped in my chest and when he came to stand beside me, I'd been filled with the inexplicable urge to turn and throw myself into his arms. But I'd forced the urge away. I didn't want him to think anything had changed from when he'd walked away the day before.

Then he'd told me about his mother and how they'd used to go walking on this beach, and in my head I could see him, a little boy running beside her as they found treasures in the sand. Then watching in delight as she drew him maps and told him of all the places they would visit.

A little boy's dream. But only a dream, because his mother had been held prisoner here and all because of his father.

My chest had tightened and it's still tight now as he presses another kiss at the base of my throat. His body is so hard and hot, a delicious contrast to the cold wind blowing around me. I can smell the smoke and cedar of his scent surrounding me, in the jacket he placed around my shoulders and on his skin, and all I want is to melt into his arms. All I want is to believe the promises he's murmuring, because right now the thought of leaving him is not one I want to contemplate.

But then I smell another scent, a feminine one, and a surprisingly sharp knife of jealousy slides between my ribs. 'So,' I whisper as he presses another kiss to my throat. 'You really meant it when you said you were going to give the emeralds to your mistress.'

He goes still for a moment and lifts his head. 'Is that jealousy I hear, *gattina*?' He's amused, but I am most definitely not, though I wish I could be.

'I know I said you weren't to sleep with anyone else on our wedding night, but even two days later it's—'

He lays a finger across my mouth, silencing me. 'I was approached, little wolf. And while I didn't encourage her, I didn't exactly push her away either. At least, not until she made her intentions known and then I decided to come home.' His gaze turns intense. 'To you.'

The jealousy eases, but I'm angry that I even felt it. I'm angry that it even matters to me, but I'm starting to realise there's a reason for that.

A reason my heart leapt when he came across the sand to me.

A reason I was disappointed he'd left yesterday.

A reason all I wanted was to throw myself into his arms today.

You are *falling for him. You idiot.*

I want to deny it. I want to deny it with all my heart, but I know the truth deep inside me. He's made me love him with his acceptance of me as I am, with his unexpected gentleness and tenderness, with his ability to join me in ridiculous arguments, and with his wicked hands and his beautiful mouth.

He's made me love him and I don't know what I can do to escape it. In fact, I have a horrible feeling I can't do anything about it at all.

His black brows draw together, and I know a moment's intense fear that he's guessed what I'm feeling right now. And he can't know, he just can't, because he promised me love wouldn't be a part of our marriage, and I don't know what he'll do if he finds out. For once, I don't want to push.

So I open my mouth and nip at the fingers across my lips and I watch his gaze flare with desire. 'I've had no sleep in the last twelve hours and I'm probably still half-drunk,' he says. 'But all I can think about is you naked in my bed, so you'd better take me back up to the villa or else you'll find yourself flat on your back in the sand.'

'That sounds uncomfortable,' I murmur.

He smiles and takes my hand. 'Maybe later we'll test the theory, but not now.'

Then he leads me back up to the villa.

In the privacy of his bedroom, he pulls me into the shower, washing the sand from my feet, while I squeeze shower gel in my hands and run it all over his body. Stroking the hard planes of his chest and stomach, then his muscled arms before turning him around and washing his powerful back. The scars from his father's belt are deep and I touch them lightly, caressing them, and he doesn't stop me. And he doesn't resist when I put my mouth to them, kissing them, because even though they're marks of pain and punishment, they are part of him and so I think I love them too.

I turn him around again, so he's facing me, his silver eyes blazing.

'I like it when you stay where I put you,' I say, teasing him.

He smiles, that one I particularly like, sexy and hot and just for me. 'And I like it when you do what I say. Get down on your knees for me, my wife. It's time for you to service your husband.'

A thrill of pleasure goes through me and I drop to my knees, because I have no trouble at all obeying his every sensual command. No, I like it. It turns me on and since my pleasure is his, he delights in it.

I take his hard cock in my hand and guide it to my mouth and draw him in, loving the way his features tense as I wrap my lips around him. His skin is smooth and velvety in my mouth, tasting of crisp salt and his own special masculine flavour.

I use my tongue and my teeth to tease him, watching him as I do, and when he slides his hands into my hair to guide me, I lean in. I grip his powerful thighs, taking him deeper, loving the way he growls in response. Then I lick and suck him, working him over, until he suddenly pulls away. His hands are hauling me up from my knees, before turning me and pushing me hard against the tiled wall of the shower. Then he lifts me straight up so I can wind my legs around his waist, and he pins me to the wall, his thick, hard cock pushing deep inside me.

I gasp in pleasure, clenching around him, loving the feeling of him inside me. His eyes are dark silver now and inches from mine, and all I can see is pleasure in them. The pleasure *I* give him.

'Let's see,' he whispers fiercely. 'Let's see if we can't create the most beautiful child right here, right now.'

And I'm so lost in the pleasure, lost in him, that all I can do is lean forward and kiss him hungrily, my thighs holding him to me as he thrusts in, deep and hard. His mouth on mine is urgent, like that first time in the pool, and I'm meeting him hunger for hunger. There's a beautiful madness in the way he fucks me, the pleasure building and building, making my nails claw at his back, catching on those terrible scars, yet he doesn't flinch.

'Harder,' he growls against my mouth. 'Scratch me, little wolf. Mark me. Give me your pain, not his.'

And I want to take that pain away from him, give him something else in return, something better, so I do. Then the orgasm comes, smashing us both into oblivion as I clutch him and whisper his name.

CHAPTER TWENTY

Vincenzo

I WAKE SOMETIME in the late afternoon, the sun shining through a crack in the linen curtains of my bedroom, turning the white sheets golden.

My Caterina lies beside me, still asleep, the black storm of her hair lying over my white pillows. The sheet has fallen off her, exposing her naked body as she lies on her side facing me. Her skin looks as if it has been gilded by a master painter, highlighting all her delicious curves, her breasts, her hips, her thighs, the delicate line of her cheek.

She is so beautiful.

I'm filled with a pleasant post-orgasmic haze, unable to stop thinking about her nails scratching my back in the shower, criss-crossing the scars I already have with the scars she gave me. I want those scars of hers. I want the pain of her nails on my skin, cancelling out the pain of my father's belt. And I want the child we hopefully created between us, new life after all these years of death.

But what if she's not pregnant? Will you keep her here like your father kept your mother?

The pleasant haze fragments as a cold thread of unease winds through me.

I wouldn't do that, of course I wouldn't. If she's not pregnant then it's fine, we can try again and I'm all for trying as many times as it will take since isn't that the best part?

I throw back the sheet and get out of bed, stalking into the bathroom. I splash some water on my face to get rid of the lingering effects of sleep, but I can't stop thinking about her, standing on the beach, looking out to sea. Her telling me that a facsimile of freedom isn't what she truly wants, no matter what I can promise her.

You know what she truly needs. That's to be free of you.

I brace my hands on the black marble vanity and look down unseeing into the basin. What she wants is impossible. She's forever tied to me as my wife now, and if she's pregnant—

You forced her into marriage, screwed her without a condom, told her that freedom for her is impossible, and that she'll never be loved. All of this is about what you *want. None of this is about her.*

I'm cold inside and getting colder, and I could lie to myself, deny that I feel anything at all for her and that there's no escaping the situation, no escape for her, but…

I'm not sure I can lie anymore or pretend she's not important to me. Act as if her feelings mean nothing, when they in fact mean everything.

She means everything.

I slowly lift my head and stare in the mirror at the man looking back. The face of the monster I've become. The Wolf of Sicily.

I have my father's eyes, his colouring and his height. I have nothing at all of my mother, except perhaps my heart, which was once as fierce and tender as hers. But it's not anymore. There's only a stone where my heart should be, hard and cold and impervious. Like my father's heart.

You know what you have to do.

Everything inside me goes tight, my chest aching as if a bullet has torn a hole right through it, but there's no escaping the truth and I know it.

I want to keep her here. I want to keep here with me forever, but if I do that, I'll be my father through and through. She won't ever taste that freedom she so badly wants. She won't ever have that little flat or a career, or a life outside the *cosa nostra*. All she'll ever have is a husband who keeps her at his side and gives her nothing in return.

I know what she needs, even though she might not know it herself. The thing that's been missing in her life since my family destroyed hers. She needs love, and that's the one thing I can't give her. Because slowly but surely the Argentis kill love. They strangle it, starve it and beat it to death. Then, once it's dead, we fill the space it left with violence and murder, with sorrow and pain.

That's the true Argenti legacy. *My* legacy.

And I can't involve Caterina or any children we may have in that legacy. I can't pass that on to the next generation. I promised myself the violence would end with me, but I know that if I keep her, it won't. It will go on and on, down through our children and there will never be an end to it. The shadow Stefano Argenti casts is too long and I can't escape it.

It has to stop. Now. Here. With her.

Ice fills my veins, my cold stone of a heart pumping it around the rest of my body, and I let it. I'm not the wolf now, I'm the man, and the man has a purpose to fulfil. He cannot let himself be distracted from it and he cannot let anyone get in his way.

I push myself away from the vanity and go back into the bedroom. Caterina is stirring, giving a sensual little stretch as she does so. Then she sees me standing next to the bed and smiles, reaching out for me. 'Come back to bed,' she says. 'I need my husband.'

But her husband is gone. I can't be him any longer, no matter how badly she wants him.

She must see something in my expression, because her black brows draw together in a frown, her green eyes full of concern. She sits up, drawing the sheet about her. 'Vincenzo? What's wrong? Has something happened?'

Hearing her say my name makes my resolve falter, but only for a second. There can be no second-guessing and no regrets, not now. This is the right thing to do, the *only* thing to do.

'Sadly, I've had a small change of heart,' I drawl. 'You wanted your freedom, so I've decided you shall have it. I'll organise a new identity for you, a new passport and a new life. You can have the normality you wanted.'

She blinks, shock slowly filling her gaze. 'What?' The word sounds blank, as if she doesn't understand what I've said.

'A new identity,' I explain patiently, my voice cold. 'That's what I gave your father and that's what I'll give you. You're right. You should have the normal life you wanted and I'm going to give it to you.'

She blinks again, understanding dawning across her face. 'But...you said that was impossible. You said that if I was pregnant—'

'I know what I said.' My voice sharpens, a hot flare of temper penetrating the ice I've surrounded myself with. 'But I was wrong. I don't want to do to you what my father did to my mother. I don't want to imprison you here.'

'I won't be a prisoner,' she says, as if it's self-evident. 'You said yourself you'll give me as much freedom as you're able to manage.'

'But you didn't want that, remember?' The cold in me is beginning to melt no matter how hard I try to hold onto it, fury coming hard on its heels, thick and hot. 'You've made no secret of the fact that it's not enough for you.'

Colour is leaching from her face, making her green eyes seem even greener. 'Yes, I did say that, but... Maybe I've changed my mind.'

My fury leaps higher. I was expecting her to grab her freedom with both hands, not suddenly decide she doesn't want it after all. Which is unacceptable.

The wolf is elemental, savage with sharp teeth and claws, and it doesn't understand what I'm doing. It doesn't understand why I'm sending her away, when all it wants is to keep her.

But I'm not the wolf now and I refuse to be Stefano, and so there's only one way this is going to go.

'That's too bad,' I say coldly. 'I've made my decision.'

She's sitting rigidly upright, the sheet now clutched

in her hands. 'I like the villa and I like you. I like being your wife.' Her tone is light, but there's a strange current running through the words.

'Since when did you suddenly like being here with me?' I shouldn't keep arguing with her, not when nothing she says will change my mind, but I can't seem to stop. 'When not a few hours ago you were telling me that it wasn't enough?'

Her mouth tightens and she looks down at her hands clutching the sheet. 'You're right. If I'm pregnant then—'

'Caterina,' I say roughly, unable to let go of the sense that she's hiding something from me. 'Give me the truth.'

She continues to stare down at the sheet for a long moment. Then abruptly, as if she's come to some decision, she lifts her head and meets my gaze. There's some powerful emotion burning in her green eyes. It's fierce, hot, determined, and it momentarily steals my breath clean away.

She lifts her chin. 'The truth? Okay, here's the truth. I changed my mind because I think I'm in love with you, Vincenzo. And now I don't want to leave you.'

The shock of it guts me. All I can do is stand there staring at her, the words echoing in my head. That thought that she might fall for me, the man who did all those terrible things to her and her family, never occurred to me, not once. And for a second I can't believe it, that she must be lying to me in some way, but there's nothing but truth in those beautiful eyes of hers.

It's too late. You've hurt her. Irrevocably.

There's an agony somewhere inside me, but I ignore it. I have to. The Argenti legacy must be more than all the violence and death my father perpetuated and it must be more than what I've perpetuated myself. And it has to start right here, right now, no matter how much she loves me.

I give her a slight but regretful smile. 'Unfortunate,' I say. 'But nothing that can't be fixed. You'll have to forget me, *gattina,* since I will not be featuring anywhere in this new life of yours.'

Her gaze is very fixed and she sits still as a statue. Then abruptly, she drops the sheet, leaps from the bed, coming over to stand in front of me. She's beautifully naked, her hair tumbling around her shoulders and falling in an inky waterfall down to her waist. Her eyes blaze with the spirit of the warrior inside her; she's ready to fight a battle and she's ready to fight hard.

'No,' she says fiercely. 'I won't go. I want to stay here with you.'

But it's a battle she can't win, because I am a warrior too, and I'm stronger. I have the scars to prove it.

'I don't care,' I say coldly, clearly. 'If you won't go then I'll make you.'

The blaze in her eyes falters as she looks at me, finding no give in my expression. 'Vincenzo...' She lifts a hand to my face. 'Please...'

I stand rigid as her fingers brush my skin and there's a part of me that wants nothing more than to kiss her palm, pull her close, tell her I've changed my mind after all.

But I can't. This is the way it has to be and after all, I'm used to pain.

'I'm going to organise some documents for you,' I say, my voice flat with control. 'Pack your things.'

Then I turn and stride out of the bedroom.

CHAPTER TWENTY-ONE

Caterina

I STARE AT the doorway as he retreats through it, shock still reverberating through me. My heart feels as if he took it between his strong hands and ripped it in two, and I can't stop trembling.

Stumbling back, I sit on the bed, my eyes prickling.

I knew when he came out of the bathroom and I saw that frighteningly cold expression on his face that he'd decided something. But I never thought his decision would be giving me my freedom. And I never thought that the moment he said it, I wouldn't want it.

Part of me is angry with myself for telling him I loved him, that I should have protected myself, kept myself safe. But another part of me, the braver part, the part of me that discovered true freedom in his arms, doesn't regret a thing.

He was never going to change his mind for me, no matter what I told him, and so the outcome would have been the same either way. At least now he knows that he's not alone, that he's got someone, somewhere, out in the world, who loves him more than she ever thought it was possible to love someone.

I close my eyes, tears forming behind my lids and falling, no matter how I try to stop them. I shouldn't be crying. He's giving me exactly what I always told him I wanted, and really, I should be rejoicing. Yet… I just wish getting what I wanted didn't come at the expense of my heart.

For long minutes I sit there as my tears fall, debating the merits of going after him and arguing with him, try to figure out a way to change his mind, but what's the point?

I'm not going to force myself on another man who doesn't want me, not after how my father treated me. And I'm tired of fighting for the things *I* want too. He gave me a taste of what being cared about feels like, so I can take that with me when I go, and anyway, perhaps he's right. Perhaps with time it'll fade. Perhaps a new life, a normal life, will make up for his loss.

You know nothing will make up for it.

But I can't afford to accept that right now, because if I do, I'll lose all hope and without hope, I'm nothing.

I weep for a bit on the edge of the bed, then I pull myself together. I go back to my bedroom and have a shower, and try to think about packing some things. But the only thing I want from here is him, so in the end I pack nothing at all.

Sometime later a meal is delivered to my room, but I don't touch it.

Part of me is hoping he'll come upstairs and knock on my door, tell me he's changed his mind, but even though I wait up till midnight, no knock comes. And eventually I fall asleep, dreaming of his hands touching me, his mouth on my skin.

The next morning a security guard finds me, telling me that my documents are ready and I'll be flying to Rome, and from there, to the US, where my new life will begin.

In my little sheaf of documents is a note on a business card. The note says: *if you are pregnant, call this number*. There's no name on the card, nothing else but the number, written in bold slashes like the note he slipped under my door only a few nights ago. It feels like a lifetime now.

So that's it. That's all I'm left with. A note and a new life, the freedom I always wanted, and yet…

Something in me rebels, something that isn't done fighting, because what will that freedom mean if he's not there? What will my new life look like if he's not in it? I'll have that career and a flat, and maybe flatmates. I'll even have a cat and one day a boyfriend, but…

I don't want it. I don't want it with everything in me. I know what I want now, what I *really* want, and it's him. His magic touch and his silver eyes. The challenges he throws me, the arguments he gives me. The tenderness and the kindness he doesn't even realise he's capable of.

Walking away would be so easy. I could take this new life he's presented me with and not argue. I could give up. Surrender. Go wherever he's decided to put me without a fight, but…

I've done nothing but fight him since I got here, so am I really going to give up now? Let him chase me away? Sure, I don't want to force myself on someone who doesn't want me, but he *does* want me. And more than that, he needs me, I know he does. He's got no one else, no one at all, no one who knows his true heart the way I know it. The way I've discovered it over these past few days.

He's never had someone fight for him. He's never had someone stay because they want to be with him, because he's more important than anything, and he *is* more important. *Love* is more important and I love him.

He is my freedom and I'm not leaving.

Slowly and with care, I rip the note up into little pieces, toss them onto the floor and then I leave the room to find him.

He's going to give me the fight of my life, but this time I'm going to win.

I'll make sure of it.

CHAPTER TWENTY-TWO

Vincenzo

I SIT AT my desk, sipping my morning coffee, every part of me concentrated on the sound of the helicopter outside on the lawn. It should be leaving any moment now, taking my Caterina away to her new life.

It was the right thing to do, the *only* thing to do. She wasn't meant to be here with me, her beautiful spirit slowly fading the way my mother's did, trapped in a life she didn't want, with a husband she never asked for.

My chest aches, a nagging dull pain that doesn't go away no matter how many times I rub it. And I can't get away from how she looked yesterday, standing in front of me so naked and beautiful, telling me she wanted to stay. Telling me that she loved me. Then the brush of her fingers against my cheek…

The pain in my chest intensifies. I drain my coffee then shove my chair back, because the helicopter is still there, it hasn't left yet and it should be on its way. I need it to leave so I can get her out of my head, and get back to the business of planning my crusade.

I go to the door and fling it open, mentally preparing myself to find out what the delay is, only to find Caterina on the other side.

She's still wearing her nightgown and her hair falls over her shoulders in a black waterfall. She blazes like a torch. Her green eyes meet mine and before I can open my mouth, she slaps her palms on my chest and shoves me back into my office. Then she steps through the doorway and slams the door after her.

I draw myself up to my full height, every muscle rigid. 'What the hell are you doing?' I demand. 'You're supposed to be leaving—'

'No,' she interrupts. 'I'm not going anywhere.' She's standing with her shoulders square, her hands now in fists at her side, and when she speaks, her voice is fierce. 'And if you think you can get rid of me that easily, you've got another think coming.'

The pain in my chest gets worse, my fury rising. 'You're leaving,' I say, trying to keep a hold of my temper. 'Get on that fucking helicopter. Do as I say!'

Her chin lifts, green eyes full of fire, a warrior about to do battle. 'Make me.'

And I want to put my hands on her hips, toss her over my shoulder, carry her to the helicopter and put her in it, except I know the moment I touch her, I won't be able to. I'll want to grip her and draw her close and keep her. Keep her forever.

'You can't, can you?' She stares furiously up at me. 'Because you don't want me to go.'

It's not a question and my jaw tightens. 'Odd. That must be why I arranged all those documents for a new life for you in—'

'Vincenzo,' she says and before I can move away,

she's lifted a hand to my cheek the way she did yesterday, her fingers brushing my skin. 'I'm not leaving you.'

Something twists hard in my chest, an agony blazing as bright as her eyes.

'You have to,' I force out through gritted teeth. 'I won't keep you trapped here with me. I won't keep you in this life you never wanted.'

'But what if I do want it?' Her palm is warm against my cheek. 'What if I want you?'

My hands close into fists as I try to keep them from reaching for her. 'You can't,' I say forcefully. 'I killed my own father. I shot him, Caterina. And there are many other things I've done, so many things—'

'I don't care.' She stares right into my eyes, seeing into the heart of me. 'You're trying to change things, trying to make things better.'

'If I keep you here,' I grit out, 'I'll be just like him.'

'You were never like him, Vincenzo.' She's suddenly fierce. 'Never. You saved me and you tried to save my mother and brother. You showed me how strong I really was, and you made me feel wanted for the first time in my life.' There are tears in her eyes now, even though her gaze still burns. 'And that freedom I wanted? I found it with you.'

I can see the emotion that lights up her face, pure and bright, making her even more lovely than she already is. *Dio*, she's always fought for what she wanted

And now she's fighting for you.

'You shouldn't,' I hear myself say, my voice full of gravel. 'You deserve better than me. You deserve more than—'

'You don't get to tell me what I do and don't deserve,'

she interrupts yet again, her thumb stroking across my cheek. 'I decide that and I've decided that what I deserve is to be your wife.'

I shouldn't be doing this. I shouldn't be letting her touch me like this. I shouldn't be letting her say all these things, each word eroding my resolution bit by bit. Eroding my certainty that what I'm doing is right. Eroding my resistance to her.

I thought I was strong enough to let her go, but I don't think I am after all. 'It won't be the life you want,' I say, trying to make her see reason. 'I don't know how long it will take to bring the families under my control, and they're not going to go quietly. There'll never be peace, which means there'll never be peace for you.'

She steps even closer, the warmth of her body and her scent surrounding me. 'Don't give me excuses, Vincenzo,' she murmurs. 'You don't have to be afraid.'

I want to tell her that I'm not afraid, that I'm not afraid of anything, but deep inside, I know that's not true.

I am afraid. I'm afraid I'm not worthy of her.

The scent of her is making me dizzy, making me want to reach out and pull her close, crush her mouth under mine. 'I can't love you,' I force out, knowing even as I say it that it's an excuse. 'I told you. Love is the one thing I can't give you.'

'It's okay,' she says as if it's nothing at all. 'I have enough love for both of us.'

I stare down into her face and a certain exhaustion winds through me as I think about what it would be like if I made her get on that helicopter. If I made her leave. There would be no more fights, no more challenges. No bright, fiery woman to come home to or to argue with.

No touches or kisses, or her warmth in my arms. No seeing that emotion, that love in her eyes.

She needs more from you than that.

I take a breath, but I can't seem to get air, as the wolf fights and claws its way out of the cage I've put it in. It wants her, it always has, and more… It loves her and the man…

Loves her too.

'Caterina…' My voice is hoarse and I don't know what I'm trying to say. It feels as if a bucket of ice water has been emptied over my head and I struggle to breathe through the shock. And I know it's true, it's always been true.

I fell in love with her the moment I saw her in the pool, floating on her back, like a mermaid. Or maybe even before that, when I married her, and I realised the worth of the woman I'd just kidnapped.

I thought Stefano had killed all love and light in my life, and yet it's here in my stone of a heart, a new tendril curling hopefully towards the sun. And as I accept that it's there, it comes to me.

It was never sending her away that made me not like my father.

It was loving her. Because he didn't know the meaning of the word.

But Caterina taught me what it meant and what it felt like. Love was her kissing the scars on my back and that look in her eyes and everything she is. Love is the warrior spirit within her, the perfect match for the wolf in me.

Love is the way she's looking at me right now and refusing to leave me, challenging me the way she's always done right from the first.

And me… I can never resist her challenge.

Without a word I turn from her and go to my desk, pull open a drawer and take out the box I had in there for safekeeping. Then I turn back to her. She's watching me, still fierce, her posture tense as if she's expecting me to keep fighting.

But I'm not. I'm done. My little *gattina* has won.

Keeping my gaze pinned to hers, I go down on one knee and hold up the box. 'Caterina Salvatore,' I say formally. 'Will you do me the honour of being my wife?'

Shock flickers over her face. 'What do you mean?'

'I'm tired, *gattina*. I'm tired of fighting, tired of pretending. I'm tired of trying to escape the shadow my father cast and I'm tired of being afraid.'

Her eyes widen. 'Vincenzo…'

'I'm afraid I'm not worthy of you, Caterina,' I say, suddenly as fierce as she is. 'But I want to be. And I realise that you're right, I'm *not* Stefano, and I know I'm not him, because he didn't know what love is. But I do. Because you showed me.'

She swallows, staring at me and I see the tears that fill her eyes.

I rise to my feet, open the box and take out the emerald rings that are still in there. The rings that were always meant for her. And I take her hand and slide them one by one onto her finger. 'I love you,' I say quietly. 'Be my wife. Stay with me. Don't ever leave me.'

She doesn't speak, giving me her answer as she goes up on her toes and presses her mouth to mine.

This time when I reach for her, I don't let her go.

And I never will again.

EPILOGUE

Caterina

I SIT ON a blanket in the shade of the great oak tree that holds court on the rolling lawns of our estate, watching as Vincenzo picks up our three-year-old son, Nico, and tosses him into the air. He's getting too big for these games, but Nico loves it and so does my husband, who indulges him every moment he can get.

I'm holding our new daughter, Elena, who is gazing up at me with her father's big silver eyes. She already has him wrapped around her tiny finger, which is exactly as it should be.

It's been five years since we left Sicily. Vincenzo and I brought the families to heel and made them agree to a truce. Then we did some succession planning. We both wanted to get away from the never-ending arguments and petty disagreements of the families, go somewhere safe to raise children together. But Vincenzo needed to be sure that the Argenti legacy he fought for would remain, and so he called the wider Argenti family to a meeting, informing them that while he would remain as head of the family, he would need someone to act for him in Italy.

He found someone—a distant cousin—who will act on his behalf, while he keeps an eye on the Argentis from a distance. We now live in England, in a beautiful country estate in the Cotswolds, which suits us perfectly.

Vincenzo arranged himself a new identity to protect us from any unwanted family attention and now goes by the name of Vincent Castle. I call him Vinny, just to annoy him.

My Wolf comes over to where I'm sitting with our son tucked under his arm. He puts Nico down and then sits beside me, looking down at our daughter, his silver eyes alight with love.

'I had a thought,' he says, reaching down to touch Elena's cheek with a gentle finger.

'Just the one?' I ask, teasing him.

'Naughty, *gattina*,' he says. 'No, I'm being serious. I've decided that the Argenti legacy was never about stopping the violence, or at least, not entirely.'

'Oh?'

He smiles and my heart skips a beat the way it always does when I look at him. 'No, the true Argenti legacy was always supposed to be love.'

I look at him and our children, and I know that of course my wolf is right. He was always right.

The true Argenti legacy is love and it starts with us.

* * * * *

Did His Forced Sicilian Bride
leave you enthralled?
Then don't miss Jackie Ashenden's
other dramatic stories!

Boss's Heir Demand
Newlywed Enemies
King, Enemy, Husband
Christmas Eve Ultimatum
His Heir of Revenge

Available now!

MILLS & BOON®

Coming next month

MY FIANCÉE PROMOTION
Emmy Grayson

Sera stares at the newspaper with horror etched onto her face.

'What...who took that?'

'One of the event photographers. Once they realised who I was, they decided to make a quick buck.' I toss the newspaper down on the coffee table on top of a stack of books.

She sighs, her hands coming up to her temples. 'The damage is done. I'll submit my resignation on Monday.'

Knots form in my chest, tighten. 'No.'

No, only something drastic will repair this.

A frown draws her dark golden brows together. 'Then...I don't understand. What can we do?'

Something stirs inside me at her use of the word *we*. I may not know the woman standing in front of me like I thought I did, but her dedication to Hawke Financial is one thing I don't doubt.

The one thing I'm counting on.

'I do have a proposal.'

'Okay.' She nods, blows out a harsh breath. 'Okay. What do we do.'

'We get engaged.'

Continue reading

MY FIANCÉE PROMOTION
Emmy Grayson

Available next month
millsandboon.co.uk

Copyright ©2026 Emmy Grayson

COMING SOON!

We really hope you enjoyed reading this book. If you're looking for more romance be sure to head to the shops when new books are available on

Thursday 21st May

To see which titles are coming soon, please visit
millsandboon.co.uk/nextmonth

MILLS & BOON

FOUR BRAND NEW BOOKS FROM
MILLS & BOON MODERN

Indulge in desire, drama, and breathtaking romance – where passion knows no bounds!

OUT NOW

Eight Modern stories published every month, find them all at:

millsandboon.co.uk

TWO BRAND NEW BOOKS FROM
Love Always

Be prepared to be swept away to incredible worldwide destinations along with our strong, relatable heroines and intensely desirable heroes.

OUT NOW

Four Love Always stories published every month, find them all at:

millsandboon.co.uk

LET'S TALK
Romance

For exclusive extracts, competitions and special offers, find us online:

- **f** MillsandBoon
- **X** @MillsandBoon
- **◉** @MillsandBoonUK
- **♪** @MillsandBoonUK

Get in touch on 01413 063 232

For all the latest titles coming soon, visit
millsandboon.co.uk/nextmonth